TRUST ME ON THIS

THE MYSTERIOUS PRESS

New York • London • Tokyo

MYSTERIOUS PRESS The Mysterious Press, 129 West 56th Street, New York, N.Y. 10019

Printed in the United States of America
First Printing: May 1988
10 9 8 7 6 5 4 3 2 1

Library of Congress Cataloging-in-Publication Data

Westlake, Donald E.
Trust Me On This

I. Title.
PS3573.E9J64 1988 813'.54 87-22098
ISBN 0-89296-176-7

For Paul Corkery, who is as amused by fact as I am by fiction, and for Dean and Richard, who first sent us kids out to play.

A Word in Your Ear

Although there is no newspaper anywhere in the United States like the *Weekly Galaxy,* as any alert reader will quickly realize, were there such a newspaper in actual real-life existence its activities would be stranger, harsher and more outrageous than those described herein. The fictioneer labors under the restraint of plausibility; his inventions must stay within the capacity of the audience to accept and believe. God, of course, working with facts, faces no such limitation. Were there a factual equivalent to the *Weekly Galaxy,* it would be much worse than the paper I have invented, its staff and ownership even more lost to all considerations of truth, taste, proportion, honor, morality or any shred of common humanity. Trust me.

TRUST ME ON THIS

THE FIRST DAY

Chapter One

Sara drove out into the wilderness. The clean new road stretched ahead, empty and white, four lanes of sun-baked concrete divided by a low gray cement barrier curled into the surfer's dream of the perfect wave. In the rented Chevette's rearview mirror, tinted slightly blue, the same empty road unreeled backward toward the city, shimmering far off in the heat-rise like a clumsily swaying backdrop.

It was nine-forty on a Monday morning. The twelve-mile-long highway cut across flat tan scrubland under a pale blue sky, absolutely alone and unused except for the maroon Chevette with glittering windows, racing west at eighty miles an hour, containing its pocket of air-conditioning and the person of Sara Joslyn. Out ahead, still far off, the building gradually appeared, sand-colored, rising up at the point of the highway. On the dashboard, the digital clock's green numbers read 9:42. I won't be late after all, Sara thought.

* * *

Jack Ingersoll said, "How long since I had a cancer?"

Mary Kate Scudder flipped through her Rolodex. "Three weeks next Tuesday."

Jack shook his head, regretful. "Too soon," he said. "Too soon." He paced his squaricle, thinking.

* * *

Sunlight glinted on an object far ahead, then not far ahead at all. Sara had time to register the dark blue car on her side of the road, parked way off on the slanting shoulder, white light fragmenting from rear window and bumper. Then her own little Chevette had shot past that place and it was only in memory that she filled in the picture: The car was tilted, right side lower than left because the shoulder fell away there toward the level of the surrounding plain. The right front door hung open. A person was lying half in and half out of the car.

A what? Sara's foot lifted from the accelerator, the Chevette slowed, she looked in the rearview mirror. But she could barely see the parked car back there, it was already no more than a tiny dark lump in all this flat world of beige and whiteness.

What should she do? Was the person hurt? Had she actually seen a person at all?

What if it's a story, she thought, and her foot moved to the brake. My first day, and I walk in with a story. How's that for starting with a bang?

But how could she get through the central barrier into the eastbound lanes? She slowed and slowed, still alone on the highway, and then it occurred to her she didn't *have* to get into the eastbound lanes. She had the road to herself. Even the parked car was no longer visible in her mirror.

Fine. A quick U-turn, spewing gravel when her tires slewed across the shoulder, and Sara accelerated back the way she'd come, the morning sun now hot and painful in her eyes as she pushed the little car up again to eighty. Be some joke if another vehicle came along after all.

But none did. The parked car grew ahead of her, increasingly distinct, and she decelerated, seeing that it definitely was a person over there, half in and half out of the car, dressed in dark clothing, head and shoulders and one arm spread on the ground like an oil spill.

She stopped just beyond the car, and when she opened her door a bundle of hot dry air rolled in and lay on Sara like a wool blanket. "Jeez!" she said, and climbed out of the car with movements that were all at once sluggish, heat-oppressed. She moved under the sun, her clothes turning to wood, her shoes making dry gritty sounds on the gravel.

The car was a dark blue Buick Riviera, a year or two old, with Dade County plates; or plate, since Florida cars don't have a license plate in the front. The rear seat was empty. A stocky man in his fifties lay sprawled face down over the front seat and out onto the ground. The engine was off, but the key was in the ignition. The car radio played salsa music, sounding like crickets on coke.

The man was dead. Sara hunkered down beside the body and touched his neck, and even though the sun had warmed that flesh, it still felt dead. Then she noticed a kind of soft-looking mound at the back of the man's head, under thin gray hair, and when she touched it she was repelled; it felt squishy under the skin. I'm a reporter, she reminded herself, swallowing bile. I'm a reporter, I'm supposed to do these things.

Hating it, she put both hands on his shoulder, stiff under the dark gray polyester jacket, and lifted enough to see his face. Gravel had embossed the skin. The face was round, tough-looking, pale, not very well shaved. The mouth was slack, the eyes closed. Above the left eye was a bruised hole, black and gray and red, with tendrils of blood.

That's where the bullet went in. The squishy place in back is where the bullet broke the skull but didn't come out.

Oh, jeepers, Sara thought.

* * *

Intrepid editor Jack Ingersoll stopped pacing. "Legionnaires' Disease," he announced. "It was guilt."

Secretary Mary Kate stared at him in repugnance. "Guilt?"

"Sure." Jack waved his arms about, fingers fluttering for handholds in the air. "They were all vets, did things in the war, never can forget, bad dreams, can't forgive themselves . . ."

Mary Kate said, "Isn't that like when Binx tried 'Legionnaires' Disease—It Was Suicide'?"

Jack frowned. "Too close? You think so?"

Mary Kate said, "Massa didn't like that other one."

Turning away, grimacing, Jack ran ink-stained fingers through thinning hair. "If only I could find the ice cream diet, the pressure would be off."

* * *

The highway funneled to a finish at the building, which bulked four stories high in the middle of nothing. Atop the structure, a monster two-story sign in red and blue neon informed the parking lots and the surrounding wasteland:

THE WEEKLY GALAXY
"THE PEOPLE, YES!"

Here the four lanes became two, which passed to either side of a stucco-and-glass guard shack. STOP said the red hexagonal on the front of the shack, and Sara stopped, rolling her window down as a brown-uniformed guard emerged, a clipboard in his hand. The Florida heat lay on Sara's face. "Hot!" she said.

The guard, an older man with dark sunglasses and a deep tan, nodded agreement. "Yes, ma'am," he said. "I already knew that."

"Do you know about the dead man?"

The clipboard quivered slightly. Behind the sunglasses, the guard did something distancing. "Which dead man would that be?" he asked.

"The one back there on the road"—she checked the odometer—"exactly two point three miles, westbound side, in a dark blue Buick Riviera, Florida license plate, Dade County 277 ZRQ. He's been shot!"

That last part sounded more excited than she'd wanted, her effort having been to be dispassionately professional throughout the entire report; still, she was pleased with her overall delivery.

The guard seemed less pleased. After frowning out at the empty road for a few seconds, he said, "Are you sure?"

"Of course I'm sure! Sure about what? That he's there? That he's dead? That he was shot?"

Slowly, the guard shook his head. "Ma'am," he said, "I'm not questioning your accuracy."

"It sure sounded like it," Sara said. This wasn't the reaction she'd expected.

"Only," the guard went on, "I don't seem to know you, ma'am. How do you happen to be out here?"

"I work here," Sara told him. "That is, I do now. I'm starting today." With a meaningful glance at his clipboard, she said, "The name's Sara Joslyn."

Back on familiar territory, the guard relaxed into routine, consulting the clipboard and saying, "Yes, ma'am, here you are."

"My first day on the paper," Sara said, unable entirely now to keep the excitement out of her voice, "and my first story!"

"This dead man," the guard said, sounding dubious again.

"He's *there,*" Sara said, sternly.

"Okay, okay." The guard held the clipboard up as a shield. "He's there, and he's dead, and he's shot."

"In a Buick Riviera."

"Yes, ma'am."

"I suppose you should be the one to call the police," Sara said, "but I'll report it inside."

"Good idea," the guard agreed. "But just hold on here." Taking a decal from the clipboard, he put the clipboard atop the Chevette, peeled the back from the decal and, saying, "Excuse me," leaned his head and upper torso in through the open window.

"Anytime," Sara said, watching him slide the decal onto the lower left corner of the windshield.

Withdrawing from the automobile, the guard collected his clipboard and explained, "That's the temporary, so you get to park in the Visitors' lot there. Once your tryout's over and you're a regular staffer you'll get the permanent sticker."

"The permanent sticker," Sara said. "It even *sounds* romantic."

* * *

Jack paced, while Mary Kate sat watching him, fingers poised over typewriter keys. Bob Sangster, one of Jack's reporters, an Australian with a very large nose, came through the door space into the squaricle and Jack flashed him a look of mingled hope, despair, rage and submission. "Senator," Bob said. "With a nose job."

Jack frowned. "North or south?"

"Nose," Bob repeated, pointing to his own large one.

"What part of the *country?*"

"Would I know? I'm a simple Aussie." Consulting a small piece of paper crumpled in his left fist, Bob said, "Where's Nebraska?"

"Nowhere," Jack told him. "Forget it."

* * *

There were no other Visitors. Sara circled through the empty space, thick white lines on blacktop defining where Visitors should park, beyond the jammed lots for staff parking, and carefully placed the Chevette between the two white lines closest to the main building.

There was such a strange feeling here, even apart from the dead man in the Buick. Not a feeling of exclusivity, exactly, but of . . . apartness. Alien. As though that building over there, seeming to hunch turtlelike in its wasteland setting as though it found the two-story-tall sign on its head painful, it was as though that building were actually a spaceship, from some universe far away. And she about to enter.

A spaceship, and a turtle, all at once. "Block that metaphor," Sara told herself, and laughed, and got out of the car.

* * *

Because Jack was in good odor at the moment—his team had done some excellent arthritis stories recently—he had a squaricle with a window, out which he now stared, contemplating the idea of flinging himself through the immovable plate glass.

Down below, in the Visitors' parking lot, a pretty girl got out of a maroon Chevette. Her short-sleeved blouse was dark blue, her linen skirt was wheat, her hair was dark blonde, long and straight. So were her legs, long and straight. In sunglasses she looked, as all women do, like Jacqueline Kennedy. She moved toward the building, and Jack liked her walk. They have ball bearings in their hips, he thought. He turned to Mary Kate, whose white rat face under the yellow Gabor wig looked alert, competent, ready. If he would speak words, she would type them.

He looked again out the window, having no words to speak. The girl was almost beyond his line of sight. "Does sex," he said, "cure gallstones?"

"Well, *I've* never had any," Mary Kate said.

Jack turned to look at her.

"Gallstones," Mary Kate explained.

* * *

Sara pulled open a tinted glass door and entered a small bare room like a check-cashing operation in a bad neighborhood, except that this place was icy cold. In the opposite wall was a wide glass window with a receptionist behind it. Both side walls were hung with framed *Weekly Galaxy* front pages in bright primary colors: annual predictions, drug deaths of television stars, invasions from outer space.

Sara crossed to the interior window and looked through at the receptionist, a rawboned hillbilly woman with black hair teased into a feathery explosion. When this person spoke, her amplified voice came from a speaker grille several feet away to the right: "Help ya?"

It was disconcerting to talk with someone whose voice came from eight feet off to one side. "I'm Sara Joslyn, I've just been hired here."

The receptionist had her own clipboard, which she consulted. "Yes, here you are," said the disembodied voice, while the receptionist's lips moved. "Take this badge," it went on, as a metal drawer below the window slid open, "and take the elevator to the third floor. Ask for Mr. Harsch."

The badge was a red and blue rectangle with many words on it, the most prominent being VISITOR. Sara took it and said, "Thank you," as a strident buzzing sound came apparently from the receptionist; that is, from the same grid that had been producing her voice. Startled, Sara looked around, noticed the door beyond that grid, and headed toward it. Pushing the door open as the buzzing stopped, she found herself wondering: Who would *visit* this place?

* * *

Jack watched Mary Kate type. He watched her stop typing. He said, "How many is that?"

"Twenty-eight."

A skinny pessimistic young reporter named Don Grove entered through the door space into Jack's squaricle, saying, "I don't suppose you want a two-headed calf."

Jack considered him. "With photos?"

"Possibly."

"Where is this thing?"

"Brazil," Don said.

"Oh, yeah? Then I want the photos signed by a priest."

"If any," Don said, and exited.

Jack stared at the window, at the ceiling, at his own clenched left fist, at Mary Kate: "The *Galaxy* clones a rat!"

"Ugh!" she said. "A rat?"

"What time is it?"

She looked at her watch—a massive intricate timepiece that could tell you everything from the time anywhere on the globe to the fifteen proofs of the existence of God—and said, "Nine fifty-eight and eleven seconds."

"Screw it. A man!"

Typing, Mary Kate said, "The *Galaxy* clones a human being."

"There *are* alligators in New York City sewers!"

"Oh, bushwah."

"Type, type."

She typed, she typed, though with a superior look on her face. All about them, movement had begun. Editors and assistants and researchers and secretaries erupted from their squaricles, striding or skipping or jogging along the hall-lanes, converging toward the elevators. Mary Kate still typed, as Jack yanked the paper from her machine, grabbed up his pads and pencils, and joined the nervous flow.

Chapter Two

Sara emerged from the elevator and looked about. It was a huge open room, almost the entire area of the third floor, without partitions. Desks and tables and people and square support pillars made an undifferentiated jumble in front of her eyes, all the way across to the far windows.

A man was bearing down on her from the right, his expression grim, his hands full of papers and pencils. She said, "I'm looking for—"

"Look *out*!" Unslowing, he shoved past her, knocking her back into the closing elevator door, heedlessly hurrying on.

Astonished, she stared after him. A bank of four elevators stood here, of which Sara had come up in the second from the right. In front of the last elevator to the left was placed a long conference table, one of its narrow ends pushed flat against the elevator door. Chairs lined both long sides of this table, with a second line of chairs ranked behind the first. Hurrying people converged now from everywhere in the room, taking seats at the table. The rude man was among them, spreading his papers and pencils at a place halfway down this side.

Sara moved out away from the elevators, deeper into the room, to get a better view of that odd scene, and as she did so—the last arrivals were just flinging themselves into their chairs—the elevator door slid silently open, and what was inside was not a normal elevator but an actual and complete office. Sara stared.

It was a large space for an elevator, but rather small for an office. Its paneled walls were decorated with framed photos. A trophy case stood at the rear, a black leather sofa to one side, cabinetry on the other containing a TV screen, video machine and stereo equipment. In the center of the room/elevator bulked a large walnut desk and behind it two men, one seated and the other standing.

As Sara continued to move sideways, staring at this apparition, a humming sound was heard and the walnut desk slid forward to *clunk* against the end of the table. The seated man was conveyed along with his desk, while the standing man stepped forward, maintaining his position just behind the seated man's right elbow.

"Good morning," growled the seated man in a raspy voice, glaring at everybody around the conference table. He was burly, about fifty, with puffy cheeks and bristly black hair and a low knobby forehead.

"Good morning, sir," or "Good morning, Mr. DeMassi," raggedly responded the people at the table. So that, Sara thought, was the boss himself, Bruno DeMassi, editor and publisher and owner of the *Weekly Galaxy*. She didn't know what she'd expected, exactly, but something rather more Perry White and less Don Corleone.

"So," growled DeMassi. "We ready to go to work?"

"Yes, sir," his subjects responded.

"Pass 'em up," DeMassi ordered, and, as sheets of paper were passed toward him from hand to hand, he picked up a twelve-ounce bottle of Heineken and downed a slug.

"Hey!" cried an outraged voice just behind Sara. She turned to see that she had almost backed into a desk at which a woman sat making grease pencil remarks on the backs of photographs. This woman, glaring indignantly at Sara and pointing her grease pencil at the floor, said, "What's the matter with you? Can't you see the *wall*?"

Wall? Sara looked down. The floor was covered with neutral gray industrial carpeting, but now she noticed that there was also a two-inch-wide black line of tape running along atop the carpet. Following it with her eyes, Sara saw that it ran straight for several feet, then made a sharp right turn. Beyond it was another similar line. In fact, everywhere she looked there were more black lines.

Possibly a hundred people were present in this vast space, in addition to the couple of dozen involved in the odd scene in the elevator, and Sara, looking around, now realized that those who were in motion moved in somewhat unnatural ways, with abrupt right-angled turns and unnecessary maneuvers that could only be explained by these black lines on the floor. The people moved around the giant room as though on tracks, as in some complex medieval mechanical toy.

"Will you get *out* of my squaricle!" the woman demanded.

"Sorry." Sara stepped back across the black line.

"Visitor, eh?" the woman said, reading the badge Sara had affixed to her shoulder bag strap. Becoming less annoyed, and pointing elsewhere with the grease pencil, she said, "If you want to talk to me, come through the door space."

"I just want to—"

"If you want to *talk* to me," the woman repeated, getting indignant all over again, "come through the *door space.*"

"Sorry."

Now *I'm* doing it, Sara thought, as she followed the black line around to the right to where it stopped, only to start again thirty-two inches later, leaving—as the woman had said—a door space. Sara stepped through. "I just got here," she apologized.

"I could tell," the woman said.

"I'm looking for Mr. Harsch."

The woman pointed with her grease pencil again, this time toward the elevator/office. "That's him over there," she said, "standing behind Massa."

Apparently it was all right to *look* through the nonwalls, even though you weren't supposed to walk through them. Looking, Sara for the first time studied the man in the elevator/office with Bruno DeMassi. Tall, thin, sixtyish, nearly bald with a low fringe of thin dead gray hair, a gaunt face with a hawk nose and ice-gray eyes, Jacob Harsch looked about as warm and appealing and human as Torquemada. Sara looked at him, head bowed, hunched forward slightly like a vulture, as he and DeMassi read the papers that had been handed forward, and she felt a little chill. "He looks busy," she said. "Maybe I shouldn't interrupt."

* * *

Massa read aloud, "'How to Give a Party.'" He looked up, glaring along the table at Binx Radwell. "Binx? What the fuck is this?"

Binx Radwell was a thirty-two-year-old blond man covered with a layer of baby fat and panic. A sheen of perspiration always lay on him, and his constant smile begged for salvation while acknowledging there was none. Teeth sparkling, eyebrows waggling up and down, he said, "That's it, Mr. DeMassi. How to give a party, right there in your own home. That survey of the readership, sir, you remember, they're a lot of very insecure people, socially inse—"

"Course they're insecure," Massa said, "they don't know their ass from a fire hydrant. What's this *party?*"

Binx jigged on his chair. "Well," he said, "we explain how to be a host, a hostess, how you—"

Massa frowned. "You mean a *party?*" Waving his hands over his head, he said, "With *hats?*"

"Well, not necessarily hats," Binx said. "We can do it without the hats. The point is, the people are coming into your house, now what the hell do you do?"

DeMassi, chewing this idea, found it without savor. His red pencil drew a line through "How to Give a Party." Only Massa was permitted to own and to use a red pencil at the *Galaxy*. That way, all orders written in red were known to be genuine. A staffer found with a red pencil on the property would be assumed to be a counterfeiter, and would be fired at once. Drawing a second line and then a third through the rejected offering, Massa said, "People don't go to parties."

Binx nodded, smiling spastically.

* * *

To delay the meeting with Mr. Harsch as long as possible, Sara continued to roam the giant room, being careful not to cross any more black lines. Away to the right, some distance from the elevators, she came upon an area where the black lines dwindled away and where there were instead eight very long tables, one behind the other. Ten or eleven people were seated at each table, all facing toward the main part of the room and looking mostly like the banks of volunteers manning the phones at a telethon. Foot-high wooden dividers spaced along the tables gave each of these people his or her own little area, and on these rather small patches of space were typewriters, telephones, cassette recorders, steno pads, cups filled with pens and pencils, ashtrays, reference books, here and there phone books, here and there a framed family photo or an African violet or a small comic statue.

These, it was clear, were the *Galaxy*'s reporters. About a third of them banged away at typewriters or jotted things in memo pads, but the majority were on the phone, making call after call. Moving unobtrusively among them, Sara listened to what the reporters were saying.

"What did the interior of the spaceship look like?"

"I'm calling from the Barbara Walters show. Of course this is the Barbara Walters show; would the Barbara Walters show lie to you?"

"And when you served the meal, you did observe that they were holding hands, is that right? Or, okay, their hands were on the table, near one another, and they were looking at one another in a very passionate way. Would you describe it as a very passionate look?"

"Professor, would you be amazed if I told you I had a three-foot-tall Saturnian in my office right this minute?"

"Doctor, as a recognizied authority on arthritis, could you comment on—I'm from the *Weekly Galaxy*, and—Doctor? Doctor?"

"Something I can do for you, honey?"

"Oh!" Sara said. "No, I'm just waiting to talk to Mr. Harsch." And she drifted away toward the conference at the elevators again.

* * *

Massa had finished with Binx Radwell. Binx mopped his brow and his neck and the tender inside of his elbows, as his spastic smile semaphored distress calls—I'm sinking! Help me! I'm drowning!—to people who had troubles of their own.

Massa was now considering Jack Ingersoll's list, and his red pencil had been working, working. Jack's manner, when things went poorly, was to become more and more still, more and more unmoving and closed in upon himself; at the moment, he could have been a granite statue, unblinking eyes fixed on Massa's furrowed forehead.

Which cleared, abruptly, like a spring day. "'Does Sex Cure Gallstones?'" Massa read aloud, and looked up with a happy smile. "That'd be good news, wouldn't it?"

"Amen to that, sir," Harsch said, in his bloodless voice, as the assembled editors feebly chuckled.

Massa swigged beer, then pointed the bottle at Jack. "Can you give me a positive yes?"

"I'll do my best, sir," Jack said.

"Don't do *your* best, boy. Do *my* best." His head lowered once more, and he read, "'The *Galaxy* Clones a Human Being.'" Awed, he looked down the table at Jack. "We do? We could do that?"

"I'd need help from the science staff, of course," Jack said. "It might—"

"Which human being?" Massa asked. "Man or woman?"

"Well, I was thinking of a man originally—"

"Where's the cheesecake?"

"We could do a woman, of course," Jack conceded. "But remember, sir, it's going to be a baby for—"

"A what?" Massa glowered. "You mean we don't start with a person?"

"No, sir," Jack said, with every appearance of calm. "Clones have to be born like anybody—"

"You mean we got a *baby* around here for twenty years?"

"Well, we don't have to—"

Binx, who at odd moments tried to help other people, even though no one ever tried to help him, said, "It might be a mascot, sir."

"Oh, no," Massa said, with a negative wag of the beer bottle. "We had that goat that time, and it didn't work out. A baby isn't gonna be better than a goat."

Jack gave Binx a quick expressionless look as Massa redlined the clone. Binx smiled like a poison victim.

Massa read, "'There *Are* Alligators in New York City.'"

"Sewers!" Jack cried.

Potentially offended, Massa glared down the table. "What?"

"New York City sewers," Jack explained. "That's where the alligators are."

"Bushwah," muttered an editor to Jack's right.

Massa waved Jack's paper. "Not what it says here."

"My secretary must have—"

"Sewers." Massa wrote it in, using a black pen, then picked up the red again, held it poised, read aloud: "'There *Are* Alligators in New York City Sewers.'" An infinitesimal pause, and the decision: "No." The red pencil drew the lines. "That's anti-Florida," Massa said. "Also, there's nobody *in* New York." It was well known that Massa had stayed completely away from the Greater New York Area for the last seventeen years mostly because three of his cousins in the garbage and jukebox industry would put several bullets in his head if he ever did go back. Before the move to Florida, the *Galaxy* had been published out of New Brunswick, New Jersey.

"Can I help you, young lady?"

Everybody looked up at the cold sound of Harsch's voice, to see him looking at an attractive but apparently nervous young woman dawdling near the table and fiddling with her shoulder bag. She was, Jack noted, the girl he had seen from the window, and she looked better close up.

Though nervous. "Oh," she said, tripping over herself by trying to back up without appearing to back up. "Mr. Harsch? I'm a new employee, I'm Sara—"

"All right," Harsch said. "Fine." To Massa he said, "What have we got left?"

"Just Boy Cartwright," Massa said, riffling papers. "He's no trouble, you go on."

Across the table from Jack, Boy Cartwright, a despicable Englishman of about forty, face puffy from years of alcohol and starch, smiled the smug smile of a winner. *Boy* was no trouble. Boy was a *good* Boy.

Massa squinted toward the new girl. He said, "She'll talk to scientists, right?"

"They do like a college girl," Harsch agreed.

Harsch left the elevator to talk to the college girl, and Massa considered Boy's list. "'The Argentine Navy Caused the Bermuda Triangle,'" he read, and lifted his head to show a happy smile. "That's terrific, Boy. Terrific."

Boy purred, eyes half closed in feline pleasure.

Chapter Three

The strange thing was, Sara had turned the job down back when it was offered. That was a year and a half ago, up in Syracuse, when the recruiters came around in the spring to talk to the journalism graduates. The *Galaxy* had a terrible reputation, a garish supermarket tabloid full of TV stars and creatures from outer space, but the recruiter had been a sensible, plausible woman, not much older than Sara herself, and she'd been tempted. Here was a chance to move from the cold dark Northeast to sunny Florida, to work in what sounded like a fun environment, to get a fabulous salary.

Too fabulous, that's what the problem had been. Thirty-five thousand dollars a year for a trainee? There had to be a catch in it somewhere. Weird scenarios of white slavery had crossed her mind—Florida was, after all, the same direction as South America—which was ridiculous, of course, but there had to be something wrong with it somewhere, or why would they pay so much? Besides, through a friend at school, she'd been offered a low-paying job on a small New England paper. It wasn't so far from home, it was real journalism on a comfortably small scale, and the editor looked a lot like Ed Asner. And the salary didn't make her nervous.

But here she was, after all, a year and a half later, and *everything* made her nervous, including the ice-eyed Jacob Harsch, approaching now from the elevator, while everybody else returned their careful attention to Mr. DeMassi. A cold smile on his cold face, Harsch made his way among the black lines—even he obeyed, she noticed—and offered a hand that Sara was not surprised to find also cold. He held hers briefly, saying, "Remind me of your name, dear."

"Sara Joslyn."

"Yes, I remember your resumé." His cold hand on her elbow, he led her away from the editorial meeting, down along the row of elevators. He was very tall, and he bent his head above her shoulder, speaking confidentially in a raspy voice. "You worked for a newspaper in Vermont."

"New Hampshire," she corrected. "It closed. Or it was merged, actually."

"We won't be closing," Harsch said, merely pointing out the fact, not speaking with any particular satisfaction. "We fulfill a need, and people come to us," he explained. They had come to a stop past the elevators, in an open space just before a librarylike area of tall bookshelves filled with phone directories and other reference books. "We think of ourselves as a community service organization."

"Oh?" Sara said politely.

"Not only in our hard news," Harsch told her, "but also in our features. Our audience is the modern woman, in all her complexity."

Remembering the gaudy front pages mounted on the entry walls, Sara nodded soberly, saying, "I see."

"Not only as a housewife and mother," Harsch went on, his manner calm and secure, "but as a consumer, a sophisticated audience for today's entertainment, and as the keeper of the flame of Western civilization. We think we here at the *Galaxy* know today's more knowledgeable, more interested, more *involved* woman pretty well, and our newsstand figures back us up. Our average weekly sale is comfortably above five million copies, which gives us sufficient financial strength to be able to go out and aggressively *get* the stories we want, the stories we know our reader is interested in."

Sara nodded, listening, keeping her thoughts to herself. This was the way the recruiter had talked, a year and a half ago, but the recruiter had spoken more passionately, selling the concept. Harsch didn't sell; he was more like a priest describing his religion. His assurance was so total that neither miracles nor agnostics could faze him. Sara, listening, wondered if the man could possibly believe what he was saying. We're all just here for the buck, aren't we? It didn't seem a good question to ask.

And what about her dead man, the man with the bullet in his head out on the highway? Her first story in the new job, and she'd imagined herself running in with the news, flinging herself into a chair in front of a typewriter, banging out the copy while co-workers in the corners of her imagination murmured, "The new kid's okay, you know?" She already had her lead: "The car radio played a sprightly melody, but the driver couldn't hear it anymore. He was dead."

Somehow, Jacob Harsch didn't seem like a person who would be *interested* in a dead body beside the road. His world was more rarefied than that. I'll tell my editor when I meet him, she decided.

Meantime, Harsch continued what was probably a set speech: "Our financial strength also makes it possible for us to hire the people we want, particularly the hardworking far-seeing young women like yourself who will help us keep the *Weekly Galaxy* brisk and alert and relevant to that ever-changing audience out there."

"Relevant," Sara echoed, no expression in her voice.

"Yes, relevant," Harsch said, smiling grimly down upon her. "We're not afraid of that word, Sara. All we're afraid of is getting stale, old, tired. That's why we *want* young women like yourself, who will challenge us, make us toe the mark, keep us . . . relevant."

"Gosh" was all Sara could think of to say.

* * *

Having passed back everybody's papers—Jack gazed in quiet despair at the many red lines now crisscrossing his own contributions—Massa finished this morning's editorial meeting with a little general diatribe, saying, "Nobody's giving me any news about John Michael Mercer. Do you people realize that man is the hottest star on television? Do you know his series, *Breakpoint*, is the number one rated series? And it's shot right here in Florida!"

Massa glared around, waiting for an answer, and finally an editor to Jack's left said, "Mercer doesn't seem to be doing anything right now, sir."

"John Michael Mercer?" Massa stared, pop-eyed. "What kind of answer is that? He's *interesting*! People want to know about him. *I* want to know about him! Last night— On the show last night, he drove that little sports car right *through* a burning barn! It was terrific! I was on the edge of my chair! You tell me he doesn't *do* anything? He drives through a burning barn, doesn't he? Why doesn't he tell us what he thinks about *that*?"

A different editor, reluctance in his face and in his voice, said, "Uh, sir, John Michael Mercer won't talk to us."

"What?" Massa was astonished. "But we're America! The *Galaxy* is the American people!"

The editor nodded. "We have explained that to him, yes, sir."

Pointing generally—but glaring, it seemed to Jack, particularly at Jack—Massa said, "I want John Michael Mercer stories." Then, using the same finger, he poked the button that caused his desk to recede back into the elevator and the elevator doors to close. The editorial meeting was over.

* * *

His cold hand once again on her elbow, Harsch led Sara back toward the conference table, saying, "Let's get you settled now. I'm giving you to one of the best editors in the shop. You'll learn a great deal from Jack."

"I'm sure I will," Sara murmured.

The editorial conference was apparently over; DeMassi and his elevator/office were gone, and many worried-looking people were getting up from the table, moving away. Harsch called, "Jack! Just a minute, Jack."

It was the rude man, who'd run into Sara on arrival. Now she could see he was about thirty, tall and well built, with thinning brown hair, and that he would probably be handsome if he didn't look so cranky and discontented. He made an obvious effort to smooth out the bad temper in his face when Harsch approached him, but failed. "Jack," Harsch said, "this is Sara Joslyn, she'll be on your team. Sara, this is Jack Ingersoll."

Jack Ingersoll was so thoroughly dislikable that Sara put on an extra-large smile to acknowledge the introduction, saying, "How do you do?"

"I've been worse," Ingersoll said, which was hard to believe.

"Jack will take care of you now," Harsch said, with a distant smile, and he left.

"You might as well come along," Ingersoll told her. He had some crumpled pieces of paper in his hand, which he waved vaguely toward the area of the black lines. "What was the name again?"

"Sara," she said, as they started off.

"I'm Jack." They walked between the lines.

"*I* remember," Sara told him, with a faint edge in her voice.

"Don't kick me, lady," Jack Ingersoll said, "I just left my bowels back there."

"What *was* all that?"

"Every morning at ten A.M.," he said redundantly, "the editors, of whom I am at least one, go to that shrine back there and lay thirty story ideas at the feet of—"

"Thirty! Every *day*?"

"Believe it or not," Jack Ingersoll said, "I came here as a young and beautiful woman. Much like yourself."

She looked sharply at him, but somehow the remark hadn't had the quality of a pass, or a compliment. That left it unanswerable, so Sara continued beside him in silence.

The result of the editorial conference was a great increase in the noise and activity within the land of the black lines. Many reporters had abandoned their tables on the other side of the room to run over here for quick meetings with their editors. Other editors were on the phone, or running back and forth between their own and their neighbors' offices; always going around to the door space, of course.

But why was that man over there putting on a Bela Lugosi mask and a black cape? Why were four women with English accents fugally singing "Row, Row, Row Your Boat" into a cassette recorder? Since today was the twelfth of July, why was one man assembling an artificial Christmas tree on his desk?

One thing about working here; it wasn't going to be dull.

* * *

Jack led the new one into his squaricle, where Mary Kate said, "What's the score, boss?"

"Five."

"Ouch." Mary Kate shook her bewigged head. Bonuses and awards and raises and squaricles beside the windows were all dependent on how many stories a team actually *got into the paper*. Jack's team usually did pretty well, but for the last week or so he'd been in a slump, and the team had reason to be worried.

"That isn't the worst of it," he told her. "One of the five is undeliverable."

"Which?"

"Gallstones. I asked the question, Massa answered it. Yes."

"Oh, boy." Mary Kate looked past Jack at the new one. "And what is this?"

"The latest keeper of the flame. Sara Something—"

"Joslyn."

"Sure." To Sara Joslyn, Jack said, "Mary Kate Scudder here is my secretary, not yours. Keep that in mind, she may be nice to you."

"How do you do," Sara Joslyn said to Mary Kate.

Mary Kate said, "I'm not sure," and gave Jack a look. "Gallstones, huh?"

"Rub it in," Jack said. "Give her the nutritionists."

As Mary Kate opened a file drawer, one of Jack's reporters, a tough broad named Ida Gavin, came into the squaricle and said, "It is definitely sex."

"Good," Jack said. To Mary Kate he said, "Also give her the goods requisition. Sign my name." To Ida he said, "Expand."

"The Keely Jones story," Ida said, referring to a currently popular television star. "She is definitely not only two-timing her husband with her manager, she is three-timing the manager with Mr. X."

"And you have Mr. X," Jack suggested.

"A swimming pool salesman."

"Okay," Jack said. "Not as good as a cardinal."

"An ex-con," Ida added.

"Oh, nice."

"Vehicular homicide. Pickup truck, pregnant woman, splat."

"Massa will want Miss Jones's reaction to this news," Jack said. "On tape."

"The little lady talks to nobody these days," Ida said. "Not even to God."

"Solve it, Ida, that's why we're here." Turning away as Ida left, Jack saw the new one standing with several papers in her hand. Taking them from her, he returned them one at a time with explanations: "This is your requisition. Take the elevator down to one, turn to the right, give them this sheet, they'll give you your typewriter, tape recorder, everything you need."

"Okay."

Pointing toward the reporters' tables on the other side of the room, Jack said, "Then you find yourself an empty oar over there, and row."

"Any one at all?"

"You're quick, I like that." Handing her two more sheets, he said, "These are tame nutritionists, they *will* talk to the *Galaxy*. You phone them and— Why aren't you writing this down?"

"Oh. Sorry." Putting the papers on Mary Kate's desk, she fumbled in her shoulder bag and produced steno pad and pencil. "Ready."

"Fine. This is your money quote. Potato—"

The girl looked blank. "My what?"

"You must be a journalism school graduate," Jack said.

She looked miffed. "Yes?"

"We talk faster here. The money quote is what you *must* get your subject to say."

"All right," she said. She was still miffed.

"This time, the money quote is, potato chips are a nutritious food, they contain all the values of potatoes plus fat *plus* salt—try to find a better word than fat—including protein. Eaten in moderation, potato chips can give you almost every known and unknown requirement of the human diet. Get me percentages; nitrate this, sodium that."

The girl looked up from her scribbling, bewildered. "But—what's it *for*?"

"The beer and potato chip diet," Jack told her, then grabbed up the papers he'd given her and drew a black pen line through one name, saying, "Don't call this one, he gave us the beer quote." He handed her the papers again.

She stood there, looking stunned. "The, the beer and . . ."

"Don't worry about it," he advised her. "Just get me the quote." He turned away as Don Grove slouched into the squaricle, looking as pessimistic as ever. "Yeah?"

"You couldn't use a Martian wedding, could you?"

"No," Jack told him. "What happened to your two-headed calf?"

Don shrugged. "They wanted the money before the pix." He sloped away, and the new girl said, "Umm . . ."

Turning back to her, Jack said, "Finished already?"

"Well, as a matter of fact," she said, "I do have a story. A different one."

Jack reared back, the better to view this wonder. "A story? Your first minute on the job? Do you hear this, Mary Kate?"

"Yes," Mary Kate said, reserving judgment.

"Tell me this story," Jack demanded, "in one brief, fact-filled, explosive sentence."

"There's a murdered man out on the road," she said, and looked smug, waiting to be patted on the head.

Jack held his breath for the kicker, though he already knew it wouldn't come. He didn't doubt her statement, not for a second—if she said there was a murdered man out on the road, there was a murdered man out on the road—but where was the fact's *usefulness*? At last Jack asked the core question: "So what?"

She gaped. "I beg your pardon?"

Okay, okay; no point taking it out on her, she's brand-new, nothing prior to this in the history of the world has been her fault. And here, in any case, is a golden opportunity for an entry-level lesson in the lower journalism. "Who is this murdered man?" Jack asked.

Wide-eyed, she spread her hands, saying, "*I* don't know, I just—"

"Who murdered him?"

"How am *I* supposed to—"

"On what series is he a regular?"

Her jaw dropped, then clenched. "Are you," she asked, "trying to make fun of me?"

"Not at all," Jack assured her, while Mary Kate shook her head in scorn. "I am merely trying to point out," he said, "that the *Galaxy* is a *national* newspaper, not some local hometown rag. We happen to be in the state of Florida, in which almost *every* road contains its murdered man, sometimes several. They're mostly grubby little crimes about grubby little people, usually connected with cocaine or the Marielistas or both. Our readers don't care about cocaine and never heard of the Marielistas, and they're happier that way. *Our* readers care about the beer and potato chip diet. They will love us and bless us and praise us as saviors of mankind when they read the beer and potato chip diet, and *you* are delaying that happy consummation. Now, you just got out of journalism school, so naturally you—"

"I did not," she said. "I worked a year for—"

"Well, now you're working *here*. Of course, if you'd rather *not* pursue the beer and—"

"I never said that!" Angry, jaw thrust forward, hands on hips, loudly she said, "I happen to be a reporter, and a good reporter, and I can follow my editor's instruc—"

"Good," he told her, meeting glare with glare, letting all the frustration and rage spill out, not caring anymore. "Because," he told her, bearing down, "*my* survival on this rag depends on my people giving me what Massa wants. If you can do it, do it. If you can't, save us all a lot of trouble and quit now." Then, realizing he was just about to go too far, that he was on the verge of firing this poor girl before she ever got a chance to go to work, he turned away to Mary Kate and said, "I'll be in the men's room, contemplating suicide."

* * *

Sara stared, openmouthed, as that insufferable man went stomping away, turning left, then right, among the black lines. The skinny little rat-faced secretary said, "Honey."

Expecting sympathy, an explanation, *something,* Sara turned her irritated expression toward Mary Kate Scudder, saying, "What?"

Mary Kate pointed across the room. "The phones are over there," she said.

CHAPTER FOUR

Coming back up to the third floor, lugging the small portable manual typewriter and the package of pens and pencils and notepads and typing paper and paper clips and Liquid Paper and scissors and Scotch tape, Sara was still furious. Leaving the elevator, she looked over across the land of black lines and there he was, Jack Ingersoll, once again in his own square, ranting at a man and a woman, pushing his fingers through his hair, pacing, ranting and ranting while the man and woman sometimes nodded, sometimes interjected a word, and the secretary, Mary Kate Scudder, unconcernedly typed.

Why would anybody ever work for such a beast? *I'll* work for him, Sara thought, but only to shove his nastiness and cynicism right back down his throat. I'll *prove* myself here, and they'll transfer me to a decent editor once they find out I can both take it and dish it out, and *then* we'll see.

In the meantime, Ingersoll was too far away to be glared at effectively, and all this stuff she carried was *heavy*, so Sara turned and went over to the rows of long tables, where the reporters still typed or jotted notes or talked, talked, talked on the telephone. There were very few empty spaces at the tables, and Sara hesitated, unsure what to do, until a young woman in the middle of it all waved and beckoned for her to come over.

There was an empty space to the young woman's left. Gratefully, Sara dumped all the stationery store stuff there and said, "Thanks. I'm new."

"You surely are," the young woman said, with a finishing school accent. She had a sharp-boned face, attractive in a patrician way. "I'm an old hand," she said, "I've been here for months and months. I'm Phyllis Perkinson."

"Sara Joslyn."

They shook hands, Phyllis Perkinson grinning like someone playing grown-up. "Who's your editor?" she asked.

"A truly terrible person," Sara said, "called Jack Ingersoll."

Phyllis Perkinson looked surprised. "Truly terrible? Jack Ingersoll's a pussycat."

"Not with me, he wasn't. I came in with—" Instinctively dramatic, Sara lowered her voice, leaning toward Phyllis Perkinson as she said, "The most incredible thing happened, on my way here."

Phyllis smiled, looking ready to laugh. "A funny thing happened on the way to work?"

"Not that funny. I found a murdered man!"

Phyllis looked puzzled through her smile, as though still looking for the punchline. "You found a what?"

"A murdered man." Sara quickly sketched in the scene out beside the road, with none of the flourishes it would have received if she'd been permitted to *write* the story, and finished, "When I told that, that, Ingersoll, he said, 'Oh? What series is he a *regular* on?' Very snotty, just like that."

"Oh," Phyllis said, frowning now as she thought it all over. "Well, maybe Jack got up on the wrong side of the bed this morning," she decided. "I mean, that was a little rough."

"I sure thought so."

"Of course, that *isn't* our kind of story, you know," Phyllis went on. "I mean, not really."

"I understand that. *Now* I do."

Phyllis dismissed the subject with an airy shrug. "Jack's my editor, too," she said, "and when you get to know him, believe me, you'll think he's great."

"I can hardly wait," Sara said, unconvinced.

"What are you working on?"

"Something called the beer and potato chip diet," Sara said, having trouble believing it herself. "Nutritive values in potato chips."

"Oh, he gave you an easy one!" Phyllis actually clapped her hands in delight. "There, see? I told you he was nice. He starts you off with something simple and easy, you don't even have to lie about who you are, and the first thing you know, you're an old pro like me." Laughing lightly, Phyllis said, "And now *I'd* better get back to work." And, with a little wave of her fingertips, she turned away and reached for her phone.

Setting up her desk space, Sara couldn't help but hear Phyllis's telephone conversation. After dialing what was obviously a long distance number, Phyllis said, with an official briskness completely unlike her previous conversational style, "Rosso Brothers? Yes, good morning, this is Miss Ballantine of Garfield Fiskin, accountants for John Michael Mercer. I understand you've taken over the gardening tasks at the Mercer est— No? Sorry." And she hung up.

Having arranged everything more or less neatly on her small desk space, Sara looked at the list of tame nutritionists, then rested her hand on the phone, but didn't immediately make a call. Instead, she listened to Phyllis talk to another gardening service and present herself again as Miss Ballantine of John Michael Mercer's accountants. Sara knew that John Michael Mercer was a television star with his own series, and so he would certainly be covered from time to time in the newspapers, but his *gardener?* What was that all about? Unable to swallow her curiosity, she waited till Phyllis's second call was finished, then said, "Phyllis? Could I ask a question?"

"He fired our other spy," Phyllis said.

Sara didn't get it. "Fired? Spy?"

"John Michael Mercer," Phyllis explained. "Massa's in *love* with John Michael Mercer, he wants stories about him all the time, but Mercer doesn't like the *Galaxy*. So we keep a spy in his house, and then he finds the spy and fires him, and then we have to plant another one. The last one was terrific, he worked for the security service, he was a guard right on the property, he knew *everything.*"

Sara said, "A private guard, working for him? And he was a *spy?*"

"The security company got all upset when they found out," Phyllis said, laughing as though it were some sort of college prank she was talking about. "So now we're going to try to go through his gardener, if we can *find* his gardener. Excuse me." And she went back to the phone.

I should leave, Sara thought. I should quit this crazy place, I should walk out right now. Oh, if only the *Courier-Observer* hadn't been merged! I *liked* working there. I'll never like this place. I should stand up this instant and walk out and never come back.

But she didn't. She picked up the phone and called a tame nutritionist.

* * *

Seated at his typewriter, Jack typed. He typed:

> Does sex cure gallstones? Go to macro, then back to micro. Does sex cure anything? Well, wait, wait, wait, a healthy sex life-- What about acne? Regular sexual activity tones the body, removes wastes-- Forget that part. Tones the body. Regular non-kinky sex tends toward mental and physical health. Can we get into it that way? Doctor, would you say a normally active sex life would tend to increased mental and physical health? Would there be some physical illnesses, Doctor, such as acne, various hormonal imbalances, that are improved by regular sexual activity? Doctor, I'm begging you here. Is it possible that certain disorders of the internal organs might be prevented or alleviated by regular normal sexual activity? The prostate, for instance. My God, the prostate! We may be onto

The new one approached the squaricle, a grim smile on her mouth and several sheets of paper in her hands. Jack tried to concentrate on the problem, but she was insistent, passing right by Mary Kate, stepping across the squaricle, slapping the pages onto Jack's desk, next to the typewriter. "The potato chip quote," she announced.

"Good, good, give it to Mary Kate."

> something here

"Don't you want to read it?"

Jack gave her a look that would have burned through a vault door. "I am *busy*," he said. "You're a hotshot reporter, as I understand it. You understood the assignment, as I understand it. You say you have completed the assignment, as I understand it. I understand. Give it to Mary Kate."

> Doctor, the prostate gland in men may be affected by frequency and manner of sexual activity. Now, is it possible

"Wait!" Jack called after her as, heavily miffed, having given Mary Kate her potato chip wisdom, the new one was about to march away. "I'll have another assignment for you in just a minute."

"As you understand it," she said.

He didn't have time to respond to that. The future of mankind itself hung in the balance.

```
that other inner organs in the human body can also
be affected, for good or ill, by sexual activity?
Doctor, is it at all possible that a combination
of mental and physical wellbeing, brought on by
normal healthy sexual activity, might reduce the
danger of developing gallstones, for example?
```

"Oh-*kay*!" Jack yanked the sheet of paper from the typewriter, and turned grinning to Mary Kate. "Give her the internists," he said. "Once again, we are snatching victory from the jaws of defeat."

"Feels more like the stomach of defeat," Mary Kate said, opening a file drawer.

"Very humorous," Jack agreed, and turned to the new one. If he admitted he'd forgotten her name she'd just get all snippy again. "Now, Champ," he said, smoothing the sheet of paper neatly on his desk, "let me describe our next money quote."

* * *

During lunch in the employees' commissary on the second floor, a broad beige room that combined all the most charming qualities of a bus depot in Newark with those of a minimum security prison, Phyllis suggested Sara move in and share her apartment. "It's *huge*," Phyllis assured her. "My salary's so ridiculous, I just went out and splurged, and there I am, stuck with the lease. It's just too large for me. Come on, Sara, it'll be fun."

"I'd love to," Sara said, having spent last night in the Holiday Inn back in the city and beginning to wonder when she'd have time to go apartment hunting for herself. So it was decided, and Sara went back to eating lunch, which was pretty good despite the surroundings, and very cheap.

Lunch happened between her successful capturing of the gallstone quote—the awful Ingersoll actually smiled when she brought it to him, or rather brought it to Mary Kate, whose comment was, "Holy shitsky!"—and her unsuccessful effort to learn which of Florida's many swimming pool care services tended to the swimming pool of John Michael Mercer. "*One* of these people is lying," Phyllis said darkly at one point, still failing to connect with John Michael Mercer's gardener. "The question is, which one? And the problem is, being service industries, they're used to lying on the phone anyway."

The question turned out to be unanswerable, at least for today, but in the process Sara learned about the reference section, an area of library stacks in a remote corner of the floor. In addition to dictionaries, encyclopedias, *Who's Who*s, almanacs and atlases, the reference section also contained what was apparently every phone book published in America, filed alphabetically by state and then by city. Sara and Phyllis alternated visits to this section, bringing back Florida phone books two at a time, calling the pool services and the gardening services, failing again. Then, at about ten to four, the workday nearly done, Sara returned to her desk space to find the white light on her phone flashing. Holding the latest phone books protectively to her chest, she said, "Why is it doing *that*?"

"Someone's calling you," Phyllis told her. "These phones don't ring, they just flash. Otherwise, could you imagine what this place would be like?"

"In a million years," Sara said, putting the phone books down, "I couldn't begin to imagine what this place already is." Picking up the receiver, holding it gingerly to her face as though it might have teeth and be of a mind to bite, she said, "Hello?"

"This is your master's voice."

She looked over toward the editors' world, and there he was way over by a window, waving at her, holding his own phone to his ear.

No. She was still angry, and she was justified. Her voice as cold as she could make it, she said, "Yes?"

"I just want to tell you," the now cheerful voice said in her ear, "you made my day with the gallstone quote. A very good beginning, Champ."

Sara knew it was risky, but she didn't care, she was still extremely irritated. "As you understand it," she said.

"Aw, come on," he said, being downright boyish now. "A little tension early in the day, that's all. Forgive and forget, Champ."

"My name," Sara said, "which you have obviously forgotten, is Sara Joslyn. And I'm sorry, Mr. Ingersoll, but you can't be both the good cop and the bad cop." And she hung up.

Next to her, Phyllis sighed. "Well, there goes a roommate," she said.

Will I be fired? Sara wondered, but couldn't guess. Do I *want* to be fired? She couldn't work out the answer to that one, either.

* * *

"She hung up on me," Jack told Mary Kate, as he replaced the receiver.

"Tough guy," Mary Kate commented.

"Me or her?"

"Both of you."

"But I'm the boss," Jack complained. "Why does some still small voice deep within me say, 'Fire the broad'?"

"You want to save her from corruption," Mary Kate suggested.
Jack shook his head. "No, that can't be it."

* * *

"You'll follow me," Phyllis said, outside the front door, at just a few minutes past four. "I'm in a white Corvette."

"See you," Sara said, and headed for the Visitor's parking lot while the hundreds of other employees all streamed the other way.

She hadn't bothered to lock the car, it being a rental with nothing personal in it, and now the glove compartment hung open. Had she left it like that? Of course not; so we have petty thieves here at the *Weekly Galaxy*, do we? There had been nothing in there but the rental agreement and the rental company's map of Florida, both of which were still present. Shutting the glove compartment, Sara drove across to the exit and waited there, watching the stream of Cadillacs, Mercedes, Jaguars, Triumphs and Thunderbirds go past the guard booth, headed for the empty highway. Several white Corvettes went by before one appeared with Phyllis's smiling face and waving arm framed in its low window. Sara waved back, slipped the Chevette into the line behind her, and drove past the guard booth. A different guard was on duty now, a short round black man who observed the passing fleet with utter boredom.

This was one of the two times a day, five days a week, when this twelve-mile superhighway was put to any kind of use. The pocket rush hour from the *Weekly Galaxy* tore along the road eastward toward the city like a mechanized tidal wave, raising pale dust, leaving emptiness in its wake.

An investigative reporter, Sara thought, could have a lot of fun digging into the history of this road, doping out what political ties, what debts and favors, had led to the construction of a twelve-mile major highway for the use and enjoyment essentially of one man: Bruno DeMassi. Pity, she thought, I'm not working on a paper that would be interested in that story.

The blue Buick Riviera was gone, and so was the body. Sara knew the precise spot where it had stood, the whole picture etched into her brain, and now it was gone, as though it had never been. So at least the local police were taking the crime seriously, even if it was beneath the consideration of the *Weekly Galaxy*.

I'll read about it, she thought bitterly, in my local hometown rag.

* * *

Phyllis's apartment was in a tall white box standing on end right at the water's edge. Out the broad windows of her seventh-floor living room, the Atlantic Ocean rolled and ran, grayish blue with foamy highlights in white. Her forehead against the cool glass—the apartment was sternly air-conditioned—Sara looked down at the beach, now in the building's shadow. "That's ours?" she asked.

"It's all ours," Phyllis told her. "The whole world is ours. Everything you can see is ours. Isn't it fabulous?"

It was. The name of the building, one of an apparently endless row of apartment buildings and condos along the oceanfront, was the Sybarite, displaying a cultural striving combined with a historical shakiness not infrequent among the namers of names along the Florida coasts. Phyllis's apartment contained, in addition to the huge stepdown living room, three large bedrooms, each with its own elaborate bath, a separate dining room with crystal chandelier at chin height, and an astonishingly large and well-furnished kitchen. Everything was a little too glittery for Sara's taste, but there surely was no appliance or mechanical convenience the builder had neglected to install.

In her few months here, Phyllis had done little by way of furnishing the place. Her own bedroom contained a king-size bed and a couple of mismatched antique dressers, plus a twelve-foot-long wall of closets stuffed to bursting with clothes. The living room featured a long sofa in white crushed velvet, a TV and VCR and stereo equipment and compact discs and videotapes all lying around on the floor amid a mass of wires, and a couple of bargain-shop lamps and end tables. The dining room was empty; Sara walked into the chandelier her first time through. One bedroom was also empty, but the other was outfitted with a double bed mattress on the floor. "You can use that until you get your own stuff," Phyllis said.

"I think I'll get my own stuff now," Sara decided. "The stores are still open."

"Good idea. Do you want to bring back a couple TV dinners, or should we order out tonight?"

I'm back in college, Sara thought, and the idea was so amusing that for the first time that day she relaxed and thought the immediate future might be fun after all. "I'll bring back a pizza," she said.

THE FIRST WEEK

Chapter One

The Peugeot smelled so *new*. Driving out to work on Friday morning, the last day of her first week on the job, the first day without the rental car, Sara reveled in the newness of the Peugeot, the slight stiffness in the steering wheel, the darkly gleaming *modern* look of the dashboard. Other cars, new and shiny and expensive, passed her as she drove, or she passed them, and it was almost as though this were a normal highway after all; until you noticed the absolute absence of traffic on the other side of the divider.

There. That's where the Buick Riviera had been stopped, with the murdered man. Sara saw and noticed that spot every morning, and the further spot where she'd made her U-turn. In fact, until Wednesday night's rain, it had still been possible to see the Chevette's tire marks on the shoulder where she'd thrown gravel in spinning around.

She wondered what had happened next, with the murdered man. Had they found his killer? She hadn't seen anything about it in the local paper, but she'd been so busy with her job, and furnishing her share of Phyllis's apartment, that she hadn't much read the local papers anyway, so it might have been in there and she'd missed it.

But probably Jack Ingersoll had been right, that first morning; the murdered man had most likely been involved in the drug world—his face had been a tough one, she remembered, even in death—and his killing would have been only marginally more interesting to a normal newspaper than to the *Weekly Galaxy*.

"THE PEOPLE, YES!" The sign reared up ahead of her, making her wonder yet again how many people besides Phyllis hadn't realized the quote was from Sandburg. How many *Galaxy* staffers, not to even think about *Galaxy* readers, would recognize the name Carl Sandburg at all?

It's a strange world I'm in, Sara thought, wondering how long she'd want to stay in it, and angled toward the single lane passing the guard booth on the right. But as she approached, the guard stepped out and held up his hand, surprising her; she'd just driven through with everybody else the other mornings this week. She stopped, wondering what was wrong.

The usual black guard was on duty at the gate, she not having seen that original white guard since she'd first arrived here and reported the murder to him. As he approached the car, she pushed the button that rolled her new window down and permitted the usual invisible blanket of hot dull air to roll in and cover her face. "Hi," she said. "What's wrong?"

No recognition touched his features: "Help you, miss?"

"I work here," Sara told him. "Sara Joslyn."

"I don't think I know you, miss," the guard said, his round black face carefully polite and impersonal, but at the same time watchful.

"I've been working here since Monday," Sara told him, feeling helpless and for some reason a little scared.

The guard transferred his careful frown from her face to the corner of the windshield. In Sara's rearview mirror, a line had formed and was lengthening; she was holding everybody up from getting to work. The guard said, "Miss? Where's your sticker?"

Then she remembered. "Oh, for Pete's sake, I forgot. That was a rented car, I bought this—"

More and more disapproving, the guard said, "You left your sticker on a rented car?"

"I'm sorry, I—"

Horns honked somewhere back in the line. The guard glowered in that direction, then glowered more specifically at Sara. "This isn't good," he said.

"I'm really sorry, I completely—"

"Park in the Visitors' lot today," the guard told her. "I'll see what I can do."

"Thank you," Sara said humbly. What a way to finish my first week, she thought.

* * *

Jack sat at his desk, eating a pencil. Beside him, Binx Radwell, sweating gently, sat on the corner of the desk and morosely squeezed a pink rubber ball. Nearby, Mary Kate typed. Jack took the pencil from his mouth, gazed somberly across the room, shook his head, took a breath, squared his shoulders, and announced, "The *Galaxy* Challenge. Who will make a replica of the Spirit of St. Louis and fly it to Paris?"

Binx considered him. He squeezed, squeezed, squeezed the pink ball. "The *Galaxy* sponsors, you mean?"

"Sure," Jack said. "The prize is three French lessons at Berlitz."

"Insurance," Binx said.

"I hate a nay-sayer," Jack said, and put the pencil back in his mouth.

Louis B. Urbiton, at fifty-one the oldest Australian reporter on the staff and frequently the drunkest, came through the black lines, entered Jack's squaricle through the door space, and said, "A stringer in Spokane says their panda died."

Jack looked up, unmouthed the pencil. "Did it leave a grieving mate?"

"I didn't ask," Louis admitted.

"Ask," Jack advised him.

Louis went away. Jack gnawed pencil. Binx squeezed the pink ball. Mary Kate stopped typing and yawned. Speaking around the pencil, Jack said, "Binx, listen, would you feel I was stealing if I did 'Legionnaires' Disease: It Was Guilt'?"

"Mine was suicide, and Massa didn't like it," Binx pointed out. "What do you mean, guilt?"

"Psychosomatic."

The phone flashed. Mary Kate answered, spoke softly. Nodding, Binx said, "Psychosomatic Illness Is All in Your Mind, Scientists Say. I tried that one once; Massa didn't get it."

"You're lucky. Okay if I take?"

Binx tossed the ball into the air, then had to scramble to catch it. "Blessings on you both," he said, and sat on the corner of the desk again.

Hanging up the phone, Mary Kate told Jack, "Mr. Harsch wants Sara when she comes in."

"Here she comes," Jack said, watching Sara approach through the maze.

"Fired?" Binx asked. "Her first week?"

"No," Jack said. "Harsch only fires on Tuesdays, so your last two days you don't get paid for."

"Maybe," Binx said, squeezing the pink ball with both hands, "maybe that's the answer. Maybe if I never come in on Tuesdays—"

* * *

In the last few days, Sara's opinion of Jack Ingersoll had softened, but she still remained wary. When Phyllis had explained at length the kind of pressure Jack and the other editors operated under, it did make his initial bad temper more understandable—"As I understand it"—though it had still been damned unfair of him to take it out on somebody arriving here for her very first day of work. Jack himself perhaps agreed with that, since he'd been much more friendly ever since; or maybe it was simply her success in getting the gallstones quote that first morning, which she now understood—"As I understand it"—had been a real coup. Not matched since, unfortunately.

Still, here was another day, another chance. Coming to Jack's squaricle, seeing Binx Radwell there with his perpetual look of terror, she told herself she'd be *much* worse off if she'd been assigned to Binx's team. He had, in the rough phraseology of Jack Minter, her former editor on the *Courier-Observer*, loser sweat all over him.

A few squaricles away, a nuclear family, Mother and Dad and Sis and Junior, loitered aimlessly, dressed in homemade spacesuits, all shiny aluminum foil, with their helmets under their arms. Looking at those people, Sara almost missed the door space to Jack's squaricle, but recalled herself just in time, made an awkward little hop to one side, and entered without breaching local etiquette. "Good morning," she said generally. "More John Michael Mercer?"

"Not yet," Jack told her. "The Lord Harsch wants you in his office, up on four."

"Then I'd better go," Sara said, wondering what this could be about. Harsch hadn't spoken to her since the first morning's pep talk. Gesturing at the astronaut family, she said, "What's with Lost in Space?"

"No idea," Jack said.

Binx said, "Something of Boy's, I think."

"That limey bastard," Jack said, his chronic bad temper suddenly resurfacing. With a gloomy glower at Sara, he said, "I'm not holding you here, you know."

It isn't personal, Sara told herself, but wanted to kick him in the balls anyway. "See you later," she said sweetly.

* * *

They watched her follow the black lines toward the elevators. "Nice," Binx suggested.

"Very nice," Jack agreed.

Binx tossed the pink ball from hand to hand, dropped it, caught it on the bounce. "Listen," he said. "Don't tell her I'm married, okay?"

"I'm listening," Mary Kate said.

"Don't," Binx told her.

Ida Gavin came striding into the squaricle. "Keely Jones," she said.

"I remember her," Jack admitted. "Three-timing her husband and her manager with the ex-con swimming pool salesman."

Binx looked up, clutching the ball. "Ex-con swimming pool salesman?"

"This one's mine," Jack warned him. "All mine. And we have Mr. X—"

"The swimming pool salesman," Binx guessed.

"—on tape."

"We are now," Ida said, "running the Mr. X tape on a loudspeaker truck in front of Keely's house in Bel Air."

"Nice," Jack said.

"I'll keep you up-to-date," Ida said, and departed.

Binx sighed. He put the ball in the crook of his elbow, bent the arm to squeeze the ball, grimaced with pain, put the ball back in his right hand, considered it like Puck considering the globe. "Invite her to our barbecue, why don't you?" he said.

Jack stared at him. *"Ida?"*

Binx looked at Jack more in sorrow than in anger. "Sara," he said.

"She'll notice you're married."

"I'll be going for sympathy," Binx said, and dropped the pink ball. He watched it roll away across a black line into somebody else's squaricle. "What do you suppose Harsch wants with her?" he asked. "Give a demonstration, do you think, on sexual technique with college professors?"

"No," Jack said. "Harsch gave up sex years ago, when he found something he really liked."

Binx waited, watching his ball at rest under the corner of someone else's desk. The silence grew. Mary Kate stopped typing. Binx sighed and accepted the inevitable. "All right," he said. "What did Harsch find that he *really* liked?"

"Roasting babies," Jack said.

* * *

Jacob Harsch's top-floor office was a large low-ceilinged room in hushed grays, with no sharp edges. Broad gray-tinted windows softened the southern view of the desert, making it into an idealized portrait of itself. Bookcases were filled with large somber tomes grouped by subject: war, pestilence, slavery, Elvis Presley. The furniture was low, bulky, dark, expensive. At a long and heavy-legged library table to one side Harsch himself stood with the *Galaxy*'s art director, Fred Mooney, a nervous paunchy balding man with a scraggly moustache. Together, they studied a number of pictures scattered on the table, Harsch's bony long fingers and Mooney's blunt fidgety fingers pushing the pictures this way and that, revealing some, covering others. "All of these women," Mooney said irritably, "have their mouths open."

"That's all right, Fred," Harsch said softly. "That's considered all right."

"Okay, okay, fine." Restlessly, Mooney's fingers pushed and shoved. "Now, these funeral pictures," he said. "These funeral pictures just don't show me a thing. It's so dark, there's no life, there's nothing."

"This was a great American, Fred," Harsch said, his gray fingernail tapping the famous chin. "Top box office for three decades. Massa wants a picture on the cover."

Dubious but scared, Mooney blinked and squinted at the pictures. "Well, I'll do what I can," he said. "We can lighten them, draw in some detail."

"A little cleavage here," Harsch said, the fingernail tap-tapping. "Widows are considered sexy."

"Uh huh, uh huh." Fleeing that topic, petulantly irritated, Mooney picked up another picture. "Now, this thing," he said. "This is the space battle story, you know? That clairvoyant in Dallas told us about it. Two spaceships had a dogfight the other side of the moon, what was it, last October, she sees space debris coming around into sight either late August or early September."

"I recall the story," Harsch agreed.

"Now, look at this thing," Mooney said.

Harsch took the picture, which was done in the black-and-white photo realist style of the *Galaxy*. "Yes?" The cold fingernail tapped. "Here's the two ships, different styles because they're different civilizations. Here's the moon. We won't see the earth, the moon hides it. So?"

"Well," Mooney said, taking the picture back, gazing at it with deep discontent, "this is very murky, like almost out of focus. The question is, is this a drawing, or is it a photo?"

Harsch lifted his gaze and looked into Mooney's fidgety eyes.

"I mean," Mooney explained, "I got to know for myself, for if we retouch or whatever, but also, what if Massa asks me?"

"Fred, how long have you worked here?" Harsch asked, not unkindly.

"Nine years," Mooney said in terror, and the intercom on Harsch's desk buzzed.

"One moment," Harsch said, and crossed to his low massive desk and pushed the button, saying, "Yes?"

"Sara Joslyn, Mr. Harsch."

"Ah, yes. Send her in."

"Yes, sir."

Turning, crossing back to Fred Mooney, Harsch said, "I think it's a drawing."

"Okay," Mooney said, nodding jerkily, holding the picture without looking at it. The door opened, and Mooney threw a glance of abject fear in that direction, as though it might be the Spanish Inquisition coming in.

* * *

Sara entered Mr. Harsch's austerely opulent office, and found him talking with a rumpled moustached scared-looking man holding some sort of picture. Mr. Harsch was saying to him, "But you could double-check. Call Accounting, see did any photographer put in for two light-years' expenses."

The rumpled man blinked, as though he'd been slapped. "Well," he said. "Okay. Okay, it's a drawing." He threw a quick glance at Sara, apparently realizing his interview with Mr. Harsch was over, and started gathering up other pictures from the library table behind him. "And we'll do what we can about that other," he said.

"Massa wants," Harsch said, in his soft cold voice.

"Okay. Sure." Pictures clutched in his arms, the man shot another scared look at Sara and hurried from the room.

This was to be the first time Harsch would talk to Sara since her arrival on Monday, and she'd spent the time in the elevator trying to guess what the subject would be. Congratulations on the gallstone quote? A special assignment? A transfer to a different editor? (She wasn't sure exactly how she felt about that last possibility.) She wasn't at all prepared for Harsch's first statement. His cold-eyed attention swiveling to her, he said, "I understand, Miss Joslyn, you've lost a piece of *Galaxy* property."

Bewildered, Sara said, "I have?"

"The sticker you were—"

So relieved that it wasn't anything serious, Sara unconsciously interrupted, saying, "Oh, that! I completely forgot—"

"Miss Joslyn," the cold voice said, bearing down, "the *Galaxy* is a fearless hard-hitting newspaper."

Thrown off balance, Sara could think of nothing to say but "Yes?"

"That means," Harsch told her, "the *Galaxy* has enemies. That's why we have security here."

"Oh," Sara said, nodding, "I see what you—"

"A *Galaxy* sticker is now out in the world, Miss Joslyn," Harsch said. "Out of our control."

Unable to believe Harsch expected her to treat this situation like a tragedy out of Shakespeare, Sara said, "But it's just a—"

"I want you to understand this, Miss Joslyn," Harsch said, overriding her. "We don't take security lightly here. Nor theft of *Galaxy* property."

Shocked, offended, Sara raised up, saying, "Mr. *Harsch*, I—"

"That's what our attorneys would name it," he said, "if we felt we had to call them in on this." Then, while Sara watched him in mingled alarm and disbelief, Harsch turned away, looking out his tinted windows at the soft gray desert. "You're new here," he said, looking at the desert, "so I'm taking that into account." Glancing back at Sara, he offered a wintry smile, saying, "Everyone gets one free error."

"Thank you," Sara said, her mind racing. Had all of this just been meant to scare her, to play some sort of petty power game on her?

"However," Harsch went on, giving her his full attention again, "we will need that sticker back."

She didn't understand. "But it's gone," she said.

"You're a reporter, aren't you?"

"Yes, sir," she said, with as much force as she could muster.

"Your assignment, Miss Joslyn," he said, bearing down again, "is to drive your stickerless car off this property and return no later than tomorrow with the sticker affixed."

Call the rental place; not impossible. Absurd, but not impossible. "All right," she said, feeling mutinous but realizing mutiny would be just as absurd as this pettiness over a windshield sticker. Captain Queeg and the strawberries, she thought.

Turning away again, moving toward his desk, speaking more quietly and thoughtfully, Harsch said, "This is a bad mark for Jack Ingersoll, and—"

"What?" Sara stared. "Why for *him*?"

Harsch looked back at her, shrugging as though it should be obvious. "You're on his team. If you don't return, it's a worse mark. And if you fail to come back tomorrow, Miss Joslyn, fail to come back."

Tomorrow's Saturday, she suddenly realized, and assumed he'd forgotten. "There won't be anyone here tomorrow," she said. "It's Saturday."

"The guard will be at the gate. He'll be expecting you."

So that's my punishment, Sara thought. I get to drive all the way out here on my day off. "All right," she said. "Is that all, Mr. Harsch?"

"For the moment," Harsch told her, as a section of wall to her left suddenly receded an inch, with a heavy mechanical *clack*, and slid away rightward behind the next section of wall, revealing Bruno DeMassi, seated at his desk in his elevator/office. He looks ridiculous in there, Sara thought, but then realized that he also looked faintly frightening, the mechanized spider in his web. Everything at the *Galaxy*, it seemed, combined those same qualities of the scary and the absurd.

"Busy, Jock?" DeMassi asked, with a quick glance toward—but not exactly at—Sara.

"No, sir," Harsch told him, his manner somehow just as cold as ever but no longer threatening. "Miss Joslyn is just starting out on assignment."

"Good, good," DeMassi said. "Golf this afternoon?"

"I'd be pleased, sir." The expression around Harsch's mouth might even have been called a smile.

Sara, moving toward the door, said, "I'll get right to work on it, Mr. Harsch."

"You," DeMassi said, waving a hand at her. "Miss Whatever."

"Joslyn," Sara said.

"Come on," DeMassi told her, gesturing for Sara to board the elevator, "I'll give you a lift."

Surprised but willing, Sara said, "Why, thank you," and crossed to enter the elevator.

Meantime, DeMassi had apparently heard the echo of what he'd said and was delighted by it. Grinning hugely at Harsch, he said, "Did you hear that? This *is* a lift! In England, that's what they call an elevator, they call it a lift! Did you hear what I said? I'll give you a lift!"

"Funny," Harsch agreed.

"Talk to you later," DeMassi said, and, with Sara aboard, pushed a button on his desk.

From within, Sara watched two wall sections close over the space, shutting out the grim figure of Jacob Harsch. The inner wall section, paneled wood with a pair of framed old hunting prints on it, snicked into place, and the elevator simply became a windowless doorless room furnished as an office. I'd go crazy in here in thirty minutes, Sara thought, as she felt the elevator start down.

"Sit down," DeMassi told her, pointing at the green leather sofa on the side wall. As she did so, he opened the refrigerator built into his desk, took out a bottle of beer, and waggled it at her. "Beer?"

"No, thank you."

DeMassi grunted, shut the refrigerator door, opened the bottle. "Good for your figure," he said. "We got a story coming up on that."

"I worked on it," Sara told him.

That brightened him right up. "Yeah? Then you know. Great story. You know why this is my office?"

"No, sir," Sara admitted.

"Watch. This is your floor."

Sara felt the elevator stop. DeMassi pushed the button on his desk and the paneled wall receded with its hunting prints, revealing the conference table and, beyond it, the editorial land of the black lines. DeMassi leaned forward, glowering suspiciously, glaring left and right at his domain out there. Then he relaxed a bit, looked at Sara, winked, and said, "They never know where I am, never know when I'll see 'em! Keeps 'em working, keeps 'em on their toes."

"I guess it would," Sara agreed. "Well, thanks a lot." Exiting the elevator, edging past the conference table, she said, "I better get to work. The boss is watching."

"You bet!" DeMassi shouted, laughing, and pushed the button again. As the elevator shut, he was drinking deeply from the beer bottle.

* * *

Jack was on the phone, helpless with rage. "Whadaya mean," he demanded, "incest isn't interesting? Incest has *always* been interesting. So what if they're giraffes?"

The tinny voice in his ear said, "No."

Jack slammed down the phone, as Sara Joslyn entered the squaricle. Not noticing her troubled expression, thinking about his own troubles, he glared at her and yelled, "Evaluators!"

She looked at him without comprehension. "Yes?"

"They hate me," Jack told her, "just out of the evil in their hearts."

"Amen, brother," Mary Kate said, not pausing in her typing.

"Evaluators?" Sara echoed. "What's that?"

Brimming over with sarcasm, punching and chopping the air in front of his stomach, Jack said, "What a happy carefree existence you do lead, Missy Sara. A life without evaluators!"

"So far," Sara said.

"You know what our bottom line is here?" Jack demanded. "What gets into the paper! And you know who carries the ball on that, every goddamn down? The editors. *Me*."

"I know that."

"You know that." Jack glared at the telephone as though it had just laughed at him. "Let me tell you what I do."

"Oh, good," Mary Kate said, typing and typing. "Now he's gonna tell her what he do."

"You be quiet," Jack told her, "or I'll tell everybody *your* secret. Underneath that wig, you're Pee-Wee Herman."

"Take it out on everybody, why don't you," Mary Kate suggested.

Turning back to Sara, Jack said, "I make up the story, or I find it in some local newspaper from East Nowhere, I sell it to Massa, that's the *first* hurdle. Then I give it to you, you check it, make it work, write it up, you give it back to me, you're done, happy as a pig at the *Galaxy*. Am *I* done?"

"I don't know," Sara said. "Are you?"

"In a word, I am not at *all* done."

"That's six words," Mary Kate said.

Ignoring her, Jack said, "My *next* task is to push the goddamn story through the fact checkers. Devil's advocate time. Do we have the quotes, the pictures, the proof? If it holds up with them, it should hold up in court. *Then* I take it up to Rewrite. You know what the cute gimmick is with Rewrite?"

Mary Kate said, "She doesn't yet, but she's going to."

"The cute gimmick with Rewrite—Mary Kate, don't you have a sick mother to visit or something?"

"She died."

"Well, that's good. Too late to keep her from having you, but still." Turning back to Sara, Jack said, "Massa likes individual initiative, so therefore the boys and girls of Rewrite get to decide *what* they will rewrite. Your story, my story, it sits there till the pages crumble. I go up, I shmooze, I cry a tear, sometimes two tears, *please* write my story!"

"Oh, my gosh," Sara said, looking shocked and sympathetic.

"Neatly put," Jack told her. "*Then,* once Rewrite has deigned to re-goddamn-write, *then* we got the evaluators. They sit up there on four, practically in Jock Harsch's left nostril, up on top of the whole shebang, they read the story, they decide is it *interesting*. It has to be interesting, and it has to be interesting to *them*. If we bore an evaluator, me and you and the fact checkers and the boys and girls of Rewrite, if all our combined efforts make an evaluator yawn, the story's dead. It does not get in the paper."

"I had no idea," Sara said. The girl's eyes were round with awe.

"A happy life." Pointing toward the conference table and the bank of elevators, Jack said, "Every week, on Massa's desk there comes the box score. This editor had six stories in the paper, this editor had nine, Boy Cartwright had fifty-seven and keeps the only corner squaricle in the known world, this editor had *two,* and that means this editor went wee wee wee all the way out of a job."

"Well, the beer and potato chip story's going in," Sara said, apparently trying to encourage him.

Jack was not of a mood to be encouraged. "One drop," he said, "in one bucket. A new bucket every week. Speaking of which—" and he picked up from his desk a paper-clipped stack of paper; Sara's first assignment this morning.

But she said, "I'm sorry."

He looked at her, not understanding. "What? You mean you *were* fired? On a Friday?"

"Not exactly," Sara said. He thought she was acting a little guilty, a little shifty.

Now what, he wondered, and put the papers on his desk again so he could give her his full attention. He said, "Who, what, when, where, why."

Sara sighed. She said, "It seems I left my parking sticker on the rented—"

"Oh, jeez," Jack said. *He* was going to get blamed again. They give him all the dimwits, and then it's *his* fault when they do something stupid. Too weighed down even to give voice, he merely sat and looked at her.

"I'm sorry," she said again, which helped a whole hell of a lot. "Mr. Harsch said I'm supposed to go get it back."

"But here we are," Jack pointed out, "having this nice chat."

Offense closed her face. Lips clenched, she turned without a word and stalked away, left and right through the squaricles. Watching her go, Jack said, "Maybe I hate women."

Mary Kate shook her head. "You're not that selective," she said.

Chapter Two

They hadn't re-rented the Chevette. Walking with the skinny young black mechanic in white coveralls through the rows of cars out behind the rental office, Sara noticed that "Z" was the first letter of every license plate back here, and she asked him about it. "State system," he told her. "Every rental, every leased car in Florida, they all got the Z plate."

The murdered man's car had had a Z plate, hadn't it? She'd jotted the details into her notebook at the time. A larger and more expensive car than her Chevette, though; some sort of Buick. Maybe he'd leased it. But that idea somehow seemed more businesslike than the murdered man's tough dead face had suggested; so maybe he stole it.

Using a single-edge razor blade, the mechanic carefully peeled her VISITOR sticker from the Chevette's windshield. "Big outfit like the *Galaxy*," he commented as he worked, "you'd think they could afford more than one of these."

"Wouldn't you," agreed Sara. "Do you read the *Galaxy*?"

"Oh, sure," he said, and grinned. "Every time. They're a gas."

Did the dread evaluators have this fellow in mind, Sara wondered, when they read each story to see if it was interesting enough to be published in the paper? Did Jack have him in mind? Am *I* supposed to?

At last he gave her the wrinkled but still intact sticker, and she gave him five dollars for his trouble, along with her sunniest smile. "I really appreciate this," she told him.

Shrugging, pocketing the five, he said, "I'da had to take it off anyways, before we rented it out again. Can't release no cars got a lotta stuff on the windows." And so much for Jacob Harsch's security.

* * *

It was barely lunchtime, and here she already had the sticker, so she got herself a ham and cheese sandwich on rye and a container of coffee from a takeout place near the rental agency, and ate it all in the Peugeot on the drive back out to the *Galaxy*. Presumably she could take the whole day off, since Harsch had given her till tomorrow to return, but this would demonstrate what a good and willing worker she was, and how heartily sorry she was to have forgotten the sticker, and all that nonsense. Maybe Jack would even lose some tiny bit of his bad temper. Besides, what else would she do with herself? She didn't know anybody yet in this part of the world except the people at work. The beach she had access to through the apartment she was sharing with Phyllis would already be in the building's shadow, and she had no interest in just hanging around the big empty apartment all day.

There. The place where she'd found the murdered man. When she'd written to her mother in Great Barrington on Wednesday night she'd described that incident, and said it was "the most exciting thing that ever happened to me," but even when writing the words she'd felt their falseness. The moment had been scary, eerie, strange, but not exactly exciting; and there'd been no follow-through. The unreality that had been in the incident from the beginning had grown and spread to cover the entire event; as though it had never been.

But there was the spot; it had happened. She looked at it on the way by, looked at it again in the rearview mirror. She was alone out here on the highway now, the same as that day, the circumstances the same as then for the first time since it had happened. Her other trips along this road had all been in the midst of the *Galaxy*'s twice daily traffic jam.

Not quite the same time of day, though. It was now just about one o'clock in the afternoon, and she'd found the murdered man at quarter to ten in the morning, her first-day appointment with Mr. Harsch having been set at ten o'clock.

Hmmm. The employees all arrived at nine, some a little earlier, some a little later. There's always a few stragglers, so it probably would have been ten past before the morning rush hour was done. Then, sometimes between ten past nine and quarter to ten—no, make it twenty to ten, since she hadn't seen the killer's car ahead of her—the murdered man had come driving out, had stopped beside the road, and had been murdered.

Well, wait. This was the first she'd actually thought about the murder since Monday, when Jack Ingersoll had so brutally disabused her of the notion that she'd brought him a useful story. But, now that she did start to think about it, driving along the empty pale road beneath the huge midday sun, there were several things she knew or could assume about the murdered man, beginning with the fact that he must have been *going to the Galaxy*. There was nothing else on this road, nothing to either side of it. So the murdered man was on his way to the offices of the *Weekly Galaxy*.

Why? To bring proof of some exposé? But the *Galaxy* wasn't that kind of paper. What she'd suspected before, she now knew for certain, after one week on the job. The *Galaxy* didn't touch real scandal at all, only marital problems of television stars, sexual peccadilloes of jet-setters, medical weirdnesses. Anything involving the mob, say, or crooked politicians, anything involving true investigative hard news, would have led the murdered man to some other newspaper, almost any other newspaper. Even the poor old *Courier-Observer* would have been a better potential place for such information.

Well, whatever the reason, the *Galaxy* must be where the murdered man had been going. So his having been killed might very well have something to do with the reason he was going to the *Galaxy*.

Unless he actually worked for the paper, of course. Maybe he was an employee. From Jack's description of evaluators, the murdered man could have been one of those.

So maybe Jack killed him, out of bad temper. Driving along, the *Galaxy* building and sign becoming visible far ahead, she grinned at that idea. The evaluator evaluated.

Well, whoever killed him . . .

Whoever killed the murdered man, he or she or they had most likely then gone on to the *Galaxy* themselves.

That's right. The body had still been warm, not yet terribly stiff. He had to have been killed no more than half an hour before she'd found him, or staffers going to work would have seen it happen. It was *possible* the killer had driven on from there to the next break in the central divider—there were such breaks every two miles—and had then turned around and driven back to the city, leaving the road at the city end a few minutes before Sara had started out on it; possible, but awfully tight. The likelihood—not definite yet, but likely—was that the killer had gone straight on to the *Galaxy*, had been waved past the guard booth because of the *employee sticker* on his car (her Chevette had been the only car in the visitors' parking lot that morning), and had simply gone to work.

Which meant the probabilities were, the killer worked for the *Weekly Galaxy*.

Had there been an employee sticker on the murdered man's car? Frowning as the *Galaxy* building loomed up ahead of her, Sara tried to remember the Buick's windshield, tried to picture it in her mind, see whether or not there had been anything on the left lower corner of the glass; but she just wasn't sure. That hadn't been part of her attention at the time, and now she could visualize the Buick's windshield just as readily with the sticker as without.

The guard was pleased when she appeared and handed him the wrinkled sticker. "Mr. Harsch sent a memo down," he told her, "said you probably wouldn't be around with this till tomorrow."

"I work fast."

"Usually," the guard said, "you wouldn't get your permanent sticker till next week, but there's no point giving you the temporary for just one more day, so . . . Excuse me."

Once again, as the white guard had done on Monday, this one took a sticker from his clipboard, put the clipboard atop her car, peeled off the sticker's backing, and leaned in through her open window to fasten it to the lower left corner of her windshield.

The permanent sticker.

* * *

Massa had liked a magnificent eleven of Jack's ideas this morning. If it weren't for the new one and her goddamn sticker, Jack's world would be a reasonably all right place today, considerably less Hieronymus Bosch than usual. And the ice cream diet, which continued to elude all search parties; those were the two clouds on Jack's horizon.

And here came one of those clouds now, a lot closer than the horizon. "Well, looka that," Mary Kate said in mild amazement, and Jack looked up, and here came Sara Joslyn herself, quartering her way through the squaricles. "Well, well," Jack said. "In fact, well, well, well."

"I'd say so," said Mary Kate.

Sara Joslyn. She went left, she went right, she advanced, she went off at an oblique angle, she turned sharply, she came straight to Jack's squaricle and entered through the door space. "I got it," she said. "Everything's fixed."

Jack smiled upon her, he couldn't help himself. "And you came back today, rather than tomorrow."

"Well, I felt bad about making trouble."

"And quite rightly, too," Jack said, as Ida Gavin entered the squaricle and said, "Keely Jones."

"Ah, yes," Jack said, swiveling around to face her. "We are playing the tape of the swimming pool salesman's story from a loudspeaker truck in front of Miss Jones's house."

"Not anymore," Ida said. "She came out and fired a shotgun at our truck."

"Oh, *nice!*" Jack said, and Mary Kate looked up with a sunny smile.

"Our attorneys," Ida said, "are right now negotiating with her attorneys."

"Be prepared, Ida," Jack said, "to sky LAward soonest."

"My fuck-you suit is already packed," Ida said. "I'll keep you informed." And she marched from the squaricle.

Jack turned again to the new one. Was it possible things would be going *well* now for a little while? Was it possible this Sara Joslyn would eventually become part of the solution, instead of part of the problem? "Your attitude is commendable, Sara," he told her. "And I shall reward it by overworking you." He selected two sets of papers from his desk and handed them to her. "I like to think of these as self-explanatory."

"I hope *I* think of them that way," she said, accepting the papers.

* * *

But first, there was the unresolved Case of the Murdered Man. What had happened there, finally? The *Galaxy*'s extensive research library did not include back issues of the local paper, so it wouldn't be easy to go back and find whatever had been reported on it, if anything. Sara believed now that Jack's first dismissive summation of the incident had been wrong, that it hadn't merely been a drug dealer story, or that if it *was* a story about drugs the trail nevertheless led here somehow to the *Galaxy*, but she had been aware of absolutely no investigation of the incident; no police presence at the *Galaxy*, none at the scene of the crime. No one had approached to question her. Were the police also dismissing the murder as unimportant? Was there such a thing as an unimportant murder?

Leaving Jack Ingersoll's squaricle, carrying the paperwork of her new assignment, Sara was distracted by this unfinished story, this unanswered question: What about the murdered man beside the road? True, it was none of her business. True, she already had too much to think about. True, there was nothing she could *do* about the problem. But it still existed, nagging at her.

For instance. Even though her next assignment was right here, clutched in her hand, she found herself wondering again about the murdered man's car's license plate; did its letters, or did they not, start with a "Z"? Making her intricate way out of the squaricles, Sara crossed to the reporters' tables, where Phyllis flashed her a bright welcoming smile while continuing to talk seriously and earnestly into the phone: "And when you met Cleopatra," she was asking, "in your previous life, did she happen to mention anything about snakes?"

To the left of Sara's desk space—Phyllis being on her right—sat Harry Razza, another of Jack's eight reporters and another of the many staffers from Australia. An aging matinee idol type, with thickly sculptured auburn hair and a roguish smile, he apparently thought of himself as being from the Douglas Fairbanks mold, and Sara had been forced to put him quite firmly in his place several times on Monday and Tuesday; since when, he'd been friendly and calm. Now, he was speaking with dogged patience on the phone, saying, "Can I quote you as saying you're glad he's dead? Well, can I quote you as saying you wouldn't bring him back if you could? Well, can I quote you as saying you feel a certain relief?"

Bob Sangster, the Aussie with the large nose, had the desk space directly in front of Sara, where he was saying into his phone, "Now, didn't the United States government *pay* for these frogs?" And Don Grove, the pessimistic young reporter who had so far this week failed to produce both a two-headed calf from Brazil and a Martian wedding from Marin County, California, in his position at the desk space directly behind Sara was also on the phone, saying, "And how old was the victim? And this midget: just how short *is* he?"

Sara had already become so used to this new work environment that she was distracted by none of these conversations. Seating herself at her desk space, putting Jack's new work assignments to one side, she rested her shoulder bag on the typewriter—there wasn't room for it anywhere else—removed her spiral notebook, and then placed the shoulder bag, as usual, under her chair. Now, the page with the murdered man's car . . .

. . . wasn't there.

She leafed through the notebook twice. Had she torn it out? She occasionally did that, when a page contained only items of the most transitory interest, like shopping lists, but surely she wouldn't have torn out the page containing the information on the murdered man's car.

That would be the same page with the details of her appointment that morning with Mr. Harsch: his name, directions to the *Galaxy*, time of the meeting. But that was gone, too.

Well, yes. That she *might* have thrown out, once the meeting was over. Had she done so without noticing what else was on that page? It was goddamn unlikely.

All right. Here's the page with the money quote about potato chips, which would be the page immediately after the one with the appointment and the car. Switching on the gooseneck lamp on her desk space, Sara held the notepad angled up so the light flooded onto the potato chip quote. Leaning in close, eyes low to the edge of the pad, she tried to look *across* the page, hoping to see the indentations pressed there by her having written on the page above it. That sometimes worked, though it was much easier when the next page hadn't already been written on. Staring, squinting, Sara could see that there were such identations, but she couldn't read them.

Well, sometimes it helped to stroke a pencil very lightly back and forth over the page, the indentations coming up paler than the rest. Sara tried that, and again she could see the evidence of lines, but they were just too slight, and too fragmented by the potato chip quote, to be legible.

Combine the two methods? Holding the page, now grayed by pencil lines, up in the glare of the gooseneck lamp, Sara peered close again, and this time it began to come clear. "Dade" first, the word "Dade," that being the county shown on the license plate, Dade County meaning Miami. Then the words "Buick Riviera." Harder was the scrawl "dk blu," meaning dark blue, the color of the murdered man's car. Hardest of all was the license plate number. It began with "2," but the next two numbers baffled her until she realized they were as simple as they looked, that they were both the number "7." And the letters? The first was "Z," just as she'd thought. Then "R." And at last one she simply couldn't be sure about, "G" or "Q" or "O."

Well, I've got it, she thought, looking at the numbers and letters written on a page from the *Galaxy*'s notepad, the one she kept on this desk. 277–ZR(G/Q/O). And now what do I do with it? Returning her own notebook to the shoulder bag under her chair, it occurred to her that almost anyone could have come over here sometime while she was in the reference section or the ladies, and torn that page out.

Had someone done that? Or had she absentmindedly thrown it away herself, noticing only the appointment with Mr. Harsch on that page? Which was more improbable?

Well, *why* would anyone throw that page away? She'd already reported the murder, hadn't she?

Hadn't she?

She was working on that question, thinking about Monday's taciturn guard and gazing at the license plate numbers she'd just written, when her telephone's white light began to flash, and she thought, with a sudden thrill of fear, *I'm being watched!* She almost didn't want to answer, but of course that was silly. Holding her breath, she reached out, picked up the phone, said, "Hello?" in a small and guarded voice, and Jack's voice in her ear said, "A special treat."

Relief made her limp, boneless. "Oh, yes?" she said.

"Because you're such a good girl," his practically cheerful voice told her, "you are being invited to a barbecue tomorrow."

"I am?"

"Binx Radwell and his wife are throwing it," Jack said, with just the most delicate added emphasis on the word "wife"; to suggest this was to be a respectable outing.

"Well, that sounds like fun," she said. "Thank you."

"Binx said I should invite you," he said, spoiling it a bit, "so thank him."

"I will, then."

"Pick you up at noon tomorrow?"

"Fine. See you then."

She hung up, obscurely pleased; a break in the routine, and some social contact in this strange new world. But now, if she was such a good girl, she should go to work. Reaching for her new assignments, she noticed the license plate numbers and car info on the pad, and hesitated. What should she do with that? Did it matter whether she kept it or not?

Feeling faintly ridiculous (but also still with that same irrational feeling: I'm being watched), she tore that page out of the *Galaxy*'s notepad and put it in her skirt pocket.

Chapter Three

Phyllis wasn't going to the barbecue. She was out all Friday night—the first time she'd been away at all, and the only indication so far that there was a man in her life—and came by briefly late Saturday morning to change, throw swimsuit and cosmetics and some clothes and a paperback novel about the French Revolution into her bright red vinyl bag, and cheerfully say, "See you mañana, my dear. You ought to try to get out."

"I *am* getting out," Sara told her, but Phyllis was gone in a flash of long legs, uninterested. Sara, irritated at being put unjustly in the position of country mouse, but at the same time just as pleased to have the apartment to herself for a while, went back to her room and her desk.

Sara's secret vice was that she was a novelist; or, that is, that she was *not* a novelist and was determined to become one. Just exactly which novelist she would eventually turn out to be she wasn't yet entirely sure—a problem which she felt was hampering her development—but she was resolutely at every opportunity practicing the craft she hoped someday to learn. That's why a desk and chair had been her third and fourth purchases for the apartment, immediately after a double bed and a tall roomy dresser.

At times it seemed to her unrealistic that a young woman in her mid-twenties like herself, with no extraordinary experiences of life, should even think about trying to be a novelist, but then she placed against that the force of her desire, and it all seemed possible. One of the reasons, in fact, that she'd taken this job after the *Courier-Observer* was merged, was that it would surely be an experience outside what she already knew; and it was definitely working out that way.

This was the first real chance she'd had to look at her works in progress and organize her thoughts since the move to Florida. Neatly stacked atop the desk were the four large manila envelopes containing the four novels she was currently more or less working on, each envelope neatly labeled: COLLEGE; SPY; CIVIL WAR; NEWSPAPER. One of these would become her project now; with luck, until it was finished.

COLLEGE (working title *I For Incomplete*) was the thickest envelope, but she hadn't worked on that one for over a year, having lost sympathy with the characters. The thinnest envelope was NEWSPAPER (no title yet), which she'd started when the word had come down about the merging of the *Courier-Observer* and on which she'd worked furiously until realizing she didn't herself much believe the villains.

This morning, she'd awakened to find herself thinking about the spy novel for the first time in months; the idea of intrigue, suspense, hidden truths, suddenly appealed to her. After her first-ever sunlit morning swim in the Atlantic, she brought out that envelope (working title *Time of the Hero*), put up on the wall the maps of Bulgaria and Costa Rica, and was just settling down to re-read what she'd already done on that book when Phyllis flashed through. That distracted her for a while, and she spent some time arranging and rearranging the other things she had up on the wall over the desk; a Polaroid shot of her mother's white clapboard house with dark green trim, up there in Great Barrington; another Polaroid, this of her mother's living room at Christmas; two favorite cartoons from *The New Yorker*; a photo of Bill Hunnicutt, the boy she'd gone steady with the last two years of college; the notepad sheet with the murdered man's car description and license plate; the letter from New England Newspapers announcing the termination of her services; a few other small things. She placed all of that to her satisfaction, read the completed pages of *Time of the Hero*, making corrections and notes to herself along the way, and then it was nearly noon, and time to change into jeans and a sleeveless blouse; appropriate wear for a barbecue, she hoped.

And who, she wondered, was Jack Ingersoll when he wasn't at work?

CHAPTER FOUR

Binx bobbled the ball. He recovered, dribbled the basketball left, dribbled it right, faked out an entire squadron of imaginary defenders, struck directly in toward the broad white garage door, went up with beautiful grace for an easy lay-up into the orange hoop, missed, and scrambled for the rebound.

"*Bii*-inx!"

That was Marcy. Binx took the rebound, leaped straight up like a Masai warrior or whoever it is, made a lovely one-hand push shot, and the basketball arced over and fell straight through the center of the hoop. "Swish!" cried Binx, though the net had rotted away from that hoop three years ago.

"*Bii*-inx! It's *your* party!"

There was something to be said for that point of view, Binx had to admit. Over there to the right was the party, and it was his, and he was expected to do something about it.

The Binx Radwell castle was a split-level ranch in a development of split-level ranches southwest of the city, half an hour from work. Here Binx lived with his Marcy and some children and a dog and probably a cat, two cats, maybe a hamster, possibly a parakeet. The plots here were half acre, the developer had left many of the scrub pines and had done other planting of his own, the roads curved and the bulldozers in their clearing had created low hills and shallow dales, and with the developer's three different models and virtually infinite capacity for options the place looked hardly like a development at all.

To the left of Binx's blindingly white house was his bottomless black driveway leading up to his blindingly white two-car garage with orange basketball hoop. Behind the garage and almost as big was his prefab metal storage shed from Sears, and behind the house was the broad expanse of rich green lawn under the Florida sun, sloping back and down to a rock garden, a trellis, some wooden fence, some metal fence and some shrubbery, all hiding the neighbor back there and all in need of work.

Here and there on the lawn were a playground slide, a set of swings, a monkey bars, a very large above-ground pool, two cabanas, and a large expensive wheeled grill, at which Marcy stood, chatting with a neighbor wife and poking sometimes with a wooden spoon at the grilling spareribs, and crying out Binx's name from time to time with that peculiarly ravenlike caw of a voice. Beyond all that, another neighbor's garage and shed and shrubs flanked the lawn on the far side, creating privacy al fresco. Lovely place for a party.

Binx's party. About twenty-five adults, a few of them neighbors, but mostly people from work, moved around the lawn, glasses or bottles in their hands, talking together and waiting for food. In among them, under their elbows and between their knees and behind their backs, several thousand children scampered, like cockroaches when the light is turned on, but louder. A smell of burning meat was in the air.

"*Bii*-inx!"

"Coming, my love!"

Here came Binx, with basketball. It was tough to dribble on grass, but when the going gets tough, the tough dribble harder. Approaching the grill, Binx yelled, "Yo, Chuck!" at a neighbor, and tried to bounce-pass the ball away, but it hit a rock or a toy or Satan's knuckle or some damn thing, and instead of going over to the waiting grinning Chuck, hands held out, one with a beer bottle in it, the basketball took a bad hop, caromed to the right, made a direct hit on the grill—scattering ribs—and bounded away toward the swimming pool.

"*Bii*-inx!"

"Sorry, Marcy," Binx said, with his sheepish grin, and trotted after the ball.

To the neighbor wife, Marcy said, "I never would have married him except my mother hated him so."

A car engine sounded on the driveway beside the house, then stopped. Car doors slammed. Binx turned, with basketball, to gaze bright-eyed toward the corner of the house. More people. A bigger party.

* * *

Sara wasn't sure what she'd expected, but somehow nothing quite as *normal* as this. The clean upper-middle-class suburb from the television commercials, complete with boys on bicycles, sprinklers spit-spit-spurrrting, station wagons stopped on sunny driveways. Riding through it all, Sara felt displaced, dislocated. Partly that was because Jack's car turned out to be an elderly red Honda Civic, the seediest, oldest vehicle she'd yet seen any employee of the *Galaxy* drive. (Jack had volunteered no explanation for the Honda, nor had she figured out a polite way to satisfy her curiosity. And at least he was appropriate to national type; she'd noticed that the Americans on the *Galaxy*'s staff tended to drive glamorous or exotic foreign cars, while the Brits and Australians preferred large boatlike American vehicles.)

But mostly Sara's sense of dislocation was caused by the person they were going to see. The sweating, panicky, endlessly striving Binx Radwell ought to live up some long steep flight of stairs somewhere. This was a neighborhood that cried out *success*.

As did Binx's house, complete with basketball hoop over the garage door. Getting out of the Honda, Sara grinned quizzically across its top at Jack, saying, "Is this the real Binx?"

"There is no real Binx," he told her. His weekend manner was exactly like his work manner; brusque, impatient, distracted. "Come on," he said.

They walked together toward the party noises around the rear corner of the house, and there was the yard, the people, the party, the *stuff*. And Binx, grinning manically at them, holding something. "Yo, Jack!" he cried, and shot a basketball in a line drive pass.

Jack wasn't ready. Before he could react, the basketball hit his chest and bounced off, leaving in its wake a reddish brown sticky stain that looked a lot like barbecue sauce. "Well, thanks, Binx," Jack said.

"Oh, wow!" Binx cried, stupendously contrite, hurrying over. "Jack, I'm sorry!"

"It's okay," Jack said, "it'll wash off." To Sara he said, "I'll be right out," and he went away toward the rear door of the house, waving along the way at an irritable-looking woman with a wooden spoon over by the grill.

"Jeepers," Binx said, looking after Jack. Then, abruptly cheerful, he took Sara's arm, saying, "Come on, I'll show you around."

She allowed him to lead her out over the yard. The woman next to the grill kept glaring in his direction. Noticing Sara noticing her, Binx explained, "Over there, that's some woman I'm married to. She's mad at me right now."

"Did you hit her with a basketball?"

"Worse," he said, shaking his head. "Far worse. Comere, lemme show you stuff."

Behind the garage was a large prefab shed. Its door stood open, revealing a full and cluttered interior. Stopping in front of this structure, gesturing, Binx rattled off, as though fulfilling a duty, "That's my power mower, that's my roto tiller, that's my tractor, that's my seeder, that's my golf cart, that's my moped, that's my shredder, that's my table saw, that's my rubber raft."

"And this is your shed."

He grinned, and pointed. "And this is my grass and that's my house and these are my friends."

"This is your life," Sara finished.

Showing alarm, Binx said, "Gee! You think so?"

Looking at the shed and its contents, somehow depressed by it all, Sara said, "All these things you own."

"You ought to own something, too," Binx said, taking her arm again. "I'll give you a beer."

"Okay."

They walked back toward the house. The woman by the grill—she probably *was* Binx's wife, actually—had gone back to her cooking now, was no longer glaring at anybody.

The house provided a narrow swath of shade across the back, in which a long folding table stood, bearing three open coolers filled with beer bottles floating in ice water. Approaching this, Binx explained, "They pay me too much, so what am I gonna do? Buy things."

"The salaries here . . ." Sara said, and shook her head, thinking of her own ridiculous income.

"You show me yours," Binx suggested, "I'll show you mine."

Startled, she said, "What?"

"Salary," Binx said. Opening a beer, he said, "Actually, I know your salary. Here."

"Thanks," she said, taking the beer.

"Thirty-five," he said, opening one for himself.

"That's right."

Binx shook his head, grinning at her. "Honey," he said, "nowhere on *earth* does a starter try-out reporter get thirty-five grand a year. You know what I get?"

Sara didn't. "Sixty?" she guessed.

"Ha ha," Binx said, without humor. "I am paid eighty-five thousand U.S. dollars per annum."

"Wow."

"I say exactly that same thing," Binx told her, "every week. Wow, Mr. DeMassi, I say, I'm not worth *half* this. I know, he says, but take it and be happy. The *Galaxy* sells five million copies every week. We got the largest editorial budget in the *world*. You see these people?"

"Yes," Sara said.

"We're *all* overpaid by the *Galaxy*," Binx said, gesturing at the partygoers with his beer bottle, slopping a little on his hand, not noticing. "You know why? You get a little scared someday, a little depressed about yourself, you think maybe you'd like to go back to the real world, guess what?"

"What?"

"You can't afford the real world," Binx said, and looked up cheerfully as Jack came out of the house and walked over, the stain on the front of his shirt somewhat paler and streakier. "Oh, good," Binx told him. "It came right off."

"Mmm," Jack said, reaching for a beer.

"You two play," Binx said. "I have to grovel with Marcy a minute."

Binx wandered off toward the grill and the woman with the wooden spoon. Watching him go, Sara said, "Binx isn't really happy, is he? Under all the joking, he's really kind of desperate."

Jack took a long swig of beer, then said, "He tried to get another job a couple years ago. Soon as people saw *Weekly Galaxy* on the résumé, that was the end of it."

Startled, thinking about her own career, Sara said, "Is that true?"

"The rest of the world of journalism looks with disapproval on the *Galaxy*," he said.

"Then he's—" Looking over at Binx, theatrically apologetic to the woman with the spoon (who was not relenting), Sara said, "He's like a slave."

"He enslaved himself," Jack commented, and shrugged.

Sara looked at him. His self-sufficiency was like smugness. Wanting to break through, she said, "And you? Are you a slave?"

"I don't own a Marcy."

"Oh, you're a tough guy," Sara said, vaguely irritated.

He returned her look at last, saying, "Am I? I don't know, I started out the softest-headed idealist you ever saw. Ever hear of the *St. Louis Massacre*?"

"Indians?"

"Newspaper, weekly counterculture. Like the *Berkeley Barb*, the *Village Voice*, all that. We were gonna change the world."

"For the better," Sara suggested.

"That was the idea. The people around me, sooner or later every last one of them sold out. And finally I figured out why."

"Why?"

"Because we weren't doing any good." Jack drank beer. "Eighty was worse than seventy," he said. "Ninety should be a real corker."

"You lost your idealism."

"I lost the baby fat in my head," he told her. "I came down here, I took the job for the big bucks and the warm sunshine, and I am retired from the fray."

"Forever?"

"They wouldn't take me back if I wanted to go. And I don't want to go."

Binx appeared next to them, looking apologetic. "Knock, knock," he said.

Jack said, "Who's there?"

"Ida Gavin, on the phone. Sorry."

"Drat." Jack put the half-empty beer bottle on the table. "Be right back."

He hurried off, and Binx said to Sara, "Sorry about that."

"That's okay," Sara assured him, but in fact things had just begun to get interesting. Looking around, she said, "None of the Englishmen are here."

"You bet," Binx said, smiling on the assembled guests as though he'd bought them, too.

"I'm always amazed there's so many Australians and English on the *Galaxy*."

"Massa likes them," Binx said. "They get their training on papers much grungier even than ours."

"But I thought you couldn't give a job to an alien if a qualified American wants it. How do they get permission?"

"You mean the green card?" Binx asked, grinning. "They don't have green cards."

"They don't? How do they work that?"

"The *Galaxy* has a nonpublishing subsidiary in Manchester," Binx told her, "over in England. All the Aussies and Brits work there, are paid out of that office in sterling, and are on permanent temporary assignment here."

Astonished, Sara said, "Is that legal?"

"I don't know," Binx said. "Do you think it matters?"

"Well, of course it— What do you mean?"

"Have you ever wondered," Binx asked her, "why the state government ran that big road twelve miles out of town, goes nowhere except Massa's house?"

"Sure," Sara said. "I've thought about it. You mean, Massa has the state government in his pocket?"

Grinning at her, Binx said, "Is that what you would say?"

"No, come on," Sara said. "Are you saying that's for real?"

Bright-eyed, teasing, Binx said, "Can I quote you as saying?"

Returning at that moment, Jack said to Sara, "Admit nothing."

"That's what I'm doing," Sara assured him.

Casually, Binx said, "Everything okay at the shop?"

"Just fine," Jack told him.

Binx looked so intently at Jack that Sara half expected him to start sniffing at Jack's clothing like a dog. "Ida had something important she wanted to talk to you about, huh?"

"She thought so," Jack said indifferently, picking up his beer bottle.

"Something more on Keely Jones?"

Jack swigged beer, then looked levelly at Binx, saying, "Does Macy tell Gimbel?"

"Probably," Binx said. "It's all a giant conspiracy anyway. Well— See you two." And he sloped off, looking harried and dejected for about seven seconds, then perking up, getting into a brand-new animated conversation with a couple of other partygoers.

* * *

Jack tried very hard not to look at his watch. There was plenty of time, and no point getting there too early, and too many of his fellow employees were present. The word that Ida Gavin had phoned him here would get around, it was bound to; if he were seen looking at his watch, someone or other would realize he was up to something.

He was patient. He pretended to drink two more beers, but switched them surreptitiously for empty bottles. He downed some of the greasy burned food and waited till Sara had clearly eaten her fill as well before he walked her casually out around the perimeter of the party and the lawn. Then, "Listen," he said, speaking very softly, looking around for eavesdroppers like a prisoner in the exercise yard in an escape movie, "what do you think? Had enough?"

Surprised, Sara said, "You want to leave?"

"You've seen it all," he pointed out, "and it won't get any better. Or would you rather stick around and see what they're like drunk?"

* * *

Driving away from Binx's party, sweeping and curving through an endless graceful spread of middle-class gentility, so neat and wholesome and sun-swept that even Jack's Honda purred, Sara couldn't seem to break herself of that final image of Binx enslaved, chained invisibly to this green and pleasant salt mine, his soft face yearning upward, oiled with panic, entreaty smearing his features. Was that what all of them would come to, eventually? Was she like a newcomer to Pleasure Island in the Pinocchio story, noticing for the first time a boy with donkey's ears?

"A penny for your thoughts," Jack said, breaking a long silence.

Startled, Sara looked over at his bumpy impersonal profile as he watched the undulations of the road; no donkey ears there, at least none that she could see. "They aren't worth a penny," she said, then remembered Binx's comments about not being worth what the *Galaxy* was paying him, and added, "I was thinking about our salaries."

Jack laughed, a rather harsh sound, and looked searchingly in the rearview mirror. "Binx thinks it's immoral," he said, "to have a dime left in his pocket at the end of the day."

"I could see that."

"What *I* was thinking about," Jack said, slowing but not stopping at a stop sign, then turning right to a straighter, cruder, more businesslike road, with a busy shopping highway visible at its farthest end, "was dinner. You got any plans?"

"Not in particular," she said, ignoring the memory of her intention to make some notes this evening on the next chapter of *Time of the Hero*.

"There's a place in Miami that's supposed to be good. Want to come along?" He glanced once more at the rearview mirror.

"Isn't that a distance?"

"Not much. The roads are good. I just have to stop by my place, pick up a couple things, we can take right off."

"I'm not *dressed* for dinner, not anywhere good."

"So we'll stop by your place, too," he told her, apparently having decided she'd already agreed. "But my place first."

Chapter Five

Sara was not surprised by Jack's neighborhood at all. There were no lawns here, no elaborate sprinkler systems, only dusty weeds baked lifeless in the sun, drooping on cracked tan dirt in front of low stucco houses the same defeated color as the ground. At every intersection stood a bar with maroon aluminum siding and opaque glass-brick windows. The scattering of slow-paced pedestrians was multiracial, democratically equal in their hopelessness and their torn T-shirts promoting beers and raceways.

Jack's house, a tiny stucco square with flat roof slanted rearward, surrounded by hard bare dirt in front and scruffy brush along the sides, looked like a place where someone wanted by the police for burglary might go to ground. Only the shiny new scarlet Jeep Laredo parked in the yard beside the front door, covered with sheets of clear plastic, seemed out of place. Seeing her look at it as they pulled to a stop at the curb, Jack said, "My bonus from Massa for a body in the box I got."

"Bonus?" Astonished, she looked from the shiny vehicle to Jack, as he started to climb out of the Honda. "He gave you a *Jeep*?"

"Massa can be very generous when he wants." Out of the car, Jack bent in to look at her, saying, "I'm selling it in the morning. Come on in while I get my tie."

Climbing out to the cracked uneven sidewalk, Sara tried to remember the strange phrase Jack had used to explain his bonus—something in a box?—but everything else about the Jeep was too insistently distracting. "Mr. DeMassi gives away Jeeps as bonuses," she said, following him across the hard-packed bare earth to the front door, there being no walk, "and you're going to sell it, and keep . . ." Not sure exactly how to describe the Honda, or her reaction to it, she merely gestured back at the car, parked so appropriately at this particular curb.

"Absolutely," Jack told her, using three keys to unlock his front door. "I'm also not going to move into that World of Tomorrow Tower with you and La Bella Perkinson."

"I don't think Phyllis is putting that accent and manner on," Sara objected. "I think that really is her background."

"I agree completely," Jack said, pushing open the at-last-unlocked door and waving Sara in first. "And she isn't slumming among us, either. This is her level, all right. This, or a little lower."

Surprised at this nasty dismissal, Sara barely reacted to the barren squalor of Jack's home, turning to say, "What's wrong with Phyllis? Doesn't she do her job?"

"Almost," he said, shutting the door. "The problem with her, the problem with a lot of these silver-spoon types, they don't know how to be scared until it's too late. Be right back."

He went on deeper into the house, and Sara now had leisure to consider both his home and his attitude toward Phyllis; both of which, she decided, were grubby. His melodramatic remark about Phyllis not knowing how to be scared simply meant he believed that people with a wealthy background didn't worry and get all sweaty about their jobs, because they weren't as dependent on their employment as poor people. Which was probably true, but so what? If Phyllis did her work—and it seemed to Sara that Phyllis did it very well—what did it matter if she didn't pull her forelock from time to time, or go around like Binx Radwell, exuding agonized uncertainty? That was just reverse snobbism on Jack's part.

And so was the house, as much of it as she could see. The living room was a barren square, the walls painted pale blue a long time ago, the woodwork painted off-white somewhat more recently. There were no curtains or shades on the windows, no rug on the floor, no pictures or other decorations on the walls. The scanty and mismatched furniture, being a Danish modern sofa, bulky sagging armchair with ugly big-flowered slipcover, rusty iron floor lamp with burn-marked shade, and old kitchen table holding the TV and stereo equipment, were all obviously bought used and with an eye exclusively to practicality, not to appearance. The room was like a set for a Sam Shepard play.

So. Unlike Binx, unlike Phyllis—unlike herself, she had to admit—Jack was not spending his lush salary, but was stashing it all away somewhere. For what?

When he came back to the living room a couple of minutes later, it was both a surprise and a relief that he was dressed now in a good-quality linen sports jacket, good slacks and shoes and shirt, and conservative tie; at least his Scrooge impulses didn't extend to his clothing. Seeing him dressed like that in this living room, Sara suddenly felt she understood. "I get it," she said.

He gave her a crooked grin. "You do? Tell me about it."

"You don't want to be like Binx, enslaved, needing the job. But you don't want to be just playing at it either, the way you think Phyllis is. You want to be serious, but not trapped."

"Sounds good," he said, watching her bright-eyed.

"You think someday they'll fire *you*."

He shrugged, still grinning. "Someday, they'll fire everybody."

"No possessions," she said, gesturing at the room. "No debts, no attachments." She'd almost said, *no romantic attachments*, but stopped in time, realizing it might sound to him like an invitation. "You'll be ready," she finished.

He nodded. "I *am* ready," he said. "I'm also hungry. Let's go."

* * *

The restaurant was Spanish, with heavy dark-wood furnishings, gigantic murky formal paintings of bullfighters posed in all their regalia, and a reputation for barely cooking its huge slabs of meat before bringing them out to the table. Sara had arrived needing to visit the ladies' room, so Jack took the opportunity to press a question and a twenty-dollar bill on the pencil-moustached, bulky, tuxedoed headwaiter, who said, "Oh, yes, they are here, but you know, we guarantee privacy."

"I wouldn't disturb them for anything," Jack assured him. "We'd just like to sit near, but not too near. Maybe we could have one of their waiter's tables."

"I'll do what I can," the headwaiter promised, Jack's twenty having already disappeared from his hand, and when Sara returned they were seated at a table precisely answering his needs. Jack placed Sara with her back to them, so he could keep an eye on them over her shoulder. Drinks were ordered, menus and wine list were studied, and they settled down into casual conversation, Jack glancing past her from time to time, not being obvious about it.

She had questions, comments about life at the *Galaxy*, which he answered easily, and then she paused, and said, "Jack, don't misunderstand me, but—" She frowned, looking for the right words.

"I will not misunderstand you," he promised. "Let me have it with both barrels."

"No, no," she said, smiling, shaking her head to assure him she didn't mean to attack. "It's just that . . . Well, do you ever wish you worked on . . . more important stories?"

He grinned at her, not misunderstanding and not taking offense. "Which ones?" he asked. "Bank robberies, mayoral elections, or snowstorms?"

She considered that. "You mean, they're all the same?"

"No. Arthritis cures pay better."

"The story *I* keep thinking about," she said, as the waiter, a short and slender Hispanic with a red bolero jacket and a pessimistic smile, brought the wine, "is the murder."

The waiter either didn't hear, or he heard such statements so often they could no longer affect him. He merely showed Jack the label of the Spanish red for his agreement that it was indeed the one he'd selected, then smiled sadly and opened the bottle while Jack returned his attention to Sara (and the couple just visible through a huge and vulgar floral assortment in hot purples and scarlets), saying, "Which murder was that?"

"The one I told you about Monday; my first day." She acted as though he really should have remembered.

Jack tasted and approved the wine—it looked like blood, smelled like laundry, tasted like wood—and said, "Oh, yeah, your famous body beside the road."

"I wonder what happened next," she said. "I never saw the police at the *Galaxy*, but they must have come out."

"Why must they? Wait a minute, Señor Wences wants to take our orders."

Jack asked for steak, and Sara shrimp. Then the waiter went away, and Jack said, "I don't know why we all don't come to Miami more often. It's right here."

She gave him a level and considering look. "Is there any special reason why you don't want to talk about the murder?"

Startled, he splayed a hand to his chest in a gesture of false innocence. By God, he thought, I've forgotten how to be innocent! Aloud, he said, "Don't want to talk about— Oh! The waiter distracted me. Of course, your body beside the road, that has to be on your mind a lot, it's something that doesn't happen every day."

"It sure doesn't," she said.

"So it looms large in your legend. Okay, what about it? Did they get whoever did it?"

"I have no idea," she said. "I didn't see anything in the *County*."

The *County*, the local newspaper, was one of those hopeless small-town amateur gazettes run as a sideline by a neighborhood printer, who cared more for how words were spelled than what they said. "I *never* see anything in the *County*," Jack said. "I hate newspapers, if you want the truth."

"The thing is," Sara said, poking at her silverware, "if the police didn't come out to the *Galaxy*, and I never saw them there, I'm wondering if maybe I ought to go talk to them."

He frowned at her, sensing she was making some sort of mistake but not sure yet which particular mistake it might be. "Why?" he said.

"Because my evidence," she explained in all seriousness, "proves the killer works for the *Galaxy*."

Jack felt suddenly very nervous; not because he thought she thought he was the killer, but because he could see she was one of those girls willing to march right out over a mine field without so much as a glance at the warning sign by its entrance. And any trouble she might make for the *Galaxy* would redound horridly on Jack. Not wanting to get caught up in some eager idiot's had-I-but-known story, he said, "Sara, don't make wild statements unless you're at work."

"It is not a wild statement," she insisted. "Would you like to hear my reasoning?"

Better me than Massa, Jack thought. "Love to hear your reasoning," he said.

She said, "It was a quarter to ten when I found the body."

"Describe this body."

"A man in his fifties," she said, "tough-looking, in a lightweight gray polyester jacket. He'd been shot just once that I could see, in the forehead. The bullet did some damage to the back of his skull, but didn't break through." She tapped the back of her own head to demonstrate.

Surprised, Jack said, "You touched it? The back of his skull?"

"I'm a reporter," she said, trying to toss off the remark as though she were being merely matter-of-fact, and not arch at all.

He let that go. "Okay. What else?"

"The car was a dark blue Buick Riviera, Dade county plate. A rented or leased car."

"How do you know that? You looked in the glove compartment?"

"No, it had a Z plate."

"Ah." He hadn't known a Z plate meant a rented or leased car, but if this ace reporter said so, he was prepared to accept it. "But did you look in the glove compartment?"

"No. Also, the radio was on, playing salsa music."

"Did the dead man look Hispanic?"

"Not particularly," she said. "Just tough."

"As though he might be somebody who'd get himself shot in the course of drug business?"

"I suppose so," she said, but reluctantly. Clearly, she wanted a more interesting mystery out of this.

"But you think," Jack said, "he had something to do with somebody at the *Galaxy*."

"I *know* he did."

"Because he was on that road? They took him there because it's empty. At night, kids do drag races on that road."

"No," she said, pretending patience. "Because he was on that road *at that time*."

"A quarter to ten in the morning."

"That's right." The waiter brought their salads, poured more wine, went away. Sara said, "The body couldn't have been there during the morning rush, with everybody going to work. *Somebody* would have seen it, would have stopped."

"I suppose so," he admitted.

"And when would the last person have gone by? Around quarter after nine?"

"Probably so. Something like that."

"And I got there at quarter to ten."

He shrugged. "So?"

"There's no exit off that road, from one end to the other." Intensity vibrated in her voice, glittered in her eyes. "I didn't see one single car coming the other way the whole time I was on it that morning. There wasn't time for someone to come out there *after* the morning rush hour but *before* I got there, kill that man, and either drive back to town in another car or walk back."

"Maybe he walked off into the fields."

"I'd have seen him," she said, and gestured, indicating a large open space. "You can see for miles there."

"True enough. So you're saying the killer didn't go back to town, and he didn't wander away across the moors, so he must have gone on to the *Galaxy*."

"Of course. Where else could he have gone?"

"It's your story," he reminded her. "But he could have been just visiting, you know."

"Mine was the only car in the visitors' parking lot that day."

He remembered then his first sight of Sara, getting out of the little maroon Chevette in the visitors' parking lot. The view of her walking was what had inspired him to the sex-cures-gallstones story; and then Sara had been the one to pull that same story out of the fire.

She frowned at him, saying, "What are you smiling about?"

"Nothing," he said. "An irrelevancy. So tell me your conclusion, Chief Inspector."

"It's obvious," she said. "The killer had to be driving a car with a *Galaxy* sticker. He shot that man, then drove on to work, parked wherever he usually parks, acted as though nothing happened."

"Possible," Jack said slowly, reluctant to permit her to bring potential trouble home to the *Galaxy*. "But there must be other possible explanations as well."

"Name three."

"I'm trying to think of just one," Jack told her, grinning, as the busboy cleared their salad plates, and the waiter, with a hopelessly muffled flourish, presented their main course. "Let me think about it," he said, "while we eat."

"Take all the time you need."

The food, though better than the wine, was probably not doing much good for anybody's arteries. Jack ate methodically, smiling at Sara from time to time, thinking idly about the murder mystery she'd presented him, and keeping one eye on the couple beyond the vulgar flowers. But say she was right; say someone connected with the *Galaxy* shot a tough-looking fellow out on the highway on the way to work Monday morning; say the police hadn't yet found the guilty party, and possibly didn't even know as much about the story as Sara did. Say all that, and the response was still the same as when she'd given him the capsule version of the story on Monday morning: So what?

In no way did this unimportant anonymous murder impinge on the life and concerns of Jack Ingersoll; no, nor on those of Sara Joslyn, either. She'd found the body, she'd reported it to the guard on duty at the *Galaxy*'s gate, and that was the end of it. Presumably, the guard would have passed the information to his immediate boss, rather than directly to the cops, so by the time the report was made the identity of the original person who'd found the body might have been lost; which would be why nobody had come around to take evidence from Sara. Or possibly the crime had immediately been solved, and no investigation needed. A small and unimportant murder, in either case, too common and minor even to make the pages of the *County*.

In any event, the murder had certainly been reported at some time and by some method on Monday, because both car and body had been removed by that afternoon. So, unless Sara started making unnecessary fusses, this was no more than a kind of game they were playing, an intellectual exercise, a fooling with what-if. And all Jack had to do was see it didn't get out of hand.

Neither of them raised the subject of the murder again until the steak and shrimp and side dishes had been dealt with and the plates removed, and they'd said yes to the waiter's offer of coffee, no to his suggestion of dessert. Then Sara said, "Well? Did you think of some other explanation, somewhere else the killer could have gone?"

"No, I must admit I didn't," he told her, "but the idea that the *Galaxy* . . ." He shook his head.

"There've been a couple of other things," she said, "since then, right there at the *Galaxy*."

"What things?"

"I don't really want to tell you," she said. "They're too silly. A note that disappeared, a different guard ever since. Nothing important, and there's a different simple explanation for everything."

"Of course there is," he said. "And for all you know, by now the whole case has been— Wait a minute. What's that?"

Following the direction of his gaze, Sara twisted around to look at the couple Jack had been watching. The girl was now making small blubbery sounds over there, one shaking hand to her face, while the man leaned across the table toward her, looking both angry and embarrassed, whispering fiercely; no doubt urging her to shut up, get control of herself, something helpful like that.

Sara spun back, wide-eyed. "That's John Michael Mercer!"

"Ssshhh, yeah, it is." Jack kept both eyes on the television star, Massa's favorite person, to see what would happen next.

Abruptly, the girl with Mercer was on her feet. A blonde, she was dressed just a little too obviously, just enough to emphasize the ripeness of her figure. Turning away from Mercer, one hand still to her face, she stumbled blindly past Jack and Sara's table, and on. Not toward the exit, that would have been the other way. So, toward the ladies' room.

Jack leaned forward, quick and intense. "Follow her! Console her. Get her story!"

Sara blinked. "Do *what*?"

"It's been dumped in our laps! Go! Quick! Massa will love us for weeks!"

At last she got the idea. Looking nervous but determined, she rose and hurried off after the blonde. Jack sat quietly for a minute or two, watching Mercer pour himself a glass of champagne, manner and expression stern but calm, that of a man who has not shrunk from an unpleasant duty. When he decided he'd given Sara long enough to make contact, Jack got to his feet, adjusted his lapels and sleeves, patted the camera in his left side jacket pocket, and walked past the garish flowers to the John Michael Mercer table, where he smiled gently, reassuringly, and said, "Excuse me."

Mercer gave him a dangerous look; the kind of look he gave lowlifes on *Breakpoint*. Clearly, he was not of a mood to suffer fans gladly. Saying not a word, he let his hostile expression speak for him, and waited with barely leashed rage for Jack to go away.

Instead of which, Jack bent slightly toward him, his voice and manner confidential as he said, "I don't know if it matters, but there's a *Weekly Galaxy* reporter in the ladies' room with your girl."

Mercer's response was entirely satisfactory. His head came up like an Indian brave hearing a twig snap in the forest at night, like a well-antlered stag when the hunter cocks his gun, like a margin buyer hearing the fall of an interest rate. "That—" he said, and rose like a thundercloud.

"Just went in there a minute ago."

Mercer left without even saying thank you.

* * *

The main question Sara had always wanted to ask girls who looked like this blonde had nothing to do with the *Weekly Galaxy* or John Michael Mercer (except indirectly) or her job at all. The main question Sara had always wanted to ask girls who looked like this blonde—busty, hippy, pouty, pneumatically soft—was if they enjoyed sex more than she did.

Oh, Sara *enjoyed* sex, that wasn't the problem, so long as the guy was someone she cared for and who cared for her and who was reasonably aware of her while the exercise was under way, but was there *better* sex somewhere, more *electric*, more *throbbing*, more exhaustingly *fulfilling*? And if there was, would these inflatable dolls know about it? And would they be able to describe it, to pass the secret along to a worthwhile sister?

Well, the question was ridiculous, wasn't it? There was no way even to phrase it without sounding silly. So, once again, Sara did not ask the truly burning question of the age—did blondes like *this* have more fun like *that*?—but instead approached the weeping girl with nothing but sympathy and concern. They were alone in the ladies' room, an intensely decorated small space with glossy wallpaper featuring orchids on a deep black background, parts of this covered by large, dark, ornately framed full-length portraits of Spanish grandes dames peering imperiously over fans. The blonde, fetchingly crumpled against the wall between the beige sink and the coral paper-towel dispenser, smeerped and gulped, little round fists pressed to her eyes. Sara took a couple of Kleenex from her bag and extended them to the girl, saying, "Oh, you poor thing. Is it really that bad?"

"He—" The girl gulped, unable to cry and talk at the same time. Fists firmly to eyes, she shook her head back and forth. "He doesn't want me," she managed to say, in a broken half whisper.

"Whoever he is," Sara told her, "he isn't worth it. No man is worth it."

Now the girl sighed, a long shuddering sound that shook her frame and made Sara truly sympathize, truly feel for this poor baby, the victim of her own lush looks and the short attention span of men. She patted the poor baby's shoulder, the tissues remaining crumpled in her other hand, and the girl turned her head slightly, right eye peering woundedly past her knuckles at Sara as she whispered, "*He's* worth it. I love him!"

"Oh, poor baby, and he's no good, is he? He doesn't love *you* the way you love *him*."

"He says it's *oooover*!"

"Oh, poor girl, poor girl. Go ahead and cry. Get it all out."

Accepting the wad of Kleenex at last, the girl also accepted Sara's willing shoulder. The head she bent there seemed terribly hot and feverish, the delicate earlobe rosy with infused blood. Sara patted her quivering back, and the girl mumbled against her clavicle, "I gave him the best weeks of my life."

"Of course you did, I know you did."

"If he wants that Felicia," she wailed, her cry of defiance belied by copious tears and broken gasps, "he can have her!"

"Felicia, did you say?" Sara asked, listening with all her ears. "Tell me about her."

"Out!" bellowed a male voice, trembling with rage.

Sara and the girl both jumped, separating, and turned to stare at the doorway, filled now with the menacing infuriated form of John Michael Mercer. "Johnny!" squealed the girl. "You can't come in *here*!"

"Out, you idiot!" Mercer yelled, advancing into the room. "That's a reporter from the *Galaxy*!"

The girl stared at Sara in shock and betrayal, then at Mercer in shock and fear. "Johnny! I didn't—"

With one last wide-eyed wet-eyed panicky stare at Sara, the girl fled. Sara stood her ground, trembling slightly, as Mercer turned his attention her way, looming over her, raising one knobble-knuckled fist, shaking it in her face. "I've warned you people," he breathed, low-voiced and savage, controlling himself with obvious difficulty. "I said, if you ever bothered me again—"

"Sara!" cried Jack's voice. "Flinch!"

She flinched, an automatic reaction, then looked over to see Jack in the doorway, a tiny camera to his face. *Click-whirr, click-whirr, click-whirr*, the high-speed shutter hit and hit, as Mercer swiveled, roaring in his fury. Then Jack was gone, the door slapping closed after him, and Mercer swung back to Sara, fists clenched, face distorted with rage, and this time Sara flinched for real.

But then, as he must have suddenly realized his former girlfriend was out and about on her own in a world newly *full* of reporters from the *Weekly Galaxy*, Mercer spun away again, toward the door, blundering through it, hitting one shoulder against the frame on the way by, bellowing, "Fluffy!" And the door swung shut behind him, leaving Sara limp and shaken.

And what a first date *this* turned out to be! Of all the restaurants in the world, they'd have to pick just the one where John Michael Mercer was breaking up with a girlfriend. And what was happening to Jack right now, in the outside world? Sara supposed she should go out and see, offer support or a witness or a calming influence or whatever seemed best, but somehow she was just in no hurry to leave this room. So she spent another three or four minutes there, soothing her own shattered nerves, fussing with her hair and makeup, half expecting the door to burst open and almost anybody come in: Mercer to pulverize her, Fluffy (Fluffy? Was that possible?) to give her another look of heartbroken betrayal, or even Jack to tell her the coast was clear.

But nobody came in at all, not even an innocent bystander. When at last boredom overcame tension, and when the face looking back at her in the mirror had finally lost its expression of just having heard a major explosion very nearby, Sara cautiously pulled open the ladies' room door, looked both ways, saw nothing that seemed to threaten, and made her way back to the table, where the red-boleroed waiter was seated in *her* chair, talking to Jack and a small cassette tape recorder.

Astonished—she'd never had her seat taken by a waiter before—Sara just stood there beside the table, not knowing what else to do, while the waiter continued to speak slowly and ploddingly to Jack in heavily accented English. After a minute, Jack looked up, acknowledged her presence, and said, "There you are. Pull up a chair."

Pull up a chair; now *there's* the benchmark of the gentleman for you. Of course Jack was deeply involved in this unexpected interview with the waiter, but still. Oh, well; Sara looked around, saw that both John Michael Mercer and his Fluffy had left the restaurant and the busboy was clearing that table, and so she pulled over the chair Fluffy had been seated in and settled herself at the side of the table as Jack said to the waiter, "As a family man yourself, would you say— Hold it a second." To Sara he said, "Write down everything that happened, so you don't forget it."

"I won't forget it. Believe me."

"Write." To the waiter, as Sara shrugged and dragged out of her bag her memo pad and pen, Jack said, "Again. As a family man yourself, would you say it shocked you when John Michael Mercer made that girl cry?"

"Oh, yeah," the waiter said.

Sara wrote a quick and simple narrative of events while Jack continued to question the waiter: "As you were serving the meal, did you observe the conversation that took place between John Michael Mercer and that young lady?"

"Oh, sure, I did."

"Was the young lady happy at the beginning of the meal?"

"Oh, yeah, sure."

"Would you say that she was very noticeably in love with John Michael Mercer?"

"Oh, sure," the waiter said, with a dirty little grin. "She was all over him."

"You would say she was making no effort to conceal her happiness, is that right?"

"She wasn't concealing *nothing*, man."

Crinkle, crinkle; greenbacks rustled in Jack's left hand, in the waiter's sight but not within his reach. Calmly Jack said, "Would you say she was making no effort to conceal her happiness?"

"Oh, yeah, that's right. Very happy girl."

"So would you say it was a shock to her when—"

"Say!" Sara, having in her narrative reached the point where Mercer had come barging into the ladies' room, looked up frowning and said, "Wait a minute. How'd he know I was from the *Galaxy*?"

"I told him," Jack said, and returned his attention to the waiter. "Would you say it was a shock—"

"*You* told him!"

"All part of the story," he said. "Now, hush, we'll talk later. I want to get Pedro's story here, while it's fresh in his mind."

Sara looked at the little tape recorder in the middle of the table. And Jack had brought a camera along, too. They'd just *happened* to sit one table away! "You *knew* about this!" she cried. "That's when— When *Ida* called! At *Binx's* house! You knew then!"

"Sara, I'm *working*," Jack snapped at her, with a look of real anger.

"When aren't you working?" she asked, understanding him at last.

"We'll talk later, all right?"

"There's nothing to talk about," she assured him, and got to her feet, and dragged the chair back to the former Mercer table, and sat there to finish the narrative in her memo pad, while behind her the drone of Jack's and the waiter's voices continued, Jack leading the man inch by inch through the version of tonight's events he needed for the story in the paper.

It was herself Sara was mad at, mostly, for having thought in the first place that there could be anything on a personal level between herself and Jack. Hadn't he made it clear he would have no personal entanglements? Hadn't he made it *abundantly* clear that his job was all that mattered to him? Hadn't she already realized—and thought she'd accommodated herself to the idea—that the only way to get along with Jack Ingersoll was to be a very efficient and very faceless little reporter, and not to take personally his bouts of bad humor and bad manners? So how had she allowed him to sucker her into thinking—

No. How had she allowed *herself* to sucker *herself* into thinking there might be anything at all other than business in his asking her to the barbecue, asking her out to dinner? True, Jack Ingersoll was a lout and a boor, but she'd already known that, hadn't she? So if she was going to get mad, if she was going to decide she'd been used, if she was going to make a fuss because the only reason he'd brought her along tonight was as protective coloration and as someone to throw at John Michael Mercer's head to make the story better, if all of that was going to upset her, the only person she could possibly blame—and this made her grit her teeth in embarrassment and anger and frustration—was, goddamn it to hell and back and hell again and back again, herself.

The busboy brought, after a while, the coffee she'd ordered before all the excitement. She drank it, she finished her narrative, and she started a self-pitying letter to her mother at home up in Great Barrington that she knew she would never finish and never send, and then Jack came over to the table, carrying his half-full coffee cup, and took the chair that had been Mercer's. He was clearly trying very hard to look concerned, maybe even a little abashed, but his true feeling of self-satisfaction glistened on him like oil. "Listen, Champ," he said. "Don't be mad."

"Forgot my name again?" But she didn't feel like playing games; before he could answer, she shook her head, ripped the pages containing the narrative out of her memo pad and pushed them over to him. "I'm not mad," she said. "Mostly, I'm just tired. Here's the story. Can we go home now?"

"Sure. Listen, I probably should have told you about the setup ahead of time, but you're new, you know?"

"I know," she said. She really was very tired, though part of her tiredness, she knew, was simply depression.

"I didn't know how you'd handle it," he explained. "I figured you'd probably do best if you didn't know anything else was going on. You could be more natural."

"It's really all right, Jack," she told him. "I *was* mad, but I figured it all out for myself, everything you want to say. I'm so completely not mad anymore, I even included the name." And she gestured at the pages of narrative.

He looked alert. "Name? What name?"

"That girl—is *her* name really Fluffy?—she told me who Mercer's throwing her over for. Somebody named Felicia."

"Felicia!" Pleased, excited, he pressed his hand palm-down on the memo pad pages, fingers spread, as though to keep the pages from flying away, or being stolen. "A new name, somebody new," he said, looking over her head, thinking out loud. "We'll have to find out who she is." Focusing on her again, he grinned broadly and said, "Great work, Champ! And I do remember your name; you're Sara the Champ."

"We do the best we can," she said, and smiled back, to show she really wasn't mad anymore.

She hated him.

THE FIRST HUNDRED YEARS

Chapter One

When Sara arrived at work Monday morning, and reported to Jack's squaricle for her next assignment, he greeted her with a harried impersonal smile, as though nothing at all had happened over the weekend. And, in one way of looking at it, nothing had.

There was just under an hour left before the morning editorial conference with Massa, when Jack would have to produce today's thirty story ideas, so that's why he was pacing the squaricle like a trapped rat, and why Mary Kate was seated so alertly at the typewriter. Clippings on both their desks, Sara now knew, represented potentially useful items from obscure journals around the world; creatures born with extra heads or other duplicated body parts came mostly from Brazil, she'd noticed, while encounters with oversexed but not unfriendly aliens took place most frequently in Scandinavia.

However, to reach that magic number of thirty, Jack would have to go beyond clippings, beyond all the bits and pieces of star bio brought him by his eight reporters, and *invent*. "The earth," he said, and Mary Kate poised her narrow fingers over the keyboard. "The earth," he repeated, pacing and pacing, staring at the gray industrial carpet, "came from another solar system. It was a, a, a, a meteor or a comet or— It was a *rogue planet*!" He straightened, as though thick leather thongs that had held him bent like an ape—rather like a Lon Chaney Sr. impersonation—had at last been removed. Beaming with joy, he intoned, "Desperate Aliens Search for Rogue Planet Earth! Collision of Solar Systems Set Our Planet Adrift!"

Mary Kate typed, her fingers snapping at the keys like tiny predators. Jack, feeling obvious relief for just this instant, smiled on Sara and said, "Good morning. You are here for your assignment."

"You want me to find Felicia?"

"No no," he said. "We have serfs dragging those ponds. You found Felicia's *name*, you flinched *magnificently* as you will see when you see the photo, and you are to be rewarded."

"I am?" Sara asked, mistrusting him deeply. "How?"

"You are going to America. In a town called—" He snapped his fingers several times impatiently at the back of Mary Kate's head. "Called, called—"

Mary Kate gave Sara a jaundiced look. Finished with her typing for the moment, she picked up a slender paper-clipped stack and read, "Whitcomb."

"Just so. In the town called Whitcomb, in the great but not overly exciting state of Indiana, are twin boys, name of Jim and Joe Geezer. Can that be right?"

Mary Kate extended to him the paper-clipped stack and he consulted it. "*Geester*. Still doesn't sound right. Anyway, day after tomorrow those boys are celebrating their one hundredth birthday together, in their nursing home out there in . . . Whitcomb, and the *Weekly Galaxy* is going to throw them a party."

"That's very nice," Sara said neutrally.

"Isn't it," Jack agreed. "And your reward, for Felicia and the flinch, is that you shall be the one in charge. You will have the Down Under Trio to—"

Sara stared. The Down Under Trio? How could *that* be a reward? Those were the three Australian reporters on Jack's team—Bob Sangster, with the big nose; Harry Razza, the lounge lizard Lothario; and Louis B. Urbiton, the oldest and drunkest reporter on the staff—and Sara had never seen any of them do anything but make trouble for themselves and others. "The Australians?" she asked. "*All* of them?"

"They are your team," Jack insisted. "They obey clear orders very well, and they'll be a terrific help if there's a problem. Also, they deserve a reward too, for a body in the box they got last month. Plus we'll—"

There was that phrase again: *body in the box*. What could it possibly mean? Jack had been given a Jeep Laredo for his part in getting one, and now the three Australians were to be sent to this birthday party as *their* reward for the same or a similar thing. Sara would have asked Jack for an explanation, but he was sailing unstoppably on, saying:

"Plus we'll send you a photographer from Indianapolis or somewhere. You go out and set up the party, see what you can do for notable names. Maybe the governor of Indiana would like a task."

"What else does he have to do," Mary Kate commented.

"Exactly. The Down Unders are super with press reps, put them to work on it. And we want a birthday cake the size of a Rose Bowl float." His hands spread wide, designing and indicating what he wanted on the cake: "Happy Birthday, Joe and Jim Thing, All America and the *Weekly Galaxy* Salute You on Your First Century. Get the words '*Weekly Galaxy*' on the cake."

"Of course," Sara said. "How much can I spend?"

"What it costs," Jack told her.

Mary Kate said, "You never ask, 'How much can I spend?' Not around here."

"Exactly," Jack agreed. "When the subject matter is truly trivial, no expense is too great. Report to Sally Forth, I told her you're on the way. And check with the Down Unders, where you'll meet them in . . . Whitcomb. They'll travel separately, you'll be happy to hear."

Sara blinked, trying to keep up. "Sally Forth?" Wasn't that a comic strip?

"Her name," Jack said, with a look at his watch, becoming nervous and impatient again, "is Sally Farber. She's in charge of travel here, down on one, and therefore . . ."

"I get it," Sara said. "Sally Forth."

* * *

Sally Forth (née Farber) was a matronly lady who never got to go anywhere except the travel office on the first floor of the *Weekly Galaxy* building. The outer room of the travel office was a barren oblong, bisected by a chest-high counter, with Sally Forth on one side and the customers on the other. When Sara entered and approached this counter, Sally Forth looked up from the paperback edition of *Marco Polo* she was reading and waited, tense and angry, obviously expecting the worst.

"Hello," Sara said. The woman said nothing. Sara wanted to ask if she was the right person, but there was no way to say, *Excuse me, are you Sally Forth?*, so she identified herself instead: "I'm Sara Joslyn, they sent me down to—"

"*Oh*, yes," the woman said, slamming down the paperback with unnecessary force. "They told me *you* were coming." Then she picked up the paperback, glaring as though she suspected Sara of intending to steal it, and carried it away to her inner room.

Alone, Sara looked around, noticing that, where one would expect travel posters on the walls, these framed poster-sized objects were merely more front pages of past *Weekly Galaxy*s. However, when she considered them more closely, she realized that one of the stories prominent on each front page involved some exotic locale: South Africa, Rio di Janeiro, Tahiti, Mars.

Sally Forth slammed back from her inner office, lugging a white shopping bag with a yellow circular smile face on the side. Her own face was the rebuttal. Lifting this shopping bag to a lower shelf on her side of the counter, "It's a nice life, I *must* say," she snarled. "Gallivanting around. Spend money like water. World travelers."

"It's my first trip," Sara said, to placate her.

She was not to be placated. Taking items from the shopping bag, slapping them on the counter in front of Sara, she announced each object in turn: "Airline ticket. American Express card. Air Travel card. MasterCard card; I hate that one. Visa card. Telephone company card. Hertz card. Exxon card. Two thousand dollars cash. Extra American Express card without the *Weekly Galaxy* name on it. Sign this."

Sara obediently signed the requisition sheet Sally Forth shoved across the counter at her, while Sally Forth sneered at her penmanship, saying, "Puss in boots, that's what it is. Seven league boots. Up up and away."

Yanking back the signed requisition, she snapped, "And what do *I* get to do? Stand here and look at this *counter*."

Trying to find something to say, some words of comfort or solace, human contact, Sara dithered and finally told the woman, "Life's unfair, I guess."

Sally Forth leveled on her a murderous but calm gaze. "So that's the news, is it?" she asked.

Sara gathered everything off the counter and fled.

* * *

Her own name was on all those credit cards. The two thousand dollars, a thick wad of used bills with a paper band around it, marked in black ink *$2G*, turned out to be a mix of twenties, fifties and a few hundreds. The airline ticket was for a first-class seat on flights between Miami and Indianapolis, changing at Atlanta. (Dead people, it was said, on their way to heaven, change at Atlanta. Or was that for people on their way to hell? Those going to heaven change at Amsterdam.)

Mary Kate's paper-clipped stack of information, now in Sara's possession, informed her Hertz would have a rental car reserved for her at the airport in Indianapolis, and a room awaited her at the

Holiday Inn on State Highway, just outside Whitcomb. All she had to do was pick up her typewriter and go.

Her typewriter? Yes. When she had, at the barbecue last Saturday, expressed surprise to Binx that the *Galaxy*'s reporters were issued manual portable typewriters rather than the word processors plugged into a mainframe computer that even the poor old *Courier-Observer* had converted to before it was merged and Sara'd lost that job, Binx had said, "Massa likes his reporters mobile." So this was what he'd meant.

The Aussies, feverish with expectation, grinning broadly and whacking one another on the back, assured Sara they would make contact immediately upon arrival at the Whitcomb Holiday Inn. Phyllis, one of those assigned to the hard slog of tracking down the unknown Felicia, expressed a heartfelt envy that made Sara glow with pleasure as she packed her typewriter and filled her shoulder bag with pens and tapes. Nearby, Ida Gavin was also packing, on her way to California to interview the elusive Keely Jones, whose defiant shotgunning of the *Galaxy*'s soundtruck had been that star's final misguided resistance of the *Galaxy*'s loving embrace. *That* was the true plum among today's journeys to America, a sunny conversation with a TV star beside a Bel Air swimming pool, but Sara felt no envy at all. Whitcomb was exciting enough, for a first time out.

What was it like? The first day of school, the first *year* of school. No, more than that; it was like the first time you ever went to the supermarket on your own, your mother's shopping list and the green paper money clutched tight in your moist fist.

Typewriter case handle clutched in her moist fist, head already filling with sentences about hundred-year-old twins, Sara ran for her plane.

Chapter Two

Whitcomb, Indiana, on a Tuesday in mid-July. Even the dogs were bored. A couple of them lying around in the shade under Edsels and LaSalles didn't even look up when the Trailways bus groaned to a stop in front of the Rexall store, farted shrilly, and opened its door to release the big-bellied sweat-stained driver and the Down Under Trio. Bob Sangster scratched his big nose, Harry Razza patted his deeply wavy auburn hair, Louis B. Urbiton gazed about the somnolent downtown of Whitcomb in mild amaze, and the bus driver opened a bomb-bay door in the rib cage of the bus to remove the Aussies' battered and disgusting mismatched luggage.

"So this is America," Harry Razza said.

"Can't say I like it much," Bob Sangster said.

"Oh, good," said Louis B. Urbiton, "there's a pub."

"Bar," Harry corrected.

"*Bahhhhh,*" Louis amended.

"Have a nice day," the driver said, and remounted his bus.

The Aussies stared after him, in astonishment and shock. "What?" demanded Bob.

"I call that cheek," Harry said.

The bus door snicked shut. The bus groaned away. The dog under the Edsel opened one eye, saw the six well-polished shoes of the Aussies, decided in his doggy innocence that these must be acceptable functioning members of society, and closed the eye again.

"We must phone the delectable Sara," Harry said, "and have her come gather us."

"Perhaps there's a phone in yonder *bahhhhh,*" Louis suggested.

"And we could wait there for her," Bob said.

Louis smiled on him. "What a good idea," he said.

The Aussies picked up their revolting saggy luggage and crossed Fremont Avenue to the Veterans' Bar & Grill, a place with neon beer signs in the window for enticement and a stubbly bit of triangular shingle roof over the entrance for decoration. They left the bright sunlight outside for the damp-smelling darkness within, and once their eyes adjusted they saw they were not alone in here, though the place was as quiet as any empty room you've ever listened to.

Fifteen or twenty people, most but not all male, were scattered along the dark-wood bar running down the right side of the joint and at the black Formica tables filling the space on the left. Everybody in Whitcomb retired from the railroad hung out here, plus a few widows and a couple of unemployed sheet-metal workers plotting a life of crime. Little was said in this room, and that little was muttered. People who hang out in the Veterans' Bar & Grill in the middle of a sunny Tuesday in July don't have much they want to say.

The Aussies gazed around this gloomy interior. "Oh, my," Bob Sangster said.

"Doctor," said Harry Razza, "can this environment be saved?"

"We're not here a moment too soon," said Louis B. Urbiton. A man of action, he dropped his bags and raised one hand. "Landlord!"

* * *

In the large main kitchen of a small local bakery, with the heat of the ovens compounding the heat of the day and a dozen white-clothed bakers punching and tearing various doughs into breads and pastries, Sara talked with the third-generation owner of the place, a fortyish pudgy man looking as sharp and hip and with-it as a huge green pinky ring and a loud check jacket permitted, and the Master Baker, an irascible genius of sixty who was good at what he did and therefore had no need to be hip, and who didn't like this lumpy interruption of Sara into the smooth batter of his life one little bit.

"It's just a birthday cake," Sara pointed out, not for the first time.

"Just a birthday cake," the Master Baker echoed, with ancient irony. He looked as though he subscribed to some primeval superstition that women were bad luck in a kitchen, and would prefer Sara to be put ashore at once.

"And our name in the paper, Gus," the owner said, showing how little he understood the wellsprings of his Master Baker's personality. "Hackmyer's Bakery," breathed this heir, almost reverently. "Gus Altervegh, Master Baker."

"Just a birthday cake," repeated the Master Baker, with the same deadly inflection.

"Sure," Sara said, pretending to ignore the sarcasm.

"Just a *twenty-foot* birthday cake!" The Master Baker looked as though he wanted to hit Sara on the forehead with a wooden spoon.

"Now, look," Sara said, turning to the owner, who was her ally. Useless, but an ally. "I've let you negotiate me down from fifty feet, but that's all. Twenty's as short as I go."

"Listen, I understand," the owner assured her. "I hear you. I know where you're coming from."

The Master Baker ignored his employer, saying to Sara, "You want to take a stroll in my ovens, lady? Walk around in there, play a little pitch and catch? Whadaya think we got here, the Bessemer Steel Works?"

"That's all right," Sara told him. "You can make it in parts, and put the parts together."

"Sure, Gus," the owner said. "With the icing on, who's to know?"

"*Look* at my ovens!" the Master Baker yelled, waving a brawny arm and a burn-pocked hand. "I can do you a twenty-*inch* cake, max max max!"

"So what's that?" the owner asked. "Maybe twelve, thirteen cakes?"

"So what's that?" the Master Baker demanded. "Two, three *days*?"

"Tomorrow," Sara said.

"They're not gonna be a hundred every day, Gus," the owner pointed out.

"If they're waiting on a twenty-foot birthday cake from *me*," the Master Baker said, "they'll *never* be a hundred."

Sara said, "What about a pizza oven?"

Horribly insulted, shocked to the very roots of his being, the Master Baker stared wide-eyed at Sara, having never in his life before seen such a dishonorable person. "Www-*what*?"

Sara was not going to let the good opinion of one small-town

Master Baker stand between her and success in her first assignment out in the world on her own. Plowing doggedly forward, pretending to see nothing odd in the man's staring eyes and ashen complexion, she said, "If I could arrange for a pizza oven, could you put together five four-foot cakes?"

The Master Baker pressed fat palms to his temples. "Five four-foot cakes," he said, with a dying fall. "I can't believe what I'm hearing."

"In the paper, Gus," the owner said, eager and avid, and to Sara he said, "With a picture, right?"

"Absolutely," Sara said. "A picture." Then she suddenly remembered: "Oh, my God, the photographer!"

Now they both stared at her. "Miss?" the owner said.

"The *Australians!*"

The owner looked like a man thinking about insurance; does it cover the nervous breakdowns of nonemployees in the kitchen? "What is it, miss?" he asked.

But Sara was already in motion. "A phone, a phone." Over her shoulder, she called, "I'll arrange for the oven, and the cake dish! I'll get back to you!" And she was gone.

The Master Baker and the owner looked at one another. "A twenty-foot cake dish," commented the Master Baker. "They put too much yeast in her head."

* * *

What a lot of fun! The regulars of the Veterans' Bar & Grill on Fremont Avenue had had no *idea* the walls of the grungy place could ring with so much hilarity. While the never-indicted Frank Sinatra sang "My Way" on the crumbling Wurlitzer, widows and retirees and sheet-metal workers all actually sat upright or even stood on their two feet, their grasp firm on their glasses, their eyes shining, their flushed cheeks cracked with unexpected laughter. Even the bartender showed a small smile from time to time, though he always remembered to cover it by turning to punch the cash register. Only one sodden bag lady in the corner remained oblivious.

Harry Razza flirted with the widows. Bob Sangster explained the real story of Ronnie Biggs and the great English train robbery to the sheet-metal workers. Louis B. Urbiton did his impressions of those various stars of stage, screen and politics which he claimed to have interviewed in his long and illustrious reportorial career. All his impressions looked and sounded like Burt Lancaster (whom he didn't do) except for his impression of Mae West, which was like nothing on earth.

"This is the most fun I've had," one ancient confessed, "since my wife's funeral."

"You fellows ought to hang out here more often," said a former railroad company timer.

Batting her eyes, until the practice made her dizzy, a widow said to Harry Razza, "So you folks are all the way from Australia."

"Drawn by the sparkle in your eyes, my darling."

"I never met anybody from Australia before," said a former fireman on the B, P & T.

Bob Sangster turned to Louis B. Urbiton, saying, "Show them your kangaroo."

A retiree gaped, slopping his Lite beer. "You have a *kangaroo*?"

The bartender lowered his eyebrows and glowered through them. "No kangaroo jokes," he said.

"Did you hear," Harry Razza asked him, "about the chap who went into the pub with a carrot in his ear?"

"Yes," the bartender said.

"No," Bob Sangster told the credulous retiree. "He *imitates* a kangaroo." To Louis B. Urbiton, he said, "Go on, Louis, show him."

So Louis showed him. The sight of a fairly respectable-looking, neatly dressed in suit and tie, fifty-one-year-old Australian leaping about the bar, up onto chairs and back down onto the floor, suitcoat tail flying, hand firmly holding drink as both hands pretended to be tiny kangaroo paws boxing, the whole while *honking,* was so captivating that everybody had to do it, beginning with the retirees and finishing with the widows. *Honk honk honk,* people jumped up and down, mighty leaps forward and back, pinwheeling their little kangaroo-paw fists; and all the while, Harry Razza continued to talk to the bartender: *"Then,"* he said, "the chap walks in next day with a stalk of celery in his ear."

"Don't tell me the punchline," the bartender said. "I'm warning you."

This was the scene Sara came upon when she entered the Veterans' Bar & Grill on Fremont Avenue: Louis B. Urbiton leading a lot of elderly dipsoes in some sort of vile calisthenics, Bob Sangster demonstrating quick-draw from a make-believe shoulder holster to a couple of unemployed sheet-metal workers, and Harry Razza chatting blithely with the bartender, ignoring the fist the man was slowly raising.

Sara called out, "Hello!" but nobody heard her, and nothing happened. She called out the Aussies' names, to absolutely no effect. Finally, seeing no alternative, she took a deep breath and screamed, "FIRE!"

Nothing. So she did it again: "FIRE!"

And a lot more times: "FIRE! FIRE! FIRE! FIRE! FIRE!"

Gradually the word penetrated, sweeping silence before it like the black death across Europe. The last of the kangaroos ceased to hop and to honk, Bob Sangster looked over at the doorway with his hand like Napoleon's inside his jacket, and Harry Razza stopped his story just short of its punchline, to turn and gaze at the red-faced Sara with pleased admiration.

Sara stopped shouting. She took a moment to catch her breath. A layabout near her said, "Lady, don't you know you shouldn't yell 'fire' in a public place?"

"Oh, yeah?" Sara told him. "You try yelling 'water' and see what you get." Pointing one by one at the Aussies, she said, "Those are mine."

"Oh, dear, it's teacher," said Louis.

"Come along, you guys," Sara said. "Where's my photographer?"

Louis gave himself a visible search, without result. "Photographer?"

A retiree urged Sara, "Have him show you his kangaroo."

"I don't want his kangaroo," Sara said, "I want my photographer."

Head on table, the bag lady had still been asleep off to one side, the only person in the room not caught up in the hullabaloo of the Aussies' descent, but now she raised her head, blearily gazed around, and said, "Photoga—? Photoga—?"

"Come on," Sara said to her team, "I need that photographer."

"Sara, darling," Harry Razza said, while the widows sniffed and looked put out, "I swear we have none of us set eyes on even a single photographer."

"Did you say *photographer?*" the bag lady cried, at last getting the name right. "*I'm* a, I can be a, I've been a—" She struggled to rise from her chair, her feet kicking at the various shopping bags around her.

"No, no," Sara told her. "Our photographer from Indianapolis."

Shakily rising, showing herself to be garbed in a motley mishmash of unacceptable clothing, inadvertently knocking over the half-full (half-empty) beer glass on the table in front of her, pointing more or less at her own self with a stubby and uncertain finger, "That's me!" the bag lady cried. "I came, I just drove down from, I'm the—"

Sara stared. "*You're* my photographer?"

The bag lady nodded hugely in happy agreement. The shopping bags around her feet were full of lenses, reflecters, work lights, folding tripods, film rolls, black cloths, light meters and actual cameras. Two more cameras dangled like lynch victims on the bag lady's person. Waving precariously, work-booted feet moving and moving among the bags of equipment, the bag lady cried, "From Indiana—Indi—From Indian— Yeah!" And backwards she toppled, thumping into a seated position on her chair, smile magnificent, arms outspread.

Sara looked at them. The Aussies. The bag lady. "My team," she said.

Chapter Three

Midafternoon, in the bustling editorial offices of the *Weekly Galaxy*. Jack Ingersoll paced his squaricle, assembling his list for tomorrow morning's conference with Massa. Pausing, he squinted one-eyed across the heaving writhing squaricles toward the battery of reporters, gnawing away at their phones. He said, "Glue on Postage Stamps Can Give You Migraine, Doctors Fear."

"Is that one sentence or two?" Mary Kate replied, but she typed, she typed.

Jack nodded, unheeding. "Jogging Causes Nymphomania," he said.

Boy Cartwright, the limey bastard, the rotten Englishman, Massa's pet editor, the only person in the known universe with a corner squaricle—walls *and* windows on two sides!—Jack's least favorite living creature, came and stood in the door space of the squaricle and smiled. Jack hated it when Boy Cartwright smiled, when that doughy baby-fat face spread its puffy pink lips. Jack would much prefer to see Boy Cartwright's unhealthy face twisted with agony, or that soft and sluglike body cowering in abject terror. The reason Jack watched *Wages of Fear* every time it came on television was so he could pretend it was Boy Cartwright being dragged down into that oozing lake of oil and squashed beneath the wheels of the straining truck.

But here was Boy at the door space to Jack's squaricle, his usual shit-eating smile smeared across his white diseased-pumpkin face.

"Listen, Boy," Jack said, "don't you have a belfry to haunt?"

"Ahsk me," Boy suggested, "what's the good word."

"Will you then go away?"

"Oh, absolutely," Boy promised.

"All right," Jack said. "What's the good word, Boy?"

"Felicia," Boy pronounced, with loving care on every syllable. Then he smiled even more horribly than before and, true to his word, went away.

Felicia! He *knew*! The bastard *knew*! Jack's face twisted with agony as he turned to Mary Kate, who was glaring poison-tipped knives at Boy's back. "How?" Jack demanded. *"Who?"*

Because it had to be a mole within his own team, a viper in his bosom. His scoop was a scoop no longer. Jack Ingersoll and his team were no longer the only ones who knew that John Michael Mercer had thrown over Fluffy MacDougall for someone named Felicia. *"Who?"*

Could it have been Sara? Could she have been that low, to take such a vile vengeance for his not having brought her into his confidence Saturday night? No; he couldn't believe it of her. She was quick and sharp enough, but not naturally mean, a flaw in her character that would keep her from rising very far at the *Galaxy*, a fact he was in no hurry for her to discover. So it wasn't her; if it had been, something would have shown on her face this morning when he gave her the reward of a trip to America, some soupçon of guilt, wisp of regret, passing shadow of conscience. So not Sara.

And not the Down Under Trio either; the Aussies despised Boy, if that were possible, even more than Jack did. As for Ida Gavin, even now skying LAward to grind her heel in Keely Jones's face, she had become who she was today as a result of Boy's loathsomeness, so not her either. So, in that case, who? *Who?*

Mary Kate? Impossible. He and Mary Kate were Siamese twins, they were joined at the hip, they had the world's first incestuous platonic relationship.

Who? *Who?* Pessimistic Don Grove, constantly coming forward with two-headed calves and honeymoons on Alpha Centauri? Phyllis Perkinson, the slumming Jaycee-ette? Chauncey Chapperell, certified lunatic, preppy Trekkie and Space Ranger, who was just this morning back from a three-week assignment to find a race of chess-playing gorillas in the Amazon delta? (They hadn't been there; too bad.)

So that was the team. Eight reporters, one secretary, one editor.

The only people in this building, the only ones, who knew the significance of the name Felicia.

Well, wait. There *was* one other possibility; slim, but possible. The waiter.

Pedro. Pedro just might already have been among those waiters, garagemen, airline clerks and others in the service trades who are part of the vast intricate frivolous network of spies and informants connected with one or another editor at the *Galaxy*. If that particular restaurant were a fairly frequent haunt of John Michael Mercer's, and if some member of Boy's team had already suborned Pedro, naturally the fellow wouldn't have mentioned the fact to Jack; particularly not when Jack had folding money visible in his fist. And Pedro, Jack remembered, had still been hanging around the vicinity when Sara had said that name "Felicia" and told Jack what it signified.

So it could be Pedro. It could be. Unlikely, *extremely* unlikely, but not impossible.

And to have to accept the alternative, that some member of his own team had been suborned by the despicable Boy, was not to be borne. So, until events proved otherwise, Jack would assume that Pedro was the source of the leak. And he would watch his ass.

At which point in the progress of his gloomy thinking, one of the absolutely trustworthy members of Jack's team, pessimistic Don Grove—could it be him? could it?—entered the squaricle to say, "I don't suppose you could use a hole opened in the earth and swallowed a garage. There was a car in it."

Back to work. Jack said, "Anybody in the car?"

"That depends," Don said carefully.

"Verifiable, Don."

"I'll see what I can do."

Don Grove started from the squaricle and Jack called after him, "Unless it's in California."

Don Grove frowned, looking back. "What's wrong with California?"

"Happens there every day."

Sighing, Don Grove went away, and Phyllis Perkinson—could it be her? could it?—entered in his place, saying, "Unless it's Felicia Farr, I just don't know."

"*Is* it Felicia Farr?"

"No."

"So you don't know, is what you're saying."

Phyllis's high clean forehead furrowed in distress. She said, "I'm sorry, Jack, I know this is important."

"About on a par with the Dead Sea Scrolls, I would say."

"The problem is, he's fired all our spies." Phyllis shook her patrician head in dismay at the baseness of humankind. "Why does Mercer have to have such a bad attitude?"

"Some people are just no fun at all," Jack agreed, as the phone in the squaricle flashed and Mary Kate answered. Jack said to Phyllis, "Strive on, girl. We must find Felicia." Rolling his eyes to indicate all the other editors in all the other squaricles, he said, "We must find Felicia *first*."

"Oh, I know, I know," Phyllis said. "I'll keep searching."

"Sara of the twins," Mary Kate announced.

"Go thou and find Felicia," Jack told Phyllis, who nodded and left as Jack picked up his phone and said, "How's Warwick?"

"Whitcomb," Mary Kate corrected, but Jack was listening, nodding, smiling, saying, "Oh, yeah, that's the photographer, don't worry about how she looks, she's really terrific, she'll give you great shots, very human."

"Oh, *that* one," Mary Kate said.

"Are the Aussies a help?" Jack asked the phone. "Don't let them drink too much." Then he looked at Mary Kate, and said, "She's laughing."

"Well, she's a cheerful girl," Mary Kate said.

"What?" Jack asked the phone, and listened, and looked sad. "No governor?" Then he looked cheerful again. "*Three* mayors! Very nice. And the birthday cake as big as the Ritz?"

"Tell her to bring me back a slice," Mary Kate said.

"It's not on your diet," Jack told Mary Kate, and then said to the phone, "Nothing, I was just chatting with Mary Kate. Twenty feet? That's not a really *big* cake, honeybunch. Tell the photographer to do a real severe angle and a wide-angle lens and whatever—well, she knows. Tell her it's supposed to look as big as that aircraft carrier, you know the one. Well, *she'll* know the one."

"The one with the planes on it," Mary Kate said.

"Have fun there, darling," Jack said, and held the smile until he hung up, when the smile was immediately replaced by a deep black scowl. "*Could* it be her?" he demanded. "*Could* it be her?"

"Of course it could," Mary Kate said. "It could be anybody. It could be *you*."

Jack stared at her. "*Me?*"

"I trust nobody," Mary Kate told him. "And I recommend you be the same."

Chapter Four

The dayroom of the Elysian Fields Manor and Convalescent Center was a large and sunny space, with gauzy white curtains drawn back from the broad airy windows so that daylight poured gaily in, sparkling on walkers and crutches, glistening on shiny heads and pale white elbows, gleaming on inhalers and syringes. The peaceful quiet calm was counterpointed, never disturbed, by the occasional turning of a card, turning of a page, or rustle of a long-drawn sigh.

Heads were lifted, eyes were rolled, fingers twitched at coverlets, as Sara returned after lunch, striding into the neat and clean dayroom with her bulging shoulder bag bouncing at her hip. The starched and ironed nurse accompanying her gestured to the farthest corner of the room, where a pair of identical wheelchairs contained a pair of identical oldsters in identical pajamas under identical blankets. Sara nodded, and the two women marched across the room to Joe and Jim Geester, the nurse saying brightly on arrival, "Hi, Joe and Jim, here's your visitor again."

"Remember me, guys?" Sara asked, making her voice as bright and chipper as the nurse's.

Joe Geester—he was the one on the right—lifted a lumpy potato head with a cranky sour face drawn on the front of it and creakily said, "Girl reporter."

"That's right!" Sara said, smiling and sparkling. "From the *Weekly Galaxy*, gonna give you guys just the *best* party ever! One hundred years young tomorrow, huh, guys?"

"Well," the nurse said, "I'll leave you to discuss the details." Turning away, she said under her breath to Sara, "Don't get too close."

"I won't," Sara murmured back, and beamed again on the birthday boys, saying, "All set for the big party?"

As the nurse marched away toward the exit, Joe's ancient scrawny hand emerged from under the blankets, making clutching motions. "Come a little closer," he said.

"Oh, I think I'm close enough," Sara said. "Now, let me tell you about the party. We found some Geesters outside Cicero, Illinois, *might* be related to you, and—"

"Liars!" Joe snapped.

"Well, anyway," Sara said, her smile insistent and undimmed, "they're coming to the party, you can compare relatives then. And guess who else is coming?"

"Cheryl Tiegs?"

Ignoring that, Sara said, "*Three* mayors! And Dr. Bark, and—"

"Butcher!" cried Joe.

Sara didn't follow that. She said, "You want me to invite the butcher?"

"Bark's a butcher!" yelled Joe, and a few quavery voices nearby said, "Right on!" and, "Tell it, brother!"

"Oh, now, Jim," Sara said, "look on the sunny side. I bet—"

"I'm Joe," Joe snarled.

"Oh. Sorry. Anyway, I bet Jim doesn't feel that—"

"Jim's dead," Joe said, and snapped his gums.

Sara blinked at him. "What?"

"Died about an hour ago," Joe said, in grim satisfaction. "Went—" And he rattled in his throat; a truly dreadful noise.

Sara, her *heart* in her throat, leaned close to the suspiciously silent Jim. Those were not living eyes. That was not a living mouth. "Oh, golly," she said.

Joe's clutching hand reached out, moving toward Sara, but too slow and too late; she was already turning away, shocked, gray-faced, moving, running, yelling, "Nurse! Nurse!"

* * *

Massa sat at his desk in his elevator/office, drinking beer from the bottle. Jacob Harsch paced back and forth in front of the desk, studying various sheets of paper. "They're getting lax, sloppy," he muttered. "A few random firings, that'll put some spirit in them."

Massa laughed. "Haven't had a good old bloodbath in quite a while," he said.

"They're getting fat, they think it's too easy, they think they *deserve* all this somehow. Chop a few heads, that'll do it."

"But not Boy," Massa said.

"No, of course not."

"Boy's worth the lot of them."

The phone on Massa's desk rang, and Massa watched Harsch pick it up and speak into it: "Mr. DeMassi's office." He listened, his lips twitching faintly, and then he looked over at Massa to say, "The twins, hundred years old tomorrow."

"Sweet story," Massa said, smiling at the thought of it. "Beautiful story."

"One died."

Massa's mouth dropped open. "Died? Before his birthday?"

"The reporter out there wants to know, do we go ahead with the party."

"Of course not!" Massa said, astonished that the question could even be asked. "What's that supposed to be? A party for one twin?"

Into the phone, Harsch said, "No party." He listened again, nodded, said to Massa, "What about the cake?"

Ridiculous; Massa knew it was ridiculous. He pushed the button on his desk that opened the elevator doors, revealing that they were at this time on the third floor, with the conference table and, beyond it out over the floor, Editorial. Way out there, among the other people, desks, chairs, filing cabinets, Jack Ingersoll stood beside his desk with the phone to his ear. But Massa didn't need a phone for this. Half rising over his desk, pointing out at Ingersoll, knowing the fellow could see and hear him, Massa bellowed, *"He doesn't get the cake!"*

* * *

On the pay phone on the street corner down the block from the Elysian Fields Manor and Convalescent Center, pickup trucks and old Hudsons puddling by behind her, Sara said unbelievingly, "He doesn't get the cake? Do you mean, not only is his brother dead, he doesn't get the party? He doesn't even get the *cake*?"

In her ear, faintly apologetic but holding out no hope at all, Jack Ingersoll's voice said, "Sorry, Sara, that's from Massa himself. He just bellowed it at me from across the room."

Sara shook her head, trying to think, saying, "I can't believe even Massa, even the *Galaxy*, would be so low that—" She broke off, blinked, licked her lips, looked desperate, and quickly said, "Yes, Doctor? Wait a minute, Jack. Yes, Doctor?"

"What's that?" Jack's tiny voice said. "Sara?"

Speaking a few inches away from the phone, sounding hopeful

but doubtful, Sara said, "Are you *sure*, Doctor?" Then, in a sudden burst of delight, "That's wonderful, Doctor!"

"Sara? Sara?"

"A miracle?" Sara cried into the phone. "Jack, did you hear? He isn't dead! He had a relapse! The other thing, I mean, the opposite. He's alive, Jack!"

The deeply suspicious voice of Jack said in her ear, "Sara, are you trying to con *me*?"

"Jack, how can you say that? The doctor's right here, you can ask him your— Oh, he had to get back to his patient. Jack, listen, I better get off, I've got this party coming up."

"With *pictures*, Sara," said that deeply suspicious voice.

"Well, sure! That's what it's all about, isn't it?" There on the street corner, out of her mind, Sara laughed girlishly, and a middle-aged couple, on their way to visit Mom at Elysian Fields, gave her a dirty look. "I'll have pictures, Jack," she said, waving brightly at the passing couple. "I'll have everything, I'll get it *all*. Bye, now!" And she hung up, clenching her teeth, not moaning in agony until the connection was definitely and absolutely broken. Then she sagged forward against the phone, resting her fevered brow on the coin slot. "I'll have pictures," she muttered. "Everything. Somehow."

* * *

Slowly Jack hung up the phone, but continued to stand there, looking at it as though it might make a sudden move, might all at once bite him. Mary Kate looked over. "Sara?"

"She's out there," Jack said. "With a questionable number of twins. Give me your reading, Mary Kate. Does that girl know what she's doing?"

"Of course not," Mary Kate said. "Why should she be any different from the rest of us?"

Chapter Five

Tann-ta-rraaa!! The Whitcomb, Indiana, Volunteer Hook and Ladder Fire Department, Engine Company 2, Fife, Drum, Bugle, Bagpipe, Glockenspiel and Clarinet Corps marched in place, blowing and plinking and whomping and wheezing, pounding the emerald green front lawn of the Elysian Fields Manor and Convalescent Home into brown muck, tearing off their rendition of "When the Saints Come Marching In" (not, perhaps, the happiest of choices, but no one seemed to notice), until Company Commander and Bandmaster J. Garrison Murchison IV shrilled his whistle, smartly about-faced, and led his seventeen widely assorted musicians in through the front door, down the wide main hall, through the double doorway at its end with the banner strung overhead reading HAPPY 100, JOE AND JIM!, and into the dayroom, alive—sort of—with the birthday celebration.

It was a dayroom transformed. Pink and white crepe streamers corkscrewed from corner to corner and from light fixture to light fixture overhead. Golden-agers seated in all manner of chairs and conveyances lined both long walls, flanking THE CAKE, whose twenty-foot length down the middle of the thirty-foot room effectively created through mitosis two parties where only one had been planned. THE WEEKLY GALAXY AND THE AMERICAN PEOPLE SALUTE JOE AND JIM GEESTER ON THEIR 100TH BIRTHDAY!!! read the cake, from end to end, in garish red letters on the pure white icing.

The cake had not as yet been broken into; in the meantime, secondary tables on the side walls contained platters of cheese sandwiches on white bread, Campbell's Cream of Mushroom Soup dip with potato chips, thawed but unheated egg rolls, a big green and red platter of crudités which everybody avoided on the assumption it was merely a decorative vegetable centerpiece, and both chocolate chip cookies and Fig Newtons. Weak coffee, see-through tea and a big bowl of Hi-C punch were the available quaffs.

In addition to the dayroom's normal occupants, shunted for the moment to the side, there were new faces here for the special occasion. Three bewildered mayors, a whole lot of intently eating Geesters from Cicero, Illinois, Dr. Bark the butcher and various other celebrities milled about both sides of the cake. The photographer, ungainly and lumpish in her brogans, gray tube socks, heavy shapeless black skirt, pilled brown sweater over torn green polo shirt, and decayed red bandana around neck, hung about with cameras and light meters, swooped and squatted around the room like some endangered species of flightless bird, now standing bent forward on one leg, now seated in a sprawl of skirts on the floor, now flat on her back under one of the tables bearing the cake, now lunging with high-kneed hops toward some new object of her magpie interest, and always with one or another of her cameras to her sweating and exalted face.

Just to the right of the doorway, as the marching band marched in (to bifurcate at the cake and finish the number marching in place all around it, while various sections of the cake slowly subsided), stood Sara with Harry Razza and Louis B. Urbiton, they drinking plastic cups of Hi-C punch which they had privately altered to their taste, she drinking and eating nothing, but smiling broadly in terror and accomplishment. This was *her* party, her creation and then some.

Of course, she'd had help. The staff and other residents of Elysian Fields, when shown the clear choice between abetting a felony or losing the party, with its attendant food and drink, not to mention publicity and visitors from the great outer world, had seen immediately and to a person which way duty lay. (In fact, when the surviving Geester boy, out of simple cantankerousness, had threatened not to cooperate, it was his fellow residents of the Manor who had swiftly ended that revolution, with graphic portrayals of what Joe's life among them would be like, however long or short, should he continue to make trouble.)

Among Sara's fellow representatives of the *Weekly Galaxy*, participation had been general, unstinting and immediate. The photographer, faced with the alternative of the long solitary drive back to Indianapolis without even the solace of sold photographs and paid expenses, had with great enthusiasm entered into the conspiracy. Harry Razza and Louis B. Urbiton, old hands at the manufacturing of news, fell in with a will and many a valuable suggestion. But the whole thing would nevertheless have been impossible were it not for Bob Sangster and his nose.

It turned out, on close inspection, that the Bob Sangster nose and the nose shared by Joe and Jim Geester were so markedly similar in both size and construction that they might actually even be related in some distant way, a concept that both Bob and Joe denied with vehement disgust. Working from that proboscal commonality, with makeup assistance from Sara and Harry Razza and the photographer, selective shaving of the Sangster head, and a set of pajamas, slippers, blanket and wheelchair to match that of the surviving twin, Bob Sangster was turned into a simulacrum of Jim Geester (or Joe, actually, that having been the model they'd worked from) so realistic that one nurse, seeing the false Jim placed in his wheelchair beside the real Joe, commented, "By God, it's like having the filthy old bastard back again."

(The real Jim Geester slept the long sleep upstairs in his room, the air conditioner turned on full and the door locked. Immediately after the party, it would be discovered that the joy and excitement had been too much for old Jim. Dr. Bark the butcher, cheerily eating Fig Newtons and chatting with the mayors, would fill out and sign and date the death certificate, and Lloyd Llewellyn of Llewellyn's Mortuary, who considered Elysian Fields Manor by far his most frequent and valued customer, could be counted on to handle the obsequies without question or fuss.)

The mayors and Cicero Geesters and other special guests were the first gulls of this cabal, and were eating it up a lot more enthusiastically than they did the mushroom soup. At the far end of the room, in subtly dimmer light, the two birthday boys sat in identical postures of slump-shouldered hopelessness, one clutching an empty plastic cup (he'd spilled the Hi-C punch on his blanket), the other feebly picking at a Fig Newton. Watching them from her post near the door, as the dismemberment of "When the Saints Come Marching In" at last clattered to its photo finish, Sara for just a second couldn't remember which was which, but then got it straight—the one who'd spilled his punch was Bob, startled at having found it nonalcoholic—and said, "By golly, I wouldn't have believed it."

"Amazing," Louis B. Urbiton agreed. "Bob's thespic qualities all these years unknown, unsung."

"They'd better stay unknown and unsung," Sara said.

"Oh, truly," Louis agreed. "Be worth our jobs, wouldn't it?"

Harry Razza knocked back his redecorated punch and said, "Looks like two of them to me anyway."

"Ladies and gentlemen!" cried Dr. Bark the butcher into the comparative quiet left when the volunteer fire department had downed instruments, "it's time to cut the cake!"

"Don't let *him* cut it!" quavered some ancient wag. "It'll never survive!"

"Ha ha," Dr. Bark the butcher said, smiling around like a searchlight, trying to find the funny fellow.

"Hold it!" cried the photographer, crashing over a number of invalids and visiting Geesters to get into just the right position. "Now!" she yelled. "Cut it now!"

"Joe and, uh, Jim," Dr. Bark the butcher said, smiling broadly in their direction and raising over his head the unnecessarily large knife, "this is for you."

"Look out, Joe!" cried the still anonymous wag.

Ignoring this interruption, Dr. Bark the butcher sliced into a somewhat underdone segment of cake and brought up a knife all gooey and runny, to which a piece of exclamation point adhered, that being the end at which the doctor's operation had begun. Gazing in revulsion at his knife, Dr. Bark the butcher said, "Who did the prep on this cake?"

Well, it didn't matter. Once the initial incision had been made, the guests fell to the cake with knives and forks and spoons and spatulas and playing cards and tearing fingers like an Islamic mob finding a heretic in its midst. In the eating frenzy that followed, no one thought to give any of the cake to the birthday boys, but that was all right; it wasn't on their diets, anyway.

* * *

The fuss around the cake woke Joe Geester from a dream in which he was at last putting it to that little Mrs. McKellahy the trolley conductor's wife in 3A; sixty-seven years dropped on him like a dead buffalo with consciousness; so who would want to be conscious? He turned his head to say something nasty to Jim, and what he saw brought near-term memory into alignment with long-term memory and gave him even *more* to be sour about. "You," he commented, without pleasure.

Bob Sangster, not all that rollicking in mood himself since discovering and spilling the contents of his Hi-C punch cup, nodded in agreement. "Me," he acknowledged.

Joe looked him over, feeling more cranky by the second, but

knowing he didn't dare do a thing to queer this deal; which only made him crankier. "You don't look a thing like me," he snarled.

"I'm not you, you old turkey," Bob said. "I'm your brother Jim."

"Don't sound like me, neither."

"Was your brother as sweet as you?"

"No," Joe said thoughtfully, looking back down the years. "I was always the good-natured one."

Bob stared at him in disbelief.

"Hold it!" cried the photographer, squatting wide-kneed in the space between them and the cake as though planning to relieve herself right then and there; but with the black box of the camera mashed to her absorbed face.

"Come a little closer," Joe told her.

"This is perfect, right here!" the photographer told him. "Hold it!"

They held it.

Chapter Six

Jack held the photo in both hands, studying it, studying the two old guys in the wheelchairs, surrounded by obvious partygoers. The two old guys were identical, with identical bad-tempered expressions. One held a floral design plastic cup, the other a crumbled cookie. Jack could see this photo, touch it, look at it; so why did he mistrust the goddamn thing so much?

"Well?" Sara asked, standing there, bobbing on the balls of her feet, filling and overflowing his squaricle with her triumphant smiling presence.

"All right," Jack said grudgingly. "All right."

Well, it had to be all right, didn't it? Here were the hundred-year-old twins. Here they were again in photos with the twenty-foot-long birthday cake, the *Galaxy*'s name prominent. Here they were with the three mayors. Here they were with the long-lost cousins from Cicero, Illinois. Here they were with the nursing home doctors and staff. Here they were with their fellow residents. Here they were looking balefully at the camera and wearing tall conical birthday hats.

Here they were, all right. And here was Jack, hip deep in

verification and authentication; so what was there about this story that made him feel as though somehow or other he'd just bought the Brooklyn Bridge?

It shouldn't matter, really. If the story was solid enough to get past the fact checkers and into the paper, that was all anybody needed. It was just that . . . it was just that . . . if there was any conning to be done, Jack was supposed to be one of the conners, not one of the connees.

Oh, well. At last, knowing that if in fact he *had* been taken for a ride it had been masterfully done, that he would never see the seams—no, it hadn't been done with mirrors, he'd already checked that possibility—he tossed the photo back among the others on his desk and said, "Well, you did it."

"I sure did," she agreed, swelling with pride. "You sent me to do a birthday party for one-hundred-year-old twins, and that's what I did. Sorry about the governor."

"That's okay," Jack assured her. "The three mayors are fine, very American."

Mary Kate paused in her typing to say, out of the corner of her mouth, "It's a real heartwarming story." And she went on with her typing.

"It was a really nice party," Sara said.

"Sorry I couldn't be there," Jack said truthfully.

Sara laughed and said, "What next?"

"Felicia," Jack told her. "The famous Felicia. Or the nonfamous Felicia, unfortunately."

"You want me to talk to her? What if she's—"

"We still need to *find* her," Jack said. "That's why you're going to be taking another little trip."

The idea pleased her, that was obvious. "Back to America?"

"Not exactly. Just to Miami, this time."

Her expression sardonic, she said, "Another restaurant?"

"Better," Jack told her, refusing to rise to the bait. "Much better, if it works out. You're new here, so you aren't known to be a *Galaxy* reporter. God knows you think on your feet," he added, tapping the photos of the birthday party. "So just maybe it'll work out."

"What am I supposed to do?"

"Apply for a job," Jack said.

* * *

Later that same day, Jack had a chat with Ida Gavin, also back from America; or, that is, from Bel Air, and the swimming pool of the overly excitable Keely Jones. The interview had gone well—when Keely Jones at last did collapse, she collapsed all the way, and Ida was precisely the right vulture to be waiting on the branch overhead at the time—and Ida had transcribed the tape and written her story on the flight back; no grass grew under old Ida's feet.

Jack's attitude toward Ida contained all the ambiguity of anyone who employs a mad dog because of the mad dog's useful qualities. At work, Ida was fast, dedicated, smart and utterly without pity. Behind the harsh expression and watchful eyes, she was a very good-looking woman of thirty-four, for whom sex was merely another weapon in the arsenal of reportorial techniques. Given her speed and single-minded dedication, she was the most resourceful and reliable person on Jack's team, more responsible than anyone except Jack himself for the team's success; but she was also the one member of the team he couldn't possibly see himself having a drink with, or a conversation with, away from the job. (As for going to bed with her, ye gods!) Ida was an android, cold and ruthlessly efficient, which made her perfect for what he now had in mind. "Your next task," he told her, when Ida came by the squaricle to drop off the Keely Jones piece, "awaits."

Ida looked alert, like a leopard smelling a deer. "Felicia?" she asked.

"No," he said. "What I'm giving you is the only thing right now that's even more important. It's industrial espionage."

Ida had engaged in industrial espionage before. She smiled thinly, perhaps at the memory of the three-week affair she'd once had with the chief surgeon of a large Dallas hospital in order to find out whether or not a hospitalized TV series star had AIDS; negative, unfortunately, but still, it was better to know. "Which industry?" she asked.

"This industry," Jack told her, waving a hand generally at Editorial. "Ida, some member of this team fed the Felicia name to Boy Cartwright."

Fire shot from Ida's eyes. Her nostrils quivered. Her fingernails grew an inch. "Who," she said.

"That is what you are to tell me."

"I will," Ida said.

She would, too. Ida's short grim history is quickly told: As a bright local Midwestern TV newsreader in her twenties, she had been swept off her feet by the sophisticated Englishman from the *Weekly Galaxy*, Boy Cartwright (less puffy and less obviously degenerate then), who had rushed her into an affair much as she would later do with such as that Dallas surgeon, swearing eternal fealty, encouraging her to abandon her well-begun TV news career with its first few useful contacts, and promising her a job as his good right hand at the *Galaxy*, while all the time he had been actually interested in nothing but some passingly newsworthy piece of showbiz info.

Her first life in ruins, Ida had followed Boy to Florida, unbelieving at first that the romance was dead, and had even managed to get herself hired by the *Galaxy*, though Boy had talked against her behind her back, not wanting the responsibility of her continued presence in his life. (He'd had less power at the paper, then, and so had failed.)

Once Ida had at last understood what had been done to her, something curdled in that body and brain. She had determined to out-Boy Boy, to become better than he at his own game, to beat him to scoops, outshine him, become the only woman in the world Boy Cartwright could admire and respect, while at all times keeping turned toward him a face of unremitting hate.

Hatred of Boy, and cold implacable efficiency on the job, begun as conscious determination, had both settled into habits, and by now these two characteristics had *become* Ida Gavin, the news machine. If she had any other facets to her personality, no one knew about them; and no one wanted to know.

"It's within the team," Jack told her. "Find out which one of them, Ida. Strip them naked."

"I will bring you," Ida said, "Polaroids of their hearts."

FELICIA

Chapter One

Felicia scraped omelette residue into the garbage and fitted the plate into the dishwasher. Johnny, having put the butter and cream away, stood in the middle of the kitchen watching her, a discontented frown on his quasi-handsome face, a face that one critic had described as "a sculptor's first draft of Adonis." Felicia, aware of Johnny's eyes on her, closed the dishwasher and looked smiling around the kitchen; not entirely spotless, but it would do. "All done," she said. "That wasn't so hard, was it?"

"Felicia, you shouldn't have to do *housework,*" Johnny said, his voice thick with the clogged fury of a man who isn't used to frustration. "And it won't be for long," he added. "I promise you."

Felicia laughed. It wasn't that she was a beautiful girl, exactly; she had pleasant and regular features, clear eyes and ash blonde hair done in a style whose cunning secret was simplicity. It was the person behind the features, the individual who animated them, that made it seem she was beautiful. When she laughed, lifting her head just slightly in that fashion, Johnny wanted to die for her; to kill for her; to live for her; to give every other creature on the planet life in her name. "Johnny, Johnny," she said (he loved her voice always, but never more than when it was saying his name), "I'm not the princess and the pea, you know. I've taken care of myself for years."

"Well, I'm taking care of you now," he said, then heard what he'd just said and laughed at himself. (One of the reasons *she* loved *him* was that, against all the odds, he frequently did laugh at himself.) "That is," he corrected, "I'm *hiring* the people to take care of you now." Laughter gone, he glowered around the kitchen. "Soon, I hope."

Her own expression now troubled, she said, "Are you really sure you had to fire *everybody*?"

"The place was riddled with spies," he told her. "I got lax, honey. Until you came along, for a long while I didn't have anything in my life I cared that much about, so I just let things happen, and that goddamn *Galaxy* bribed its way into my *closets*, into my *bathroom*. There was no way to tell who hadn't sold out, so the only thing to do was start all over, and be *sure*."

"That's so hard on the innocent ones, though."

"Everybody got a first-rate recommendation," he pointed out, "and fat severance pay. And if any of them were innocent and got hurt, that's something else for the *Galaxy*'s conscience, if it has one."

"I don't even see," she said cautiously, knowing how strongly he felt about this, "why they're so *important*. It's just a trashy gossip paper, nobody believes it or pays it any attention."

"People pay it attention, yes, they do," he told her grimly. "But that isn't the point. The things they say, the intrusions, the violation of the simplest standards of decency and privacy. You don't have the thick skin, Felicia, you aren't toughened." He crossed the room to put his arms around her, looking at her as solemnly as a child. "They'd tear you apart, my darling. I'm not going to let that happen. I want you never in this world to be anything but happy."

"I am happy," she said, and kissed him. Then she laughed again, saying, "And when we have a whole new staff here, screened and guaranteed by that *brilliant* employment agency man—"

"Reed. Henry Reed is his name. And he is brilliant."

"And when he's done his work," Felicia said, laughing at Johnny, but fondly, "and we have a new cook, and a new maid, and a new gardener, and a new butler, and new security people, and a new secretary, and a whole *army* of new people, then you'll be happy, too, *mon général*. Isn't that so?"

"Stay with me, Felicia," he told her, his arms tight around her waist, "and I'll be happy. That's all it takes."

Henry Reed rested his palm on the employment application form and looked at the young woman across the desk. In a few minutes, if it seemed worthwhile, he would study the answers she'd written on that form, but at first, as was his invariable practice, he would simply talk to her, ask her questions and listen to the answers, and watch her, become aware of her on a person-to-person basis. That was much more valuable than all the filled-out applications in the world, and it was his skill at reading people rather than reading forms that had made Henry Reed Personnel Inc. *the* premier-quality placement service (*never* employment agency, nothing so blue collar and crude) in south Florida, for both the better corporate clients and the most discriminating private individuals. There's a lot of money in south Florida, and it was Henry Reed's service to that money to provide for it the upper echelons of discreet, practiced, highly trained servitors.

"So, Miss Henderson," he said, "you're looking for work as a personal secretary."

"That's right." She was attractive, in her twenties, neatly and personably dressed; she met Reed's searching look clearly, without fuss. "I prefer not to work in offices," she went on, and smiled. "I'm afraid I get bored too easily, though maybe I shouldn't admit that to you."

"Not at all," he murmured. So far, he was impressed. There were several clients he could think of—one in particular, in fact—who would perhaps be very grateful for his introduction of this young woman into their lives.

"For me," she was saying, "it just seems to work out better if I work for one specific person in a more informal setting, be he an entrepreneur, an artist, a venture capitalist, or whatever he might be." Laughing lightly, she said, "Or *she* might be, I have nothing against working for a woman. In either case, that's what's more likely to give me the kind of varied work experience that keeps me happy."

Reed nodded. "Would that include," he asked, "well-known people?"

She looked alert, but uncomprehending. "I'm sorry?"

"Celebrities, you might say."

"Oh." A sardonic expression crossed her face. She crossed her legs, crossed her wrists on her lap, leaned back slightly in the chair; all body language for rejection. "Oh, I've had my celebs," she said. "Yes, sir."

"And would you prefer a well-known employer again?"

"*Oh*, no," she said, with a palm-down right-hand sweeping movement away to the side.

"No?" Reed watched her with great care. "Would you mind saying why not?"

"I'm a good personal secretary," Miss Henderson said, and gestured at the application form on his desk. "And those people will tell you so. But celebrities have great big heads and they're the *worst*."

"They are?"

"They think they're all that matters in this life, and it's *my* job to convince the rest of the world they're right. No more movie stars for me. Give me a nice doctor's wife, an importer, a grapefruit heir."

Reed smiled, sympathizing and to some extent agreeing; he had his own celebrity clients, and the grapefruit heirs were considerably easier to deal with. "You sound very certain," he said.

"That's because I am."

"So if I *had* a celebrity, you'd absolutely turn the job down?"

She frowned, as though faced with a difficult decision. "Well, not absolutely," she said. "I suppose it would depend. But my feelings are, I'd rather not get in that rat race again."

"The person I'm thinking of," Reed told her carefully, "is John Michael Mercer."

"Oh." She looked rather taken—and taken aback—by the idea. "Well, I don't know," she said. "He *is* famous, and . . . I'd hate to turn a good job down, but . . . I suppose I'd have to talk with him first, see how we get along."

"Of course," Reed said. Smiling thinly, he glanced at last at the application form. It would be solid, of course, every reference would check and double-check. Still smiling, at the perversity and cleverness of the human mind, he folded the form in half, then again, then leaned over to make an elaborate show of dropping it in the wastebasket. "Thank you, Miss . . . Well, I'll go on calling you Miss Henderson, shall I? Thank you for stopping in."

The young woman stared in blank astonishment at his face, at the wastebasket, at him again. "What are you *doing?*"

"Not that it matters," Reed said, "but just out of curiosity, who are you with? The *Enquirer*? *People*? *Sixty Minutes*?"

"I have no idea what—" she spluttered. "I'm just—"

"It's a very cute approach," Reed assured her, not wanting to entirely ruin her day. "Not absolutely original, of course, but then what is? Nevertheless, a nice approach. And you did it very well."

The young woman, her expression on the brink of outrage, studied him a few seconds longer, then abruptly shifted; her posture became looser, her expression more frank, her mouth more sensual. "So what went wrong?" she said.

Reed smiled; he liked her, really. Too bad he couldn't seduce her away from her present employer, place her with someone really good. But of course, he'd never be able to trust her; no one would. "You switched," he explained, "just a *teeny* bit too soon."

Rising, nodding, smiling back at him, she said, "Well, I'm new at the game."

"You are?" Reed viewed her with honest pleasure. "You'll be something, when you get your growth," he said.

* * *

"Homosexuality Linked to Atheism, Experts Say," Jack said.

"Massa hates faggots," Mary Kate informed him, as she typed.

"No no," he assured her. "It's true, he won't touch *lesbianism* with a rake. Remember when I had that great one?"

"I remember."

Jack looked up, seeing it in lights. "Famous Writer's Wife Leaves Him for Affair with Actress."

"Massa went away and washed his hands when you told him that one," Mary Kate recalled.

"I had *everything*," Jack complained. "I had tapped phone calls, I had best-friend affidavits, I was covered more completely than J. Edgar Hoover."

"And Massa said no," Mary Kate pointed out. "He hates faggots."

"He hates *dykes*," Jack corrected. "It's because he can't figure out how to sell them anything. What we're talking here is male homosexuality, which he doesn't give a shit about, and a *positive* religious story, which he loves. You wait and see."

"The red pencil lines," Mary Kate said. "I can see them now."

Ida Gavin entered the squaricle. "Industrial espionage," she said, with a glance at Mary Kate.

Jack also glanced at Mary Kate, and nodded his head at her, and said to Ida, "Have you cleared her?"

"Yes."

"Then you can talk in front of her."

Mary Kate gave Jack a long slow look, as Ida said, "I have found no one who has a special relationship, or a relationship at all, with Cartwright." She never called Boy "Boy." "As for people potentially in a position to be blackmailed, I have nothing solid, but there's one area that might be explored further."

"Which area is that?"

"Phyllis Perkinson."

Jack looked away across the room toward the banks of reporters. Phyllis was visible over there, lying on the phone, with gestures, throwing herself into it. Jack looked back at Ida. "Tell."

"She worked two years on *Trend* magazine."

Trend magazine was a glossy yuppie magazine based in New York, one that had put together a successful formula composed mostly of lists of the best sixty places to get a pizza in the United States and high-finance real estate scandals; a how-to magazine for young MBAs, in other words. Nodding, Jack said, "I knew that."

"She was on special projects there, under David Levin."

"That I didn't know," Jack admitted. "What next?"

"She left," Ida said. "She didn't get fired, there was no suggestion of trouble. She finished a piece on ham in kosher hot dogs, turned it in, quit, came down here."

"At an increase in salary?"

"Of course," Ida said.

"And better weather." Jack shrugged. "Everybody's story, Ida. What bothers you about it?"

"I'm not sure yet."

"You want to pursue?"

"Yes."

"Pursue, then," Jack said. "You know I trust your instincts."

"Thank you." Jack might have turned away then, but Ida wasn't finished. "John Michael Mercer," she said.

Jack gave her *all* of his attention. "Speak, Ida," he said.

"Yesterday he flew to Boston, on the network's jet."

"Alone?"

"According to our contact at Logan, he was with a woman named Felicia Nelson," Ida said, with no change in tone or expression.

Jack lit up like a video game. "Felicia *Nelson*! Oh, Ida! Where are they staying?"

"This morning," Ida reported, "they both returned from Boston and closed themselves once again in Mercer's house in Palm Beach."

Mary Kate half turned at her desk to look searchingly at Ida. Jack viewed Ida through narrowed eyes. "Up there yesterday?" he asked. "Back today? What is our reading on this, Ida? What is this telling us?"

"So far," Ida said, "we have no line into the Hall of Records, there in the state capital of Massachusetts. We're working on it."

"A marriage certificate, Ida? Is that what's at the end of this rainbow? Or is that just wishful thinking?"

"We'll know," Ida said, "very soon. You want me to follow up on Felicia Nelson, or on *Trend*?"

Jack thought. "*Trend*," he said. "But mention nothing about Felicia Nelson to our co-workers."

"Right."

"Nor Boston."

"Never heard of the place," Ida said.

Chapter Two

It was because she was getting nowhere with *Time of The Hero,* and couldn't even look at the manuscripts of the three other partial novels buzzing away reproachfully at her in their desk drawer, that Sara was reading the wall over the desk in her bedroom at the Sybarite Saturday morning, and came again upon the license number and description of what, if she'd been writing it up, she would surely have called "the death car."

After yesterday's failure at Henry Reed Personnel—gosh, that fellow was good; how *had* he caught on so fast?—Sara had phoned Jack from Miami, feeling very brought down, particularly so after the heights she'd been flying on the impetus of the twins coup. He must have heard it in her voice because, when she'd asked him what she should start on next, he'd said, "Nothing. It's Friday. Go home, Champ, take it easy for the weekend. Monday morning, we'll meet at the coalface."

That had been handsome of him, but by the time she got home from Miami it was mid-afternoon and the beach she had access to was already in her building's shadow, so that was when she'd gone off to the local library to do some necessary research for *Time of the*

Hero. There were so many spy-novel details she didn't know; descriptions of guns, names of airports and railroad stations, histories of remoter Eastern European provinces.

Sara had spent a few absorbed hours in the fairly adequate library, then had returned home to find Phyllis back from the paper, changing into cutoffs and a T-shirt, packing pretty weekend clothes into her overnight bag. With a cheery inconsequential word tossed in Sara's direction, off she had blithely gone, leaving the apartment to Sara for the weekend. (Phyllis had never said a word about the man she was presumably going away with each of these weekends, nor had Sara ever seen him, so she took it as given he was married.)

Friday evening was spent alone with frozen food and television, but Saturday morning dawned sunny and hot and with less of summer's humidity than usual, so Sara at last logged in some beach time, swimming away the muscle stiffness brought on by travel and by sitting so long at desks. On the beach she met a guy named Bob, a good-looking stockbrokerage employee from Boston, down visiting his grandparents for a week, they having an apartment at the Sybarite (most of the Sybarite's residents were considerably older than Sara and Phyllis), and they were getting along very well until, at his question, she told him what she did for a living, and he made fun of it.

It wasn't so much his infantile humor, as it was his assumption that she would *agree* with his simpleminded put-downs. Did he think working at the *Galaxy* didn't take *brains*? didn't take cleverness and quick thinking? didn't take nerve? Over five million copies of the *Galaxy* were sold every week, so they must be doing something right. She tried to say all this, in fact even tried to tell him the story of the hundred-year-old twins—her greatest triumph so far, by God—but his scorn had simply become more and more mixed with incomprehension. "You're putting me on!" he said, so many times that she finally answered, "Oh, no, I'm not. Not even for a test drive." And she cut her swim-and-sun session short, leaving him gaping and openmouthed on the beach.

Back in the apartment, she made an early lunch, half muttering various deadly remarks she should have thought to say to that Boston half-baked bean, and she was about to settle at her desk with the results of yesterday's research session at the library when the doorbell rang.

Could it possibly be *him*, the Wit of the Beach? It was extremely unlikely, but wouldn't it be nice to have a second shot at him, to actually *deliver* all those killer lines she'd thought of too late? Mind swirling with deliciously snide remarks, she hurried to the living room, pulled open the door, and confronted a telephone repairperson.

Yes, that's right, a woman. She was as young as Sara, and stunningly beautiful, with great masses of red hair around a perfect oval face. She wore a T-shirt, cutoff jeans, green-striped tube socks, heavy brown work boots and a broad work belt laden with tools. "Sorry about this," she said. "We've got a little problem one flight up, and I need to get at the wire outside your kitchen window."

"Oh, sure," Sara said. "Come on in." And, because when a deskful of work calls, any distraction will do, Sara followed the repairperson into the kitchen to see what would happen next.

What happened next was that they got into conversation. Sara's curiosity got the better of her, and she just simply had to ask it: "How did you wind up with a job like *this?*"

"Oh, I love it," the repairperson said. "My father and my brother both work for Bell, too. I hate offices and all that, and this is interesting, it gets me out, I meet people, have all different kinds of things to do."

Sara watched the girl perch on the kitchen windowsill and do things with a junction box on the outer wall of the building. "I can't quite think of the angle," she said, "but there's got to be a story in you."

The repairperson grinned quizzically at her. "A story?"

"Well, I work for a paper, you see, and—"

"A paper? Which one, the *County*?"

"No." Half embarrassed, sorry she'd even started this, Sara said, "The *Weekly Galaxy*, as a matter of—"

"No kidding! I *love* that paper!"

Sara stared. "You do?"

"I read it every week! You really work for them?"

"Well, yeah," Sara said, making the adjustment from embarrassment to a kind of weird pride.

The repairperson glowed, inside her forest of red hair. "And you think you could get *me* in the *Galaxy*?"

"Well, I'm not sure, I don't have the angle yet, the specific— Maybe we could talk a little, uh . . ."

"Sure! Just let me take care of this thing."

"I'll get my camera."

The repairperson's work on the junction box was brief, and during it Sara took three or four pictures. As a woman and a feminist, she was opposed to cheesecake on general principles, but this girl with the long bare legs ending in heavy work boots, the slender body encased in a thick belt hung with all kinds of tools, somehow raised the genre above itself. How to be a sex object while not being a sex object.

Then they sat at the kitchen table with cups of coffee and talked for fifteen or twenty minutes, while Sara tried to find the hook that would turn this girl into a *Weekly Galaxy* story; that is, into a story *she* could sell Jack Ingersoll, which *he* could sell Massa, and which all of them could then sell to Rewrite and the evaluators. Not easy.

In fact, not at all, at least not right now. The girl—Betsy Harrigan, her name was—was somehow just too cheerful and sunny and *competent* to be good copy. She had no problems, she didn't get hit on by the customers or resented by her co-workers, she had no manifesto she wished to share with the world, and no miracles had helped her attain her present position in life. "There's *something*," Sara finally said, "I know there's a story in you somewhere, but I just can't seem to figure out what it is. Let me think about it and call you, okay?"

"Sure," Betsy said. "Anytime at all."

"In the meantime, I'll get these pictures developed and talk it over with my editor, and see what I can come up with."

"I'm real excited," Betsy admitted, with a huge sparkly smile. "If I was in the *Weekly Galaxy*, my mom would just about flip like a pancake."

"I imagine she would," Sara agreed. "I'll call you, I hope, in the next few weeks."

Then Betsy left, and Sara went back to her desk and did a brief memo about Betsy Harrigan, telephone repairperson, in order to have *something* on paper while it was all still fresh in her head. And then, at long last, she turned to her novel, *Time of the Hero*.

And it just wouldn't come. The damn book simply refused to happen.

Is there anything more frustrating? Here on paper was the book so far. Here on other papers were the research items, the data, the factules out of which to construct the rest of the story. Here in her brain lay the rest of the story, awaiting, at least in broad outline. But she just couldn't *concentrate*, couldn't think about the book for more than a few seconds at a time, couldn't seem to compose sentences that would push the story further into existence. Everything distracted her, as of course Betsy Harrigan had distracted her; now it could be a stray passing cloud beyond the window, or merely the blue of the cloudless sky; the sharpness of her pencils; the various cartoons and messages and photos tacked to the wall over her desk. And at last she found herself reading once again about the dark blue Buick Riviera, Dade county license 277–ZR(G/Q/O).

What had ever happened in that situation? Why hadn't the police interviewed her? It had been nearly two weeks now; was the murder solved?

Here was a distraction worthy of the name. With hardly any guilt feelings at all, Sara reached for the phone directory, looked up the number for the local newspaper, dialed, asked for Editorial, and got nowhere. No one she talked to knew anything about anything, and when the third person suggested she call back during business hours on Monday—the sentence "There's nobody here right now" suggested a pretty miserable level of self-image—she gave up, went back to the phone directory, and called the police.

Here the problem was one of too much eagerness, rather than the newspaper's too little. Sara had the hardest time convincing the man she wasn't trying to *report* a murder. "It happened twelve days ago," she insisted. "It's *been* reported."

Not, however, to the town police. When Sara finally made her question clear, the answer was that there was no record in that department of the crime. "*Where* did this take place?" the man at last asked her, and when she described the location, out on the highway leading to the *Weekly Galaxy,* he said, with obvious relief, "Oh, *we* wouldn't have that anyway. That's not our jurisdiction. Try the state police." And he hung up before she could thank him.

But the state police didn't have it either, and suggested the county sheriff, who also didn't have it. "I really don't understand this," Sara said to the man at the sheriff's number. "*Somebody* has to know about a dead man beside the highway."

"Did you call Shore Hospital? Sometimes they—"

Knowing instantly that calls to all the area hospitals would *really* be a waste of time, Sara said, "The man was shot in the *head*. He was *dead*. A hospital would have reported a gunshot homicide without—"

"Gunshot?" A faint echo of disbelief twanged through the phone wires and into Sara's ear. "Are you absolutely sure of that, ma'am?"

"Of course I am," Sara said, being calm with an effort, displaying her professional poise. "He was shot once in the forehead. The bullet broke the skull in back, but didn't come all the way through."

"And this was— I'm sorry, when was this?"

"Monday, the twelfth of July. I reported it to the gate guard at the *Galaxy*, and I suppose—"

"You reported it *where*?"

"The guard on the gate at the *Weekly Galaxy*," she repeated, remembering that she hadn't seen that guard since that morning. A stray wisp of question in her mind wondered if the guard's disappearance were meaningful, but the thought was interrupted by the sheriff's office man's next question: "What were you doing *there*?"

"I work there. I'm a reporter, that's why I'm so certain of my—"

"Oh, for Christ's sake," the voice said, in sudden disgust. "Don't you people know better than to set up your bullshit with *us*?"

"What?" Sara was too astounded to be insulted, at least not at first.

"We tape all incoming calls, Ms. *Joslyn*," the voice said, dripping with scorn. "If we hear from you again, you're in trouble." And he slammed the receiver real loud.

* * *

Phyllis, looking troubled, entered Jack's squaricle at 10:45 on Monday morning. "About Felicia Nelson," she said.

Jack was feeling moderately human at the moment, having had nine yesses at this morning's editorial conference and having been singled out for public praise by Massa for the large number of items he had generated in last Friday's *Galaxy*. Therefore, he neither snarled at Phyllis nor moaned in despair at the sight of her, but merely said, "Tell me everything, Phyllis dear, tell me everything about Felicia Nelson."

"There *isn't* everything," Phyllis said. "That's the trouble. There's almost nothing, in fact."

"Everybody's somebody, Phyllis," Jack told her. "That's a rule of philosophy. So tell me, now. Who is Felicia Nelson, what is she?"

"Well," Phyllis said, "she was born and raised in Whittier, California."

"There, see?" Jack said. "Already, we're filling in the picture. I don't suppose there's any Nixon connection."

"What?" Phyllis looked deeply lost.

"Never mind," Jack told her. "Probably wouldn't fly anyway, not past Massa's red pencil." Generally speaking, Massa preferred Republicans among politicians, except for reform Republicans, whom he thought of as unnatural and loathsome, like hermaphrodites. "Go on, Phyllis," Jack said. "Give me background."

"There is none, that's the trouble," Phyllis said. "That girl's led the emptiest life since Princess Di. Never been married, no recorded abortions, never been fired from a job, never been sued."

"What a tedious existence," Jack said. "I quite feel for the girl. But *something* must have happened to her prior to that singular day when she met John Michael Mercer."

"Not that I can find out," Phyllis said. "She went to secretarial school. She works for an insurance agent."

Mary Kate looked over, raising an eyebrow. "Wears white underwear all the time," she commented.

"Wouldn't surprise me," Phyllis said.

"All right," Jack said. "Time, place and circumstances of the aforesaid singular day."

Phyllis did the blank look again. "What?"

"Where and when did she and Mercer meet?"

"I don't know," Phyllis said.

"That *is* unfortunate," Jack told her, "because if *you* don't know, then *I* don't know, and Massa is going to *want* to know."

"I'm doing my best," Phyllis said, looking and sounding harried.

"I'm sure you are, dear. Do we happen to know the name of the lucky Miss Nelson's employer?"

"Feingold and Robinson Insurance in Fort Lauderdale," Phyllis said, with excellent promptness.

"Very good," Jack said. "Perhaps Mr. Mercer had a claim to be adjudicated. What does Miss Nelson do for Messrs. Feingold and Robinson?"

"She's a secretary."

"Hmmm." Jack considered various of his options, then said, "All right, Phyllis. Continue to dig for background on Nelson. *Something*. Does she subscribe to *Hustler*? Is she in analysis? Find me something that will make Felicia Nelson as fascinating to me as she is to John Michael Mercer. Can you do that?"

"Do you want me to find out how they met?" Phyllis asked.

"No, we'll put another of our tireless researchers on that one," Jack told her. "Be off with you, Phyllis, and consider yourself lucky. Had you brought me this little news on a Friday, you'd be leaving here with toothmarks."

Phyllis attempted a light laugh, but it didn't quite make it past her harried look. "I'll do my best," she said, and hurried away.

Jack watched her go. When she was out of earshot, he muttered, "As Massa says, don't do *your* best, do *my* best. I wish I had the brass to actually tell somebody that."

Mary Kate paused in her typing to look at him. "When I think," she commented, "of all the things you *can* bring yourself to say."

"Oh, pish and tush, Mary Kate," Jack said, reaching for the phone. "I'm just a jocular type, everybody knows that." He punched out a number, and far away across the room Sara reacted to the white light flashing on her phone. When she answered—"Hello?"—Jack told her, "This is your master's voice. And guess what? You're going to love Fort Lauderdale."

* * *

On her way out from the *Galaxy*, Sara braked the Peugeot to a stop at the guard shack, even though she'd been waved through. As her window slid down, defeating the air conditioner she'd just turned on, the guard came over to see what the problem was. It was the usual round-bodied black man. He said, "Yes, miss?"

"Remember me?" Sara asked him. "Week before last, I'm the one left her temporary sticker on the rental car."

The guard smiled faintly, saying, "Yeah, I remember. And you come back on Friday 'stead of Saturday."

"That's right," Sara agreed, nodding, smiling at him to thank him for remembering. "But here's the thing," she said. "You weren't the one who gave me that temporary sticker in the first place."

He looked at her, having no idea where she was going. "I wasn't?"

"No. That was another guard on duty here that Monday morning. Two weeks ago today, it was."

The guard offered another faint smile, this one subtly different, this one suggesting Sara was up to something and he was seeing through it. He said, "You mean, he should have told you about holding on to that sticker? It's *his* fault, is that it?"

"No, no," she said, reassuring him, "I'm not blaming anybody but myself for that, honest. It's forgotten anyway, I'm not in trouble anymore."

"I'm glad to hear that," he said, his manner neutral.

"It's just that, when I came here that first morning, there's a *fact* I told that guard, and I want to talk to him to be sure I got it straight. I know this sounds weird," she added, rushing on, meaning that she knew it sounded counterfeit and false and untrue, "but he'll know what I'm talking about. Anyway, I keep waiting to see him again, but it seems like it's always either you or that tall skinny fellow—"

"My relief man," the guard said, nodding. "Wasn't him, huh?"

"No, he was an older man, very tanned, with a very lined face."

"Oh, that'd be Jimmy," the guard said, nodding, looking displeased at some memory. "Yeah, he quit just about then. Two weeks ago? Yeah, that's when he went. Made a real mess for *me,* let me tell you."

"He quit?" Sara echoed, then hurriedly asked the reporter's question: "Jimmy's his name? Jimmy what?"

"Taggart. But you don't want to use *him* to prove anything around here, his name is mud at this paper. Just up and walked off the job. They caught me on the phone just as I was going fishing."

"And he did that two weeks ago?"

"Yeah, just about— Wait a minute."

The guard went back into his stucco-and-glass shack, and Sara wrote on the open memo pad on the seat beside her, *Jimmy Taggart*. Then the guard came back, nodding in satisfaction, and said, "Yeah, I thought so. That was the day. Monday, July twelfth. Monday's supposed to be my day off, but here you see me, here again on a Monday, we're still shorthanded. Tough to find reliable people, you know."

He quit that day, Sara thought. That is *not* a coincidence. She said, "So I guess I better find some other way to verify this fact of mine. Thanks anyway."

"Good luck, now," the guard told her, stepping back from the car.

She thanked him again, slid up the window, and drove away to Fort Lauderdale, where she became a brisk young businesswoman named Alice Tucker. Having a used jeans boutique in Boston, she was thinking of expansion, of opening a shop in the Fort Lauderdale area, where she was also looking at homes to buy. She didn't make her livelihood from the jeans boutique, of course, that was just the fun thing she did; her livelihood came from alimony, and was therefore rock solid and dependable. However, she was very serious about the business side of her life, and so she wanted to discuss both business and personal insurance in Florida at great length, knowing that each state's insurance laws are unique.

In the course of two hours at Feingold & Robinson Insurance, Sara talked with four bright and helpful employees, fended off two passes, learned an incredible amount about both personal and business insurance in Florida, and neither saw Felicia Nelson nor learned a single thing about her. (The one picture of Felicia Nelson in the *Galaxy*'s possession, taken from a ship at sea off the John Michael Mercer property in Palm Beach and using a telephoto lens, was blown up to a grainy grayness, but a specific individual was still identifiable there, standing in a light short skirt and dark polo shirt on Mercer's dock, smiling down at Mercer in his powerful cigarette-style speedboat, the *Zoom Lens*. If Felicia Nelson had been present at Feingold & Robinson, Sara would have known it.)

Drat. It wasn't possible in the insurance office to ask about Felicia Nelson or even mention the woman's name; that would blow her cover for sure. So, when she could stall no longer, when there was no single question left for her to ask and not one possible insurable eventuality left for the folks of Feingold & Robinson to describe to her, Sara smilingly took her leave, promised to keep in touch, and spent the rest of the day in her parked car down the block, the blowup photograph on the seat beside her.

And no Felicia.

* * *

Jacob Harsch didn't often enter Editorial, and when he did, it was always something of a surprise that he obeyed the pattern of black lines on the floor. One would expect Jacob Harsch to walk through walls as a matter of course. And yet, he didn't; he turned left, he turned right, he followed the walls and corridors indicated by those black lines, quartering across the large open space like any normal human being, and every time he did it everybody in Editorial came that much closer to a heart attack. Because, of course, until the last second, no one could know for sure just which one of them Jacob Harsch intended to visit.

Jack Ingersoll. Today, Jack. "Afternoon, Mr. Harsch," Jack said, smiling brightly, blinking hard as Harsch came through the door space into his squaricle. (At her desk, Mary Kate made one of her very few typos.)

"Afternoon, Jack," Harsch said, in his thin cold voice. He looked out over the writhing mass of Editorial as though he stood on a mountaintop and were about to offer Jack the world. Instead, he said, as though referring to some really complex estate before the probate court, "In the matter of John Michael Mercer."

Jack rose to his feet, hearing the *Galaxy*'s national anthem. "Yes, sir," he said.

"This time," Harsch said, with a sort of gloomy satisfaction, "he apparently intends to marry the girl."

"Ida Gavin thinks it's heading that way, yes, sir."

"There are other sources of the rumor as well," Harsch said. "Boy Cartwright has been building a file."

"So have I," Jack said quickly, while Mary Kate made a rictus of death and, behind Harsch's back, pretended to throw up in the wastebasket.

"We'll want the girl's bio," Harsch said, looking away across Editorial again, dissociating himself from the conversation. "And the touching story of how they met, this famous television star and this girl behind the notions counter."

"You'll get it," Jack said.

"We'll want it in this week's paper," Harsch said, with a brief cold glance at Jack. "By next week, *everyone* will have the story."

"I'm on top of it, sir."

"If you'd rather Boy did the backgrounder—"

"Oh, no, sir! We've already got most of the material on hand, just need to whip it in shape."

"Good." Harsch smiled, never a pretty sight. "Massa wants," he said, and left the squaricle, and made his way like the Windsurfer of Death out of Editorial.

Jack sat down. His face was greasy with perspiration. "Christ on a bleeding crutch," he said.

Ida had been waiting some distance away, not wanting to interrupt Harsch, but now she entered the squaricle and said, "Phyllis Perkinson."

"No," Jack told her. "John Michael Mercer and Felicia Nelson. Where and how did they meet?"

Ida shook her head. "Nobody knows. We've bought everybody we can buy, but our people just don't know that story. One day he didn't know her, one day he did."

"I need it," Jack said. "I really need this one, Ida."

Ida came as close to looking troubled as her bitter face could manage. "Jack, you know me," she said. "I don't give up easy. The origin story just isn't known by any third party, and that's it."

"They gaze in each other's eyes," Jack said. "There's that moment when they know; *this* time it's for sure. Ida, do we want to lose this to Boy Cartwright and his Mongolians?"

"He won't get it either," Ida said, with a curl of the lip. "Believe me."

"All right," Jack said. "All right. Desperate measures time. Find me a best friend for hire."

"Hers or his?"

"Doesn't matter."

"There's a fishing boat guy we've used before," she said. "He and Mercer go deep-sea fishing together sometimes, get drunk, play boys will be boys. We can use him if we don't give him attribution by name in the paper; just for backup."

"That's the guy, then," Jack said. "Get in touch with him, put him on standby."

"Will do."

"I'll write the meeting and the romance, you have this fisherman read it to you on the phone, then we have the tape, our ass is covered."

"Easy as falling off a house," Ida said.

"Good. *Now* Phyllis Perkinson."

"She used to work for *Trend*."

"I know that."

"She *still* works for *Trend*."

Jack looked at her. Mary Kate stopped typing and turned slowly in her chair to look at Ida, who stood silent, a killer robot waiting for the word of command.

Softly, Jack said, "What is she doing for *Trend*, Ida?"

"I don't know yet. But she draws the salary."

"In addition to ours? That *is* greedy."

"On her Sprint bills, she makes calls to a number in Greenwich Village, in New York. That's David Levin's home number, and he's the special projects editor at *Trend*."

"What are you suggesting, Ida?"

"I think I ought to go to New York," Ida said. "I think I ought to squeeze David Levin's balls, see what happens next. But there's the Mercer problem."

"No no, forget that, I can't get myself blindsided by Phyllis Perkinson. Follow up on that. Do you think this is connected to the Boy leak? That is what you're looking for."

"Don't know yet," Ida said. "But that's the only window so far with footprints outside it."

"So follow those footprints," Jack said. "As for the Mercer best friend, turn that over to . . ." He considered his available team. "What about Sara Joslyn? She's rooming with Perkinson, is she part of it?"

"No proof so far," Ida said. "She and Perkinson definitely didn't know one another before this. Joslyn has no link I can find with *Trend* or David Levin. It's still possible, but not likely."

"Then give it to her," Jack said.

* * *

"I'll be a little late getting home," Sara said, crossing the employees' parking lot with Phyllis and a lot of other people whose Tuesday work stint was done.

"That's okay," Phyllis answered. "I'm in the mood for a real gourmet meal. I'll stop at the supermarket and get something frozen. Could you bring wine?"

"Red or white?"

"White," Phyllis decided. "I'm feeling fishy."

So that was that. They separated at their cars, Phyllis hopping into her white Corvette in a swirl of skirt and flash of leg, Sara entering her Peugeot more staidly, feeling tired and slow.

It had been a strange Tuesday. In the morning she'd talked with a heavyset bad-tempered Italian woman in Lantana who had been Felicia Nelson's landlady last year; before, unfortunately, the girl had met John Michael Mercer. There was no subterfuge this time, no phony name or background. Sara had simply identified herself as the reporter from the *Weekly Galaxy*, the one Jack had mentioned to the woman on the phone, and the woman had demanded five hundred dollars. Sara's budget was two hundred, which she'd fully expected to spend, but the woman was *so* bad-tempered that Sara haggled more fiercely than she'd ever done in her life before, and forced the woman all the way down to one-fifty. *Then* they talked, and as far as Sara was concerned, even at one-fifty the woman had been overpaid. No scandal, no juice, no clues to the Mercer connection, nothing. Still, it was further confirmation of the good girl they were all getting to know, and it was solidly down on tape, and she had saved the *Galaxy* fifty bucks, so everybody should be reasonably happy.

Tuesday afternoon was the telephone call from the best friend. Ida had explained that situation to Sara this morning, before leaving for New York on some mystery mission of her own, so when the fellow calling himself Rusty Scanlan phoned at two o'clock Sara knew she was just supposed to grunt and say yes at the appropriate points. Rusty Scanlan began by saying, "You want to know how my buddy Johnny Mercer and that real nice girl, Felicia, met, is that right?"

"That's right," Sara said.

"Well, I'll tell you," he said, and did, in a slow and stumbling monotone, while Sara sat and listened and occasionally said, "Uh huh. I see. Right." There was no point even taking notes, since the whole reason for the phone call was to have the story on tape, verifiable for the fact checkers, and defense evidence against any attorneys who might come along in the future.

After the monologue from the best friend, there had been a miscellaneous series of calls to make, all having to do with Felicia Nelson's background, all dull stuff—the high school in Whittier, California, that sort of thing—in the middle of which she'd taken time to look in the local telephone directories, where she'd found a James Taggart listed, and copied down his address. That former guard here at the *Galaxy* was of interest to Sara, more so than the current principal at Whittier High. Why had the man quit so abruptly, the same day Sara had told him about the murder? Why hadn't he passed the report on to the police?

Was he the murderer himself? Then why had he left the body there to be found, only to become panicked when the discovery was made? And if he wasn't the murderer, why had he just happened to quit his job with no advance notice on the same day Sara told him about finding the body?

So that's where she was going now, on her way home, to beard James Taggart in his den, which turned out to be a small house in a dusty poor neighborhood, rather reminiscent of Jack Ingersoll's house and neighborhood, but in fact miles away. There was no one in sight when Sara parked the Peugeot and stepped out to the late afternoon's sodden heat.

At 5:30 P.M. in late July, the sun was still halfway up the western sky, glittering on the dead-looking venetian-blinded windows of the Taggart house. Sara could hear the doorbell echo inside the house, but no one came to answer. The sagging floor of the little porch had been painted deck-gray years and years ago, and was now worn and flaky; Sara crossed it to peer in at the windows, but the blinds were closed tight, leaving no gap at all to look through.

Around back?

Tire marks and an oil stain showed where a car was usually parked on the packed earth beside the house, amid a scraggle of weeds. Sara walked around that side to the back, seeing every blind lowered and shut, and in frustration more than hope she rattled the knob of the back door, which yawned silently open at her touch.

The kitchen was beyond, in dim gray light, like a cave beneath shallow water. Sara extended one foot forward, touching the old pre-Mondrian linoleum lightly, as though expecting alarm whistles or a trapdoor. When nothing happened, she shifted her weight slowly to that foot, and then she was inside, and it was all right.

Well, not all *right*; but at least she was successfully within. She brought the other foot along, and stood in the entrance with her hand still on the doorknob as she leaned forward slightly to call, "Hello?"

No answer. The spoken word sank into the house as into black cotton. There was a kind of fuzziness in the silence that suggested a long-empty house. "Mr. Taggart?" Sara called, getting more personal, and when that produced no response as well, she released the knob, committing herself to the invasion, and took another step into the kitchen.

Should she close the door? No, leave it open; otherwise, it could make her look like a burglar.

To whom? To anybody. Pushing mythical interrogators from her mind, Sara looked around at the kitchen, which was plain and ordinary and old-fashioned. A white plastic table and four chairs, the usual appliances, a small portable electric fan atop the refrigerator. Closed venetian blinds over the double window above the sink. No dirty dishes, no messes. An oval-arched doorway on the other side showed parts of a dark hall.

Sara crossed the innocent kitchen and stood in the oval doorway. The hall was plain, with dull blue walls, bare wood floor, pale sound-absorbent squares on the ceiling, and the front door at the far end. No furniture, no pictures, no hooks for coats. A broad doorway on the left, with rounded upper corners to echo this oval doorway, showed a corner of living room. Three gray wooden doors were closed on the right.

A combination of the silence in the house and a lifetime of movies and television led Sara to expect a dead body behind every door she opened, which made her move very slowly indeed; but there were no dead bodies here. The first door on the right led to a narrow bathroom with old white china fixtures and a black and white tile floor. The second led to a Spartan bedroom, with clothing in the closet and in the bureau drawers, all of it well used and shabby, but neat. A sweater and shirt were tossed over the chair, a pair of slippers leaned together on the worn small rug, and an empty glass stood on the bedside table with last month's *Penthouse*. Clearly, Taggart had not moved out.

The remaining door on the right led to a tiny front bedroom with drawn shades and no furniture, but crammed with cartons, suitcases and bits and pieces of junk, including one automobile tire and an empty aluminum beer keg. On the other side of the hall, the living room's used and mismatched furniture was grouped around a large console television set.

There was nowhere else to look, no basement, no garage, no sheds. Taggart was not home. He was at work, or on vacation, or in a nearby bar, or at the movies. Somewhere with his car, in fact. Sara went back to the kitchen and copied down the number from the wall phone beside the refrigerator before departure, so she could call from time to time until she found him in, then took one last look around that room, and opened the refrigerator door.

Still no bodies. Several jars—ketchup, pickles, things like that—a package of All-Bran kept in here to protect it from the prevailing humidity, a blue-fuzz-covered half lemon on a saucer, and a quart carton of milk.

It was the rotted lemon that made Sara pick up the milk to see if that had gone bad, too, but she didn't have to bring it all the way to her nose to tell. Just squeezing the carton in lifting it released a putrescence strong enough to close her throat. She quickly put it down and slammed the refrigerator door, and stood there feeling sick.

How long had it been since Taggart—or anyone—had looked in there? Sara turned away and ran her fingertip across the white plastic tabletop and left a new bright road in the dust. She crossed to the sink and turned on the cold water, and orange rust ran for a second or two before the water turned clear.

Taggart hadn't been home in a couple of weeks. He hadn't moved out, but he hadn't come home either, not since— Probably, not since the day Sara had reported the murder.

Had he run away? Was it because he was the guilty party after all, had she actually done the absurd thing of reporting a murder to the murderer? Or did he have reason to believe he too was in danger? Had Sara's report of the dead man in the dark blue Buick Riviera been the signal to Taggart that trouble was coming his way? Or had someone bribed him to disappear?

It did seem certain by now, one way or another, that Taggart had *some* sort of knowledge of what was going on. Now more than ever, Sara wanted to talk to him. But where had he run?

There was no indication in the house, not in a cursory look-through; no notes on a pad by the phone, nothing like that. In his employee file back at the paper there'd be more information on Taggart, at the very least a listing of next of kin; surely there was a way she could get a look at that. Deciding to check into that tomorrow, Sara left the house by the kitchen door—pulling it shut but leaving it unlocked behind her, as it had been—walked around to the front, and found there a woman in running shoes, blue jeans, a faded apron, a cartoon T-shirt and dark sunglasses, who was leaning against the fender of the Peugeot, arms folded in a declaration of grim and implacable determination. "Hello," Sara said, when it seemed certain the eyes hidden behind the sunglasses were focused on her.

"Hello, yourself," the woman said. "And where's Jimmy Taggart?" She was probably about forty, stringy and bony as range cattle, and with a cigarette-and-whiskey hoarseness in her voice.

"Well, I—" Sara said, nonplussed. "Who are you?"

"The landlady," the woman said. She continued to lean on the Peugeot, arms folded, making it clear Sara would not leave here until given permission. The woman said, "What are you, a daughter or something?"

"That's right," Sara agreed. "Sara Taggart. How do you do?"

"Pissed off, that's how I do," the woman said. "Carol Bridges is my name, and your father owes me two weeks rent, thirty dollars cash loan, and one hell of an explanation."

He was sleeping with this woman, Sara thought. It always astonished her to run across evidence that people more than a few years older than herself still engaged in sex. And still made a mess of it, too. "I really don't know where, uh, Pop is," she said, the hesitation caused by her realization at the last second that any child of Taggart's would surely call him Pop rather than the Dad she'd been about to say. Hurrying on, she said, "He didn't know I was coming, in fact I didn't know myself until just, uh, I'm just driving through, just thought I'd take a chance, and, uh . . ." I'm just babbling, is what I'm just, she told herself. You do this for a living, you lie to people seven hours a day at the *Galaxy*; get back into gear. So she clamped her mouth shut, having already said too much.

The woman's manner was suspicious, certainly, but it seemed a generic unfocused suspicion rather than one specifically aimed at Sara. Squinting behind her sunglasses, "Maybe you should give me your phone number," she said. "In case I have to get in touch."

"In touch? For what?"

"You want to pay the back rent," the woman suggested, "bring us up to date, that's okay, too. Otherwise, there's gonna come a point when Jimmy's stuff goes *out*, and I rent this place to somebody else."

"Oh, sure, of course," Sara said, thinking there might be some advantage to having this link with Taggart's last known address. "And you can give me your number, too."

"Sure." The woman unfolded her arms, reached into her apron, and brought out a Holiday Inn memo pad and Sheraton Hotel pen. "I just live down the block here," she said.

And you're keeping an eye on the house, Sara thought. She said, "I'll only be around a couple of days, I'm actually working up in Charleston now, but I can give you the number where I'm staying."

"That's fine." Her expression behind the sunglasses was alert, but not dubious. She quickly wrote her own name and address and phone number, ripped that sheet off the memo pad, and handed it to

Sara, who said, "My friend is Sara Joslyn, you could ask for either of us." She reeled off her home number, which the woman wrote down, and then said, "If Da— Pop does come back, would you give me a call?"

"Well, I'll tell *him* to," she said. "He's your father."

"Yes, but you know how he is," Sara said, smiling, trying to make them co-conspirators. "A little forgetful, a little flaky sometimes."

"That's your father, all right," the woman agreed, falling in with the conspiracy at once. "All right, I'll call the minute I see him."

"Thanks a lot," Sara said, and started around the Peugeot toward the driver's side.

The woman turned, facing Sara, no longer leaning on the car. "But," she said. "If he doesn't come back by this weekend, you be prepared on Sunday to come get his junk, or I'll just dump it in the street. I got bills of my own, you know. I got to rent this place."

"Oh, I'm sure he'll be back by then," Sara said. "You know Pop."

Chapter Three

Ever since his divorce, David Levin, special projects editor at *Trend,* The Magazine for the Way We Live This Instant, had lived in a fine little apartment on Bank Street in Greenwich Village, on a quiet block of small brick houses and slate sidewalks, all so yeastily authentic that movies were being shot there all the time, which was just about the only drawback the place had. That, and the fact that David was not himself living in one of the charming old nineteenth-century brick houses, but in one of the mid-twentieth-century postwar apartment buildings the old brick houses were being torn down for before the Landmarks Commission had come along. Still, when *he* looked out his window it was charm he saw; if the people who actually lived in the charming houses were reduced to having his dull apartment building in their view that was just tough patooties.

The mail was delivered on David's block every morning between nine-thirty and ten, and his position at *Trend* was sufficiently powerful that he could more or less define his own hours, so he left the house every morning at about ten-fifteen, picked up his mail, took the 7th Ave IRT up to midtown, and was in the office before eleven, leaving plenty of time to deal with all phone messages and other problems before lunch.

This particular Friday morning at the end of July, with the temperature and humidity both hovering around 86, and it's still *morning,* for Christ's sake, David was a bit later than his usual routine, which annoyed someone he didn't even know yet, and which he would pay for in ways he would never understand. It was after ten-thirty before he took the elevator down from his top—sixth—floor apartment, keyed open his mailbox, withdrew his daily clump of mail, tossed in the wastebasket kept here in the lobby for that purpose all the throwaways and pitches and catalogs and CAR-RT SORTs that flesh is heir to, and stepped outside onto quiet Bank Street, looking at his remaining mail so intently that he never saw her coming, on her bicycle, on the sidewalk, until a horrible squawling voice scrawked, "Watch it!" and she smashed into him hard enough to bounce him into the air and send him sprawling over the ranked masses of garbage cans lining the building front. (That was his punishment for being late. Originally, Ida Gavin had meant merely to bump him a little.)

The garbage cans toppled, and dumped David to the quaint but nevertheless hard slate sidewalk. The bicycle, riderless and on its own, wobbled an amazingly long time before it fell on him. His mail was strewn far and wide. And some woman, sitting splay-legged on the sidewalk in front of him, was yelling, "Why don't you watch where you're going?"

David stared at her in stunned surprise, battered and confused and totally unable to catch up. "What?" he managed. "But I was—"

"How long you been in New York, you idiot?" the woman shrieked. What a loud and grating voice she had. "Are you a *tourist?*" she yelled.

Like most New Yorkers, David was from Omaha, Nebraska, but was a real New Yorker now. (All together: "Oh, he's from O-ma-ha Ne-bras-ka, But he's a real New Yaw-kuh now.") An accusation of being a tourist, therefore, struck at the very core of his most deeply hidden and most powerful insecurity. (All together: "Oh, Man-hat-tan's in his vision, But Ne-bras-ka's in his blood.") Pushing the bicycle off himself so he could sit up and affect a bit of dignity, "Certainly not!" he cried. "I live here, that's my buil—"

"Are you looking up my *skirt*?"

Astonished, David looked up her skirt. That color is called peach, isn't it? "No!"

"Well?" she yelled, sitting there on the slate, legs wide, hands on hips, voice bouncing and echoing off the building fronts, "are you going to help me up or *what*? You knock me over, you sneak looks at—"

"Never!" Embarrassed, frightened, in physical pain, wanting only for this horrible experience to be *over,* David struggled to his feet, vaguely aware of surprise that all his parts seemed to be working. "I'll be happy to help you," he said, clambering through her bicycle, praying she wouldn't yell anymore, "I certainly never intended to—"

"Watch that!" she yelled, as he slid his hands under her armpits to help her up. "Don't get grabby!"

Oh, enough was enough. Releasing her, "Madam," David said (a deadly insult, that), "you *asked* me to—"

"Wait a minute," she snapped, utterly self-absorbed, twisting around. "You broke something, I know you did. You live here?"

Bewildered again, thrown off balance yet *again,* "Yes," he said, pointing vaguely upward, "on the top—"

"Okay, okay, carry me in," she ordered, still as loud as ever, bossy, self-important, paying attention to nothing but herself, "carry me in, we'll see what— Carry me *in*!"

He reached for her again, not knowing what else to do, anything to shut her up, and she glared hot rage at him, yelling, "And *don't* get grabby!"

Recoiling, he said, "I don't see how you expect me to—"

But she never listened to a word he said, never. Staring upward, she said, "You're on the top floor? All right, we'll make it. There's an elevator in there?"

"You want me to carry you to my *apartment*?"

"So," she yelled, volume and outrage both reaching new peaks, "*that's* the way it is! You knock me down, now you'll just *leave* me here for muggers and rapists and white slav—"

"All right, all right, all right," he said, desperate to stop that awful voice, lunging forward again to help her to her feet. And this time he managed it without any more shrieks and squawks about his being grabby, even though his right hand did inadvertently touch her right breast for one second before he hurriedly shifted position.

Take her inside, that was the plan, sit her down, get her away from the public street and calm her down, give her some coffee—or a drink, if she wanted one at this time of the morning—phone the office, get rid of her as soon as possible, wait a good five minutes—no, a good ten, maybe even fifteen minutes—after she left before essaying another departure, and *still* get to the office in plenty of time for lunch. (Lunch today, he remembered, was with their Mafia specialist reporter, a man always full of wonderfully unprintable stories. He was looking forward to it.)

The woman leaned heavily on him, and they staggered to the building entrance, and were halfway through the outer door when she started screaming and shrieking again, yelling, "Don't leave my *bike*! Now you're gonna get my *bike* stole!"

Take the dreadful harridan's *bicycle* up to the apartment? Oh, anything, anything, just let this terrible sequence be over, let it be something to laugh about with Nick at lunch. "I'll get your *bike*," he said, exasperated but flummoxed, and propped her against the inner door while he went out for the damn thing.

What a way to start the day.

* * *

What a way to start the day, Jack thought in no little satisfaction. *Nine* yesses from Massa and his red pencil, *six* stories from the mighty Jack Ingersoll team in this week's brand-new *Galaxy* just arrived here on his desk, and an actual smile from Jacob Harsch this morning as the man murmured, "Well done," in connection with the John Michael Mercer/Felicia Nelson meeting-and-romance story. Back in his squaricle, basking in unfamiliar contentment, Jack dictated a letter to the rapid and nearly cheerful Mary Kate: "I have reassured myself that there is no reporter by that name at the *Weekly Galaxy*. We of the *Galaxy* maintain the highest standards of journalistic integrity, and would never stoop to the . . ."

Jack trailed off and looked up as Binx entered the squaricle, holding the new *Galaxy* in his hand and looking troubled. "Hello," Binx said.

"Morning, Binx," Jack said. "Rough this morning." Only three of Binx's story ideas had survived Massa's red pencil.

"Well, that's what happens," Binx said, shrugging it off with uncharacteristic calm. Had Binx given in at last to his despair? It would certainly be restful for him.

"Next week," Jack promised him, and moved a hand vaguely.

"Sure." Binx held up the new *Galaxy*. "Jack," he said, "this romance story about John Michael Mercer and Felicia Nelson."

"Isn't it nice? The Harsch smiled upon me, it was quite an experience."

"It's a real coup," Binx agreed. "But when I was reading it, something kept bothering me."

"It went through the fact checkers like prune juice," Jack assured him. "I've got a best friend on tape."

"Sure you do. But I was reading it, you know," Binx said, holding the paper up, frowning at it as though he might read it again in Jack's presence, to show him what the process looked like, "I was reading it, and I kept thinking, this is familiar, I *know* this story. And then I got it."

Jack gave him a careful look. "Yeah?"

"It's *me*," Binx said, staring at Jack wide-eyed, like the steer in the stockyard just after it's been given the stunning blow. "This is *my* meeting with Marcy," Binx said, rattling the paper, "the mix-up with the car keys, and getting the street wrong, and all the rest of it. Jack, you sold the paper my life story!"

Jack took a deep breath and faced Binx honestly and squarely. He was aware, in the periphery of his vision, of Mary Kate, not looking at him. "Binx," he said, "ask yourself this question: Would my best friend do a thing like that to me?"

Binx nodded. "I have, Jack," he said. "I have asked myself that question." Poker-faced, he dropped the *Galaxy* on Jack's desk and left the squaricle.

Jack watched him go. He sighed. This too will pass. Turning to Mary Kate, he said, "Where were we?"

Mary Kate leaned forward over her typewriter and read: "We of the *Galaxy* maintain the highest standards of journalistic integrity, and would never stoop to the." She settled back into her chair and looked at Jack. "You stopped there," she said.

* * *

Ida Gavin, in a big blue terry-cloth robe, poked and pried around David Levin's apartment, ignoring the view out the living room windows of charming old nineteenth-century redbrick houses. Much of this living room was lined with bookcases. The furniture, low and pale and bulky, had been chosen by the consultant at Bloomingdale's to suggest a nonaggressive but self-confident masculinity, but in fact it made the room look as though self-indulgent Munchkins lived here. Ida opened drawers and leafed through magazines and looked in cabinets, casual but relentless, and continued to poke and pry when David Levin walked in, one towel wrapped around his waist while he briskly rubbed his hair with another. She was aware of him, but ignored him, and kept on searching.

David wrapped the second towel around his neck. His expression was satisfied, even smug. "Hello," he said.

"You, too," Ida said. She opened an end table drawer, pushed and prodded with busy fingertips at the book matches, playing cards, pencils, obsolete credit card, and other junk within, and shut that drawer again.

"What are you doing?" David asked her.

"I'm nosy," Ida told him, and turned to give him a challenging stare. "Suppose I'd make a good reporter?"

"You just did." David smirked.

She turned away, ignoring that, and opened another drawer. He crossed the room, put his arms around her from behind, and kissed her hair. She studied the junk in the drawer. "I'm glad you're not hurt," David said.

She shrugged him off, and shut the drawer. "It'll take a bigger man than *you*, fella," she said, and picked up a copy of last week's *Galaxy* from the coffee table. "I thought you worked for *Trend*."

"I do."

She waggled the *Galaxy* at him. "You *read* crap like this?"

Simpering, David said, "That's a secret."

Ida dropped the paper on the coffee table and considered him, looking him up and down. "*You* don't have any secrets from *me*," she said.

Chapter Four

James Taggart had no secrets; at least, none Sara was likely to care about.

Taggart, the runaway guard, had for a while gone out of Sara's mind as though he'd never been. She'd been to his house last Tuesday, had gone to work on Wednesday morning planning to find some way to get a look at the man's employment record, and had been given by a harried Jack the urgent and all-consuming assignment of finding out just exactly where in Massachusetts John Michael Mercer and his Felicia planned to marry. "We need this, Sara," Jack had said, looking like a man with tapeworms. "Boy Cartwright is on the trail."

"But *we* got Boston."

"That was yesterday," he'd said, and so the race was on, and Taggart was forgotten completely until ten o'clock on Sunday morning, when Sara, home alone for another weekend and already plotting the phone calls she would arrow Massachusettsward on the morrow, received a phone call from an angry-sounding woman who said her name was Carol Bridges.

Which meant nothing to Sara at first; she was too deep in Massachusetts to remember much about Florida. But then the woman said, "Well, Miss Taggart? Have you heard from your father?"

"Oh! No, I haven't. You neither, huh?"

"Today is August first," Carol Bridges said. "I have a chance to rent the house, and I'm taking it. I just wanted you to know that."

"Oh, well, I guess . . . I guess you've been pretty patient. I don't blame you."

"Unless you want to bring the rent up to date?"

"Oh, I couldn't afford that. And I don't know what, uh, what Pop would want, exactly."

"Well, if you want his *things*," Carol Bridges said, with angry emphasis, "you'll find them on the curb. You can come get them, or the trash collector can take them away."

The trash collector can take them away, Sara was thinking, when all at once she interrupted her own thought with a realization: Some clue to Taggart's whereabouts, or to his motive for disappearing, might very well be in his possessions from that house.

"Except the TV," Carol Bridges went on. "I'll take that in lieu of back rent, and if Jimmy wants it back, he knows where to find me."

Remembering that large console TV set dominating the living room—the only expensive item she'd seen in the whole house—Sara said, "That sounds fair. I don't see how Pop could complain about that."

"I don't see how your father could complain about *anything*, Miss Taggart," the rejected Carol Bridges said.

* * *

Carol Bridges was nowhere in sight when Sara, at just after noon, stopped the Peugeot beside the pile of shabby goods in front of Jimmy Taggart's former home. There were a number of items here she remembered from her earlier walk through the house: the automobile tire, the aluminum beer keg, the window fan that had been atop the refrigerator. (But not the refrigerator itself, which apparently belonged to the house.) The white plastic table from the kitchen was here, surmounted by stacks of unmatched plastic plates and cups, chipped glasses, and an assortment of tired flatware, all looking like the world's most hopeless yard sale. The bureau from the bedroom stood here, its drawers full of shirts and socks. The mattress and box spring leaned against the table legs and the back of the bureau, with their metal frame folded on the ground beside them. A few lamps lay about like a surrealist's version of ninepins. A couple of sagging armchairs bore loads of suitcases and cartons and the small worn rug from the bedroom floor.

What could there be, within this shabby postmodern sculpture, to tell her anything about the present whereabouts of Jimmy Taggart? Climbing from the Peugeot, which looked almost indignant to find itself next to such a display, Sara stood a minute looking at the piles of junk, and was half ready to turn right around and go home, without touching a thing.

But what if there *was* a clue somewhere in here? Wouldn't a man's possessions inevitably say something about the man? Possibly something about where he went, or who he was, or why he ran?

Well, if she was going to take any of this stuff she ought to get started. She wasn't anxious for another conversation with Carol Bridges, who was probably watching out some window right now. But where to begin?

She couldn't take it all, certainly. For one thing, the Peugeot wouldn't hold half of this pile. For another, she was here in search of clues, not furniture, so the bed and chairs and lamps and all that sort of stuff could be left for the trash collector, or whatever neighborhood scavenger would follow her here. Ditto the tire and beer keg and other weirdnesses. Which left cartons and suitcases, and possibly the nonclothing contents of bureau drawers.

Feeling she shouldn't start a search right out here on the sidewalk, Sara briskly opened the Peugeot's trunk and side doors and started loading. The bottom bureau drawer appeared to be filled mainly with papers and documents of some kind, so she removed the drawer entire and put it in the trunk, leaving the bureau with a wide blank across the bottom that gave it an expression of disgruntled surprise.

Was that all? Looking around, Sara noticed a small table lamp with a delicate narrow glass base and clean pale linen shade; somewhat nicer-looking, in fact, than its companions. I could use a lamp on my dresser, Sara thought. She squelched a little pang of guilt by remembering Carol Bridges and the TV set. Besides, this way she was saving the lamp from the trash collector.

As she was slamming the trunk and right side doors, preparatory to departure, the Peugeot as jam-packed as a circus car full of clowns, she looked up to see Carol Bridges crossing the street toward her, looking grim. Oh, dear, Sara thought, and moved toward the Peugeot's driver's door, a friendly smile pasted to her face. "Hi," she said.

"That's all you're taking?"

"Well, I can't . . . I don't have . . ." Sara gestured vaguely at the encumbered Peugeot and the remaining pile of property.

"Well, that's strictly up to you," Carol Bridges said. "I talked with my lawyer, and *I'm* absolutely within the law. If this stuff is thrown away, it's not my responsibility. I've had no word from the tenant, and I've informed his representative that I'm putting his things out on the street."

"You did?" Sara asked, thinking, a clue, someone who might know where Taggart's gone. "Who?"

"You, of course," Carol Bridges said. "You're his daughter."

"Oh," Sara said. She looked at Taggart's possessions, piled on the curb, about to be lost forever. Her responsibility. "I really wish," she said honestly, "I knew where Pop was."

* * *

This was one time Sara was just as glad Phyllis disappeared every weekend; there would be no awkward questions about the pile of near-trash she was introducing into the apartment. Conversely, another pair of hands would have been nice, to help move all this stuff from the Peugeot first to the lobby of the Sybarite, and from there to the elevator, and from there to the apartment entrance, and from there at last to her own bedroom. When she finally lugged the last two suitcases in and plopped them on the floor, her overcrowded bedroom looked like the bus station in a Depression movie. And now, to sort through it all.

It felt so odd to be this close to an older male's private property. In college, and since then with roommates like Phyllis, Sara had grown more or less used to the idea of being around the personal possessions of other young women—and here and there a young man—but this stuff was *different*. It was as though she'd brought it back from some other planet, or an earlier civilization.

Her first move was to open every box and every suitcase, to see what sort of thing she'd caught, and so her first deduction about Jimmy Taggart was that he was a man who never threw anything away. (Which increased the oddity of his having disappeared, thereby putting *all* his possessions at risk.)

Clothing. Despite the bureauful of clothing she'd left behind, here was more and more of the stuff. One cardboard liquor store carton was full of shoes; all of them old and battered, most with holes in the soles, all with badly creased uppers, some without laces. Another carton was full of tattered shirts with missing buttons, or with ripped pockets; some of these were work shirts, with names sewn on: HAL, JERRY, FRANK. But no JIMMY.

Then there was an old cardboard suitcase with broken locks, which turned out to be full of radio parts; that is, various parts of a disassembled old-fashioned radio. And a box of jelly jars full of used nails and screws sorted into their various sizes. And a box packed with beat-up old games: Mille Bornes, Waterworks, several dog-eared decks of cards. Time to clear a lot of this *out* of here.

Down the hall from Sara's apartment toward the elevator, a black metal door opened to a kind of shallow closet containing the hatch to the garbage chute. Items too large for the chute were to be left in the closet for the super; Sara piled up boxes and luggage in there, then went back to see what was left.

Papers; this was more like it. Feeling like a reporter on the trail at last—a *Galaxy* reporter, in fact—Sara settled down with James Taggart's history on paper, his old checkbooks, income tax statements, correspondence, army records, paid bills, leases, contracts. Now, she thought, Jimmy Taggart, let's see who you are, and where you've gone.

* * *

By nine that night, after a break for a quick dinner thawed from the freezer, Sara was finished at last. She had typed out what she now knew about Jimmy Taggart, and it looked like this:

Born Oct 13, 1931, Brandon, Missouri. Graduated Marshallsburg Consolidated High School, Missouri, June 1949. US Army, January 1951 till October 1954. That would be the Korean War, but his army records show he spent one year in Italy and the rest of his tour of duty on army bases in the southern United States.

Suspended sentence, Elmford, Illinois Municipal Court, drunken driving, March, 1963.

Suspended sentence, Tulsa, Oklahoma Municipal Court, drunken driving, leaving the scene of an accident, August, 1966.

Divorced from Ellen Marie (Neustadter) Taggart in Oklahoma in 1968.

A creased and tattered sentimental Christmas card without its envelope, with ''Dad,'' handwritten above the printed message, and ''Jill'' below, is the only indication of children.

Employment records from the Galaxy show he started there four years ago. Next of kin, Jack Taggart, phone number and address in Hagerstown, Maryland. Prior to that, according to copies of tax returns going back ten years, he'd been employed three months by Gulf Coast Supermarkets, Fort Myers, Florida; before that for seven months by US Plastic Novelties of Orlando, Florida; before that for at least six years by Colonial Furniture Company, Lexington, Kentucky. The tax returns show no dependents.

Correspondence: A few letters over the years

from worried-sounding women, a few letters -- none recent -- from army friends, two old letters from a counselor in Tulsa telling Taggart his basic problem was low self-esteem, and a notice dated July 8th of this year from Shamrock Liquor Stores saying that James Taggart had won the one hundred dollar third prize in the Lucky Shamrock Drawing; he should present this letter by July 31st at the Shamrock Liquor Store Outlet where he'd filled out his entry, to receive his check.

Address book, mostly empty: bank, movie houses, take-out restaurants, Carol Bridges, a few local people who are probably co-workers, two neighbors, and a Jack Taggart in Hagerstown, Maryland. No evidence of longterm ongoing friendships with people in other parts of the country.

Unpaid bills and magazines and other mail from the three weeks since he left, including a notice from Shamrock Liquor Stores that he has only until July 31st to pick up his one hundred dollar check. Which was yesterday.

Why hadn't he ever picked up his hundred dollars? The first notice was dated the Thursday before he'd disappeared, so he'd probably received it on the Saturday and would have planned to bring it to the liquor store the next time he went shopping there. Why hadn't he?

For the first time, Sara considered the possibility that Taggart hadn't disappeared on purpose. Either he'd been bribed so lavishly that Shamrock's hundred dollars no longer mattered, or he'd been forced to leave.

Was Jimmy Taggart dead?

The thought was a long time coming, mostly because Sara didn't want to think it. To begin with, that way lay melodrama, and she had enough of *that* at work. But there were also the implications, if in fact Jimmy Taggart really and truly was dead.

What's going on here, she wondered, feeling the emptiness of the dark apartment all around her. The silence behind her head, the dark silence in the apartment's other rooms, had a muffled quality, as though something were being concealed. But what?

Does Taggart's disappearance have something to do with the dead man beside the road? And if it does, what does that mean for *me*? Taggart only heard about the dead man; I was there, I saw him.

There has to be another explanation. It's been three weeks, nothing else has happened. If Jimmy Taggart . . . disappeared, died, whatever . . . because of what I told him, that wouldn't have been the end of it. Something else would have happened, but nothing has happened. The lost license number doesn't count, that's not an event. Nothing has happened.

Nothing is *going* to happen.

All right, all right. *Is* there another explanation? If there is, by golly, let's find it. It was still not yet nine-thirty at night; Sara dialed the number of the Jack Taggart in Hagerstown, Maryland. After three rings a gravelly voice said, "Yes?"

"Mr. Taggart? Jack Taggart?"

"That's right."

"I'm looking for a Mr. James Taggart."

"Oh, Christ," said the voice, sounding disgusted. "What's he done now?"

"Nothing," Sara said. "I'm just looking for him. Do you know where he is?"

"No, I don't, and I don't want to," the voice said, and hung up.

CHAPTER FIVE

Monday afternoon, the second of August. Massa's office was parked on four at the moment, doors open to Harsch's larger and more dramatic room, with its desert views. While Massa leaned back in his chair, feet up on his desk as he occasionally sucked on a bottle of beer, Jacob Harsch paced slowly and methodically along an invisible and slightly bowed line between Massa's desk in the former elevator and his own desk in his own room. Seated on the sofa to Massa's left, legs casually crossed but pad and (black) pencil alertly at the ready, was Boy Cartwright, smiling like the school snitch in the principal's office.

They had been talking, these three, but then a silence had fallen, broken by the glug of Massa's beer, the faint brush of Harsch's black shoes on the gray carpet, the creak and twitch of Boy's smile. *Tonk,* said the beer bottle when it kissed the desk top. *Grugg, gergg, gug-gug-guggle,* said Massa's stomach. "If we only knew *when,*" said Massa.

"Well, sir," Boy said, with that light and airy display of omniscience-now which was his trademark, and which was mostly the effect of his diet of Valium and champagne, "it must be soon, mustn't it? They do have the license and so on."

"There's also," Harsch said, pacing by, "the question of *where*. Massachusetts is a fairly large place."

"We have our people, sir," Boy said, mostly to Massa, "following them everywhere. They'll lead us to the place, as soon as they're ready."

Massa's hand caressed last Friday's *Galaxy*, lying faceup on his desk, containing the story of the meeting and romance between John Michael Mercer and his little Miss Nobody. "Real nice story, there," Massa said, a sentimental curl passing over his eyebrows. "How they met, and all."

"I was quite touched by it," Boy said. It was his policy never to denigrate a competitor unless there was a clear and unequivocal immediate gain to be made; thus his reputation for fairness and acumen among those where it mattered, like Massa and Harsch, a reputation that made his occasional slurs and slices doubly potent.

Massa said, "Suppose Jack Ingersoll has the where and when?"

"No," Boy said, and permitted himself a faint smile. "I have a . . . *friend* on Jack's team. What he knows, I know."

Massa grinned; he loved intrigue, except against himself, and encouraged it among the staff.

Harsch, returning among them like Halley's Comet, said, "Whatever the date and place turn out to be, the point is to be ready."

"Oh, but of course," Boy said to Harsch's back, as the *Galaxy*'s number-two man receded again into his own office.

"Jake's right," Massa said, turning serious, putting his feet on the floor, replacing them with his elbows on the desk. "What it comes down to is: What's our story?"

Surprised, Boy spread his hands and said, "John Michael Mercer gets married."

Harsch, circling back, said, "That's the door, that's not the house."

"That's right," Massa said, nodding, shaking the beer bottle. "It's the door, not the house."

"Yes, of course," Boy said. He drew a little door on his pad, almost got lost in the reverie of a complex doorknob, and pulled himself back to the mundane plane by his shirttail. "We must enter the house," he said, extending Harsch's metaphor as far as he dared.

Massa said, "*Who* is he marrying? Is that our story?"

Now that they were talking again, the orbit of Harsch's pacing had contracted, so he could remain a part of the conversation. Drifting left and right, but never very far away, he said, "Who is Mercer marrying. A nobody from nowhere."

"Maybe *that's* our story," Massa said, while Boy looked alert, ready to agree whenever a decision was reached.

Not yet, though. "She's a bore, Bruno," Harsch said, and kept moving.

"All right, then," Massa said, accepting that. "*Why* is he marrying? What do his friends think? What does the network think? Is there a story in any of that?"

Massa was now staring straight at Boy, who felt constrained to answer. "We're working those angles, of course, sir," he said. "So far, not much of interest."

"Then *Mercer* is the story," Massa said, and spread his hands. "Why not?"

"Interesting," Harsch said, while through his brave expression Boy looked scared.

"The exclusive interview with John Michael Mercer!" Massa announced, and read the headline off a giant marquee: "Why I Finally Decided to Tie the Knot!"

"Ah, yes," Boy said. All on its own, his pencil drew a great X on the door.

"*You* can do it, Boy," Massa said. "If anyone can."

"Ah, yes," Boy said, and made his sunniest smile. "Yes, indeed."

* * *

Near the barricaded finish of a four-mile-long dead-end road running parallel to the beach between bay and ocean, within the city limits of Palm Beach, an avenue flanked on both sides by increasingly large and well-protected waterfront houses, a small side road choked by encroaching pine trees was marked with official city signs reading, ONE WAY—DO NOT ENTER. But this was a lie, since the road was in fact an entrance as well as an exit, and the only entrance/exit by land to the compound containing the home of John Michael Mercer, star of TV's *Breakpoint*.

A low sprawling white house done in modified Spanish style dominated this compound. It was open on all sides to the breeze and to eye-filling views of the ocean, the pool, the tennis court, the gardens. In the open, airy, comfortable, beautiful main living room of this house, John Michael Mercer stood and said, "I want them to suffer."

"But there's really nothing to be gained by suing them, Johnny," said the lawyer seated on the couch.

"Oh, yes, there is," Mercer said. Earlier in the conversation, he had thrown the *Weekly Galaxy* on the floor, where it had separated into several overlapping sections, on all of which he now stomped as he paced back and forth in front of the low and comfortable sofa where the lawyer and the lawyer's attaché case were seated.

"We know the way they work," the lawyer said, spreading his hands and shaking his head. "They'll have backup for that entire story."

"There isn't a word of truth in it!"

"Of course not. They—"

"All that *crap* about mixed-up car keys, and all that other *shit*, as though we're mental retards in some slapstick movie!"

"They're quoting a quote longtime friend unquote," the lawyer said. "They'll have someone, you know, someone you're acquainted with socially at some level or another. For a few hundred dollars that person read off that ridiculous yarn into a tape recorder. If we sue, they'll produce the tape in court. If it's false, it isn't *their* fault. They accepted the friend's word in good faith. You won't be able to touch them, and in fact they might very well have a valid countersuit, which wouldn't be at all pleasant."

Mercer stopped pacing to stand with both feet planted on multicolored segments of the *Galaxy*. Looming over the lawyer, he said, "If we sue, they produce the tape. Then we *know* who the friend is."

"Oh, Johnny, what's the point?" the lawyer asked. "It won't be anybody close to you or important to you. If you sue *him*, or try to get even in some other way—"

"I was thinking," Mercer said, "of the death of a thousand cuts."

"Legally inadvisable," the lawyer told him. "All you can do is demean yourself and raise this anonymous pip-squeak into importance. Forget it, Johnny. Treat it as the unimportant dreck it is."

Mercer frowned down at the paper beneath his feet. "I can't do anything," he complained softly. "I hate these people, loathe and despise and detest them, and I can't do *anything*. I'd like to express my opinion of this rag down here on the floor right here and now, and I can't even do *that*, because I like the rug too much."

Laughing, the lawyer said, "That's right, Johnny. As long as you keep your sense of humor, they can't beat you."

"You can get further," Mercer said, "with a sense of humor and a gun."

Rising, closing his attaché case, the lawyer said, "You have money, success, fame and the love of a good woman. And what do they have? Envy, viciousness and a terminal case of small-timer's disease. Bask in your comforts, Johnny, and forget them."

"I guess, the next time I want legal advice," Mercer said, walking with his lawyer to the door, "I should call a psychiatrist."

"Not a bad idea," the lawyer said, unruffled.

They shook hands at the door, said a few more inconclusive words, and then Mercer shut the door, walked back through the house, looked out a window, and saw Felicia sunning herself in her bikini on a chaise beside the pool. The wise man would join her.

* * *

Sunning herself in her bikini on a chaise beside the pool, Felicia idly watched the new groundsman work among the roses in the garden. A tiny gnarled Oriental man of indeterminate age, he was just beginning today, and Felicia found a fascination in watching the way he acquainted himself with the flowers, touching them lightly, muttering to them, poking tentatively with fingertips around their roots. Here was an honest son of toil, as brown and twisty as an old shrub himself—though not exactly an ornamental—and to Felicia it seemed the man was letting the flowers grow used to *him* as much as he was getting to know them.

Johnny came out in his swimsuit and dark glasses, smiling in that tough self-confident way that was second nature to him and was so much of the reason why the camera loved his face. "Nice," he said.

"Very nice," she agreed. "I'm ready for a day like this to go on forever."

"I meant you," he said, grinning, sitting on the other chaise next to her.

"I meant the day. And you, of course." Looking around, sighing, she said, "But it is too bad we can't be married in this beautiful place."

"No way," Johnny told her, an edge in his voice. "The press would be all over us like bedbugs. We're going to be someplace not connected with us at all, have a good private ceremony, just our closest friends, no circus, no cheapness. Thank God for Martha's Vineyard!"

"Johnny!" she exclaimed, with a quick look toward the groundsman. Even though she knew she was just picking up Johnny's paranoia, she couldn't keep herself from saying, "We're not alone!"

"Don't worry," he said. "He doesn't speak a word of English, I have it absolutely guaranteed by Henry Reed."

"He might know Martha's Vineyard," Felicia said doubtfully.

"Not a chance," Johnny said, waving the idea away. "Come on, let's do some laps."

So they swam together in the pool, two of the beautiful people in sparkling sunshine, making rainbows as the water splashed all about them. The new groundsman continued to work for another half hour, then pottered off, out to his messy rattly truck, where he put his tools away, cleaned his hands, activated the electric gate blocking the driveway as Mr. Mercer had demonstrated, and drove away. His little truck jaunted all the way out the four-mile-long dead-end road, then turned right and came to a stop at a gas station where the groundsman climbed from behind the wheel, went to the pay phone in the corner and made a long distance call to another part of Florida, where Boy Cartwright languidly picked up his flashing phone and said, "Are you there?" a Britishism he'd retained through all these years in exile because he knew the Americans hated it.

"Istu mintacko kuminish," said the groundsman.

"Ah, my little brown friend," Boy said, sitting up straighter at his desk. "Stendoko mirik?"

The groundsman nodded. "Dako maku," he said, "chinchun mookako Martha's Vineyard."

"Ahhhh," said Boy. "Moko chicku watto."

When he hung up, he was smiling.

Chapter Six

Sara was learning so *much* about Massachusetts, and none of it worth a good goddamn. For instance, Massachusetts, forty-fifth of the states in size—it lost most of itself in 1819 when Maine was separated off and became its own state—is also one of only four American states officially designated a commonwealth, the other three being Kentucky, Pennsylania and Virginia. But, since "commonwealth" is merely an old-fashioned word that actually means "state," so what? I mean, so *what*?

This was the kind of thing Sara was learning, along with the potential venality and gullibility of certain functionaries and employees and residents within the state, along with much information about the tourist attractions and scenic wonders therein, and absolutely *everything* about Massachusetts marriage law. But what she wasn't finding out, no matter how hard she tried, was *where* in that great and glorious state—motto: *Ense petit placidam sub libertate quietem*, or, "By the sword we seek peace, but only under liberty"—did the Mercers-to-be intend to become the Mercers-that-were? And *when* would that happy event take place? And *where* would they be staying in Massachusetts, either on the wedding night or the pre-wedding night, whichever turned out to be more newsworthy? And in just what manner—religious, civil, large, small—did they intend to be wed?

Today was Tuesday, August the third, and in the last four working days Sara had been, on the phone, everything from Felicia Nelson's pregnant sister to the Atlanta-based offices of the National Disease Control Center. And *never* in all her life—which is to say, in the three weeks and two days she had been an employee of the *Weekly Galaxy*—had she run up against so thoroughly *blank* a blank wall as in this case. Her entire attention was tuned to this problem, so thoroughly that she could do nothing with her evenings but talk to Phyllis about potential further schemes and stratagems. She was even *dreaming* about it, coming up with wonderful ideas from her subconscious that turned out the next day to be of absolutely no help whatever. And once again the question of Taggart, the missing guard, with no further incidents to fuel her interest, had faded away. His remaining papers lay ignored in the back of her closet.

Today, Sara almost didn't take time for lunch, but Phyllis insisted. "You have to *eat*, silly," she said.

"But what if Boy gets there first?"

"Oh, what if he does?" Phyllis said, shocking Sara. "Honestly, Sara, I never thought *you'd* get caught up in it like this. A month from now, what will any of this matter?"

"*Something* will matter."

"But it won't," Phyllis said, laughing at her in surprise. "It's not as though we're uncovering Watergate, for heaven's sake. The *subject* is a TV star getting *married*, and honestly, dear, that is not earth-shattering. Now, come to lunch."

So she went to lunch, with Phyllis, in the commissary, but all through the meal she kept thinking of calls she could be making, and could barely pay attention to Phyllis's blithe conversation at all, except for when Phyllis said, "Of course, one nice thing if our team does get the assignment, we'll all get to travel away from *here* for a while."

"Yes," Sara said fiercely, "but *when?*"

"Oh, eat your pie," Phyllis said.

But she couldn't eat her pie. She gulped down her coffee, abandoned her pie, hurried back up to Editorial, and when she saw the white light flashing on her phone she felt only irritation that an incoming call would delay her getting back to work.

More than delay, though; the game was over. "Forget it," Jack's voice said in her ear.

She knew what he meant, of course, but tried not to know. "Jack? What do you mean?"

"Ohly ohly in free," he said, "come on home. Massa just gave the Mercer wedding to Boy."

"No! Why?"

"Massa has spoken," Jack's grimly calm voice said. "It has become Boy's exclusive. We may be called on for some sidebars."

"That isn't *fair!*"

"I don't believe fairness was a significant factor in the decision," he said. "Come over to Mary Kate to get your new assignment."

"All right."

"And while you're here . . ."

"Yes?"

"Don't sympathize," said the cold calm voice.

* * *

As Jack dropped the phone onto its receiver, Ida entered the squaricle, wearing her fresh New York pale. "Phyllis Perkinson," she said.

"She works for us," Jack said, "and she works for *Trend*."

Ida nodded. "She does."

"And what is she doing for *Trend*, Ida?"

"Us," Ida said. From her shoulder bag she took half a dozen audio cassettes and dropped them on Jack's desk. "She is doing a *Galaxy* on the *Galaxy*," she said.

In the periphery of his vision, Sara arrived and spoke quietly with Mary Kate. Jack's attention was focused on Ida, very very very exclusively. Breathing, nearly whispering, he said, "An exposé? Of *us*?"

"On those tapes," Ida said, "we got you claiming to be the State Department. We got Sara claiming to be a rape victim, an arthritis victim and an extraterrestrial's common-law wife. We got Binx explaining all about how the Brits and Aussies work here without the green card. We got Massa talking about John Michael Mercer and the beer and potato chip diet."

Wide-eyed, Jack said, "She's got *Massa*?"

"She's got Harsch doing his hatchetman." Gesturing at the tapes, she said, "What you got there is nine hours of high crimes and misdemeanors."

Jack spread his hands over the tapes. "Are there other copies?"

"No. I left him blanks." Smiling like a polar bear, Ida said, "I'd like to be at that editorial conference, when he plays them. He's been keeping them at home for safekeeping."

"Oh, yes?"

"In the same bedside drawer with the condoms."

Sara, having accepted a wad of papers from Mary Kate, was on her way back to her station. Watching her work her way through the black lines, Jack said, "What about Sara? She a part of it?"

"No. This is all the Perkinson."

"If this gets out," Jack said, "even if we've killed it, if this gets out, I am a nonperson. She's on *my* team. Never trust a woman, Ida."

"I never do," Ida said, and Mary Kate said, "Binx just called."

"He isn't talking to me, for some reason," Jack said.

"He didn't want to talk to you," Mary Kate said. "He just wanted to let me know, he's been called up to Harsch's office."

"Oh," Jack said, paying insufficient attention, his mind still turning over the Phyllis Perkinson problem. "Boy must have this," he said.

"The spy," agreed Ida.

"He found out— Some way, he found out she was a spy for *Trend*, and turned her, and made her a spy for him."

"We'll never prove it," Ida said. "I'd love to, even Massa wouldn't be able to stomach somebody who lets a spy stay here so she can spy for *him*, but you know as well as I do Cartwright's too good, he'll never leave a footprint."

"But he can't blow the story on us either," Jack said, "not without showing his own knowledge. So we're safe from Boy, if we can only blow Perkinson out of the water without the reason getting known."

"Or leave her in and neutralize her," Ida suggested.

"Here? Everybody here talks, Ida, they talk all the time. Information is our most important product."

"She could have a fall and break her leg," Ida suggested.

"Two or three months in the hospital?" Jack considered the idea. "The only problem is, things like that tend to backfire, and then the situation's worse than it was be—" He stopped, frowned at Mary Kate, and said, "Harsch called Binx to come up to his office?"

"That's what he said," Mary Kate agreed.

"What day is it?"

"Tuesday," Mary Kate said.

Jack looked across the room toward Binx's empty squaricle. "That poor bastard," he said.

* * *

Binx was back in his squaricle, packing his personal possessions into a briefcase and a shopping bag, under the impersonal gaze of a brown-uniformed guard maintaining a discreet distance, when Jack came in and said, "Jesus Christ, Binx."

"Crucified in Jerusalem," Binx responded. "Rumored to be a faggot."

Jack stuck his hands in his back trouser pockets and walked around and around inside the squaricle. "Shit, Binx," he said. "We've been friends."

"Memories I'll treasure always," Binx said.

"What *I'm* sorry for," Jack said, "is stealing your life for the Mercer piece. I was scrambling, you know?"

"Water over the grave," Binx said, "not to worry. I probably would have done the same thing."

Jack stood still and considered him. "Well, no," he said. "No, you wouldn't, Binx."

"Why do you say that?"

"Because I haven't been fired," Jack said, and hurried on, saying, "Do you have any ideas?"

"Oh, thousands," Binx said. "Carbon monoxide, mostly." With a nod toward the guard, he said, "You know, mostly, when people get the push and the guard shows up, other people don't come around. They don't want the contamination."

"Fuck that, pal," Jack said. "I'll be your friend as long as you want me."

"No ulterior motive?"

"Like what? Buy your thesaurus cheap? Listen, seriously, Binx, do you have any other job ideas lined up?"

"Not actually in a line," Binx said, and paused in his packing to say, "I'm trying to figure out what to put on my résumé."

"Ah."

"Eight years at the *Galaxy*. Not a selling idea."

"A real problem," Jack agreed.

"I was thinking, maybe I'll claim I was in an asylum the last eight years, but I'm better now. What do you think?"

"It's even almost the truth," Jack said.

"I'm looking at it from the employer's point of view," Binx explained. "A man can be cured from being crazy, but there's no cure for sailing with the *Galaxy*."

"I'm glad to see you're taking this in a positive upbeat manner," Jack said, then stopped again, struck by some sort of incredible idea that caused him to go, "Ah!" and smack himself on the forehead.

Binx looked at him mildly. "Square root of two?"

"You could—" Jack started, hope in his face, but then abruptly changed his mind and turned away, saying, "No, forget it, I don't know what's the matter with me, thinking about my own problems when you've got, oh, hell, this is really rough, Binx."

"What?" Binx asked.

"You being fired!"

"No. What can I do for you?"

"No, don't even think about it, I'm sorry I even mentioned it. Listen, this weekend, why don't we get together, do a list of people we know in the business, papers and magazines, I bet we could find people who'd back you up here and there, so you could put together a real nice résumé, worked this place, worked that—"

"What," Binx said.

"Huh? No, forget it, Binx, I mean it."

"I don't have much energy today, Jack," Binx said. "Let's just go to it, okay? What is it I can help you with?"

"Well— If you're *sure.*"

Binx, energy level low, didn't respond, but merely waited.

Jack shrugged hugely, spreading his arms, shaking his head, absolving himself of responsibility. "Okay," he said. "*Okay*. If you insist. I got a problem, and it's Phyllis Perkinson, and if I try to fire a member of my own team it'll give me a black mark with Massa, so I don't know what to do. But you're leaving *anyway.*"

"So?"

Jack took a deep breath, clearly reluctant to wash this dirty linen in public. "Phyllis Perkinson made lesbian overtures to two members of my team. Now, you know how Massa feels about—"

"Who?"

"What?"

"Which two members of the team?"

"Ida and Sara. Now, this is going to have a bad effect on—"

"That's the story you want me to bring to Harsch," Binx said. "What's the real story?"

Jack stared at him in utter innocence. "*That's* the real story! Jesus, Binx, do you think it's *easy* for me to talk about this, under any circumstances at *all,* much less with my best friend being kicked out on his ass? Holy shit, Binx!"

"Let's see if I've got it," Binx said. "Sara and Ida, not sure how you'd take the news, came to me for advice and I told them not to make any waves, not to tell anybody else. So they didn't. But now that I'm gone anyway, I might just as well come clean and tell Harsch what's happening to those two poor girls in *his* workplace."

"Gosh, Binx," Jack said, "if you could do that, we'd all be so grateful. It *has* been rough on the girls."

"Do Sara and Ida know about this yet?"

Jack gaped at his friend. "Didn't you hear me? *They're* the ones with the problem!"

Binx took a deep breath. "Jack," he said, "I don't ask for much honesty in this old world, but unless you are straight with me on at least *one* miserable detail I will not carry your shit bucket to Harsch's office for you, and that's that."

"Binx, I can't believe you'd—"

"I'm leaving," Binx said, picking up his briefcase and shopping bag. "Goodbye."

Jack glared at him. "They'll *know*!" he yelled. "All right? If they have to know, they'll know!"

Binx put his briefcase and shopping bag down again and said to the guard, "I just have to go upstairs for a minute." To Jack, he said, "I'm sure glad you didn't forget why you came over here."

Chapter Seven

When Sara walked into the apartment at the end of that day, she passed Phyllis's bedroom, and through the doorway saw Phyllis standing in the middle of the large room, hands on hips, frowning at her wall of closets. All the doors were open, revealing a soft, colorful, jam-packed miscellany of clothing, enough to initially stock any new boutique in a suburban mall. More cloth billowed from open-sagging dresser drawers. The room looked as though it had just had an orgasm; Phyllis, however, looked like someone with a problem. "Hi," Sara said. "What's up?"

"Oh, hi," Phyllis said. "Listen, could I borrow your suitcases a couple days? I'll ship them right back United Parcel, I promise."

"Sure," Sara said, bewildered. "How come?"

"I had all that money," Phyllis said, with a pretty shrug, "I bought all these clothes, I never bought suitcases. You don't think about suitcases when you buy clothes. Listen, I won't stiff you on the apartment."

"You won't?" Sara said. She was beginning to get it.

"It's just barely the beginning of August," Phyllis said, "so you wouldn't expect me to pay my share of the whole *month*, but I'll split it with you, okay? Give you half."

"You quit," Sara said.

"*Oh*, no," Phyllis said, with a perky laugh. "I was definitely fired, by Mr. Harsch himself. You would have thought I was the undead or something, the way he looked at me."

"Fired? Buy why?"

"Well, they must have found out about *Trend*," Phyllis told her, then frowned as perkily as she had laughed. "But how? Boy wouldn't have told them."

"Phyllis, none of this is—"

"Oh, *I'm* sorry," Phyllis said, "I'm just all caught up in my own problems here, and I'm not making sense at all. The fact is, I've been doing undercover work."

"Well, we all have," Sara said.

"No, not for the *Galaxy*, for *Trend*." Phyllis stood straighter, pride showing through. "I'm a staffer with *Trend*," she announced. "And I was sent down here to do an inside story on the *Weekly Galaxy*, and just *wait* till it comes out!"

"Oh oh," Sara said. "Poor Jack."

Phyllis raised an eyebrow. "Poor Jack? What's that supposed to mean?"

"Well, you're on Jack's team," Sara pointed out, "or you were, and the editor's responsible for his team."

"Oh, pooh," Phyllis said, dismissing that with a wave of her slender hand. "The best thing that could happen to Jack would be to get fired."

"But that isn't up to you, Phyllis," Sara said. Anger and tension were making her neck hurt.

"Personalities can't enter into this," Phyllis said, as though repeating a lesson she'd learned in a Social Sciences class. "We're talking about a very serious First Amendment issue here."

"We are? Which First Amendment issue?"

"Well, the *Galaxy*, of course," Phyllis said. "The very existence of gutter journalism like that is a threat to decent news media everywhere, you surely don't disagree with *that*."

"You mean," Sara said, "the existence of Hostess Twinkies and Froot Loops is a threat to sirloin steak."

"Oh, now you're being silly," Phyllis told her.

"One of us is," Sara agreed. "You tell me one thing we could do down here, the *Galaxy* could do down here, or even any combination of things, that would threaten the existence or reputation of, for instance, the *New York Times*."

With a pitying smile, Phyllis said, "So the *Galaxy* is just a harmless enterprise?"

"No, I don't mean that," Sara said. The memory of Binx Radwell leaving the office this afternoon, briefcase and shopping bag hanging from his arms, brown-uniformed armed guard trailing him, employees along his route turning their backs and studying reference books and doing anything they could not to meet poor Binx's eye, was still fresh in her mind. "The *Galaxy* is very harmful in one way," she said. "It eats its young. That part scares me sometimes, but I think maybe I'm smarter and tougher, and it'll come out all right. But our arthritis cures and our interviews with people from outer space don't hurt the First *Amendment*, for Pete's sake!"

"We have a difference of opinion," Phyllis said, shrugging again.

Sara said, "What it comes down to is, you want to do the same kind of muckraking we do, but you want to feel holy while you're having your fun. Like television movies about the evils of teenage prostitution."

"*Isn't* teenage prostitution evil?"

"So are the crotch shots on TV."

"Oh, really," Phyllis said airily, "if you can't see the difference between the *Weekly Galaxy* and *Trend*—"

"That's right, I can't."

"—then there's really nothing more to be said."

"You're right." Sara turned away, leaving the bedroom, but then reversed and said, "Wait a minute. What was that about Boy?"

Phyllis had already returned her attention to her major holdings in recent styles. "Mmm?" she said.

"You said something about Boy before, about him not telling on you."

"Well, he wouldn't," Phyllis said, "so Mr. Harsch must have found out some other way."

"You mean, Boy knew about it."

"He's very forceful, Boy is," Phyllis said, with admiration in her voice. "I kept this little cassette recorder in my bag, going all the time, and I'd always go to a stall in the ladies' to switch tapes. One of his reporters heard a click in there—I thought I was alone, stupid me—and she thought she recognized the sound, and she told Boy, and do you know what he did?"

"He didn't go to Mr. Harsch," Sara said. The full extent of the infamy here was unfolding itself to her.

"Not Boy," Phyllis said, laughing. "He arranged with the girls on his team to cover for him, and he came right into the ladies' and into the stall just when I unlatched the door and he just overpowered me. He sat on *me* on the toilet, and listened to some of the tape, and went through my bag, and found my *Trend* ID, and then he told me if I didn't tell him the absolute total truth he would send photos to David Levin of me doing oral sex on him in the stall in the ladies', and he had a girl in there with a camera, and he was *serious*."

Shocked, outraged, Sara said, "He couldn't do that! You should have screamed, you should have refused, you should have *bit* him!"

"Too bad," Phyllis said dryly, "you weren't there to offer moral support. As it was, I told him the truth, I told him everything. And then he said all right, he'd let me alone on two conditions. First, that nobody on his team ever showed up on a tape or in the story, that he wasn't connected with me in any way. And second . . ." Phyllis finally wavered, and looked away toward her closets, and cleared her throat.

Sara couldn't imagine what enormity might be coming next. "Second?" she urged.

"All I had to do," Phyllis said, not meeting Sara's eye, "was tell him anything interesting that Jack's team might find out about anything."

Sara stared. "You mean, spy on Jack's team for Boy?"

"I was already doing it for *Trend*," Phyllis pointed out, "so it hardly seemed to make much difference."

"What a nasty little bitch you are," Sara said.

Offended, Phyllis said, "Oh, now, no need to get personal!"

"*That's* why Boy got the Mercer wedding!"

"Actually," Phyllis said thoughtfully, nodding, "you're probably right about that."

"You can just go to Mr. Harsch right now," Sara announced, pointing vaguely westward, "you can *destroy* that Boy Cartwright for good and—"

"Well, no," Phyllis said delicately. "Boy insisted on insurance. There *are* pictures. I'm sorry about Jack, of course, but you'll never get a word out of *me* against Boy."

"Then *I'll* stop him," Sara said, filled with a clear white flame. "Jack's life is tough enough without being betrayed by a smug, self-righteous, mental lightweight little *snip* like you!" Then, astonished at herself, she reared back and said, wonderingly, "Snip. I never used that word before in my life."

"I am *not* a snip," Phyllis said, deeply insulted.

"That's just the beginning of what you are," Sara told her, and pointed a trembling finger at the girl's nose. "You owe me the entire month of August rent, and if you don't pay me, I'll see you in Small Claims Court, and *I'll* bring a photographer, and I'll just casually mention the tricks you were turning in this place. As for loaning you my suitcases, ask me again, why don't you, what you should do with your clothing! I'm going to make a phone call now, and if you spy on *me*, you snip snip *snip*, I'll make you regret it every time you look in the mirror the rest of your life."

"That's a *horrible* threat!"

"And you're a horrible person," Sara told her, and went away to save Jack Ingersoll. And she was so intent on the phone call she had to make, she never noticed that the sheet of memo paper containing the license plate number of the murdered man's car was no longer amid the clutter on the wall over her desk.

CHAPTER EIGHT

In his small and messy kitchen, Jack Ingersoll, wearing an apron and a fine dusting of flour over his jeans and polo shirt, baked a cake. It was Wednesday, the fourth of August, and yet he was not at work, and fuck it. Humming a slow and erratic version of "Moanin' Low," Jack stood at his kitchen counter and combined flour and eggs and sugar and butter and, oh, just lots of good things. White flour floated in the air. And fuck it.

The doorbell rang. Jack frowned in that direction. "More good news," he muttered and reached for the measuring cup, and the doorbell rang again. "Life calls," he told himself. Grabbing up a floury dish towel, he made his way through the house, drying his hands, while the doorbell rang yet a third time. "Very impatient, this life," Jack told himself, and opened his front door, and Sara was standing there, looking awfully goddamn chipper, under the circumstances. "Yeah?" he said.

She looked him up and down, apron and flour and dish towel and all. "Which one are you?" she asked. "Laurel or Hardy?"

"I gave at the office," he told her.

"So did I." Unbidden, she entered the house past him, saying, "Mary Kate said you took the day off because you were gloomy."

"That Mary Kate," Jack said. "She just talk and talk and talk." Accepting the inevitable, he shut the front door.

"She wanted to phone you the good news," Sara said, "but I said no, I wanted to tell you myself, in person."

"Good news?"

"We have a free vacation," she said, grinning at him.

He looked at her. "A free vacation. I'm fired? That's the good news?"

"To Martha's Vineyard, an island off the coast of New Bedford, Massa—"

"I *know* where Mar—" he said, then woke up. "Martha's *Vineyard?* The Mercer Wedding?"

"You got it."

"But— But *Boy's* doing the Mercer wedding!"

"Not anymore," she said. "The Jack Ingersoll team is running that story now."

Jack stared at her. "*You* did this thing?"

"It is true, she said modestly," she said modestly.

"Next," he said, rubbing his hands on his apron, "you'll tell me you got Binx his job back."

"No, sorry, my powers don't reach that far. I wish they did. Binx is still fired. On the other hand, so is Phyllis."

"Ah, well, the living must go on. Tell me what you did, Sara."

Reaching into her shoulder bag, she brought out a manila envelope, saying, "First, there's a little story we *must* get into the paper. And we've really got to get this one in there, Jack."

"Tell me," he said cautiously.

"Twenty-four years ago," Sara said, opening the manila envelope, "a Mrs. Kathleen Harrigan was about to have her fourth child, when in a dream she saw that she would have a daughter, which was all right, but then in the dream it seemed to her she could see that daughter hanging from a pole, which was less all right."

"Discomfiting," Jack agreed.

"Twenty-four years later," Sara said, "that dream has come true in the nicest possible way. Mrs. Harrigan *did* have a daughter, named Elizabeth, called Betsy by family and friends, of whom she has many, being such a sweet and sunny girl—"

"My my," Jack said. "Sign me up."

"And Betsy Harrigan," Sara said, taking a number of eight-by-ten glossy photos from the envelope and handing them to Jack, "became a telephone company repairperson."

Jack looked at the pictures. "Mmmm," he murmured. "Baby, baby, fix my phone."

"Enjoy the pictures," Sara told him, with a faint edge in her voice. "Take your time."

Jack looked up from the pictures, comprehension dawning. "Telephone repairperson," he said. "You tapped Mercer's phone!"

"My own extension," she corrected, "in a car out on the street. I can now tell you"—she checked each item off on her fingers—"what *date* the lovebirds are flying out over the ocean, what *hotel* they're staying at, the wedding date, the name and religious affiliation of the person who will perform the—"

"Sara!" Jack cried, knees buckling. "Don't make jokes!"

Plucking the photos of Betsy Harrigan from his nerveless fingers, Sara said, "You want more? I phoned the minister. We have an exclusive interview with him right after the wedding, and all we have to do is publish a little piece he's written about the Irish question."

"Taking which side?"

"Does it matter?" Sara asked. "But *I've* got the date and the hotel. It turned out Boy already had Martha's Vineyard, but that doesn't matter anymore. *I've* got the exclusive with the minister, and I'm *your* reporter, and that means *we* are going to Martha's Vineyard!"

His look of delight dimmed, as a cloud passed over. "The interview," he said.

"It's in the bag," she assured him. "He's the darlingest old minister you ever—"

"Not that one. Massa, remember? He decided already what the wedding story is. The interview with John Michael Mercer on why he finally after all these years decided to get married. The exclusive interview with *us*."

"Oh," Sara said, going under the same cloud.

"When John Michael Mercer sees the *Galaxy*," Jack pointed out, "he doesn't give interviews. He calls the dogs."

"I remember," Sara agreed. But then that pesky cloud passed on from her face and she brightened again, saying, "One day at a time, right? We got this far, didn't we? So we'll get the rest."

Jack looked at her. "You really think so?"

"What I really think is," she told him, "this is *fun*. This is the most fun I've ever had in my entire life. Absolutely nothing in this world matters except that we beat Boy Cartwright to the John Michael Mercer wedding."

Grinning crookedly, Jack said, "Not even your murdered man beside the highway?"

Sara laughed. "On what series is he a regular?"

"None."

"Then forget him! We're on our way to Martha's Vineyard, that's all, and whatever Massa wants from us, we'll *get* it!"

"By golly, Sara," Jack said, gazing upon her in wonder, "you are *not* the girl who walked into the *Galaxy* office last month and told me you were a real professional reporter."

"You're darn right I'm not," she said. "I don't have a serious bone in my body."

"I want to put my arms around you," he said, looking down at himself, "but I'd get you all over flour."

"Flour from a gentleman is always nice," she said.

* * *

Hours later, in bed, in the semidark, he said, "Tell me one thing. Were those twins legit?"

"Of *course* they were," she said.

THE WEDDING

Chapter One

Have you ever tried to find a hotel room on Martha's Vineyard in August? Martha's Vineyard, be it explained, is not a vineyard and doesn't belong to Martha, but is a twenty-mile by ten-mile island in the Atlantic, off the Massachusetts coast, four miles south of Cape Cod, with a year-round population of fewer than twelve thousand souls. The moneyed literary, showbiz and other celebrity sorts of the American Northeast, or at least those of them too dignified for the Hamptons, invade the Vineyard every spring, quintupling its population, only to be driven back into the sea every fall, and August is the absolute height of their incursion. Every ferry making the three-quarter-hour trip across from Falmouth Heights or Woods Hole carries another forty or fifty cars and as many people as the law will allow. Most of these people have made their housing arrangements months or years before, but now and again an innocent disembarks, asks where a room might be found, and is answered with rolling eyes and pitying smiles.

There are three airfields on the island, only one of them normally open to commercial aircraft, and the visitors who arrive there also sometimes amuse the local cabbies by asking to be taken to "a nice hotel, not too expensive, but on the water." *Everything* on Martha's Vineyard is too expensive, but then again, everything is on the water. And everything is booked solid until Labor Day.

Just after four o'clock on the afternoon of Wednesday, August the fourth—not very long after Sara Joslyn, fifteen hundred miles away in Florida, put Jack Ingersoll's mind at rest in re those hundred-year-old twins—a small charter plane from Boston landed at the main airport on the Vineyard, and its three passengers not only wanted rooms for themselves starting today, they also wanted rooms for *twenty-four people* starting tomorrow. In addition, for purposes other than accommodation, they wanted a house. They also wanted a number of rental cars and telephones and other things. And they wanted everything *now.*

Most people would have gotten nowhere with such a quixotic quest, but most people are not Ida Gavin. She was accompanied, as the advance guard of the *Galaxy* invasion, by Harry Razza and by a Boston stringer of the *Weekly Galaxy* called Sherman Sheridan. Ida left the plane moving fast, and when she returned to the airport at one o'clock the next afternoon, to meet the larger charter plane containing Jack and Sara and the entire Ingersoll team, plus several photographers and a lot of equipment, it was with only the faintest edge to her voice—residue of combats won—that she greeted Jack with the words "All set."

* * *

All set. Through bribes, bluff, blandishments and browbeating, Ida had managed to secure nine rooms in the motels along Main Street and West Chop Road in Vineyard Haven, the town where the ferry comes in. Three more rooms—these very expensive, and exceedingly tough to get hold of—had been obtained in inns down around Edgartown, the posh heart of the island. The house they also needed for their nefarious purposes had been found and rented, and was even now being adapted for their use, over in Oak Bluff, the other side of Vineyard Haven Harbor. (Oak Bluff is—I'll have to say this quietly, and away from the children, because of course such things don't exist anymore—the black neighborhood on the island. *Rich* black, but black.)

To be put into all these rooms, assembled with such grim determination, a motley crew indeed had now descended on the Vineyard. There was, to begin with, Jack Ingersoll and his team: the eager Sara Joslyn, the arid Ida Gavin, the pessimistic Don Grove, the irrepressible Down Under Trio and even the team's resident spaceman, Chauncey Chapperell, who this time had been called back from Port Radium on Great Bear Lake in Canada's Northwest Territories, where he had been sent in pursuit of the North

American cousin of the Himalayan yeti. (A tall, cadaverous, wild-haired, huge-eyed creature who appeared to have been put together with low-quality rubber bands, Chauncey Chapperell might readily have been mistaken for a yeti himself, if he would wear a fur coat and if anyone knew the sound of the yeti's mating cry.)

Supplementing this core group were eighteen more Galaxians of various sorts. There were nine photographers, two of them full-time employees of the paper from Florida, the other seven sometime contract workers from New England, all nine of such a level of disreputability and disorganization as to make Sara's bag lady photographer of Indianapolis look like Meryl Streep playing Greer Garson. Also from Florida were four secretaries from the secretary pool, known for their efficiency and silence and loyalty and low self-esteem and miserable sex lives, while also from New England were five more stringers, or local pieceworkers for the *Galaxy* and other publications, these last all similar to Sherman Sheridan, the stringer who'd flown in with Ida and Harry Razza yesterday. That is, all were hairy, sloppy, distracted, and probably infested with bugs; all were themselves failed scientists or philosophers or mathematicians, whose occasional work for the *Galaxy* consisted of speaking about *Galaxy*-type scientific concerns—extraterrestrials, cancer cures, unlikely pregnancies—with members of that vast unworldly technocracy of professors and scientists and engineers in the greater Boston/Cambridge area; and not a one of them knew *the slightest thing* about American popular culture of the second half of the twentieth century. They could describe the theory behind the invention of television—if television hadn't already been invented, they could probably invent it—but none of them ever actually *watched* anything on it. To them, "John Michael Mercer" and "*Breakpoint*" were words in some foreign language they had no desire to learn. So they stood about, scratching and blinking, and waited to obey orders they already knew they would not comprehend.

Once all these stray molecules had deplaned and were standing around amid their discreditable luggage, Jack gestured at them and said to Ida, "You've looked the area over. Will they have any trouble blending in?"

Ida considered the question. "K-Mart," she decided, "meets J. Press."

* * *

Four P.M. Jack and Sara, having reassured themselves that their rooms at the inn in Edgartown were adjoining, with a connecting door, drove over to Oak Bluffs to look at the house Ida had found. Jack's rental car was a maroon Chevette, the same model and color as the car Sara had driven that very first day in Florida, when she'd gone out to the *Galaxy* to find work, so new and naive she'd thought the people there would give a damn about a murdered man beside the road. That seemed so long ago! She'd learned so much, she'd done so much, she'd even managed the hundred-year-old twin con under the very eyes of Jack and the fact checkers and Mr. Harsch and *everybody.* This maroon Chevette on Martha's Vineyard was a symbol. It said to her: "You've come a long way, baby. By golly, you're *good.*"

Driving across the island, remembering, Sara said, "Do you know what Henry Reed said to me?"

"Huh? Who?"

"The man who does John Michael Mercer's hiring."

"Oh, him. He said no, didn't he?"

"When I told him I was new, he said, 'You'll be something when you get your growth.'"

Jack laughed, and looked at her, and then looked thoughtful, and then grinned. "He was right," he said.

Sara returned the grin. She felt he was proud of her. "I *am* good," she said.

* * *

In front of the address in Oak Bluffs were parked three phone company trucks, a rental furniture company van, a Land Rover, a few more rented cars and a chrome-quilted small truck blazoned with the name CADET CATERING. Phone company linemen, none as pretty as Betsy Harrigan, worked on the roof. Two burly bruisers carried a long table into the house. Jack parked among all the other vehicles, and paused to sing, "Just be-*fore* the battle, Mother." Then they got out of the car.

The house itself was a small two-story gray-shingled place with white trim, in a very New England fishing village style; appropriate enough, Oak Bluffs having originally been a fishing village, and the whole island still being in New England. The house was among the less desirable properties roundabout, however, being a good seventy feet from the ocean and less than a mile from the public state beach.

The little house had a narrow porch, with gray floor and white railing. Jack and Sara followed the bruisers with the table across this, Jack held open the charming old front door with beveled-glass lights, and they entered the stateroom scene from the Marx Brothers' *A Night at the Opera.*

The original living room furniture, down to the carpet, had been removed, toted upstairs and stored in the bedrooms up there. The rented furniture replacing it, and still in the process of being delivered, consisted mostly of long plain tables and innumerable folding chairs, plus a few tall metal filing cabinets and a number of large clunky wooden wastebaskets. More of these items had been rented than could fit into the house, but that was all right; they shoehorned everything in anyway.

And among the furniture moved the people. To one side, at the moment, Ida was nailing a large map of Martha's Vineyard to the wall with huge common nails. Beyond her, two men wearing silver warm-up jackets that made them look like the Cadet Catering truck outside—and that even said CADET CATERING on the back—were dealing out onto one of the long tables plates and trays of sandwiches and doughnuts and other inedibles. At the other tables, reporters and stringers and photographers and secretaries sat and ate or typed or drank coffee out of cardboard cups or played with their photographic equipment or talked to one another or (in Chauncy Chapperell's case) slept snorily, sprawled forward with one cheek pressed to the table. Three phone company installers crawled around on the floor as though looking for any number of lost contact lenses. The furniture rental bruisers opened table legs that kept bumping into people who were either too intimidated or too disassociated to complain. And Bob Sangster, thoughtfully scratching his big nose, sidestepped his way through it all to say to Sara, "There's a priest for you next door, in what was once the dining room."

"A priest? You mean a minister?"

"How would I know?" Bob asked. "I'm just a simple Aussie."

"Don't you have ministers in Australia?"

"Certainly not, they're all poofters. Yours is a very clean old body, though."

"My minister," decided Sara, nodding at Jack.

Jack said, "The officiator at the wedding?"

"And solver of the Irish question. See you."

Sara went away to the other room, and Jack crossed through the scumble and flux to a long table bearing a dozen identical black rotary-dial telephones. He picked one up, and spoke into it: "Watson, come here, I want you." Then he did it to the second: "Watson, come here, I want you." Then the third: "Watson, come here, I want you." Then, with grim patience, a man wanting to know the worst, insisting on knowing the worst, demanding to know the worst, he went on through the rest, telephone by telephone: "Watson, come here, I want you. Watson, come here, I want you. Watson, come here, I want you. Watson, come here, I want you. Watson, come here, I want you. Watson, come here, I want you. Watson, come here, I want you. Watson, come here, I want you. Watson, come here, I want you." Then, rather than hang up this last phone, he waggled it at the nearest kneeling installer, saying, shouting over the general hubbub, "Why all this peace and quiet?"

"Just a few more minutes, sir," the installer said, from the floor. "They're bringing the lines in from the road now."

And even as he spoke, there was a tremendous *crash*, and plaster dust drifted down onto the people and the food and the phones and everything else, and when Jack looked up there was now a metal pipe sticking down through the ceiling, and out of the metal pipe was emerging telephone line. "There it is now," the installer said.

"So I see."

"We were told a rush job," the installer said, finally getting up off his knees. "Otherwise, your lines wouldn't be so noticeable."

"Ah."

Ida, her nailing of the map to the wall completed to her satisfaction, made her way through the mob to Jack and said, "You like the place?"

"It's so *much* like home," Jack told her, "I keep looking for old Shep, the faithful hound."

"He's around here somewhere," Ida said, frowning at the installers all over the floor.

The front door opened and a man with a moustache stuck his head in to shout, "Telly!"

"Kojak?" cried a photographer, reaching for her cameras. "Where?"

"Tele*vision*, madam," said the newcomer frostily.

"A passing fad," Jack told him.

"The rental television that was *ordered*, sir," the man explained.

Jack looked around his overcrowded realm. "Oh, really?"

Ida said, "That goes in the next room."

"Thank God," Jack said.

"Thank *you*, madam," the rental television man said, and disappeared, only to reappear leading a tiny Oriental man carrying a huge television set on his back. Wires trailed from the television set down the Oriental man's legs and along the floor. The rental man, the Oriental man and the television set moved on into the next room as Sara came out of that room, looking dazed, holding a slender manuscript rolled into a tube in her right hand, and smiling imperfectly at a roly-poly white-haired smiling saintly man who looked like Santa Claus disguised in a minister's suit. "Well, Reverend," Sara was saying, "it's a fresh approach."

"Thank you *very* much," the reverend said, with an angelic smile.

"I'll see it gets prominent placement in the paper," Sara promised him, gesturing with the tubular manuscript.

"Oh, that would be nice," the reverend said, and pressed his clean pink pudgy hands together.

"With the same photo of you that we use for the interview."

"Oh, a photo!" The reverend's smile had a halo of pleasure around it; but then he became more serious, with an obvious effort, saying, "But that can't be till *after* the wedding, you know."

"No, of course not," Sara agreed.

"Mr. Mercer wants the whole affair kept absolutely private."

"Of course."

"He would be *quite* upset," the reverend went on, with an impish little grin, "if he even knew I was here, talking to you."

"I'm sure he would," Sara said.

"So I'd best run along," the reverend said, with a little bobbing bow. "Thank you again."

"Thank *you*, Reverend," Sara said.

Sara saw the reverend out, her own smile holding till she'd shut the door, when it got all wrinkly around the edges. Turning, she waded through the rising tide of rentals and reporters to Jack, and handed him the roll of manuscript. "The Irish question solved," she announced.

He handed it back, his expression dubious. "Can you give me a summary?"

She looked at the manuscript, which she thought she'd given away. "Well," she said, "it's not too coherent . . ."

"Good."

". . . but it *seems* to suggest that all the Protestants in Northern Ireland should be relocated."

"Where?"

"Mars," Sara said.

Jack nodded thoughtfully, looking at nothing in particular. "I see," he said.

"To work in the mines there," Sara explained.

"Uh huh, uh huh." Jack nodded some more. "You know," he said, "Massa might actually like that."

"That's what I thought, too," Sara agreed, and all twelve black telephones began wildly ringing. Everybody stopped doing everything to stare. RRIYYYINNG!!! said the phones, in unison. They took a deep breath to say it again, and in that interval the head installer beamed proudly at Jack and said, "All set, sir."

Jack said, "What's—"

RRIYYYINNG!!!

Jack said, "What's *this*?"

"Your phones," the installer said. "All—"

RRIYYYINNG!!!

People started answering phones just to stop the ringing, picking up the receivers and putting them back down again. "Not bells!" Jack cried. "*Li*—!"

RIIINNG!!

"What?" asked the installer.

"*Lights!*" Jack shouted at him. "Not be—"

RING!

"What?" asked the installer.

"Look on your order sheet!" Jack yelled. *(Ring.)* "*Lights* on the phones! How are we supposed to know which is which? How are we supposed to *think* around here?"

"Oh," the installer said, as another installer came over with a clipboard, showed it to the first installer, and pointed at something. The two installers muttered together, looking like men trying to figure out a way to blame somebody else and not succeeding.

"Jack?" asked Sara.

He raised an eyebrow at her. "Yes?"

Sara spread her hands to encompass it all, the phones, the installers, the rented tables, the map nailed to the wall, the caterer's men and their food, the television rental man and his faithful Oriental companion just now leaving, the reporters and photographers and stringers, the filing cabinets, themselves. "Why?" she asked.

He shook his head. "Why what?"

"We have such nice hotel rooms," she said. "Why did Ida have to come on ahead to find a private house? Why do we have all this *stuff* here? Why are we in this dump in the first place?"

"No hotel switchboard, for one," Jack told her. "No nosy guests. No other media climbing all over our exclusives." Holding his closed hand to his cheek to simulate a phone call, he said brightly, "Hi, this is Jack Ingersoll of *Newsweek*. Sure you can call me back, I'll give you my number."

Sara said, "Do we really need that much security? I mean, who really *cares*, besides us?"

"The world cares, my darling," Jack assured her. "Everyone else pretends to be more sophisticated than that, to *really* care about international arms control, but when it comes right down to it, they'll all be here. The newsmagazines, the gossip magazines, the fan magazines, the networks, cable news, the wire services, the entertainment editors of every newspaper in the United States with a travel budget, *everybody*."

"But we're the only ones who know about the wedding," Sara said.

"Today," Jack said. "This is Thursday, the wedding's Sunday, we probably have a twenty-four-hour jump on the rest of the world. *We* have first pick of the rental cars and motel rooms and photo labs, and first shot at bribing the bellboys and ministers, but no later than tomorrow the locusts will descend. Believe me."

Sara couldn't help grinning. "And John Michael Mercer," she said, "thinks he's going to be all alone."

Chapter Two

Security. Secrecy. Privacy. A *Breakpoint* production assistant made the two first-class Miami–New York American Airline reservations in false names, then phoned American's security twenty minutes before flight time to reveal who would actually be using those tickets. The limousine service between Kennedy Airport in Queens and Teterboro Airport over in New Jersey was arranged for by an assistant in John Michael Mercer's accountant's office in New York, who also reserved the chartered plane from Teterboro to Martha's Vineyard, paying for it with a credit card with her own name on it. A private car and driver had been ordered to drive down from Boston and across the ferry to the island, an arrangement made by the network's New York office, so that when John Michael Mercer and Felicia Nelson landed at the Vineyard Friday afternoon the car was waiting for them, driven by a deferential man with a black chauffeur's cap, a funny accent, and a large nose. " 'Ere we are, sir," he said, with a sweeping gesture. " 'Ere we are, madam. Your chariot awaits."

"Are you English?" Mercer asked, getting into the rear of the black stretch Caddy.

"Australian, sir," Bob Sangster told him. "I'm just a simple Aussie."

* * *

As they left the airport, the driver expertly steering them out to West Tisbury Road and turning east, Mercer said, "So far, so good."

"This is a beautiful place," Felicia said, this being her first time on the island.

"And private," Mercer said, relishing the word, stretching his long legs out in the roomy car, relaxing. "And secluded. And remote."

"Sir?" said the Australian driver.

Mercer looked at the face in the rearview mirror. The eyes in that face were firmly fixed on the well-traveled road. "Yeah?"

"I don't mean to intrude, sir," the driver said, with a little stiffening of the shoulders to indicate the distance he knew he was expected to keep, "but if at some point you wouldn't mind to give me just a little autograph for my daughter, it would be the thrill of her life."

"Of course," Mercer said, smiling, while Felicia squeezed his hand. "What's her name?"

"Fiona," the driver said. "She's your biggest fan."

"Is she?"

"But we all are, sir, if truth be told. The whole family, we wouldn't miss a thing you do. Not just *Breakpoint*, you know, but everything. That blind rodeo rider in the movie for television, *Study in Courage* was it? That was beautiful, sir, if you don't mind. Beautiful."

"I *am* proud of that one," Mercer agreed, nodding in manly acknowledgment.

"Not to intrude, sir."

"Not at all, not at all."

* * *

Of the exclusive hostels on Martha's Vineyard, the Katama Bay Country Club is perhaps the most exclusive, limiting its clientele almost totally to the friends and guests of island residents. Over the years, these friends and guests have included a full range of the famous, from politicians to rock singers, from Pulitzer playwrights to movie stars, and as a result, the management and staff of Katama Bay have had long practice at developing the style and substance of their relationship with the media. To journalists of print and picture alike, as well as the putative biographers and other camp followers, the face Katama Bay turned was unfailingly polite, and unfailingly unforthcoming. Never to be rude, yet never to give them a goddamn thing, that was the unstated motto of Katama Bay, always honored.

Even in the presence of the *Weekly Galaxy*. The manager, a smooth sleek man named Ferguson, looked at the card this fellow had given him—John R. Ingersoll, *Weekly Galaxy*—moved it delicately between his fingers as though unobtrusively looking for slime, and with perfect politeness said, "Just how may we be of assistance, Mr. Ingersoll?"

"Well, I doubt you read the *Galaxy*, Mr. Ferguson," Ingersoll said, with an understanding smile. Ferguson bowed, admitting the charge, and Ingersoll went on, "Probably very few people on this entire island read the *Galaxy*. A place like this—the Vineyard, Katama Bay—this is a fantasy world to our readership."

Faintly surprised at Ingersoll's frankness, wondering what deviousness it concealed, Ferguson said, "I suppose that must be true."

"A part of the *Galaxy*'s appeal," Ingersoll said, "is that we take our readers, in fantasy, into places like Katama Bay that they'll never see in real life."

"You want to do a piece on the hotel, is that it?"

With another self-deprecating smile, Ingersoll said, "I realize it won't be the kind of publicity that can do you any real *good*, but it can't harm you either, and of course we would clear all text and pictures with you for approval before going to print."

They know about Mercer, Ferguson thought, nodding thoughtfully, turning Ingersoll's card over and over in his hand, between his long fingers. "No personalities, in other words," he said.

Ingersoll gave the alert look of a man who didn't understand the question: "I beg your pardon?"

"No . . . stars, or famous names. Just the hotel itself?"

"Oh, of *course*!" Ingersoll beamed with happy relief, clearly seeing that the only possible objection had now been surmounted. Dropping his right hand into his jacket pocket in order to take an insouciant stance, confident, smiling, he said, "We wouldn't dream of bothering *any* of your guests. You'd set the ground rules, and we would absolutely abide by them." In taking his hand from his pocket, to make an all-inclusive gesture, Ingersoll pulled from the pocket, as though accidentally, a thick banded wad of money, which fell with a padded sound to the terra-cotta tile floor of the lobby. "Woops!" Ingersoll cried, and stooped at once to pick it up.

Ferguson's faint sense of amusement abruptly left him, and he became very angry. Nothing changed on his face. He waited till Ingersoll had straightened again, and stuffed the money back into his pocket, and was once again meeting Ferguson's eye. Then, as Ingersoll was just about to say something else, Ferguson said, very quietly, "Mr. Ingersoll, if you have some idea of offering me that cash, do let me assure you I have any number of bellmen who would be pleased to tear you limb from limb."

Ingersoll looked shocked, stunned. "What?" he cried. "A bribe? From the *Galaxy*?"

Turning his head, Ferguson caught the eye of Eddie, the dark-green-uniformed doorman on duty at this moment. Eddie, in response to that glance, strode rapidly across the quiet lobby from the door, saying, "Yes, sir?"

Ferguson gestured at Ingersoll with the hand holding the fellow's card. "This," he said, "is Mr. John Ingersoll of the *Weekly Galaxy*."

Eddie turned a fish eye on Ingersoll. "Yes, sir?"

"He's just leaving now," Ferguson said, "but if he comes back . . . hurt him."

"Yes, sir," said Eddie.

"Goodbye, Mr. Ingersoll," Ferguson said.

"I hope someday, Mr. Ferguson," Ingersoll said, "you'll know just how deeply you've wronged me."

But Ferguson was finished with Ingersoll; leaving the fellow to Eddie, he went off to concern himself with hotel business.

"Goodbye," Eddie said.

Ingersoll gave Eddie an irritated look. "Don't play tough guy, okay?"

"I was eleven years a cop in Boston," Eddie said. "I used to tell people the same thing. Don't play tough guy. Not unless you really know the part."

Ingersoll considered Eddie briefly, then turned his head, looking around the large discreet lobby. Eddie, following the guy's thought processes as though they were a schematic printed on his forehead, said, "Not a one of us. You won't find one employee in this whole place to give you the time of day."

Ingersoll turned back, and gave Eddie a pitying smile. "Now *there*," he said, "you're wrong."

* * *

The man from the *Weekly Galaxy* went out the front entrance of the Katama Bay Country Club under his own steam, and walked around the curving entrance driveway toward his waiting maroon Chevette, just as a long black stretch Cadillac arrived, purring in around the curve toward the entrance. The driver of the Cadillac, involved in deferential but friendly conversation with his passengers, and the man from the *Galaxy* walking away from his rout and defeat, didn't so much as glance at one another. The man from the *Galaxy* did smile, though, when he saw the florist's delivery van turning in at the hotel entrance; he it was who had composed the effusive greeting to Mr. Mercer and Ms. Nelson accompanying the six dozen roses that were about to be delivered to the happy couple.

Welcome, John and Felicia! May all go well with thee!

* * *

"No," Mercer said, and hung up the phone.

"What was that, Johnny?"

"Nothing," Mercer said, and prowled the large sitting room saying, "What do you think of it?"

"The place? It's beautiful."

And it was. At the very end of the curving brick path through trellises of climbing vines and flowers, this separate little shingled structure managed to combine all the charm of the eighteenth century with all the comforts of the twentieth. In addition to the large and pleasantly beige sitting room, there were two cosy bedrooms, each with its own bath, one including an indoor-outdoor hot tub. The front of the cottage was all small-paned windows and gray shingles, but the rear was open, with sheets of plate glass commanding the view from Chappaquiddick on the left to Norton Point on the right and the Atlantic beyond. Sliding glass doors led out to a brick patio and a narrow brick path down to their own private bit of beach.

Here they would spend the next two nights. Today there was nothing much for them to do but settle in, and have dinner this evening with friends who had a small rental house over by Gay Head, at the other end of the island. Tomorrow was the rehearsal at the church in Edgartown, and the next day, Sunday, the wedding. Just under one hundred guests had been invited, most of them flying or driving in for the day, a few staying on at the Vineyard. After the wedding, all would return here to Katama Bay, where the banquet room had been reserved for the reception. Then, at seven on Sunday evening, just in time to fly off into the sunset—a touch Mercer liked—their chartered plane would take them away to their honeymoon far down the coast on Hilton Head.

A lovely plan, a lovely setting, lovely people, lovely church, lovely weather. And only the press was vile.

* * *

The main room in the *Galaxy* house in Oak Bluffs no longer looked like the primary staging area for the evacuation of the planet Earth. Order had been obtained; a noisy, sloppy, messy order, but order nevertheless. All the installers and deliverers had departed, the rented furniture had been arranged so as to leave twisty trails and pathways through the room, and a sheet of acetate tacked over the map of the island nailed to the wall was beginning to fill up with grease pencil remarks. The photographers and all their equipment had been banished to one of the bedrooms upstairs, the stringers were all out looking for local color, and most of the regular reporters were off in search of employees—hotel employees, laundry employees, utility employees, all kinds of employees—to suborn. The dozen telephones were now distributed to key points around the room, and all featured lights that flashed politely to indicate an incoming call. At one of these, Sara, seated on a folding chair, elbows on the table, made an outgoing call, to but not through the switchboard at the Katama Bay Country Club: "Ms. Nelson, please."

"May I ask who's calling?" the switchboard person answered, already sounding snotty.

"This is Ms. Blanchard of *Mademoiselle*," Sara told her. "Our interviewer, Countess Marguerite Orvieto, would like to make an appointment with Ms. Nelson at her earliest—"

"I'm sorry, they've asked not—"

"I beg your pardon?"

"*Not* to be disturbed. Could they call you back?"

"Of course they can," Sara said. "That was Ms. Blanchard of *Mademoiselle*," she repeated, then spelled both "Blanchard" and "Mademoiselle" and read the number off her phone. "I'll be here for the rest of the business day."

"I'll pass the message on," the cynical voice said in Sara's ear, as Jack loped in from the outer world, looking like a carnivore trapped in a produce market.

"Please explain," Sara said, shaking her head at Jack as he loped in her direction, "that this is *Mademoiselle* calling, and we do have a deadline."

"I'll pass the message on," the uninterested voice said, and the connection was broken.

Hanging up her phone, Sara said, "They won't call back."

Jack nodded. "Stonewalling us, eh?"

The white light flashed on Sara's phone. Raising a surprised eyebrow at Jack, Sara picked up the receiver and said, "Ms. Blanchard here."

A hasty hushed whisper sounded in her ear: "Lemme talk to Jack Ingersoll."

"Hold on." Sara extended the phone to Jack: "It's a breather, for you."

"Oh, good." Into the phone he said, "Tell me." He nodded, listening hard. "They're on their way to Edgartown? Anybody mention a hotel? Good." Hanging up, he looked around the room, saying, "Where's the Down Under Trio?"

"Well, Bob Sangster's still being Mercer's driver."

"They haven't scoped him yet?" Jack asked in surprise. "Beautiful."

"I think Louis and Harry are in the kitchen. No, here they are."

Louis and Harry, carrying coffee and Danish, strolled into the room, talking Austriylian at each other. Jack called, "Men!" and they stopped their conversation to look around in mild curiosity, not seeing any.

"Comere, comere, comere," Jack told them, and they came over, eyes full of mischief and mouths full of Danish. Jack said, "Our friend at the airport just called, and the world's press has arrived."

"Ah," said Harry Razza, patting his matinee idol hair.

"Stop them," Jack said.

"Duty calls," Louis B. Urbiton said. He shook his Styrofoam coffee cup, frowned at it when he didn't hear any ice tinkling, and handed the cup to Jack. "Ever ready," he announced, "ever willing, and ever able."

"Good men. Green's Hotel in Edgartown was mentioned. When Bob's cover gets blown, I'll send him along for reinforcements."

"We'll hold the fort," Harry said, and beamed at Sara. "As lovely as ever, Sara," he said.

"Thank you."

"Come, Harry," Louis said, "there's work to be done."

Harry winked at Sara, and the two Australians left, moving at what for them was a fairly rapid pace. Sara said, "What was that all about?"

"We have an employee out at the airport," Jack told her, "who will tell us interesting events. Two planeloads of press just reached the island."

"And?"

"The Down Under Trio—or the Down Under Duo, I guess—will stop them, hold them off while we get our work done."

Sara shook her head. "I don't get it. How do they do that?"

"Mostly," Jack said, "by getting everybody drunk."

* * *

A number of cabloads of press arrived at Green's Hotel simultaneously. Both large and garish by island standards, Green's Hotel was the sort of place that would have corporate rooms and suites reserved on a standby basis for the convenience of executives passing through. Given the cat's cradle of interlocking corporate structure in today's free-enterprise America, most of the media had access to this mothball fleet of rooms in an emergency, and so it was to Green's Hotel that the nation's press repaired when it became necessary for just a moment to set aside thoughts of nuclear winter, municipal corruption, African famine, rampant inflation, the eroding American industrial base, urban crime, racial violence and presidential aspirations to turn their attentions to the wedding of a TV star.

It was probably this sense of momentary respite from the weighty problems of nation, species and planet that made the assembled journalists seem so jovial as they tumbled from their taxis and flooded into the lobby, cheering and chortling and calling out to one another. Perhaps a score of them were there, both male and female, gathered around the desk, calling out good-natured gibes at the hardworking registration staff, when Harry Razza wandered aimlessly by, drink in hand, amused smile on face, and viewed the rear elevation of his fellows of the press. "Chester?" he called. "Chester, is that you? And Bullock, you old sod!"

A couple of the reporters turned around, to see who and what this was, and then a few more turned, and then a few more. "Why, it's the Razzer," said the one who'd been called Chester. "What do you say, Harry?"

"Nobody's safe now," a woman reporter said accurately, "with the *Galaxy* here."

Harry smiled upon his compeers, more and more of whom had diverted their attention from the flustered hotel staff to his own person. Innocently, he said, "And what news brings you all out, boys and girls?"

Laughing, the reporter called Bullock said, "Forget it, Harry, we all know about John Michael Mercer."

With a dismissive shake of his drink, Harry said, "Oh, that. There's no story in it."

Hoots and catcalls.

"No, you're welcome to it," Harry told them. "He's at the Katama Bay right now with the girl. Felicia Nelson, from Whittier, California. A registered nurse."

The woman reporter who'd announced the end of safety said, "A registered nurse? I didn't get that."

"They met in Africa, you know," Harry said airily, throwing the information away. "Come on in the bar, I'll tell you all about it, some of the other chaps are here."

Bullock, looking alert, looking like a man set to start memorizing things, said, "Africa? When was she in Africa?"

Unobtrusively shepherding his charges toward The Nineteenth Hole (what else would you call the bar in a tacky hotel called Green's?), Harry said, "Oh, there's nothing in it, the whole thing's a poor lame excuse for a story, but the editors don't care, do they? Send us out to the rubbish tips of the world. Then it's up to *us* to prove them right. Come along, come along, first round's on me."

"Ho ho!" cried Chester. "Harry Razza's buying!"

And so they all receded into the bar, where Louis B. Urbiton was lying in wait.

* * *

Eddie the bellman walked out the front entrance of the Katama Bay Country Club, carrying a Polariod camera. He walked stolidly and unhurriedly around the curving drive to where the stretch limo was parked, engine off, windows open, with its driver absorbed in a paperback of *Middlemarch*. Eddie tapped on the windshield. The driver immediately closed his book, looked alert, reached for the ignition and gazed past Eddie for his charges back by the entrance, but Eddie shook his head, waved his hand, and said, "No, no, no, I just want to take your picture."

The driver leaned his head out the window, squinting in sunlight. "My picture?"

"For the night man," Eddie explained. "So he'll know you're the real driver, not a ringer. Not somebody from one of those rags like the *Weekly Galaxy*."

"*Weekly Galaxy*," echoed the driver, musing, as though those were words in a foreign language. "Never heard of it. I'm a simple Aussie myself."

"If you'd just step out of the car for a minute," Eddie suggested, "so I can get a good clear shot."

"Take two, mate," the driver said, cheerfully climbing from the car. "One to send home to me mum in Sydney. You want me right here, next to me rickshaw?"

"That's fine, that's fine," Eddie told him, crouching like a linebacker on a must-pass play, peering into the black box of the camera. "Just lift your head a little into the sunlight. *There*, that's got it." Smiling, Eddie took the extruded print from the front of the camera and tucked it away in his shirt pocket.

"Is that it, then?" the driver asked, reaching for the door handle. Then he stopped himself, saying, "No, you were going to do me another."

"For your mum," Eddie agreed. "Let's just wait and see how this one comes out."

"Wonderful machines, those cameras," the driver said. "Takes all the guesswork out. Snap your picture, just like that you know what you've got."

"Oh, I know what I've got," Eddie told him. Taking the picture from his shirt pocket, he saw that the ambers and sepias were beginning to rise, that the picture was going to be good and clear and identifiable. "Oh, that's nice," he said, and put the picture away again.

"Could I have a look, then?" the driver asked, stepping closer.

"Let's take the other one," Eddie said. Shifting the camera to his left hand, he took one step forward and drove a mean hard right fist into the driver's body, just above the belt and just below the rib cage. Then he stepped back, put the Polaroid to his eye, and snapped an excellent photo of a man not breathing.

"*Hnghnghnghnghng,*" said the driver, mouth open wide, arms folded across stomach.

"Now, don't you throw up on hotel property," Eddie told him, and tucked the second photo into the breast pocket of the fellow's dark blue jacket. "For your mum," he said. "Down in Florida, wasn't it?"

"*Hhhhhhhhhhhhh,*" said the driver.

"Our manager here," Eddie explained, "that's Mr. Ferguson, he does everything he can to keep his guests comfortable and happy. So he phoned up to Boston, to the limo company, and he asked about their driver, and it turns out you ain't him."

The driver, having remembered how to breathe, breathed. His face became less purple, his eyes less distended, his posture less pain-wracked. "That was," he said, still gasping, "an unnecessarily cruel act."

Eddie nodded, agreeing with that appraisal. "Think what I'd do if I got mad," he said.

"Die of apoplexy, I hope." The driver's voice stuttered and rasped.

"Don't count on it." Eddie pointed, away from the hotel. "Out to the public highway, bo. Leg it."

"May I at least call a taxi?"

"From somewhere," Eddie said. "Not from here. All you can do from here is leave. And don't come back."

"Oh, not to fret," the driver assured him. He'd regained some of his jauntiness along with the ability to breathe. "*I* won't be back. Someone will, but not me. What *I* will do, I believe, is go to Green's Hotel, and give myself a drink."

Chapter Three

Ida said, "Jack tells me *you* got this. Took it away from Cartwright."

"He did?" Pleased, Sara smiled at Ida for possibly the first time in her life. They were seated near one another in the command center living room of the house in Oak Bluffs, late that same afternoon, several hours after arrival on the island. A routine had already been established, controllable chaos wrestled from pure chaos, and several of the staff were now lounging about—never very far from the phones—waiting for whatever would happen next. Surprised and pleased that Jack would go out of his way to give her credit for their being there, Sara said, "It was just luck, really."

"You hooked a telephone girl," Ida said, nodding. "On your own."

"I was just mad at Phyllis, mostly," Sara told her. "I got mad enough, I guess, to really start *thinking*."

"You doing anything else on your own?"

She's jealous of me! Sara thought, with a little thrill, looking into Ida's icy eyes. She knows I'm competition. And I am, doggone it, I really am! "No, nothing else," she answered, "not right now. But if I think of something, I'll land running."

Ida nodded slowly, absorbing and accepting the challenge. "You came along pretty fast," she said.

"I guess I did." Sara smiled again, very happy about herself. When this wedding is over, she thought, Jack will just have to give me a couple of days off, he'll have to, I'm so close to home, I'll go over to Great Barrington and see Mom, and tell her . . .

Sara's smile slowly faded to a look of puzzlement instead, as Ida looked away, picking up a pen and starting to make tiny precise notes to herself. Sara frowned, as she tried to figure out just exactly how to tell her mother about these triumphs. How to make them sound . . . heroic. Brilliant. Fun.

Maybe, she thought, maybe you just have to be there.

Over by the side window, next to the big Vineyard map crucified to the wall by Ida, Jack stood, looking out. Turning, he waved a pair of binoculars toward Sara, calling, "Comere. Take a look at this."

Sara rose and threaded her way through the room. When she reached him, Jack handed her the binoculars, pointed out the window, and said, "Take a look."

Straight ahead, outside the window, were some pine trees and shrubs, and beyond them faint indications of another house. At an angle to the right, beyond the last trees, some distance away, Nantucket Sound could be seen, the arm of the Atlantic Ocean hugging this island on the east. Looking out in that direction, adjusting the binoculars for her own vision, Sara found herself looking at a beautiful white yacht, at least forty feet long, with royal blue trim and bits of gleaming honey-colored woodwork. The ship was lying offshore, in fact was moving very slowly southward along the coast, the late afternoon sun lying on it from this direction like a coat of lacquer, heightening its elegance and beauty, making it stand out from its surroundings like a perfect slide of itself. "That's beautiful," Sara murmured, gazing at the ship, holding the binoculars close against her eyes. "I wonder whose it is."

"Ours," Jack said.

Sara slowly lowered the binoculars and turned to look at him. She knew him well enough by now to know he didn't joke, or at least he didn't joke in any normal and expected way. "Ours?" she echoed.

"Not to keep," he told her. "Just to give away."

"I didn't know we were that nice. Who are we—"

She was interrupted by Don Grove, sounding more terrified than pessimistic this time, as he called from across the room, "Jack! It's Mr. DeMassi!"

"Come along and listen," Jack suggested, grinning.

Sara followed him over to where Don Grove sat, holding up the telephone receiver as though it were a poisonous snake he'd been lucky enough to pick up just behind its jaws, so it couldn't get at him, but had no idea how to put down. "Mr. DeMassi," he whispered, as Jack took the phone.

"Thank you, Don." Holding the phone to his ear, Jack took a folded sheet of paper from his pocket as he said, "Mr. DeMassi? Good afternoon, sir. Yes, sir, everything's under control. I have the text of the telegram right here and"—he looked quickly at his watch—"Mercer should be reading it just about five minutes from now."

The word that Massa himself was on the phone from Florida had spread immediately through the building, and people were gathering around Jack as though he were an accident victim; with the same morbid fascination and unstated relief that it hadn't happened to them. They all, Sara included, watched and listened in total silence as Jack shook open the folded sheet of paper in his hand and said, "Yes, sir, here it is here. Shall I read it? Yes, sir." Clearing his throat, holding the paper up in the air, Jack read, "'John Michael Mercer, Katama Bay Country Club, Martha's Vineyard. Dear John Michael Mercer. All of America is thrilled and delighted at the news of your impending marriage to Ms. Felicia Nelson of Whittier, California, and Miami, Florida. Knowing how important privacy is for you at this major turning point in your life, the *Weekly Galaxy* wishes to give you, all expenses paid, two weeks on the first-class yacht, *Princess Pat*, which you can at this moment see outside your window.'"

Sara, mouth hanging open, turned to stare out the window—she couldn't see the Sound at all from here—then stared at Jack again.

"'You may travel,'" Jack was saying, continuing to read from the sheet of paper, "'anywhere in the world you wish on this yacht, safe and secure from all interruption. In this brief period before your nuptials, the *Weekly Galaxy* would be proud to present to the American people your thoughts at this important milestone in your life.'"

My gosh, Sara thought, my *gosh*! We can do *that*? This organization, *my* organization, we have that much money, that much power, that much determination? The last tiny shred of nostalgia for the poor old, fusty old, ineffective old *Courier-Observer* fell away from Sara's brain at that point like dead ash days after the fire.

"'Our discreet interviewer,'" Jack was saying, continuing to read into the phone, "'will be available at your convenience. With warmest wishes and sincere congratulations, John R. Ingersoll, Senior Editor, *Weekly Galaxy*.' And I put this address, Mr. DeMassi, so he'll know we're really here."

We're really here, Sara thought. She was so excited she kept bobbing up and down on the balls of her feet.

"Yes, sir," Jack was saying, smiling at the phone. "I'll be right here, sir, and I'll relay the information to you the instant we get Mercer's answer."

* * *

"No," John Michael Mercer said, and slammed the door.

Chapter Four

It was 4:45, nearly the end of the working day at the *Weekly Galaxy*. Mary Kate Scudder, the only member of the Jack Ingersoll team still in Florida, holding the fort, typed a letter to her sister, a WAF at Landsruhe Air Base in West Germany. "Not much news from here," she had just written, when a general stir made her look up.

There was a flurry of activity all about her in Editorial, people rising, moving with startled expressions in the direction of the elevator bank. Something was going on over there, something disturbing. People trotted toward that disturbance, alarmed, calling out to one another, but still obeying the black lines on the floor, still quartering this way and that through the maze. Abandoning her sister, Mary Kate rose and called to a staffer rushing by this squaricle, "What's up?"

"Massa's stuck between floors!"

And Jack is missing this, Mary Kate thought, not without some satisfaction, as she joined the flow, hurrying over to the elevators, where a pair of sweating editors struggled vainly with the door facing the conference table. As Mary Kate arrived, so did an officious janitor, jangling a handful of keys above his head like a symbolic gesture in some religious service, and crying, "Don't break the door! Don't break the door!"

The janitor forced himself through the gathering crowd, Mary Kate slithering along in his wake in order to assure herself a good view, and the futile editors stood back, brows damp and hands filthy. The janitor dropped to one knee and inserted a long narrow key into a small round hole near the bottom corner of the door. The *click* was clearly audible to Mary Kate above the excited hubbub of the crowd. The janitor stood, and the elevator doors slid back to reveal only the top third of Massa's office, with its roof and machinery and cables above. Looking down past the janitor's elbow, Mary Kate could see Massa down in there, red-faced, staring upward, standing on top of his desk and hopping up and down in his agitation. "Don't worry, Mr. DeMassi," the janitor called. "We got Maintenance on the way!"

But the stuck elevator didn't seem to be what was agitating Massa. Ignoring the janitor, still hopping up and down on his desk, kicking over papers and empty beer bottles and framed testimonials from service organizations, Massa yelled, "Get me Boy! Get me Boy Cartwright!"

The janitor, bewildered, stepped back as Boy pushed himself through the crowd and dropped to one knee at the edge of the floor, the better to look down into the office. He looked, in that position, like one of the viler vassals of one of the baser barons of the Age of Chivalry. "Yes, sir, Mr. DeMassi," he called down to his liege. "Did you want me to help you up, sir?"

"I got it, Boy!" Massa yelled, waving his fists above his head. "I got the John Michael Mercer story!"

Boy looked pleased, but puzzled. "The interview, sir? You have that?"

"He won't *give* us an interview!" Massa roared. "The son of a bitch! If he won't take the goddamn yacht, there's no *way* to get to him!"

"No, sir," Boy agreed. "Looks like no one up there can get to him."

You snake in the grass, Mary Kate thought, I wonder if I could just accidentally step on your hand while you're down there.

But Massa was saying, "*No* one could get to that ungrateful son of a bitch, Boy! We need a different story, and I've got it!"

"Yes, sir?" Boy asked, alert and eager.

"The wedding album!" Massa cried, dancing on his desk like Rumpelstiltskin when nobody could guess his name. "The wedding pictures are the story!"

"Yes, sir!" cried Boy. Still on one knee, he waved his own fists around in imitation of his master.

"Go up there, Boy!" Massa shouted, while Mary Kate stared in shock. "Go up there and get me those pictures!"

"Yes, *sir*!

"If anybody can do it, Boy, *you* can!"

"Yes, sir!"

Boy was up and away. Mary Kate, still in shock, stared down at Massa, wondering if she dared speak up for Jack, knowing in her heart it would be much too dangerous, seeing Massa look around himself, frowning at the position of his office in relation to the floor, frowning at his own feet on his desk. "What *is* this?" he demanded, just now noticing the fix he was in. "Get me *out* of here!"

"Yes, sir!" cried the janitor. "Here comes Maintenance now!"

And as Maintenance came, Mary Kate left, running across Editorial, this way and that through the black lines, the shortest route to the Ingersoll squaricle where she flung herself on the phone and called the house in Oak Bluffs, on Martha's Vineyard.

Jack was out, nobody knew exactly where. Don Grove was the one who answered. He took Mary Kate's message, and it didn't decrease his pessimism one little bit.

* * *

The first shot woke Sara, startling and frightening her but leaving her bewildered, aware only of the after-sound of breaking glass, not sure what she'd heard that had brought her up from sleep. Jack shifted sluggishly beside her—the news about Boy's imminent arrival had caused him to drink just a teeny bit too much at dinner—his arm moving heavily on her rib cage. *What?* she thought, but drowsily, eyes half open, brain not yet really at work.

But then came the fusillade, and snapped them both back into the world, sitting bolt upright together in the darkness. A thunder of shots, closely spaced, intermixed with more chitters of falling glass, and then silence, a silence full of round silent implosions, sharp silent junctures, furry silent menace, and the drifting scent of gunpowder. "Wha—?" started Sara, but Jack clapped a hand over her mouth, his breath in her ear whispering, "Sshhhhhhh . . ."

Distant noises, people shouting, doors banging. Sara and Jack clung together, her arms around him, his right arm around her, left hand cupped to her mouth. Moving her head under that hand, she looked to her right, to the dim red glow of numbers from the clock-radio provided by the inn and bolted to the bedside table: 3:07 A.M.

They were in Jack's bed. They might have been next door in Sara's bed, but the teeny bit too much Jack had taken to drink had caused him, when they'd returned to the inn tonight, to totter directly toward his own room, so Sara had followed, through the connecting door, and their comforting of one another over the bad news of Boy's resurgence into their lives had led to one thing and another, all in this room, in this bed, as slowly solace became sleep. And so here they still were, four hours later, when the night was blown apart with gunshots.

Sara moved her head again, freeing her mouth from his grasp. Softer than soft, she murmured toward his ear in the darkness, "Revolution? Starting in Martha's Vineyard?"

His lips touched her ear. His warm breath whispered, "It was in your room."

She stiffened, holding him tighter, feeling chilled. The connecting door still stood open. Was the person with the gun still in there?

A sudden banging sounded at the hall door in that room, and a male voice called, "Miss Joslyn! Miss Joslyn!"

"Wait here," Jack whispered, and disengaged himself from her, and slid out of bed. She heard him pulling on trousers, and could just make out his form crossing past the drapes over the sliding glass door. Then he opened the hall door of this room, leaned cautiously out, and called to someone outside, "Down here."

Light-spill from the hall, passing Jack, gently illuminated this room. Sara threw a fearful glance toward the doorway to her own room, the blackness in there still total. Nothing seemed to move in there. While Jack and one or more other voices murmured in the hall, she found on the floor the jeans and shirt she'd discarded just a few hours ago, and pulled them on.

"Just a minute, let me see," Jack said firmly, and shut the door over what seemed to be protests. As Sara stood, Jack came running around the bed, grabbing her arm, whispering rapidly as he propelled her toward the frightening darkness of her room, "You were in the bathroom when it happened."

She didn't want to go into that black rectangle. Pulling back, she whispered, "No! Jack!"

Glaring at her, a stranger, he pointed fiercely downward, at the floor of his own room, rasping, "You weren't in *here*! You were in the bathroom. You're afraid to come out."

Then she caught his meaning at last, and allowed him to drag her into the darkness and through it to the bathroom, switching on the harsh fluorescents in there—a frightened backward look showed her the surface of her bed all puffed and torn, like a scale model of a mountain range—and then she was in the bathroom alone, the door shut, turning the lock with shaky fingers. She leaned against her robe hanging on the back of the door, its terry-cloth softness her only comfort.

Of *course* she couldn't have been in Jack's room. If Caesar's wife must be above suspicion, how much more must a staffer on the *Weekly Galaxy*. The follies and foibles they reported on must not be shown to exist in their own lives. If she were alive now only because she'd been in Jack's bed rather than her own, Massa would fire them both in the morning.

She could hear Jack out there, talking to someone he'd let into her room from the hall. "She isn't here," his voice said, sounding honestly puzzled. "Unless she's in the bathroom."

Another voice approached this door, saying, "Let's see. Miss Joslyn?" *Rap rap rap* against the door, vibrating against the cheek she'd pressed to her robe. "Are you in there?"

Jack's voice, awed, said, "Look at that bed. Somebody emptied a gun into it. Look, through the window here, fired right through the glass door."

The doorknob rattled. *Rap rap rap* came the knocking again. "Miss Joslyn? Are you all right?"

It was true. She *was* afraid to come out.

CHAPTER FIVE

After the police left, Mercer and Felicia looked at one another in wordless silence until yet another goddamn discreet tap at the suite door announced the return of Ferguson, the manager, behind a sad and apologetic smile. "I couldn't really keep the authorities out," he said.

"No, of course not," Mercer agreed, and gave the man a comradely pat on the arm. "I'm not blaming you, believe me I'm not. It's my own big mouth I blame, mostly."

Felicia, clearly troubled, said, "Johnny, nobody believes *you* shot at that person."

"I have been quoted, and not inaccurately," Mercer reminded her, "as having threatened the life and limb of *Galaxy* reporters before. As the cops just now pointed out."

"Nevertheless," Ferguson the manager said, "as Miss Nelson says, no one actually *believes* it was you."

"And nevertheless right back at you," Mercer told him, "the cops have just requested I not leave this goddamn island until they say it's okay."

"Oh, dear," Ferguson said. "And I imagine, at this point, you would very much like to leave."

"You're damn right I would. Nothing against your place here."

"Oh, I realize that. I know what the problem is." Looking past Mercer, out the living room's picture window, Ferguson said, "I see that yacht is still there."

"They won't give up," Mercer said grimly, not looking toward the damn yacht. "Which is only one of the fifteen or so reasons why I wouldn't actually take a gun to the sons of bitches. On the other hand, I can see why somebody else might, and I'll tell you the truth, I'm not that happy they missed."

"Johnny!"

Mercer patted the air in Felicia's direction. "This is just between us," he assured her. "These particular walls *don't* have ears."

"Well, as to that . . ." Ferguson said, delicately.

Mercer frowned at him. "As to what?"

"Unfortunately," Ferguson said, "so far this morning I have had to let two employees go. The maid who would have cleaned this suite was found to have come to work with a tape recorder, and one of the night girls on the switchboard offered one of the day girls five hundred dollars to record any phone calls either of you two might make."

"That's crazy!" Felicia said, staring at them both.

"You see?" Mercer said, with an angry shrug. "They don't give up."

"And the suborning of employees," Ferguson said, his lip curling a bit, "seems as natural to them as breathing. I feel confident of perhaps ninety-five percent of my people here, including the girl who refused to be bribed, but there's no doubt the *Galaxy* will find the other five percent. And if they don't, others will. I'm reliably informed that Green's Hotel has now filled up with members of the press."

"Locusts," Mercer said.

"Oh, Johnny," Felicia said faintly. "And we were going to have such a nice, quiet wedding."

"If I may make a suggestion," Ferguson said, and waited.

They both looked at him. "Go ahead," Mercer said. "Make it."

"I feel quite badly," Ferguson told them, "that I cannot guarantee the privacy and security you should have at Katama Bay. I wouldn't at all blame you for leaving."

"But the cops say we can't."

"You can't leave the island, at least not yet. But you could leave the hotel, much as I would consider that a personal defeat."

Mercer shook his head. "Leave the hotel? *This* is the most secure place on the island."

"Actually, it isn't," Ferguson said. "And this morning I took the liberty of phoning the person I thought might be able to help you, if she would. She has agreed. May I bring her in?"

Mercer and Felicia looked at one another, then back at Ferguson. Mercer said, "You've got somebody outside there? Sure, bring her in."

"Thank you." Ferguson turned toward the door, then looked back to say, "Let me explain first, she is not exactly au courant on current affairs. I don't believe she even has a television set. She has no idea who you are, except a nice young couple I've vouched for, who merely want a simple private marriage and are being hounded by the gutter press."

"Won't know who I am, eh?" Mercer said, with a half-disbelieving smile. "Well, that ought to be a breath of fresh air. Bring her on in."

* * *

Sara was still scared. *Could* it have been some goon hired by John Michael Mercer? Shades of Keely Jones and the shotgunning of the sound truck! But that had been the passion of the moment, and the destruction was aimed at property, not at lives. And in any event, why would John Michael Mercer pick on *her* in particular? It didn't make any sense.

But if the attack didn't have anything to do with Mercer, what did it have to do with? Someone had come around to the back of the inn at three in the morning, had come to the glass doors leading to the ground-floor terrace off Sara's room, had aimed through the glass and the closed curtains—she'd never drawn the heavy opaque drapes in there last night—and had emptied some sort of handgun into the bed she was supposed at that moment to be asleep in.

Was it meant to be a warning, made by somebody who knew the bed was empty? But how could anyone have been sure she wasn't asleep there? The room was dark, the curtains not easy to see through. And *what* warning would it have been, anyway, and from whom?

Somebody tried to kill me, Sara thought, unable to concentrate on anything else, unable to even think about the activity swirling all around her here in the Oak Bluffs command center. Jack, galvanized by the thought of Boy Cartwright coming up to take over this campaign with a new and different concept of the lead story, was madly still trying to make the initial concept fly. If there was anything to be done to save the situation, Jack would do it.

So. All day today, the Mercer suite at Katama Bay Country Club was being buried beneath a cornucopia of largesse, an amplitude of gifts; every red rose from every florist on the island, cases of champagne, original watercolors by local artists, the finest fishing equipment. The hotel, clearly at Mercer's orders, was intercepting every gift and turning it away before Mercer even got to see it, but

Jack continued anyway, manic, driven, feeling the dusky wings of Boy Cartwright on the back of his neck.

And that wasn't all. Every employee of Katama Bay Country Club was being researched, all the way back to high school and all the way out to first cousins; where there were handles, they would be grasped. The Down Under Trio, gray-faced and red-eyed but game as ever, continued to hold forth in the Nineteenth Hole at Green's Hotel. The *Princess Pat,* bearing its load of telephoto-lensed photographers, continued in the offing beyond Katama Bay. Sophisticated long-range microphones purchased some time ago from a disaffected CIA ex-agent and just expressed up from Florida were being beamed at the Mercer suite from every possible direction and were recording nothing but the cricker and ghee of insects, punctuated by the occasional slamming of a telephone.

And through it all Sara sat, haunted, hunted, hunched, thinking only about the eight bullets that had fluffed her bed into the soft-sculpture equivalent of a psychotic interlude. Who had done it? Why? What would they do next?

There was no reason why she should think of the dead man beside the road, nearly four weeks ago, fifteen hundred miles away in Florida. So she didn't.

* * *

"We really appreciate this, Lady Beatrice," John Michael Mercer said, while Felicia clung to his arm and beamed in delight on their benefactor, and Ferguson the hotel manager stood to one side washing his hands together and smiling on one and all like a lesser saint on a good day.

"Think nothing of it," Lady Beatrice said, with an accent Mercer and Felicia recognized as English, but which any normal class-conscious Brit would have known right away was certainly county, definitely landed, and probably from within thirty miles of Banbury. A gnarled and ageless ancient in an outdated but excellent riding habit, Lady Beatrice appeared to have been fashioned long ago out of fine old leather, well oiled and still sound. "My late husband," she went on, "General Sir Eustace Romneysholme, Earl of Romney, believed all journalists should be horsewhipped on sight."

"Your late husband and I would have got along, ma'am," Mercer told her, unconsciously countering her British accent by becoming more Western than he had ever been.

"My late husband," Lady Beatrice said, her agate eyes glinting, "used to say there were three extraneous classes of life on this planet: tsetse flies, male ballet dancers and journalists. An enemy of any of those three is a true friend of mine."

"Lady Beatrice," Felicia said, "this is really the nicest thing that ever happened. I was so unhappy before you came in."

"I too have had romance in my life, young lady," Lady Beatrice told her. "How could I stand by and see it spoiled? Of course I have to take you into my heart, and my home."

"If we're puttin' you out, ma'am—"

"Nonsense," Lady Beatrice told him. "If you were putting me out, Mr. Murphy, I wouldn't—"

"Mercer," Mercer said gently, with a little pained smile.

"Mercer, then," she agreed impatiently. "And if you were putting me out, I wouldn't permit you to. It's as simple as that. Now clearly, however unfortunate it may be, your original thought of a church wedding here is just not on, so of course we'll have the wedding at my home."

"But—" Mercer said.

Felicia said, "Lady Beatrice, we have *one hundred* people coming!"

"Well, no, they can't all stay the night," Lady Beatrice agreed. "Possibly, with doubling up, we could house perhaps half of them, but the others would have to make their own arrangements. You'll give me your A and B lists." A sudden and surprisingly girlish smile creased her morocco-bound face. "It will be just like house parties in the old days," she said, a lilt in her voice.

Gently, Ferguson explained, "Lady Beatrice's home, Romney Hall, is, uh, rather extensive."

"I guess it must be," Mercer said, looking more carefully at this dotty old lady.

"We shall maintain security," the dotty old lady said, rubbing her shagreen hands together in plotter's satisfaction, "by not informing your guests of the change in plans until the very last moment. Once they've arrived on the island, we'll redirect them to the site of the happy occasion."

"Yeah, but right there's the snag," Mercer said, grimacing and shaking his head and automatically looking out at the damn yacht in the damn offing, even though he'd *sworn* to himself he would never look at that ship or acknowledge its presence ever again. "The press is all over this island like maggots on a dead horse," he said. "Any move I make, they'll know it in a second."

"Ah, but we are prepared for these maggots," Lady Beatrice said, and smiled with approval on Mercer, saying, "How my late husband would have enjoyed you. He too had a colorful way with a phrase."

Ferguson said, "We have a van without side windows that we use for picking up supplies at the airport. We can get you into that, with your luggage, absolutely unseen. On your way toward the airport, the van will turn off on Pohoganut Road as though the driver had to—excuse me, Lady Beatrice—relieve himself. One of Lady Beatrice's limousines will be there to pick you up."

"The one with the side curtains and the little venetian blinds in back," Lady Beatrice added.

"By the time the press finds out where you are," Ferguson assured them, "you will be man and wife. And may you have long years of happiness, contentment and privacy."

"Hear hear," Lady Beatrice said.

* * *

"Gone?" Jack cried, like a mortally wounded yak. *"Gone?* They can't be gone!"

It had been Don Grove's sad task to bring this unhappy news to command center late that afternoon, a duty that did nothing to lift his normal cloud of pessimism. "They're gone," he repeated. "Disappeared without a trace. The manager had a lot of fun with it, let me know the *Galaxy* could rent that suite for as long as we want. Eleven hundred dollars a day."

"You took it, of course," Jack said.

"Sure I took it," Don agreed. "But they won't let me in until the maid's done. Really *done.* I don't suppose she'll leave anything."

Ida and Sara, the latter still looking mostly like a trauma victim, came over to the scene of the disturbance, Ida saying, "What's up?"

"The love birds have flown," Jack explained, with bottomless bitterness.

"Impossible," Ida said. "We're all over them like acne. We've got stringers hanging from their ears."

Sara's attention, too, had been fairly caught, for the first time today. "Gone?" she echoed. "Gone where?"

"That is the question, all right," Jack agreed.

"Gosh," Sara said. "They wouldn't try to leave the island, would they?"

"Leave?" Jack stared madly around the command center. "Leave Martha's Vineyard? You mean, when the love birds fly, they *fly?*"

"There's no more flights out today," Ida said.

"There's such a thing as charter," Jack answered, and pointed a trembling finger at Don. "Go you to the airport," he started.

Don frowned. "What about the suite?"

"Ida can do that. She's the best searcher in the business. You go to the airport, you hire every charter pilot they got, you put everybody on standby. Nobody flies tonight."

Don managed to nod and shake his head at the same time, as he said, "What am I hiring them for?"

"Potential emergency. We have this small sick child here."

Sara, coming fully back to life at last, said, *"All* the pilots?"

"A class," Jack decided. "The whole first grade has this mystery illness."

"Doctors are baffled," Ida suggested.

"Aren't we all," Jack agreed. "Go," he told Don.

Don, the true centurion's underling, went. Jack turned to Sara and Ida, saying, "Now, we have to find those two."

"That son of a bitch," Ida said, low and angry. "Running out on us. Who is he without us, anyway?"

"That's right," Sara said, as fierce in her own way as Ida. Jack stared at her in ambivalent surprise—did he want Sara to *become* Ida? What a thought!—as the girl shook her fist and declared, "What do people like John Michael Mercer have, except their celebrity?"

"That's right," Ida said, glaring at Sara in aggressive solidarity.

"And where do they *get* their celebrity?" Sara demanded.

"From *us*!" Ida snapped.

"That's right!" Sara cried, in full voice. "When they want publicity, we give it to them. And when *we* want, *they've* got to give!"

Finding this new fierceness—not that new, actually—of Sara's both encouraging and disturbing, Jack said, "Sara, my darling, I can hardly wait for you to get the opportunity to make that point to John Michael Mercer face-to-face. But before that happy event can occur—"

He broke off to glance at the door, and in came Boy Cartwright, pasty and unhealthy and diseased and smiling. Gazing around command center, "Charming little hovel," he said.

I'll have to get along with this toad, Jack reminded himself. "Hello, Boy," he said. "Welcome to Martha's Vineyard."

"Ah, Jack," Boy said, with his puffy squidlike smile. "How's the old interview coming along?"

I'll have to tell him we've lost Mercer, Jack thought, and listened to hear how he'd phrase it, but all he heard from himself was silence.

Ida, who would not stay in the same room with Boy Cartwright if she could avoid it, turned away, saying to Jack, "I'll go check the suite."

"Good."

"No more long faces," Boy announced. From the laziness of his eyes, he must be taking Valium by the bottle these days. "We'll all have to be much jollier, now that I'm aboard."

"And where's Paul Revere," Ida was heard to mutter, on her way out, "now that we need him?"

Chapter Six

A fierceness held Sara like a sheathing of blue flame, warming and protecting her, as she made phone call after phone call. "This is Henrietta Nelson," she would say, a quaver in her voice. "Is my niece Felicia there? Her mother has been taken suddenly ill. No? Oh, dear. If we don't find poor Felicia in time"—a little break in the voice at that point—"I'll never forgive myself."

The calls ranged far and wide across the island, from East Beach to Lobsterville, from Scrubby Neck to West Chop. Mercer and his bride were in no hotel on the island, but they were definitely still *somewhere* on the island—the wedding guests were still scheduled to be here for tomorrow's ceremony—so that meant they had to have gone to ground in someone's private residence. Home owners and home renters and house sitters, beginning with showbiz people Mercer knew or had worked with, spreading to showbiz people Mercer *might* know, spreading to anyone with any sort of celebrity at all or any sort of potential connection with Mercer at all, every one of them was being approached by Sara on the phone. And at the same time, the same list was also being investigated by various of the New England stringers by foot and in cars—selling magazine subscriptions, reading meters, *anything*—and by a couple of photographers by air, via charter pilots already on the *Galaxy* payroll.

Sara's fear, following last night's attack, had paralyzed her all day long, but had disappeared like smoke with the news of Mercer's disappearance. Rage can be stronger than fear, and Sara's rage at John Michael Mercer was now both wide ranging and intense. She was furious at him for complicating the already complicated life of Jack Ingersoll. She was indignant with him for causing the descent into their midst of Boy Cartwright. And she was wrathful at the son of a bitch for *not playing the game*. Just who did he think he was?

We're quicker than you are, John Michael Mercer, Sara thought, as she dialed her numbers and told and told her story. We're tougher than you are, we're meaner than you are, we're more determined than you are, and we *do not give up*.

"This in Henrietta Nelson . . ."

* * *

The Mercer suite was clean. Just to make absolutely certain that no clues had been inadvertently left behind, the maid had gone so far as to remove notepads, matchbooks, room service menu, magazines, TV listing sheet and all other such materials from the suite and replace them with brand-new. The medicine chests in both bathrooms smelled of Lysol. When Ida lifted the carpet in the living room, she saw that the maid had already done so. When she lifted the mattresses on the beds, the maid had been there first as well. When she took the drawers out of the dressers, to see if perhaps something had fallen down inside, she smelled Pledge; the maid had done this, too.

There was nothing here, that's all, nothing to be seen but the empty gesture of the *Princess Pat*, the yacht still pointlessly floating offshore, centered in the picture window. Giving that useless tub a cold look, Ida left the suite, wandered the curving brick paths in the late afternoon air, and finally saw ahead of her a wheeled maid's cart, piled high with tissue boxes and soap. It stood in front of another small shingled separate structure, another cabana suite like Mercer's.

The maid, busily at work in the sitting room, was short, skinny, bony-faced, pale-skinned, gray-haired and fiftyish; no doubt the wife or widow of a fisherman, daughter of fishermen, member of a longtime family along these waters, proud and poor and dismissive of the rich summer people who had taken over their world. Ida, who quite naturally looked more like this maid than like the rich summer people, entered this suite and said, "Hi."

The maid looked at her, a flat and waiting look, not yet suspicious. "Yes, ma'am?"

"Did you clean the Mercer suite?"

Now the expression *was* suspicious. "Yes, ma'am."

Ida extended toward her a folded green bill, saying, "You dropped this."

"Oh, no, ma'am," the maid said, calm and positive in her competence. "I couldn't have."

"Well, it was there," Ida said, brisk and impatient. "Do *I* look as though I need a dollar? I work for the *Weekly Galaxy*, they pay me plenty. A lot more than my sister, she's a waitress. Here, make sure."

The maid doubtfully took the bill, which Ida had folded so that all the numbers were inside, and so that the bill was already in the maid's hands when she opened it and saw those repeated digits: 100. "Oh, *no*, ma'am," she said, almost in a panic, trying to push the bill back into Ida's hands. "This isn't mine!"

Ida backed away, lifting her hands as though the bill scared her, too. "That's a hundred!" she cried. "It isn't *mine!* We're in enough trouble with the management here, I don't want anybody saying I took money."

"But—" The maid looked at the hundred-dollar bill in her hand, looked hopelessly around the room as though for a place where she could safely put it down, then looked back at Ida. "I don't know what to do," she confessed.

"I tell you what," Ida said. "Maybe it was dropped by whoever was here with the Mercers just before they left. If I leave it with you, you could pass it on to— Who would that be?"

The maid looked keenly at Ida. The bill crackled in her fingers.

* * *

"Lady Beatrice Romneysholme," Ida announced, her mouth curling around the syllables of the name. "Widow of an army general known as the Dunce of Dunkirk."

Jack frowned. "I thought Dunkirk was a success."

"A successful retreat," Ida pointed out. "He made it necessary. The British press gave him the horse laugh the rest of his life, so naturally the widow hates reporters."

Jack nodded, sad but noble. "They always blame the messenger," he said.

"Sure," Ida agreed. "Lady Bee has kind of a castle over on the west side of the island. Up on a bluff over the water. Very tough to get into."

"Servants?"

"Old retainers," Ida said. "Been with her since Magna Carta."

"I look ahead of me," Jack said, "and I see oblivion."

Boy, with his dreamy infected smile, floated over to say, "I understand the happy couple have been rediscovered."

"You're quick, Boy," Jack told him. "You've got what I call a nose for news."

Ida studied her nails. They were long and sharp.

"They're with a compatriot of mine, I understand," Boy went on.

"In a manner of speaking," Jack agreed.

"I suppose, really," Boy said, "one ought to drop in on dear old Lady Beatrice."

"That's a great idea, Boy," Jack said.

"I'm sure we'll get along famously," Boy said, drifting toward the door. "Ta."

Jack watched him leave. Slowly, a smile overlaid the lineaments of despair on his features. "Now, why," he asked, "do I find myself feeling this unreasonable sense of happiness?"

* * *

Amid that mix of New England fishing village, undeveloped sand dune and elegantly rustic architected homes of the rich and famous which combine to give Martha's Vineyard its aura and ambiance, a kind of Frankenstein castle rose on a bluff overlooking the western shoreline, a tall building of stone and stucco and shingle, surrounded by well-tended and well-watered greensward, neatly placed ornamental trees, smooth stone patios and a croquet field, all enclosed by a thick stone wall, with a grand stone gatehouse at the only entrance, and a gravel drive curving in and up to the fieldstone portico at the broad front door.

Inside, Romney Hall was furnished in great part from the original Romney Hall, a similarly sprawling stone structure beside the Thames near Wallingford. When, after the war, Romney Hall was given to the National Trust as part of some sort of complex tax deal, and when for a variety of reasons it had seemed best for the Romneysholmes to remove themselves from England, this furniture, these carpets, these paintings and sconces and tea sets, all made the move as well, first for a brief, mistaken, unfortunate stay in Bermuda—Little England, indeed!—and then on here to Martha's Vineyard, where people's memories were blessedly shorter and the weather wasn't so boringly perfect all the time. "Hate to be in a place where only man is vile," the General used to say, on the cold bleak days of winter, standing on his bluff overlooking the sea, with the sharp icy wind and the stinging salt spray in his face.

Since the General's demise—Lady Beatrice found herself at times saying he'd "been put down," as though he were one of his own dogs, or a case of his favorite vintage port—Lady Beatrice had sometimes considered a return to the old country, but when she read the news in her airmail edition of the *Times* and saw what her countrymen looked upon as a "conservative" these days, the decision to go back just kept being postponed. And so she stayed, and the old family retainers stayed with her, and generally speaking she was content. And from time to time there were little events—

like this hounded young couple and their upcoming nuptials—which enlivened her landscape and put the roses back in her cheeks.

How sweet they were, as from her upstairs window she watched them stroll hand in hand across the lawns, he with his rugged good looks, she clearly a practical girl of the sort Lady Beatrice had always approved. Apparently Mr. Mercer was something in show business, but so many people on the Vineyard were, and in fact, at a certain level, there were any number of acceptable people in that area of endeavor. Sir Larry back home, for instance, and the Rossellini girl, and perhaps Mr. Reagan (though Lady Beatrice harbored the suspicion that Mr. Reagan was a climber). In any event, they had been so harried and unhappy and tense when she'd met them, and now look how relaxed and joyous they were, laughing together, strolling without a care in the world.

The phone near Lady Beatrice's elbow tinkled, the sound of an in-house call. Still gazing out at the lovebirds, she picked up the receiver and spoke: "Lady Beatrice here."

"It's Jakes, Mum."

Jakes was the man on duty at the gatehouse, the one whom traders and visitors and other callers had to get through, and whom no one got through if Jakes did not approve. "Yes, Jakes?"

"There's a *chap* here, Mum," Jakes said, with a faint but unmistakable edge of disapproval. "He'd like a word with you."

"What about?"

"Well, he says he's from a newspaper, Mum." Faint murmurings off: "He says he's from the *Weekly Galaxy*, Mum, it's a sort of servant-girl paper, all in color."

Lady Beatrice's eyes glinted. So the villainous press had traced the fair couple, had it? Well, it would not be permitted to destroy their happiness. "And the scamp," she said, "has the effrontery to come to my front *door*?"

"He asks if he can have a word with you, Mum."

"Put the villain on."

"Boy Cartwright here, Lady Beatrice," said the villain, and the instant she heard that glutinous voice, that style of Uriah Heep after assertiveness training, Lady Beatrice placed the fellow precisely and unerringly in his proper pew in the great English pecking order. A tradesman's son from somewhere like Bradford, a redbrick university dropout, the sort of fellow who in Manchester or Liverpool sells used cars to Pakis. "If I could have a bit of a chat, Lady B," this mongrel said, "I'd be most appreciative."

You've had your bit of a chat, my lad, Lady Beatrice thought, and said, "Put Jakes on."

"I beg your pardon?"

"That large strapping fellow there with you. Jakes. Put him on."

"Oh, of course, of course. See you in half a tick, then," the creature said, and Lady Beatrice heard him, away from the phone, say snottily to Jakes, "Your mistress has instructions for you."

"Mum?"

"That wide leather belt you usually wear, Jakes," Lady Beatrice said. "Are you wearing it today?"

"Yes, Mum."

"Then use it, man!"

Lady Beatrice hung up, and smiled out at the happy couple still strolling around the lawn, saying little private things to one another. To the right, the gravel road curved down and away. Almost out of sight through the ornamental trees was the gatehouse. All at once, from down there, came the sound as of someone crying out, "Woop!" And then again: "Woop! Woop! Woop!" The couple down below seemed not to hear it, and rapidly the *woops* receded into silence, and all was well.

Chapter Seven

Jack couldn't sleep. Usually, no matter what happened in the course of a day, no matter how much warthog dung was dumped on his head, it all sloughed away by beddy-byes, and he slept like an innocent babe; which just goes to show. But tonight, in the dark, with Sara's dear head on his breast and the sound of her slow respiration soothing to his ears, tonight for some reason he just couldn't seem to lose consciousness.

When in doubt, make a list. What's bugging the old brain, then, that it won't let go of Saturday?

Well, let's see. Outside this room, out there beyond the repaired glass doors and new curtains, a Massachusetts state trooper patrolled, or was alleged to patrol; with a second wandering the halls of the inn. No one could figure out why those shots had been fired into this room last night, so there was a general effort to keep more shots from being fired tonight. Had someone been trying to kill Sara, and if so, why? Had they been trying to kill someone else, and got their targets mixed? Had it just been a random shooting, without sense or meaning?

Hmm. Whatever the cause of the shooting, the *fact* of the shooting was item number one on Jack's list, and he studied it, turned it over and over, poked at it with his brain as his tongue might poke at an aching tooth. Is that why I can't sleep? Because somebody emptied a gun through that window into this bed last night?

No. Doesn't feel right. Not my problem, to begin with, plus we have police protection, plus the shooting didn't accomplish anything. So, no.

Boy Cartwright, then; item number two on the list. I am now in a subservient position to Boy Cartwright, my assignment to get an interview with John Michael Mercer having been superseded by Boy's assignment to get the wedding pictures. Is *that* why I can't sleep?

Certainly not. The worst day of his life, Boy Cartwright couldn't keep me awake for a second if I wanted to sleep. So, no.

The wedding itself, then, the whole problem of John Michael Mercer and his marriage and Martha's Vineyard and the very wild card of Lady Beatrice Romneysholme. Yes?

No. The job does not keep us awake. No.

In her sleep, Sara murmured slightly, sighed, shifted position, her palm warm on Jack's chest, her hair pleasantly tickling his chin.

Sara.

Yes.

Jack pondered that idea, found it surprising, found it discouraging, but reluctantly admitted he also found it plausible. The reason he couldn't sleep was because he was worried about Sara.

Not Sara being shot at. His worry was much sillier than that, much more ridiculous, too absurd even to look at straight ahead; which is why he'd been unable to think about it and deal with it and ignore it and go to sleep.

He was afraid Sara was getting too good at her job.

It had probably been happening from the very beginning, or at least from the time of the hundred-year-old twins, but it hadn't been out front and obvious until here in Martha's Vineyard, until Sara's reaction to frustration had been to get steadily tougher and tougher, stronger and stronger, more and more ruthless and determined. When Jack had seen her with Ida today, had seen how well the two women meshed, had seen how Sara was *becoming* Ida, something terrible had happened inside his brain, something awful, something he had thought himself safe from, something he had believed could never again get its clutches into him:

Ambiguity.

If Sara's getting better at her job, if she's becoming ever more useful, there's only the one reaction possible, isn't there? Pleasure. Satisfaction at the development of another powerful member of the team. So whence, damnit, this ambiguity, these doubts, this brooding inability to sleep?

With what trouble and difficulty Jack had rid himself of extraneous emotion several years ago he could barely stand to remember. A thoroughgoing romantic in college and beyond, slopping over with empathy and fellow-feeling, as naive as a CIA man at a rug sale, he had been hardened, *annealed,* by circumstances too harrowing to store in the memory banks, and since that time he had been safe.

It had been a conscious decision he had made, four years ago, to retire from the human race, to care about nothing, to become as self-sufficient as Uncas. He had chosen deliberately an environment where emotional attachments of every kind, from the greatest to the smallest, were literally impossible. It was not conceivable to *care for* one's fellow workers at the *Galaxy,* for instance. One amusedly pitied a Binx Radwell about as meaningfully as if he were a puppy with a thorn in its paw; one used an Ida Gavin and then washed one's hands; one rather relished a Boy Cartwright as so thoroughly *representing* the environment.

Equally, one could not become emotionally involved with the job. Not *this* job. Nor could one care about the pip-squeak transitory celebrities on whom they all lived their parasitic existence. Even the state of Florida helped; anyone who managed to sing the glorious rocks and rills of *that* sunny buttcan needed psychiatric care.

Too thoroughly a burnt-out case even to relish the romantic self-image of *being* a burnt-out case, Jack Ingersoll had retired to Florida and the *Weekly Galaxy* and the likes of Ida Gavin and Boy Cartwright to lick his wounds and care never again about anything at all. Not even possessions; his Spartan life not only gave him more money to put into blue-ribbon investments, the better to prepare for that inevitable day of involuntary retirement, it also kept him from falling—like puppy Binx—in love with *things.* He who has nothing has nothing to lose. And he who has nothing to lose has already won.

Unlike Sara. I don't want to care about her, he thought. I want to be pleased that she's getting better and better at the job. I want to be happy that I have a second mad dog on my team, nearly as good as Ida, and potentially even better. I want to be amused by the knowledge that she lied to me *in bed* about the hundred-year-old twins, and that I'll never be able to prove it. I cannot save myself because I do not want to save myself, and therefore I cannot save Sara, so I should merely find contentment in her transformation.

And what do I mean by *save,* anyway? That's pretty goddamn

melodramatic, isn't it? Sorry, buddy, I didn't notice the halo when you came in.

Thus Jack tried, with sardonic contempt, to whip himself back into shape. And lay in bed awake, Sara's head warm on his chest. And failed.

Chapter Eight

Gloomy Sunday. The morning of the Mercer-Nelson wedding dawned bright and sunny, with a light offshore breeze, temperature in the low sixties, expected to rise to the low seventies by nuptial hour at 1:00 P.M. In the Oak Bluffs command center of the *Weekly Galaxy*, crammed with Jack Ingersoll and his entire team, plus Boy Cartwright and the riffraff and scum of his group, plus assorted stringers and photographers and secretaries, the gloom was as palpable as a bad smell.

There were also actual bad smells, of course, which everyone was too depressed to complain about, some rising from Boy Cartwright's assorted vermin, but most emanating from the Down Under Trio, recalled at last from the trenches of Green's Hotel (where Phyllis Perkinson, representing *Trend*, had been among the happy distractees). It no longer mattered that the world's press was here; *Trend* or *Newsweek* would get as short shrift from Lady Beatrice Romneysholme as the *Weekly Galaxy*. (It was, in fact, a *New York Post* team, attempting a landing on Lady Beatrice's private beach via rowboat, who had been driven back into the sea with their legs and behinds riddled with birdshot by ancient but unerring marksmen on the household staff, thus ending any idea Jack might have had of trying the same stunt.)

And now, the final nail had been driven into the coffin of their hopes by the arrival of Ida with yet another bit of bad news. "I found out who's taking the wedding pix," she told Jack.

Boy, nearby, raised his head and looked mildly at her stony profile. "You'll want to talk to me, then, dear," he said.

Ida ignored him, continuing to look at Jack, who said, "Would this photographer be bribable?"

"I doubt it," Ida said. "Lady Beatrice is a rather well-known amateur photographer, it turns out."

Jack clutched his forehead. "Oh, don't do this to me."

"Not to you," Sara said. "To Boy."

"Thank you, dear," Boy said.

Still talking exclusively to Jack, Ida said, in a fake la-dee-da voice, "Her flower photos are in all the *best* magazines."

"Then I wouldn't have seen them," Jack said.

Bob Sangster, fondling his large nose, which had become quite a bit redder the last few days and possibly larger as well, smiled sadly and said, "Time for Ida to arrange another fire."

Ida gave him an icy look. "I didn't *arrange* the first one."

"Just a manner of speaking, love," Bob told her, but then retreated to another table, still within earshot.

Sara, looking alert, eager to learn, said, "What fire?"

"Nothing," Ida told her. "Doesn't matter."

"As a matter of fact," Jack said, "that was about the quickest thinking I've *ever* seen, and that's saying something."

"It sure is," Sara agreed. "Tell me about it."

"What's happening right now," Ida said, "is what we should be thinking about."

"Ida," Jack said, "what's happening right now is failure and defeat. Speaking for myself, I'd much rather think about a triumph of yesteryear than the rout of today." To Sara, he said, "It was a body in the box last year, George Hamler, I think, somebody famous who—"

Sara, frowning in bewilderment, said, "Body in the box?"

"That's right, you haven't been along on one of those, have you? That's a—"

"Tell her about the *fire,* man," Harry Razza said. "She's a bright girl, maybe it'll give her an idea."

"Right." Jack said, "It was a situation just like this. We couldn't get in, no matter what we tried, we just couldn't get that picture, and we *needed* it. We're all standing around outside, we had a Mayflower moving van down the street with our headquarters inside that, and all of a sudden there's a fire breaks out up in the main house. We barely hear the sirens and see the smoke when Ida's right *there* with a fireman's outfit. I put it on, I take the camera, I'm in with the first bunch of firemen running in, I get my picture, by then the cops were there—"

"By then," Harry Razza said, "the cops were checking the *firemen*, they were already on to the idea of the stunt."

"We only made it because Ida was so fast," Jack said. "She heard that siren, she saw that smoke, she was *there*."

"Then, when the old lady died," Harry Razza said, "we couldn't use the picture after all. Such is life."

Sara, bewildered, said, "Old lady died? Is that the body in the box?"

"No, no," Harry said, "his *mother.* She died in the fire."

Louis B. Urbiton raised his hoary and battle-scarred head from a nearby table. "Mother-in-law," he said, and subsided.

"Right you are," Harry told him. "Mother-in-law it was."

Don Grove said, "I don't suppose lightning'll strike that house, or anything nice like that."

"Well," Sara said slowly, "but what if there was a shipwreck? Washed ashore."

"No," Jack said. "Lady Bee is not your basic humanitarian type."

"If people are *drowning?*" Sara insisted.

"Lady Bee," Jack told her, "would turn the hose on them."

"Something else, then," Sara said, thinking hard. Jack, watching her think, tried not to be troubled, tried to be proud of this prodigy. "An airplane crash?" Sara thought aloud, and shook her head. "Maybe a quarantine? A terrible infectious disease, nobody allowed off the property until the health department gives everybody shots?"

"Medical science baffled," Jack suggested. "But Lady Bee would give the shots herself."

"There *has* to be a—" Sara started, but Boy interrupted, saying mildly, "Is this a light I see before me, flashing off and on?"

It was the light on the phone on Boy's desk. Everyone in the room watched him pick it up and speak into it, with calm self-assurance: "*Family Circle.*" Then he sat abruptly to attention, even the dead suety flesh of his cheeks seeming to stiffen. "Yes, Mr. DeMassi!" he announced, and *everybody* stiffened.

"Yes, Mr. DeMassi."

"No, Mr. DeMassi, I'm afraid not."

"Well, Mr. DeMassi, they do take our money. We have, I'm afraid, enriched several of Lady Beatrice's servants. However, having taken our money, they then refuse to honor our bargain. Instead, they run us off with shotguns and dogs."

"Absolutely, Mr. DeMassi, that is immoral and unethical behavior, but—"

"No, sir, the authorities in this area are absolutely no help at all."

"Well, sir, I've just managed to find out who's going to do the official wedding album—"

Ida looked daggers.

"—and I'm afraid there's no comfort there, either. Lady Beatrice herself is going to—"

"I'm afraid so, sir, yes. Yes, indeed."

Boy's eyes widened. He sat even straighter than before. The knuckles of the doughy hand holding the phone receiver to his leprous ear were seen to whiten. "Yes, sir!" he cried. "Yes, sir, we will! Absolutely, Mr. DeMassi! Thank you, sir!"

Boy hung up. Greasy globules of perspiration stood on the fishbelly flesh of his forehead. He stared about at all the people staring at him. "Well, well," he said in a kind of awe.

"Well?" demanded Jack. "What did he say?"

"He said—" Boy cleared his throat. A nervous smile flickered spastically across his face. "Massa said— Mr. DeMassi said— He said . . . *storm the wedding!*"

Chapter Nine

"The bride on her wedding day," Lady Beatrice said firmly, "must not see her intended until the actual moment of the ceremony."

John Michael Mercer humbly accepted this pronouncement. "I left my tie in there, is all," he said.

"A servant will get it for you." Lady Beatrice patted Mercer's arm, to get him walking away from the door to the chamber in which—Lady Beatrice was not *entirely* unworldly—the bride and her intended had spent the prenuptial night. As they walked down the sunlit corridor she said, "I understand you're nervous."

"Yeah, I am." Mercer seemed surprised by the idea. "Not much has scared me in my life, Lady Beatrice," he said, as they walked along, "and I don't say that to be boastful. It's just the truth. I guess I have a high imagination threshold or something. But *this*. This is different."

They came to the end of the corridor, where a broad window overlooked the south lawn and the sea. A great gleaming green and white striped tent had been erected there, full of white chairs and round white tables on a carpet of green Astroturf to protect the real lawn. Green and white pennons fluttered in the breeze from the peak of the tent and from poles flanking its four broad entranceways. Long tables extended in an L from two corners of the tent, suggesting an enclosure without confinement. White linen cloths were spread on the tables, their hems swaying in the breeze, and at the moment down there Lady Beatrice's staff busily distributed dishes and cups and glasses and silver on those long white expanses. The food awaited in the caterer's trucks—Cadet Catering—parked down on the road, and when the time came, the household staff would carry everything in through the gatehouse and up the gravel road to the reception, saving the caterer's men from having to step on the property. (Galling for those three catering employees who had been suborned by the *Weekly Galaxy*.)

The early guests had already arrived, surprised and delighted, the men in lightweight jackets, the women in any number of fanciful costumes, all light and airy and flirting with the breeze. Old friends called cheerfully to one another across the lawns, their voices rising like birdsong in the clear air. Today, the civilians among them—the relatives of the bride and groom, the old friends from school days—looked as glamorous and beautiful and happy and eternally young as the showbiz folk.

A few of the guests had arrived in their own boats, which stood offshore in a cheerful gossipy little fleet, nodding companionably together, their own banners snapping in the breeze, their brightwork polished for the occasion, while their fresh-painted dinghies, having carried those guests ashore, now waited all in a row on the beach below the bluff, like a hitherto unknown Monet.

The whole panorama, spread out below them, was a scene from a medieval romance, and Lady Beatrice nodded at it in satisfaction. "This *is* different," she agreed. "Getting married is unlike anything else you will ever do."

"I guess it is."

"But do you know why it is?" Resting her hand on his arm, Lady Beatrice said, "It's because, for the first time in your life, you're taking another person seriously. And that means, for the first time, you're taking yourself seriously." Looking up at him, she saw the reminiscent grin that flickered on his lips, and she said, "You're remembering those other girls, aren't you?"

He looked guilty, sheepish, but nevertheless pleased with himself. "I guess I am," he said.

"*Do* think about them," she told him. "And remember, with them, you acted as though *you* were nothing but a toy."

"I did?" He thought about that, not totally pleased, but accepting it. "Maybe so," he said. "Maybe so."

"Today," she said, "you become a real boy."

He laughed, and said, "This is my first time, you know. Felicia's, too."

"Oh, I could see that." Lady Beatrice pointed a bony leathery finger at Mercer, saying, "And the last."

"We'll give it our best shot. I know that much." He looked out at the day, the tent, the people, the sea, the few small white clouds in the blue sky. "One thing," he said. "We're sure getting a great start for it."

* * *

In the dry-earth yard of Rudy's Riding Academy, near the inland border of Tisbury, Sara and Jack stood side by side, watching Don Grove pass by on top of a large black horse. The horse cantered a bit, made cheerful by activity and good weather, and Don bounced madly atop it, head dangerously flopping about. "I think," he cried, clutching to saddle, bridle, mane, his own knees, "I think this one's broken!"

"Maybe it's got a flat," Jack suggested.

All around them, other Galaxians were mounting up, with more or less success. Bob Sangster, smilingly at ease atop a big-chested roan, looked amazingly like a train robber, while Chauncey Chapperell, virtually crossing the ankles of his long legs beneath the belly of the modest gray he'd been assigned, looked more than ever like a transient from some other star cluster.

All in all, sixteen staffers and stringers had been dragooned into the *Galaxy* Dragoons. Hung about with cameras, dressed in bulky clothing meant to absorb falls, blows and birdshot, riding their steeds with lesser or greater grace, they looked mostly like the remnants of a defeated punitive expedition making its way back through the Khyber Pass. But when Sara was efficiently aboard a small and frisky pinto mare, she cantered over to where Jack sat stolidly atop a big chestnut gelding and said, with excited eyes, "Look at them! Our cavalry!"

"I see them," Jack agreed.

Sara seemed not to notice his lack of enthusiasm. "They won't get away from us this time!" she cried, with a fierce rallying wave of her arm.

"No, they won't," said Jack.

* * *

The *Galaxy* attack was three-pronged, being by land, by sea and by air. While those with the slightest pretense to equitation formed their posse in Rudy's Riding Academy, a group led by Boy Cartwright and featuring Louis B. Urbiton and Harry Razza and every other Galaxian who could be made to look reasonably appropriate in formal wear (or who could simply *not* be safely placed atop a moving animal) had been garbed in formal wear and ferried out to the *Princess Pat,* waiting now in Vineyard Haven Harbor. As the nuptial hour neared, the *Princess Pat* would ease on down the roads, past West Chop and Lake Tashmoo and Makonikey Head and Lambert's Cove and so on down the coastline to slip itself as unobtrusively as possible in among the ships already in attendance below Lady Beatrice's castle. If the plan worked, these uninvited guests would slide ashore and mingle, snapping surreptitious pix with the tiny cameras concealed on their persons.

At the same time, Ida Gavin was boarding the helicopter at the airport, at the head of a troop of photographers augmented by several freelancers borrowed for the moment from other segments of the press currently on the island. It was a big transporter helicopter, with side doors that opened wide, and half a dozen photographers would be able to shoot at once from each side of the ship, some lying prone, some kneeling above them, some leaning out from the corners of the openings.

By land, by sea and by air. One way or another, Massa would get his wedding album.

Chapter Ten

The wedding began beautifully. The Reverend Alfred Wimms Hookey, a bit bewildered by the change in venue, and privately feeling just the teeniest bit guilty at having agreed to speak to those newspaper people, nevertheless represented in excellent fashion both the local and the transcendent authorities whose invocation and approval were at the heart of the ceremony. The bride was so beautiful, so ethereal, so radiant and so nearly translucent one looked behind her for wings, and the groom had become for today a true gentle giant, courtly but strong. The guests, the weather, the setting, all rose to the occasion, and Lady Beatrice, in lavender lace, moved through it all like Tinkerbell's grandmother, discreet camera ever snapping and snapping and snapping.

The *Princess Pat* eased in among the waiting yachts. Well-dressed but indefinably scruffy people started over its offshore side, out of sight of the wedding guests on the bluff, clambering down into the *Princess Pat*'s two small motor-driven dinghies.

Jakes, with two of his mates down in the gatehouse, looked out past the caterer's vans and the caterer's men and on down the road. "Looks like horses coming," he said.

"Dearly beloved," the Reverend Alfred Wimms Hookey began, and the rest of his opening statement became increasingly hard to hear as a hum began somewhere eastward, rapidly increased to a *roar*, and proved, when the startled bride and groom and reverend and guests all looked upward, to be a huge black helicopter, with many mechanical faces dangling from it on both sides.

"Go on!" Lady Beatrice cried to the reverend, waving her camera at him. "Go on! Go on! Speak up, and get on with it!" And, while Reverend Hookey shakenly nodded and tried to recapture his equilibrium and his place in the proceedings, Lady Beatrice called to one of the servants waiting back by the tables, "Benson! *Stop* that thing!"

"Mum!" cried Benson, with a kind of salute, and he moved off at a run for the castle.

Offshore, crew members of one of the waiting yachts, people who had chosen to stay aboard and take care of some necessary maintenance during the actual ceremony, looked out and saw the two dinghies rounding the prow of the *Princess Pat*, headed toward shore. "What the fuck's *that*?" one of them asked, and another answered, "Reporters!"

Don Grove, having fallen twice from his steed in the early going and having become determined to make up for those lapses once he'd figured out how to stay on top of the goddamn hairy creature, was the first Galaxian to gallop through the entrance beside the gatehouse, and so was the one to discover the rope Jakes and his mates had just put across there, higher than a horse's head but not higher than a man's torso. While Don, suddenly alone up there, did a number of interesting and seemingly impossible things in midair, his mount hurried on to the party without him.

In his efforts to stop from following Don into disaster, Bob Sangster so confused and bedeviled both himself *and* his horse that the beast stopped dead, turned on a dime, and went back where it had come from while Bob sailed over its head and continued on through the gatehouse entrance alone, traveling several feet over Lady Beatrice's property before touching any of it; with, as it happened, his nose.

Forced to bellow over the howl of the helicopter, now hovering directly above the wedding group, its rotors creating too strong a wind for comfort down below, Reverend Hookey did his best to inform the assembled guests just why they had all been gathered here.

"Over the wall!" shouted Jack to the surviving members of his cavalry. Caught up in the action, forgetting his recent doubts, free for now of the curse of ambiguity that had descended upon him, he spurred his gelding on and jumped a horse over a wall for the first time in his life, thereby learning why it's generally considered a difficult thing to do. While the gelding trotted on up the slope without him, Jack rolled to the booted feet of Jakes, who looked down on him without kindliness.

The wind of the helicopter rotors tore off ladies' hats, strained the moorings of the tent, knocked over pennons and flipped from one of the tables its load of linen cloth and china dinnerware, while the roar of its engine caused the wedding guests to cower and hunch as though beaten by giant cat-o'-nine-tails. Tears started in Felicia's eyes as her veil was ripped from her head, but Mercer held her close and Reverend Hookey kept shrieking out the words of the service.

The dinghies of the *Princess Pat* all at once found themselves amid a swirl of boats. Fast boats roared at them and then, at the last possible instant, veered off, slewing away, creating great wakes that threatened to swamp them. Larger boats bore down, forcing them to turn away from shore. "Avast!" cried the *Princess Pat* crew members steering the dinghies. "Belay!" they cried, and other nautical terms, none of which did any good. The dinghies shipped water. The Galaxians' feet got wet.

Jack's cavalry, unhorsed, fled before Jakes and his club-brandishing mates, and fled even faster before Jakes's fang-brandishing dogs. Jack and Sara, on the property but on foot, scampered up the slope from the gatehouse, not directly toward the castle—there were too many defenders in that direction—but at an angle that would lead them through ornamental trees up toward the clearing inland of the house and just higher, overlooking the entire wedding scene.

Benson extended an over-and-under shotgun from an attic window, *boomed* twice, and turned the helicopter's windshield into an opaque shower curtain. The startled pilot, leaning out to look around this sudden expanse of pebbled glass, caught a glimpse of Benson rapidly reloading, and cried, "*Oh*, no! No more wars for me!" He swung the stick, and the helicopter veered up and away, with many a shriek from his photographer cargo.

One dinghy made it back to the *Princess Pat*. The other sank, in seven feet of water. Those from the swamped dinghy who swam back to their home yacht were not further bothered, while those who swam for shore were intercepted, hooked out of the water, thrashed severely, and dumped back into the sea next to their yacht.

Ida screamed at the helicopter pilot to return to the wedding, but he flatly refused. Navigating by keeping his head outside in his own wind, he ran up the coast till he came to a bit of flat empty beach, where he set down and ordered everybody off his ship. "Make me," Ida said, with an icy glare. He considered that idea, shrugged, said, "You fly the fucker, then," deplaned, and went slogging off through the sand, while a dozen cameras clicked away behind him, recording the moment.

"We have to get through!" Sara cried, totally committed to this quest. Panting in desperation, she struggled upslope past the ornamental trees, Jack hurrying in her wake, the both of them forced again and again to turn aside, every time they tried to move closer to the wedding party, by stalking retainers armed with shotguns and large sticks.

"I do!" announced John Michael Mercer, in a loud and ringing voice, no longer overpowered by the roar from above.

On the slope inland from the house, Sara slipped and almost fell, but Jack grabbed her around the waist. Holding her, he looked down at the wedding party. "Look," he said.

The air attack had been routed. The naval invasion had been driven back into the sea. The cavalry had been unhorsed, muddied, cudgeled and bitten, and now riderless horses grazed peacefully here and there in the middle distance, adding to the bucolic beauty of the scene, while their former riders continued to leg it back across open country toward North Road.

"I do!" said Felicia Mercer, née Nelson, smiling through her tears.

"I see them," snarled Sara, answering Jack, staring down at the couple hand in hand before the minister. The bride was disheveled, her veil and train torn, her bridesmaids all in a heap like a pile of discarded bouquets, the wedding guests stunned and tattered, the reception tables upended, tent listing, Astroturf torn and bleeding mud. Sara glared, breast heaving, eyes still flashing with the heat of the battle. "They beat us, the bastards!" she cried.

John Michael Mercer kissed his bride. The wedding guests cheered.

Jack felt Sara's tense body quiver within the curve of his arm. "Bastards," she muttered. "Bastards. Bastards."

Chapter Eleven

Oh, somewhere in this favored land the sun is shining bright. The band is playing somewhere, and somewhere hearts are light. And somewhere men are laughing and little children shout. But there is no joy in the Oak Bluffs command center on Monday morning; the *Weekly Galaxy* has struck out.

Boy, who had been beaten soundly twice yesterday afternoon by the large, bluff, hearty, healthy crew of a ship called *Big Daddy*, once for trying to swim to shore after his dinghy sank and the other for protesting this treatment in an English accent, sat at his table in the command center sullen and silent and more puffy-faced than ever, while his lieutenants and Jack's disheartened team kept bringing in further gobbets of bad news. The helicopter had been traced to the *Galaxy*, and several lawsuits were being threatened. An ex-telephone receptionist employee of the Katama Bay Country Club had gone to the police with a story of blackmail and intimidation on the part of a *Galaxy* staffer which was unfortunately supported by a tape recording surreptitiously made by the little bitch. And, in the confusion and disorganization of yesterday's rout, they'd lost the Mercers, who had apparently been spirited away on one of those damn ships anchored offshore. They could be anywhere in the world by now, and no one the wiser.

The *Galaxy* had nothing. The *Galaxy* could not produce one word, one picture, one *inference* about the John Michael Mercer wedding that a reader couldn't find just as easily in *Time* or *People* or even the goddamn *New York Times*!

In the general gloom of last night, Jack had been a solitary mourner, lamenting a tragedy other than that being bewailed all around him. It wasn't the loss of Sara's innocence, such as it had been, that so touched him with melancholy, but the loss of his own corruption. How *pure* Sara's fury had burned, as she had stared down at the bedraggled wedding party, and how weak had been his own yielding to shame and pity. What did John Michael Mercer care about Jack Ingersoll, eh? Eh? Keep *that* in mind, can't you?

He can't. He couldn't. That the Mercer marriage was trivial and unimportant in itself didn't bother him, since he'd accepted that idea from the beginning. But that there might still be in this life, and on this earth, things that *did* matter, that *were* important, was disturbing and deeply unsettling. Have I become spoiled for this job, he wondered? And if the answer was yes, he was in serious trouble, because he was already spoiled for everything else.

Late last night, rash with drink, he had tried to broach these thoughts to Sara, but every reminder of the Mercer nuptials just set her raging again, so much so that fortunately she never did hear what it was Jack had been trying to say. She was already up and gone when he'd rolled, sodden and remorseful, from the sack late this morning, and he hadn't yet seen her today, but he was pretty sure she hadn't noticed last night his separate reasons for despondency.

The light flashed on the phone on Boy's table. He looked at it as though it were hemlock. It flashed again. Everybody in the room looked at it, as though it were Alfred Hitchcock's glass of milk. It flashed again. Amid a general sigh, as of the sound of the unshriven departed moving through the upper branches just before sunrise, Boy picked up the receiver and said, with simple unwonted honesty, "Boy Cartwright here."

"Yes, Mr. DeMassi."

Another general sigh.

"No, Mr. DeMassi, I'm afraid we—"

"We tried, Mr. DeMassi, we—"

"Yes, sir, we did try that. And a helicopter."

Sara's voice, loud and confident, grabbed everyone's attention: "Just a minute."

Jack gaped at her. Everybody gaped at her. She marched in from the front door, head held high, eyes clear, tread firm. Calling to Boy, she said, "Is that Mr. DeMassi?"

Boy, too stunned to do otherwise, nodded. Other people murmured confirmation and tried to hush her, but Sara marched by them all. "Let me speak to him," she said, and on her way by she dropped a bulky envelope on the table in front of Jack. It was white, with blue and orange sections.

Boy stared, unable to believe it. *Reporters* don't talk to Massa, not directly, not unless Massa initiates the conversation. Reporters do not interrupt conversations between Massa and *editors*. Reporters do not make their presence felt in any way when Massa is in conversation with an editor other than their own. Sara was violating so many conventions that when she reached out and plucked the phone receiver from Boy's nerveless hand, he didn't even make an attempt to stop her.

"Mr. DeMassi? Mr. DeMassi, this is Sara Joslyn, a reporter on Jack Ingersoll's team."

Jack pressed a hand to his hot dry forehead.

"Yes, sir, that's what I want to tell you. I have just this minute given to *my* editor, to Jack Ingersoll, the official wedding album of the John Michael Mercer marriage."

Jack stared at the envelope. He tore it open.

"Yes, sir, Mr. DeMassi, the photos taken by Lady Beatrice Romneysholme. We may have to negotiate with her, but *we* have the pictures, so it shouldn't be impossible."

Onto Jack's table, out of the envelope, spilled four black plastic film containers with gray plastic caps. Inside each was a roll of 35mm film.

"Yes, sir, Jack Ingersoll has the film now. He'll be bringing it back to Florida with him. Thank *you*, Mr. DeMassi." She extended the phone toward Boy: "He wants to talk to you again."

As Boy began to stutter and whimper into the phone, Sara crossed to Jack, smiling, nodding, accepting the silent signals of congratulation and joy from her co-workers. Jack whispered, almost afraid to hear the answer, "What did you *do?* How did you—"

"It was easy," she said. She was a good three inches taller than yesterday. "Lady Bee's an amateur photographer. Where do amateur photographers get their film developed? At the drugstore."

Jack gazed at the torn white-orange-blue envelope on his desk.

"So I waited for her this morning," Sara went on, "and I followed her when she was driven away from her house in one of her limos, and I watched which drugstore in Edgartown she went into, and twenty minutes later I went in and said I was there from the lab to make the film pickup."

"Sara," Jack said, and stopped, at a loss for words. He shook his head in wonder.

"Oh, Jack," called Boy, looking more and more like something that should have been given decent burial a week ago, "Jack, Mr. DeMassi would have a word with you."

Jack blundered to his feet, painfully bumping a knee and sending the film containers rolling. Sara slapped a hand over them, and Jack limped quickly across the room to take the phone from Boy's decaying hand. "Yes, Mr. DeMassi?"

Jack smiled modestly. "Thank you, Mr. DeMassi, but you know me. I think my whole team's special."

Jack's eyes shone. "*Thank* you, Mr. DeMassi! Yes, sir. Yes, sir." Grabbing a pen from Boy's jacket pocket, a piece of paper from under Boy's elbow, Jack made quick notes. "Yes, sir. Right away. Thank *you*, Mr. DeMassi."

Jack hung up. He turned his back on the moldering Boy, and smiled upon his team. "We have been given our reward," he said.

"Yes? Yes?"

Doubt was vanquished, certainty triumphant. "We have been given," Jack said, "a body in the box."

THE BODY IN THE BOX

Chapter One

There. The dead man beside the road, that's where she'd found him. Sara glanced in the rearview mirror at the spot, realizing how long it had been since she'd even thought about that incident, and then she looked forward again, through the windshield at the *Weekly Galaxy* building, rushing closer.

Late afternoon, Monday. While Jack and the rest of the team had gone on to Norfolk, Virginia, to set up the next command center, something to do with this mysterious body in the box, the *Galaxy* had chartered a plane to fly Sara and the precious rolls of Mercer wedding film to JFK, where a commercial flight for Orlando had been held for her—she merely accepted this sort of thing as her due by now—and at Orlando another chartered plane had waited to bring her down here, where she'd reclaimed her Peugeot from the airport parking lot and was now zipping out Massa's road to the *Galaxy*, well ahead of closing time.

She nodded to the regular guard, parked as close to the employee entrance as possible, and went first to the Picture Department on the second floor, where the staffers fell on the rolls of film with cries of joy. Sara then went on up to Editorial to get whatever material Mary Kate might have for her to bring to Jack.

It was while she was talking with Mary Kate that she glanced across the squaricles and saw Binx Radwell walking by, looking sadder and more hopeless than ever. "Isn't that— Isn't that Binx?"

"The very same," Mary Kate agreed.

"But— So he wasn't fired, after all?"

"Sure they fired him," Mary Kate said. "The story is, he begged Massa for a second chance. Wept real tears, and like that. So Massa hired him back, as a reporter."

"A reporter!"

"At reporter's starting salary."

"Ow!"

"And assigned him to Boy Cartwright," Mary Kate said dryly.

"Oh, poor Binx," Sara said, watching the slope-shouldered booby settle himself at one of the long reporters' tables on the far side of the room.

"They fired him as an example," Mary Kate said, "and then hired him back as a long-term example."

"And he can't afford the real world," Sara said.

* * *

It was amazing how large and deserted the apartment seemed. It was only last Tuesday that Phyllis had moved out, and only last Thursday that Sara herself had left on the trip to Martha's Vineyard, and yet the big cold place felt like a mausoleum that had been deserted for years. Sara moved through it, lowering the air-conditioning, looking out at the restless Atlantic Ocean, at the beach in the building's shadow, and the silence in the apartment just went on making her uncomfortable.

Yet, there was nothing to do but stay the night here, as planned, and take the morning flight to Washington, D.C., as planned, where a commuter flight would bring her back down to Norfolk. It was too far to drive overnight, and if she looked for a flight heading north now there wouldn't be a place for her tonight in Norfolk. And how would she explain it to Jack? "I didn't like my apartment."

There was food in the freezer. The television set worked. She could make it through the night. And in any event, here was a chance to go look at her novels-in-progress. She had the feeling she was still too keyed up from the Mercer wedding to settle down to any serious work, but at least she could touch the manuscripts, glance at them, remind herself that *here* was what she wanted from life, the real goal.

The business in Martha's Vineyard had been exciting, had caught her up in the rush and flow of it, but she could see how that sort of high could become dangerous. What if *all* you wanted in life was the pictures of the Mercer wedding, or the party for the hundred-year-old twins, or the body in the box, whatever that turned out to be? No; the rush and the high were fun, but the novels were real life.

It was while seated at the desk with *Time of the Hero* spread out in front of her, but really while she was not actually paying close attention to the manuscript, that she noticed the empty space among the items taped and tacked to the wall above her desk. The information about the dead man's car was gone.

She stared at that space while a chill of fear spread through her body. She remembered taping it there. She remembered the parentheses around the uncertain final letter of the license plate (G/O/Q). She remembered putting it there, but she couldn't remember the last time she'd *seen* it there.

Am I alone in this place?

She was. Of course she was. Hesitantly at first, but then more rapidly, she moved in silence through the apartment, whipping open closets, peeking around doorways, terrified but willing herself to be brave, and of *course* she was alone in the apartment. The piece of paper must have been removed some time ago from above her desk.

By Phyllis.

That's right. Who else was there? No one else had ever been in this place.

Phyllis had been at Martha's Vineyard.

Phyllis had been seated next to her at the reporters' table when the first sheet about the dead man's car had disappeared.

Hurrying back to her own bedroom, Sara pulled open her closet door, pushed skirts and blouses out of the way, and saw the two boxes of Jimmy Taggart's papers still back in there, on the floor, where she'd left them. So Phyllis hadn't found *those.* But Phyllis had been gone from here only two days after Sara had brought those papers in, and Sara had—luckily—hidden Taggart's papers, while the license number had been left right out in plain sight. For Phyllis to see, and understand.

Did Phyllis try to kill me, shooting through that window? Or was she warning me off, because she'd seen that piece of paper in this apartment, over my desk?

What's the connection between Phyllis Perkinson of *Trend* magazine and the dead man beside the road?

Sara hurried back to her desk, cleared the manuscripts out of the way, readied the typewriter, rolled in a sandwich of two sheets of paper and a carbon, and began to type:

On July 12th, on my way to work the first day at the Weekly Galaxy, I found a dark blue Buick beside the empty road, with a dead man lying on the ground beside it. He had been shot once in the forehead. I reported this to the guard on duty at the *Weekly Galaxy* gate. That guard, whose name is or was James Taggart, disappeared that same day and has not been seen either at work or at his home ever since. So far as I have been able to determine, no official report was ever made to any police department about the murdered man I found beside the road.

The data on the murdered man's car was on a sheet of paper in a notebook I keep at all times in my bag. After I was introduced to my editor that first morning, I took a place at one of the reporters' tables, next to a young woman named Phyllis Perkinson. (She called me over; it wasn't coincidence.) I did not meet Phyllis Perkinson until some time after I arrived at the *Weekly Galaxy* building. It is absolutely possible that she arrived at the building after I did that morning.

That day, Phyllis Perkinson invited me to share her apartment in the city, and I agreed, and continue to live there.

On Friday of that first week, four days later, I discovered that the page with the information about the murdered man's car had been ripped from my notebook. I make it a habit to leave my bag under my chair when I am away from my place at the reporters' table, either in the research section or the ladies' room. It would have been very easy for Phyllis Perkinson to have removed that information from my bag.

With some trouble, I reconstructed the information, which I put on a sheet of paper taped to the wall over my desk at home; that is, in the apartment I shared with Phyllis Perkinson.

One week ago, on Tuesday, August 3rd, Phyllis Perkinson was fired from the *Weekly Galaxy*, it having been learned she was actually working for *Trend* magazine on undercover assignment to do a smear article on the *Galaxy*. While at the *Galaxy*, her secret had been learned by an editor named Boy Cartwright, who had not exposed her but had forced her to be a spy for him against other editors at the *Galaxy*.

Last week, while I was on assignment in Martha's Vineyard, somebody fired a pistol several times through my hotel room window into my bed. Fortunately, I was in the bathroom at the time.

I have now discovered that the dead man's car information has disappeared again, this time from the apartment.

1) It would have been easy for Phyllis Perkinson to take the information from my bag at the Galaxy.

2) Phyllis Perkinson was in Martha's Vineyard, on assignment for Trend, when the shots were fired into my room.

3) Only Phyllis Perkinson could have taken the information from the wall over the desk in the apartment we shared. No one else has been in here.

I have no idea who the murdered man was or what his link was to Phyllis Perkinson. I do know she seems at all times to be living some sort of double life. Every weekend while we shared this apartment she went off by herself, as though to spend time with a boyfriend, but she never said anything about this person, so I have no idea where she was really going.

I think it's clear that Phyllis Perkinson murdered the man beside the road, that she did something to or about the guard named James Taggart to keep him from reporting the crime, that she removed the information from my bag in hopes that I wouldn't be able to do any follow-up on the case, and that when she saw I'd reconstructed the information she (a) removed it again, and (b) fired into my hotel room either deliberately to kill me or to scare me off.

I am determined now to find out who the dead man was, and what his link was with Phyllis Perkinson.

She signed and dated both the original and the copy, and then—feeling self-consciously melodramatic and yet determined—she typed TO BE OPENED IN THE EVENT OF MY DEATH on two envelopes, put the two copies of her statement in the two envelopes, put the envelope with the carbon copy inside the large manila envelope marked I FOR INCOMPLETE (college novel), put the other envelope with her luggage, to take with her to Norfolk, and then sat in the living room to think things over.

I have no proof of any of this.

I am a staffer on the *Weekly Galaxy*, and I have no proof of any of this.

I am a staffer on the *Weekly Galaxy*, and I have no proof of any of this, so it would be a mistake to go to any police department about this.

Does Phyllis still have her key to this apartment?

She spent the night at a motel out by the airport.

Chapter Two

The death of Johnny Crawfish stunned the civilized world. The thirty-eight-year-old country singer who had risen from poverty and squalor as the child of migrant farm workers, the gravel-voiced balladeer who had found both God and his muse in a Tennessee prison where he'd been sentenced for manslaughter, the self-taught millionaire songwriter/businessman who by his thirty-fifth birthday had appeared in command performances before both Queen Elizabeth and President Reagan, died that Saturday morning of at first unknown causes in The Shack, his palatial thirty-room waterfront estate on Chesapeake Bay north of Newport News, Virginia, and when the news was flashed round the globe it was as though four billion human beings had just lost their best friend.

The media—most of the media—were not informed for more than twenty-four hours after the abrupt darkening of this star in the firmament, first because of the extraordinary attempts being made by the world-class team of Crawfish doctors to bring their patient back to life, and then because the family and business partners wanted to know exactly what had caused Johnny's demise before the news was released. As a result, though Johnny Crawfish passed from his reward on Monday morning, it wasn't till Tuesday evening that his death became the lead story on the network newscasts. Wednesday's *New York Times* began its coverage on page one, below the fold, with a photo of Crawfish performing at the White House, and included a second photo—an early Crawfish concert—with the bulk of the obit deeper in the paper. Photos of Crawfish—not identical photos, but identically smiling—made that week's covers of *Time* and *Newsweek*.

Official statements were made in response to the awful news. "A great American, a fine musician and a source of inspiration to rich and poor alike," said President Ronald Reagan, Archbishop John J. O'Connor of New York, motion picture and television producer David Wolper, fellow artist Frank Sinatra, Virginia Senator John Warner and evangelist Billy Graham, in separate press releases.

* * *

The *Weekly Galaxy*'s primary spy at The Shack was a carpenter named Moe Kerlie, employed to make some necessary repairs and expansion on the boathouse and docks along the property's bay frontage. Almost no one was allowed inside the razor-wire-topped walls of the grounds around The Shack other than Johnny Crawfish's extensive family and his ex-con old pals, who served him as chauffeurs, bodyguards, executive producers and pinochle partners. But carpentry was not a skill any of Crawfish's cronies had picked up in the pen, so an outside man from time to time had to be called in.

Moe Kerlie had worked off and on for Johnny Crawfish for nearly seven years, and every time he did so he was simultaneously on the payroll of the *Weekly Galaxy*. Early indications of Crawfish's travel plans were sometimes picked up from Moe, and changes of girlfriend or the occasional falling-out among the buddies and hangers-on, but until the Monday morning when Johnny Crawfish said, "This coffee tastes like shit," and toppled forward into his apple-and-Jarlsberg-cheese omelette, Kerlie's information had been barely worth the rather modest retainer the *Galaxy* gave him. On that Monday morning, though, Moe did his suborners proud.

Hearing a fuss of some sort up at the main house, seeing maids (cousins) and butlers (parolees) running back and forth and in and out of the many French doors, Moe moseyed on up there, ostensibly to say he needed somebody to drive the pickup into town to pick up some more A/C plywood, and he found the household so distracted and unaware of his presence that he wandered freely and heard the whole thing. Crawfish dead; doctors sent for; Crawfish *dead*; carried to his bed; *Crawfish dead!*

"I gotta go to town," Moe told a former mob enforcer, "get me some more A/C plywood."

"Go, go," the enforcer said, looking old and gray and worried, hurrying off on errands of his own.

Which is how the *Weekly Galaxy* became the first to know.

Chapter Three

In Norfolk, Virginia, at number 147 Edger Street, not terribly far from the Naval Station but several blocks from the sea, stands a small yellow clapboard house, two stories high, in a depressed area of similar small houses, vacant lots, concrete block buildings containing auto body shops, and liquor stores. This particular house, with full basement and cramped triangular attic, with one bathroom, three bedrooms (upstairs), living room, dining room and kitchen (downstairs), had stood empty for not quite two months since the last tenants, a family in desperate need of birth control information, had skipped out owing three and a half months' rent.

Now, however, to the landlord's bemused delight, a new tenant had been found, a short-term tenant who was paying, *in cash*, for one month's occupancy, the equivalent of ten months' rent. The landlord, a retired Polish pipe fitter living out near Richmond on the income from twenty-seven rental properties in depressed parts of Norfolk and Portsmouth, had asked only two questions on the Monday afternoon the deal was cut: "Is it a whorehouse?" "Is it gambling?" Being assured the tenants had neither prospect in mind, and being given half his rent in advance—five months' worth!—the landlord had been pleased to withdraw back to his home near Richmond and think no more about it.

Much activity immediately ensued at number 147. A professional cleaning service swept through like the sorcerer's apprentice on a good day, followed by trucks from an office furniture rental place up in D.C. delivering desks, wastebaskets, filing cabinets, library tables, bulletin boards and a refrigerator. Simultaneously, the phone company arrived to install fifteen telephones with fifteen separate lines (and *lights*; no bells), a beverage distributor brought in cases of beer and soft drinks and a water cooler with large blue jugs of bottled water, and electricians came to add two new circuits to the first floor. These were meant to accommodate the rented air conditioners and copiers and television set also being delivered at that time. Meanwhile, teams of plumbers and carpenters were hard at work converting the kitchen to a photographic darkroom.

And while all that was going on, the *Weekly Galaxy* was on its way.

* * *

From Dulles International, they took a chartered bus down Interstate 95 from the nation's capital through Richmond and then on I-64 toward Norfolk. It was Tuesday morning, the team having left Martha's Vineyard early in the day, spending the previous day and night cleaning up after themselves, distributing bribes and reparation money, cooling out the victims where possible, eliminating the traces of their presence where more blatant felonies might be involved. Now, with yesterday's news already forgotten, with the New England stringers returned to their dusty ivory towers, the team looked forward to the challenges ahead.

Jack sat by himself behind the driver, yellow pad on lap, considering approaches; the body in the box was never an easy goal. A few miles below Richmond, Ida joined him, dropping into the aisle seat to say, "Sara Joslyn."

"A trusted assistant," Jack said. "Who shall rendezvous with us later today."

"She wasn't in the john when her bed was shot up," Ida said.

Jack looked at his mad dog carefully. "She wasn't?"

"I checked the room last night, after she left," Ida said. "There's a ventilation space under the john door. With the door closed, you can see from outside when the light's on in there."

"Ah," Jack said. Ever the investigative reporter, this Ida. "What does this say to you, Ida?"

"If she was in the john, whoever fired the shots would know it," Ida said. "And with the lightspill under the door, they'd know there wasn't anybody in the bed."

Jack nodded. "Maybe that was the point," he suggested. "Maybe they did it as a warning, some kind of a warning, and didn't want to kill anybody."

Ida gave that the look it deserved. "*One* shot is a warning," she said. "You don't empty a gun into a hotel room unless you're trying to be sure the person you're shooting is really dead. You don't take the extra time, make the extra noise, for a *warning*. And you don't take the chance she'll come out of the john and see you and identify you later."

"Hmm," Jack said. "So what are you suggesting, Ida?"

"She was in bed with *you*," Ida said.

"Ah," Jack said. "That would explain it, all right."

"The lie's because Massa'd fire you," Ida said, "if it went public that she was in bed with you."

"Moral turpitude," Jack agreed. "Are you handing this story to me as your editor, Ida?"

"For myself," Ida said, "I don't care if you fuck goats, just so it doesn't change anything on the team."

"Ida," Jack said, in absolute sincerity, "I would never never *never* alter my editorial judgment for the sake of a piece of ass. I hope you know me better than that. I hope you know my values are higher than that."

Ida said, "She *was* in bed with you, wasn't she?"

Jack gave her another long considering look. "Ida," he said, "are you taping this little conversation?"

"Yes," Ida said.

"In case you ever feel badly treated later on?"

"Yes."

"Sara was in bed with me, Ida," Jack said, clearly and distinctly. "We lied."

"Thank you," Ida said, and went back to her own seat.

* * *

It almost looked like home. Sara walked into the house on Edger Street, and it was a definite *Weekly Galaxy* command center, full of photographic equipment, empty bottles, paper plates, people on phones, manic conversations. Presiding over it all, impersonating an unexploded bomb in the front room, was Jack.

He probably doesn't want to hear about Binx, Sara thought as she crossed to where he was in tense conversation with the regular members of the team. As she arrived, Jack was saying, "No, that isn't a story, we don't have— Hello, Sara. Sit. —a story, we have a load of horseshit."

"Horseshit cousins," Harry Razza said.

"That's one of our problems," Jack agreed. "Johnny Crawfish's family and friends are as scuzzy a lot as we've ever come across."

"There's a couple of them around," Don Grove said, "trying to sell Crawfish's *hair,* saved from four years of haircuts."

"Swept from four dozen barbershops," Jack suggested.

Nodding, Don said, "From what they showed me, Johnny did grow hair in quite a variety of colors."

Louis B. Urbiton said, "I wonder. Could the very awfulness of these people be our story? The incredible muck that Johnny Crawfish rose out of to become the so on and so forth we drop our trousers for today."

"I'll tell you what's wrong with that, Louis," Jack said, shaking his head regretfully. "Look at it from Massa's point of view, and you'll see those creeps and cruds around Crawfish act just exactly the way the *readers* would if they suddenly found they had a rich and famous cousin. The reader identification is going to be with the scumbags, so we'll never be able to call them by their rightful name."

"Which is Cretin," Louis said.

"Very true."

"They do all have their little stories to sell us," Bob Sangster said. "So far, I've got three completely different sets of last words, all sworn to and vouched for by different cousins."

"I saw Johnny enter heaven," Harry Razza said, "up through a big white cloud, Elvis leading him by the hand. I have a cousin who'll swear to it."

Chauncey Chapperell, stretching his long legs up and over a desk, said, "I've got a UFO sighting over Chesapeake Bay just before he died."

"*More* horseshit."

Ida said, "What about cause of death?"

"Sorry, Ida," Jack said. "In the first place, Massa's a Johnny Crawfish fan, he doesn't *want* to hear Johnny OD'd, or had AIDS, or committed suicide because he couldn't read music, or anything with juice in it. And in the second place, they've had half the American Medical Association up in that place. If it *wasn't* an embolism, they've had all the time and talent in the world to rig it so we'll never prove a thing." Spreading his hands, he said, "Come on, gang, where's my *story*?"

Baffled, Sara said, "He's *dead*. Isn't that the story?"

"It is not," Jack told her. "What's our headline? Crawfish Dead. Our paper hits the supermarket Saturday, we're a *weekly*. By then, unborn Ubangi tribesmen will already have the news. The *Galaxy* needs to go beyond that simple fact, into the realm of excitement, romance, adventure and the totally fantastically unexpected."

"The body in the box," Sara suggested, hoping at last to find out what that could be.

"That, too," Jack agreed. "But that's just the cover, the front page. We still need a headline." He made a sweeping arm gesture, to suggest headlines: "Crawfish Was Victim of Foul Play. Except he wasn't. Crawfish Had Premonition of Own Death. Except he didn't. Crawfish Was in the CIA. Except he wasn't."

"Well," Sara persisted, "what *about* the body in the box?"

"We'll get to that," Jack assured her, "once they lay him out. One problem at a time."

Ida said, "Sara and I can get that, when the time comes."

Looking surprised and hopeful, Jack said, "You think so? Fine, it's all yours."

Oh, good, Sara thought, I don't even know what it is, and I've just been volunteered for it.

Chapter Four

Tuesday afternoon, in the command center. The meeting around Jack had ended inconclusively—where's the story, what's the story, give us our story, who's got the goddamn STORY?—and everybody was now on the phone:

"Doctor, this is Maurice Fischback of *Psychology Today*. Do you anticipate mass suicides as a result of the recent death of popular idol Johnny Crawfish?"

"Would you say Johnny was a source of comfort to the other prisoners? Did you fellas all sort of look up to him, is that your memory of that period?"

"Can I quote you as saying you're glad he's dead? Well, can I quote you as saying you wouldn't bring him back if you could? Well, can I quote you as saying you feel a certain relief?"

"When he was a little boy, did the rest of the family *know* somehow the greatness that was in him? Are there incidents from that period you would like to share with our readers at *Modern Maturity*?"

Amid them all, Sara was also on the phone, but not in precisely the same way. On *Galaxy* time, using the *Galaxy*'s long-distance phone service, she was selfishly not plugging along in the *Galaxy*'s best interest, but was egocentrically trying to save her own life. It wasn't enough to surround herself with envelopes to be opened in the event of her death. It was time to take steps to avoid having those envelopes opened. It was time to counterattack. "Theft Record Transcript?" she asked the lazy voice that answered her most recent call, and when assured that Theft Record Transcript of the Dade County, Florida, sheriff's office was indeed what she had reached she said, "This is Officer Helen Sonoma, Norfolk, Virginia, Public Safety Division. We're trying for verification on a suspect's story here."

"You're Norfolk Police? What was that name again?"

Sara repeated the same false information, spelling the last name and saying, "Like the wine county in California." She had learned that unusual names create for some reason an aura of believability, as though anyone who claimed to be called Helen Sonoma was unlikelier to lie about other things than someone who said her name was Helen Smith.

"Okay," Sara said briskly, when her credentials had been accepted, "what we've got here is somebody claiming a kidnap in a stolen rental or leased vehicle, Florida plates. Dade County."

"Kidnapping?"

"That's the claim, but it's a weird story, and we're not sure we want to follow through on it. We need verification."

"What kind of verification?"

"Okay," Sara said, still being brisk and a little irritated, as though if she'd been a *man* she'd be out on patrol or stakeout somewhere, and not stuck in this police headquarters making these dumb phone calls. "The vehicle description is a dark blue four-door Buick, two or three years old, with a Z plate. The complainant doesn't know anything more than that, but she states it was a stolen vehicle. And it would have been stolen within the last four weeks."

The voice said, "So you want to know, do we have a listing for a dark blue four-door Buick, a lease or rental vehicle, on the sheet in July or August?"

"Right," Sara said. It had taken her four phone calls, beginning with the Florida state police, to finally get to the place where such records were kept, so the slight edge of irritation in her voice wasn't at all difficult to maintain.

"Hold on," the voice said. "Or do you want me to call you back?"

"Either way. I can give you my number. How long's it gonna take?"

"If I do it now—"

"Let's do it now," Sara said, sounding peeved and being peeved.

"Two, three minutes," the voice said. "Hold on."

So Sara held on, and when Jack walked past she said into the silent phone, "But on that first date, if you could sense the power he was going to have someday, why didn't you sleep with him?"

"Huh?" said the voice.

"Talking to somebody here," Sara said, Jack having moved on out of earshot. "You got it?"

"The answer's no," the voice said.

Sara was surprised. "No? No stolen Buick?"

"Fantasy kidnappings," the voice said. "They happen all the time. It's something with the full moon."

"Okay, fine," Sara said. "Thanks."

She hung up and sat there a moment, hand on the phone. So the murderer—or somebody—had returned the Buick to the renter, after getting rid of the body. Or, if it was leased, the murderer—or somebody—still had it. And this time, Sara had no way to recapture the car's license number.

So what next?

* * *

Night on Edger Street. The house at number 147 remained brightly lit, crackling with activity. Aerial photos of The Shack, Johnny Crawfish's compound on Chesapeake Bay, taken earlier today and blown up to monstrous size, were taped and tacked to the living room walls. In one of the upstairs bedrooms, photographers and stringers and various deeply dubious individuals tried on any number of costumes and uniforms, becoming serially policemen, nuns, ambulance drivers, mailpersons, priests, nurses, United Parcel deliverymen, Girl Scouts (with cookies) and U.S. Navy frogmen. In the former kitchen, now a nascent darkroom, any number of small and easily concealable cameras were being loaded with very fast film. At the dining room table, artists sat and forged a variety of identity documents. On the front porch, the Down Under Trio chatted and drank with a scabrous assortment of Crawfish cousins, all of whom listened with their mouths open.

Since all soundings had failed to indicate any Crawfish story worthy of the name, meaning the body in the box was probably all they'd be able to set at Massa's altar at the end of this expedition, and since the body in the box was *not* going to be easy to get this time, it was the aerial photos of the Crawfish estate that mostly held Jack and the key members of his team. "Look at those guys," he said, tapping the large color picture yet again. Sara, Ida, Don Grove, Chauncey Chapperell and a couple of photographers (one dressed as a Washington Redskin, with his camera in the helmet under his arm) all obediently looked. "Those are armed guards in jeeps," Jack said, "buddies of Crawfish, patrolling the perimeter."

"They're violating their parole, those guys," Don Grove said. "Carrying guns like that." He sounded aggrieved.

Jack considered him. "You want to go tell them that, Don?"

"I don't think so, no."

"Good."

Jack contemplated the photo again, without love. "This is razor wire, all along here," he said. "See that whip antenna on the jeep? They're in constant contact with each other."

"From the sea," Ida suggested.

Jack shook his head. "Like in Martha's Vineyard? It didn't work there, and those people weren't homicidal. These are." He pointed to spots along the shore. "In the big double boathouse here, a cigarette boat, big and fast and mean, with a reinforced prow, it's already been used twice to ram strangers who got too close. And a big twenty-six-foot inboard in there too, they can put an *army* on that, chase us across to Cape Charles, *maim* us. And they'd do it, too."

"Parachute," Chauncey Chapperell offered.

"They'd shoot you out of the air," Jack told him.

"I wasn't thinking of doing it myself, actually," Chauncey said.

"The problem is," Jack said generally, "in life, Crawfish surrounded himself with thugs and killers, and they're all still there. And the cousins are the same thing, only dumber."

Ida said, "Why don't Sara and I go up there tonight, look it over?"

"He isn't laid out yet, Ida," Jack pointed out. "If you *did* get in there tonight, what's the point? You can't get the body in the box until tomorrow anyway."

"Excuse me," Sara said.

Politeness? Jack upraised an eyebrow and looked out at Sara from under it. "Yes, Sara?"

"I hate to sound dumb," she said, "but people keep talking about the body in the box, and I don't know what it is."

Jack stared at her. "You don't know what we've been talking about all this time?"

"True," she said.

A fleeting memory came to him, of his night of fretfulness concerning the descent into the maelstrom of this young woman. Okay, here's another step down; let's see how she handles it. "The body in the box," he explained, "is exactly what it sounds like. It is a photograph of a dead person in his or her casket."

Sara looked at him, waiting for more. "And?"

"No and. When a celeb goes down, Massa wants the body in the box, and we go get it."

"But— But *why*?"

"Because America wants it," Jack told her. "Don't ask me to explain, I'm just telling you the way it is. When a major pop figure dies, particularly if they're fairly young and still at the height of their success, America wants to see a photograph of that person in the casket. Never mind pictures of the guy at the White House, pictures of him dancing, laughing, eating pizza, fucking beautiful women. What America wants is the dead body, on its back, hands folded over shriveled balls, lips sewed shut, eyelids with that special *caved-in* look, puffy silk casket lining all around."

"That's disgusting," Sara said. "Who could want something like that? Why would anybody want that?"

"Ask them, next time you're in the supermarket," Jack suggested. "Every week, the *Galaxy* sells about five million copies. When the front cover's a body in the box, a major star that just went down, we sell six or seven million. When Elvis went down, we sold eight million. We'd *still* be selling that one, only they had to replate the presses for the next week's paper."

"It's like—" Sara floundered, hands moving vaguely. "I don't know what it's like. Something primitive, tribal. It's like cavemen. It's like the missing *link*, for God's sake."

"Sara," Jack said mildly, "who did you think our readership *was*? The senior class at MIT?"

CHAPTER FIVE

Sara sat up in bed, watching the red numerals on the television/radio/clock slowly slowly change. 7:08. 7:09. 7:10.

She had been awake for well over an hour, as the light grew and changed in this spacious but anonymous hotel room and her mind teemed with a confusion of thoughts. The untraceable dark blue Buick. The ugliness of the body in the box. The idea of Phyllis Perkinson as a person who empties pistols into hotel rooms.

As to that last, *this* hotel room was surely safe. It was on the seventh floor, with no balcony outside the drape-covered windows. Every possible means of locking the door had been used and then double-checked by Sara last night. She was, as well, registered in a different room on a different floor, and she'd made sure last night to go in there and muss the bed, leave some clothing and spare bits of makeup around, to give the impression she was really in residence there.

As to the body in the box, why had that shocked her so? Weddings, funerals, wasn't it all the same? The picture of the event. What do family and friends do, as their last interaction with the deceased? They view the remains.

So the body in the box was merely the great American public wanting to be treated like family; the outsiders pressing their noses to the windowpane, trying to see what the insiders see. If the body in the box was a little more ghoulish than a wedding album or a hundred-year-old birthday, wasn't it nevertheless still merely another element in that great cycle of happenings among the select Few at which the Many stand outside the ropes and pay obeisance by their gawking?

I wonder, Sara thought, unwillingly, what picture Massa wants when a major female star gives birth. She averted her gaze from that question, to consider another, being the question of Jack's attitude toward her. It seemed to Sara that, in some way, Jack was testing her, had been doing so for some time. When he'd told her about the body in the box last night, she could sense the intensity with which he'd watched her, as though still wondering, after everything she'd already done, if she were up to this. She'd deliberately done what she could to hide her revulsion, to show how quickly she could adapt to whatever he might choose to throw at her. She'd even joined enthusiastically in the final part of the discussion about just how to get into the Crawfish viewing.

Had he appreciated that? It was hard to tell. He hadn't raised the subject again in here afterward, had made no further comment at all. But Sara found herself, rather against her will, wanting Jack Ingersoll's good opinion, and if that meant being cool about the taking of pictures of dead bodies, so be it. As cool and capable and unaffected as he wanted, that's who she was.

She peeked at him, still asleep in the bed beside her. It was awfully early—7:17, 7:18—but she wanted to talk to him. She couldn't go back to sleep herself, and she didn't want to just sit here and brood forever. She needed to talk to Jack. Not about the body in the box, about the dark blue Buick.

How do I find it now?

Wake *up*, Jack.

* * *

Awake, Jack studied Sara's profile through slitted eyes. What is she thinking about? The body in the box? Christ, she took to that quick enough. She had the normal first reaction—ooo, that's disgusting, all that—but then immediately she was with it, helping to think up ways to get into the Crawfish compound, get next to the Crawfish bier, get above the open Crawfish casket.

What's the problem here? Why do I want this girl to fail at her job? I look inside my heart and I wonder if I'm simply making her a surrogate for myself, giving her all *my* unused innocence and pushing her out to sea on this small thin cake of ice here, just to prove to myself yet again how far innocence will take you. But why her? If I like the girl—and I do, I do, let's let it go at that—so if I like her, why do I keep measuring her for the sackcloth and ashes?

Particularly since she's shown not the slightest interest in wearing them. So what's it all about? Sometimes I don't understand me.

Sara was growing restless, sitting there beside him, shifting around, readjusting her pillows, occasionally as though by accident kicking him in the shin. She wants companionship, he thought, and decided it was time to awaken. With a huge yawn, he thrashed about in the bed, managing to kick *her* once, half opening his eyes, peering up at her and saying, "Is it morning?"

"Yes," she said.

He lifted himself a bit and looked across the room at the red numerals above and to the right of the dead television screen. 7:23. "Sara," he said. "It's awfully *early*."

"I want to ask you about something," she said.

He propped himself up beside her, blinking fuzz out of his eyes. "Good morning," he said. "You're beautiful."

"You're beautiful, too," she commented off-handedly. "I haven't brushed my teeth yet."

"Neither have I."

"I know. Listen, I have a question."

"Okay," he said. His hand, under the covers, rested on her thigh. "Ask away."

"How do I find a car," she said, "if I know it's a rental, and I have a decription of the car, and I know it's registered in Dade County, but I don't know the license number?"

"Hmmmm," he said. He thought about the question. He also thought about the question behind the question, or: Why does she want to know? He said, "Would this have anything to do with the dead man you found beside the road, your first day on the job?"

"I'm not asking for the job," she told him. "I'm asking for me."

"I understand that. Do I take it, then, you think the gunfire in Martha's Vineyard is connected with that dead man?"

"It's possible," she said.

"How come you didn't say anything? When it happened, I mean."

She gave him a clear-eyed look. "Why should I? On what series am *I* a regular?"

"Oh, come on, Sara," he said, pulling his hand away from her thigh as though it had burned him. He sat up straighter and said, "If somebody's trying to *shoot* you?"

"I should try to do something about it," she said. "I know, I agree with you. But *I* should. Not you. Not the *Galaxy*."

"How about the cops?"

"Do you know how interested in the case they were in Martha's Vineyard," she asked, "when I told them I worked for the *Galaxy*? My attempted murder just wasn't a crime they could get all that excited about."

"The down side of being beneath notice," he said. "We're also beneath contempt. All right, tell me about this car."

"A dark blue Buick, I think a Riviera. Two or three years old. Lease or rental, Dade County plate. I checked with the Dade sheriff, and it wasn't stolen."

He frowned at the gray TV screen, thinking about it. "Two or three years old," he said. "And a Buick, at that. Clean, good-looking?"

"Kind of scruffy, actually," she said.

"Okay. Probably not a long-term lease, then, that's mostly new cars, this one's beyond most lease agreements. And not one of the big regular rental outfits like Hertz. Some kind of Rent-A-Wreck outfit, local company with cheaper rates. How many of them could there be?"

"In Dade County?" she asked him. "In Miami? Thousands."

"Well, no. Hundreds, maybe. I tell you what, I'll call Mary Kate, have her collect an IOU from somebody, put a reporter on it, call every off-brand rental outfit in the Miami yellow pages."

"That would be terrific, Jack." She was looking perkier and perkier.

"Too bad Binx got himself fragged," Jack said, musing. "He was always good for crap like this."

"Uh," Sara said.

Jack frowned at her. "Was that a noise of pre-revelation?"

"Binx is back," Sara said.

Jack was astonished, delighted and depressed. "Back? That's amazing! Massa *never* brings them back from the dead. Back in his old squaricle, is he, cheerful as ever?"

"Well, no," Sara said. "He was hired as a reporter, at starting salary."

"Oh, *shit!*"

"Assigned to Boy Cartwright."

"And he *took* it?"

Sara just let that one lie there. Jack looked at it, sighed, nodded, and said, "We work for an evil empire, darling. Don't ever forget that."

"I don't intend to."

"Anyway, I'll call Mary Kate as soon as we get to the command center. Maybe Binx can play hooky today."

"I appreciate this, Jack," she said. "I really do."

"Ah, it's nothing," he assured her. "Besides, you're a good enough reporter, valuable enough member of the team, if there's a chance to keep you alive, what the hell, I say go for it."

She smiled at him. "You are a nice boss, after all," she said.

"After all what?"

"Wait right there," she told him, "while I go brush my teeth."

Chapter Six

Copy poured from the house on Edger Street, messengered swiftly to Massa down in Florida. UFO sightings at both Johnny Crawfish's death *and* birth; premonitions; reminiscences from suspiciously articulate jailbirds; incredible parallels drawn with the lives of Mozart, Thomas Jefferson and John Lennon; thoroughly bogus romances with three television series stars; a little known (because nonexistent) tale of Johnny's service as a Peace Corps volunteer; other odds and ends of detritus. Some of this sludge would be summarily dealt with by Massa's own true red pencil, some would fail to make it through the fact checkers or Rewrite or the evaluators, some would actually appear in the paper. But none of it mattered, one way or the other, just so long as they got the body in the box.

It wasn't going to be easy. Virginia state police patrolled the only public highway that went past the compound, and they'd already been rather aggressive with Don Grove when he innocently stopped his car beside the fence to clean bugs from his windshield. Within the compound, the cutthroats and brigands with whom Johnny Crawfish had liked to idle away his free hours were belligerently on guard, having already hospitalized three ordinary fans of the late great man who had in their innocence thought they might be forgiven for sneaking in to say goodbye.

The main hope was the cousins. Johnny Crawfish had risen from a teeming and scrofulous family, any one of whom would have sold his sister to orangutans if the price were right. ("Don't worry, Sis, they promised you'll get your own fur coat.") Singly and in groups, the cousins were approached, coated with a promissory sprinkling of money, trained in the operation of the simple and concealable cameras, and promised vast additional moneys should they return with a usable photo of their dead departed relative, entire, recognizable, in focus, and in the box.

There would be two viewings, neither public; both were meant for family (cousins), friends (thugs) and showbiz peers exclusively. Printed invitations were jealously guarded and eagerly sought after. (Chauncey Chapperell's visit to the printer of these invitations produced, instead of the duplicate ducats hoped for, a fresh swelling under Chauncey's left eye and a little difficulty with his voice for a few days.) The two viewings—Wednesday, 5:00 till 10:00 P.M., Thursday, 6:00 till 9:00—were democratically divided among the various categories of invitees, so that cousins and thugs could hobnob with the great and near-great on both occasions.

The idea of buying invitations from a couple of cousins, and sending Don Grove or somebody to pretend to be a Crawfish, was scotched, much to Don's relief, when it was learned there would always be a relative or two on duty at the entrance, looking out for just that sort of substitution. With the obsequies taking place indoors, there was nothing for a *Galaxy* air force to do. With the Crawfish fleet at the ready, the *Galaxy* navy must needs stay in port. And with razor-wire-topped walls and armed thugs in jeeps to contend with, there was no thought of the cavalry this time coming to the rescue.

It was all up to the cousins.

* * *

Wednesday, 4:30 P.M. The first camera-equipped cousins had been sent off, but no result as yet was known. Sara sat as quietly as everybody else, at her desk in the command center, and when the white light on her phone began to flash she couldn't at first think why on earth anybody would call her at this particular moment. Then she picked up the receiver and said, "Yes?" half expecting a wrong number, and it was Binx:

"Is that the lovely and charming Sara Joslyn?"

"Binx! How are you?"

"Reasonably well," he said. "Sitting up, taking nourishment."

"Did you want Jack?"

"I don't think so," Binx said, "I never have before. Actually, it's you I'm calling. I've got your Buick, I think."

Heart quickening, Sara reached for pen and paper. "You do? Great!"

"Mary Kate was pretty closemouthed about the purpose of all this," Binx said, complaining gently, "so I'm not sure exactly what you need, so I just got whatever I could."

"That's great," Sara said, being just as closemouthed as Mary Kate. "That's fine, whatever you can get is exactly what I need."

"Okay. The Buick was rented from A-Betta Car Rental, out near the airport." Binx spelled the name of the rental company. "The renter, who used an American Express card, gave the name Michael Hanrahan."

"Irish?" Sara said, surprised. The salsa music, the toughness of that face, all had made her think he was Latin in some way. Dope dealers, something like that. So what was this? Gun-running?

"If Hanrahan is an Irish name," Binx said, "and if he wasn't fibbing when he gave it, then I guess he's Irish. Is this significant?"

"I have no idea," Sara told him truthfully. "What else do we have? Anything?"

"Mr. Hanrahan gave a corporate address in Los Angeles," Binx said. "On Sunset Boulevard." He reeled off the address, and said, "I think from the number it's way east, out of the good section. And the company is called Western States Investigations."

Sara absorbed that one, then said, "Private detectives?"

"I think so." Binx said, "I called there, and they said Michael Hanrahan doesn't work for them anymore."

"Did they say when he left, or why, or any—"

"Sara, Sara," Binx said. "I am only human. In fact, barely that."

"Yes, you're right, I'm sorry."

"I can tell you when the car was turned in, if you'd like."

"I'd like," Sara said.

"July twelfth."

The same day she'd found the dead man; the car was turned in the same day. "Ah hah,"Sara said.

"The interesting thing," Binx said, "anyway I guess it's interesting, is, that was the second day of a one-week rental. They hadn't expected it back until the weekend."

"Well," Sara said, "I guess Hanrahan didn't need it anymore."

"And that," Binx said, "is all I could learn. I hope it helps, with whatever you're doing."

"Thank you, Binx, I'm sure it will," Sara said. "I really appreciate this."

"De nada. See you when you get back."

"Right."

"Oh, and Sara . . ."

Sara listened. "Yes?"

"I've been thinking, you know," Binx said, hemming and hawing and sounding very nervous and embarrassed, "and I'm pretty sure the time has come and I've just got to leave Marcy. I mean, for everybody's sake. And I was thinking, uh, uh, when you come back, uh, maybe you and I could have dinner or something, uh, talk about it, you know, and, uh, you could give me the woman's point of view."

"Uh huh," said Sara.

"I think maybe you like understand my situation," Binx said. "You know, a sympathetic ear."

"Uh huh," said Sara.

"A shoulder to cry on, you know, kind of thing."

"Uh huh," said Sara.

"Well," Binx said, and cleared his throat, and said, "See you, then."

"Uh huh," said Sara.

Chapter Seven

If a man from California is murdered in Florida, won't someone in California notice his absence?

Yes. The Los Angeles Police Department, Missing Persons Bureau, confirmed to Sergeant Helen Sonoma, Dade County sheriff's office, that one Michael Xavier Hanrahan had been reported missing on August third by his brother, Nicholas Hanrahan, of 27500 Banetree Drive, Northridge, California, home phone 818-555-6904, work phone 818-959-9999. It being just on five o'clock in the afternoon in Norfolk, Virginia, and therefore just on 2:00 P.M. in Northridge, California, a distant Los Angeles suburb on the north side—as the name suggests—of the San Fernando Valley, Sara immediately phoned Nicholas Hanrahan's work number, where a woman's voice answered, saying, "All-Day Parking."

"Nicholas Hanrahan, please."

"Nick doesn't come in till later. Try after six."

So she called his home number, and got his answering machine, a pleasantly gravelly voice, suggesting a middle-aged tough guy with a sense of humor: "This is Nick Hanrahan, and I'm out somewhere. Leave your message after the beep."

"This is Helen Sonoma," Sara told the machine, after the beep, "of A-Betta Car Rental, Norfolk, Virginia. We're trying to locate Michael Hanrahan because of property left in a vehicle rented by him from our Miami location on July eleventh of this year." She gave the number of the phone she was calling from, and said, "Please call collect."

As she hung up, the first two Crawfish cousins came bursting into the house, both laughing and excited, adrenaline flowing, unable to stop talking and crowing about their success, waving their cameras around, crying, "We got it! We got it! You can forget about it, we got it, we got it, we got it right *here*!" And on and on like that, while a couple of dispassionate technicians plucked the cameras from the cousins' waving hands and carried them away to the darkroom. The cousins were persuaded to wait on the front porch, and things got very quiet, everybody looking toward the former kitchen.

Another cousin, this one as nervous and jittery as a rat in a dog pound, sidled in and produced another camera, which Jack took from him, saying, "You got the picture?"

"Yeah. Gimme my money and I'll go."

"First we look at the picture."

"It's there, it's there, don't worry."

"I like to worry," Jack told him. "Wait outside."

Ten minutes later, a technician came from the darkroom/kitchen with word on the first cousins' pictures: "No."

"No?" Jack said. "What do you mean, no?"

"The in-focus pictures are mostly of an ear," the technician said, "and the rest are of the casket lid. I think one of those guys turned the camera the wrong way and it's *his* ear we're getting."

"Give me the pictures," Jack said, and took the wet smelly things and went outside and dropped them in the lap of the cousins, who cried, "This isn't our stuff! You're trying to cheat us!"

"If you're on this porch one minute from now," Jack told them, "large men will come out with baseball bats and turn you people into dog food."

The cousins flung the pictures of ears and lids onto the porch floor and stalked off in dignified disgust. The rat-faced cousin stood by and smoked a cigarette cupped with total secrecy in the palm of his hand. He watched Jack without blinking.

Jack went back inside, and a few minutes later two more cousins arrived. These didn't have pictures or even cameras anymore, but they were bleeding from various parts of their heads and hands, and they insisted the *Galaxy* pay their cab fare. While Don Grove, shaking his head, went out to give money to the cabbie, Jack listened to the cousins' story. Through all the defensive verbiage and unnecessarily graphic descriptions of physical mayhem practiced upon their bodies by the guards at The Shack, the basic story was a simple one: The cousins had been careless. They had let other people see them wave their cameras around in the same room with the remains. Jack gave them one hundred dollars and directions to a hospital with an emergency room.

The rat-faced cousin's pictures were extremely out of focus, every one.

Worse was to come. Two giggling female cousins seemed to have been unable to concentrate on anything but their departed relative's crotch: seventy-two pictures of gray folded hands with pinky rings. An elderly cousin had managed to obtain five excellent, clear, in-focus pictures of the casket from the other side of the room, with not one hair of Johnny Crawfish in sight. A teenage cousin had taken pictures of the exterior of the house—floodlit for exclusive taped ABC television coverage and a Crawfish Productions filmed documentary—as well as pictures of the grounds, the guards, several attending celebrities, the sideboards loaded with food and drink in the main entrance hall of The Shack, the built-in organ in the Music Room where Johnny Crawfish had penned such monstrous hits as "Bedroll Woman" and "My Semi-Drivin' Heart's in a Demihemiquaver Over You," the breakfast nook where Johnny died, and that was that: By the time he got to the remains, he'd run out of film.

And he was the last to have any chance at all. Enough cousins had been ineptly showing their cameras by then to alert the pluguglies guarding the entrance that something was afoot, and from then on every cousin was searched upon arrival. The discovery of a camera produced an immediate beating as well as revocation of the entry card. Soon, the highway outside The Shack was littered with abandoned cameras, the hospital emergency rooms of Hampton and Newport News and Norfolk were awash in battered Crawfishes, and *Galaxy*-inspired traffic through the Hampton Roads Bridge–Tunnnel connecting Hampton with Norfolk was all one way: south, away from the Shack. Retreat had become rout.

"Screw it," Jack told Sara. "Let's go have dinner."

* * *

"The problem is," Jack said, over scungilli and a side order of spaghettini in butter-and-cheese sauce, "too many of these celebs now are aware of the body in the box, and they don't like it, and they try not to let it happen."

"How?" Sara asked, over scampi fra diavolo and zucchini.

"Cremation's one way," Jack said, and sipped Chianti. "There are actual no-fooling legit movie stars in Hollywood right now that have instructions in their wills that when they die they want *no* viewing, *no* publicity, and cremation within twenty-four hours. That's on account of us."

"But the fact that they *know* about it," Sara said, surprised.

"Sure they know about it. Celebs are among our most fanatic readers. We guarantee their fame and importance. The more bullshit they read about themselves in the *Galaxy*, the more assured they are that they still have that audience."

"And they don't want themselves, dead, looked at by eight million people."

"Very narrow point of view," Jack said. "One that does make life tough for us at times." He grinned. "But it has its high points, too."

"It does? Like what?"

"Like a little piece of videotape I've kept," Jack said. "I'll play it for you sometime. It shows me dressed as a priest, being interviewed on network news in front of the Bel Air mansion of a very famous singer that just went down. I'm Father Mulroney, and I say—" Looking pious but impish at the same time, Jack folded his hands over his scungilli and said, "At a time like this, speaking as an old family friend as well as spiritual counselor, I believe it is *so* important that the family be left alone by the media, your good selves included. Leave them to the privacy and dignity of their grief." Jack laughed and sat back. "I had that bastard so ashamed of himself for being a reporter on their lawn he was practically in tears. And I'd just come out of the house with the camera in my pocket."

"The body in the box."

"The very same."

"Didn't we send somebody up to The Shack dressed like a priest?"

"We did," Jack said. "And they tried to turn his head around to match his collar. They aren't very religious up there."

"What are some other things you've done?"

"You mean, to get the body in the box?" Jack looked thoughtful and reminiscent. "Ida was an unwed mother once," he said, "clutching in her arms the deceased's bastard child. She was *determined* the infant would get to gaze upon his daddy just once."

"Oh."

"Another time," Jack said, "Chauncey was the long-dead son of the family who it turned out *didn't* die after all when he disappeared in that Swiss avalanche but made his way home after all these years just in time for Dad's funeral."

"Oh, my God."

"Yeah, that one got a little hairy afterward," Jack agreed.

"I should think so."

"Then there's Ida's fire," Jack said, "when I was the fireman."

"No way to burn The Shack, though," Sara said.

"Unfortunately not."

Sara said slowly, "Jack? What if we don't get it?"

"What's that?"

"The body in the box. Sometimes we fail, don't we?"

"Never!" Jack sat up straight over his scungilli. "If there's one thing Massa wants more than anything else on this planet—or any of the near planets, either—it's the body in the box. Every time. The twenty-four-hour cremation is the only acceptable excuse."

"Gosh," Sara said.

Jack shrugged. "Ida says she's got something," he said. "She tends to come through. We'll find out when we get back."

* * *

The gray station wagon parked in front of 147 Edger Street was surmounted by an official red flasher light, not at the moment in use. The licensed plates were official, and the white lettering above the seal on both side doors read COMMONWEALTH OF VIRGINIA, BOARD OF HEALTH. "By golly," Jack said, "they're closing us down."

"I can't find it in my heart to blame them," Sara said.

Inside, they found Ida dressed like a Gray Lady or something; a round gray pillbox hat with some sort of brass symbol on the front, a severely tailored pearl-gray suit with high-lapelled white blouse, black stockings and disgustingly sensible black shoes. "*There* you are," she said to Sara, and gestured at a plastic dry cleaner's bag draped over a chair. "Your uniform. Try it on."

Jack said, "Ida? Is that car out there yours?"

"It's the real thing," Ida told him. "It cost us."

"Doesn't matter," Jack said. "Not if you have a way to get in."

"We'll get in," Ida said.

Sara picked up the plastic bag by its wire hanger and saw inside what appeared to be a uniform identical to Ida's. A package of black stockings and another round hat and a pair of those tugboat shoes were also on the chair. "I'm supposed to wear this stuff?"

"We don't have much time," Ida pointed out. "It's after eight, and the viewing stops at ten."

"All right." Sara wandered off into the empty dining room to change. While transforming herself into something as repelling and bloodless as Ida, she wondered what Ida's idea was, and whether or not it would work. The people guarding The Shack; were they capable of beating up women who looked like *this*? Feeling excited, but also a bit queasy with apprehension, Sara went back out to the living room, clomping along in shoes that actually fit. In fact, all the clothes fit, and so did the hat.

"Ravishing!" Jack said. "My darling, fly with me! You've never looked lovelier."

"Thank you, Jack," Sara said.

Don Grove called over from his desk, "Sara? Did Ida tell you about your phone call?"

"Phone call?" Before leaving, Sara had Scotch-taped to the

receiver of her phone the names "Helen Sonoma" and "A-Betta Car Rental," so that anyone answering the phone if its light flashed would know which scam was being pulled. Now she said to Ida, "Who was it?"

Impatient, Ida said, "The info's on your pad there, you can take care of it when we get back."

"Just let me look," Sara said, moving toward her desk.

Ida said, "Jack, we don't have much time."

"This'll only take a couple minutes," Sara promised.

"Go ahead," Jack told her, while Ida looked *very* impatient.

The message was from Nick Hanrahan at his home number. Sara called, identified herself as the person from A-Betta, and Nick Hanrahan's pleasantly raspy voice said, "You're not the only one looking for Mike. I'm looking for him, too. His landlord called me the first of August. When did he rent that car from you people?"

"He returned it the twelfth of July."

"Yeah, he flew to Miami the eleventh," Nick Hanrahan said. "That was on his desk calendar when I went into the place. But I got nothing on him after then. What did he leave in the car?"

"A gun," Sara said.

"Oh," Nick Hanrahan said. "Jesus. Yeah, I guess you people could get a little uptight, something like that."

"It would help," Sara said, "if we knew why Mr. Hanrahan might have been carrying that gun."

"Well, he's a private eye," Hanrahan said, and then laughed self-consciously and said, "Not like it sounds. Not like in the movies."

"I'm not sure I understand," Sara told him.

"See," Hanrahan said, "where he works— Well, let me start with me. I'm a partner in a bunch of parking garages."

"All-Day Parking."

"That's us. We got a bunch of locations around the greater Los Angeles area. Now, you've got a lot of cash operations, a business like that, you've got guys sometimes try a little hustle, so we hire a company like Western States—that's who Mike works for—"

"Yes," Sara said, "that's what he listed on the rental form. Western States Investigations."

"Right. They're mostly industrial security, like for people like us. Put in undercover people, whatever, anytime we think we're getting a short count. And with stuff like this, you don't go to court, you know? So Western States, they make the point for us, you know?"

"We have similar situations in our business," Sara said.

"Yeah, I suppose you do," Hanrahan said, "a car rental place, so you know what I'm talking about. So anyway, Mike works for them, through me recommending him when he moved out here, and when they've got these occasional regular investigations, not this employee scam stuff, he usually does it."

"So he really is a private detective," Sara said, being careful to speak of Michael Hanrahan in the present tense.

Hanrahan laughed. "More than Western needs, sometimes. He's only supposed to go through the motions, you know? Keep the client happy. But like this trip to Miami, he told Klein—Klein's his manager, at Western—he told Klein he had to show some expenses anyway, for this rich client—"

"Which client?"

"I dunno," Hanrahan said, "some rich woman, some star's widow or something. Anyway, Mike said he had to show expenses anyway, and he'd like a couple days out of town, so he flew to Miami. And now he's disappeared, and you tell me there was a gun in the car. What gun, do you have a description?"

Sara had made herself ready for this one. She read off a description she'd culled from a firearms magazine: "A .38 Special Colt Cobra."

"Huh," Hanrahan said. "A concealment gun. I dunno, maybe, doesn't sound like any weapon I've ever seen around him. But could be. Leave anything else?"

"No, sir."

"What local address'd he give?"

"None," Sara said. "Only Western States, on Sunset Boulevard."

"Okay, look," Hanrahan said. "I've reported Mike missing to the L.A. police. I'll tell them about this new thing, they'll get in touch with the Miami cops, they'll come pick up the gun. Okay?"

"Fine," said Sara. "Thank you for your cooperation, Mr. Hanrahan."

When she hung up, Ida was standing there looking bad-tempered. "That was more than two minutes," she said.

"Sorry. I'm ready now."

Jack said, "I wish you both every success."

"Thanks," Sara said. "I just wish I had jeans or something to change into when I get back."

"I'll get you some stuff from the hotel," Jack promised, and turned to Ida to say, "Ida, is it permissible to know what you're doing?"

Ida picked up from her desk a black leather old-fashioned doctor's bag. "We're shutting the viewing down," she said.

"Why?"

"The corpse has AIDS," Ida said.

Chapter Eight

The Shack flamed white, a great colonnaded columned antebellum plantation house gleaming alabaster in the black depths of space. White lights flared at it, banks and walls and towers of light, washing the tall broad structure with color-destroying glare. Within that light, wood turned to porcelain and paint to frozen milk. Windows could show nothing against that blaze; they stood black within the ivory walls, reduced to the architect's idea of windows.

Grass surrounding the main house was gray, the winding path to the front door black, the mourners moving slowly on that path both black and bent. Within the dazzle of the lights, it seemed there was no sound, no color, barely any movement possible. But beyond them, in the gray ordinary night of the world behind the lights, thousands moved, tens of thousands moved, alive with color and noise.

The manifold mourners of Johnny Crawfish, uninvited, unneeded, crowded the highway along the edge of the compound, trembled close to the razor-wire, and called out the names of still-living celebrities they saw step out into the field of light and make their bent way under that brilliance up to the main house and their farewell to "the troubled troubador of our troubled times" (*Newsweek*). Uniformed police, on foot and on horse and by car, patrolled the outer perimeter, keeping the highway open, keeping the Unwashed from the Elect, maintaining order in this "hour of national grief" (*Time*). Old compadres of the deceased, rough and ready men, served as ushers within the grounds, escorting the "peers of the peerless" (*People*). Tape cameramen for ABC and film cameramen for Crawfish Productions turned the ghastly lunar landscapes they saw inside their machines into images of somber beauty, filled with famous faces thinking long thoughts about "the Prodigal Son America took to its heart" (*USA Today*). And all around was the hubbub of life, the surge and swell of the crowd, the murmurs of the invited guests, the brief comments and directions of the ushers, the halloos back and forth among the cousins.

At first, in all that shifting and sonorous throng, the sound of the oncoming siren could barely be heard at all. First one police officer, then another, looked up from his endless chore of crowd control to see that flashing red light coming, and to realize at once it wasn't just another ambulance. (There had been several ambulances already this evening, for those overcome by emotion or the ushers, and for a few who had mistaken their footing and fallen beneath the crowd.) But this was something else, official, and moving fast.

"Back there! Back there! Keep clear! Clear this area! Get out of the *way*!"

The gray station wagon roared into sight, and past the gaping mob, who had no idea what to make of the two grim-faced women they just barely saw within it. The station wagon flashed by, screaming, strained into a hard tight rubber-shredding turn at the entrance, and jolted to a stop just inches from the side of a Crawfish jeep blocking the drive.

Officials and guards and television producers came running from everywhere, as the two women stepped from their car, as gray and grim as the backspill that lit them.

"What's going on?" screamed a State Police captain. "Who are you people?"

"Court order," Ida snapped, slapping onto the hood of the station wagon documents it would take hours to prove false. "This place is shut *down*."

* * *

In the hotel room they shared, while looking for clothes for Sara to change into later, Jack found beneath her underwear an envelope marked TO BE OPENED IN THE EVENT OF MY DEATH.

What? Jack fingered this envelope, trying to decide if it was a gag or not. Was Sara the kind of person to hide in a drawer an envelope like this containing itching powder or some sort of joke remark or something like that? No; it wasn't her style.

So what was this? Jack thought it over, and came to the conclusion that it probably had something to do with Sara's dead man again. Also, he told himself, as her editor and companion, he had certain rights and privileges in a situation like this. And finally, realizing he was aflame with curiosity, he stopped arguing with himself and ripped the damn thing open.

He read slowly, with mounting surprise and then mounting unease. Something was wrong here. When he finished, he read the paper again, and this time he saw where Sara had made her mistake. Phyllis Perkinson wasn't the killer of the dead man beside the road, or the shooter of bullets through the hotel room window. There was one assumption Sara had made in this letter that was absolutely wrong.

Which meant—

"Good God!" Jack cried aloud, and ran from the room.

Chapter Nine

It was so strange to be alone in this entire huge house, with all the light glaring in from outside, distorting the shapes, turning the furniture into science-fiction versions of itself. Sara walked wonderingly through it all, sensible shoes clacking, echoing in all the empty rooms.

Ida, armed only with ruthlessness and forged documents and a black leather doctor's bag, had emptied this house as though with a machine gun, had sent people backing away from all this light with shocked faces and twitching hands. AIDS? Johnny Crawfish? Here was horror compounded; no one wanted to be anywhere near the merciless killer disease. And no one wanted to believe that *Johnny Crawfish* had carried it.

"Contagious disease," Ida had said to the State Police captain, her tone cold and official and just slightly contemptuous, as Sara had stood beside her, trying to make her own face that cold and impenetrable. "Death from contagious disease," Ida had said. "State law prohibits public viewing, prohibits *any* services of any kind until after the autopsy. This property is closed by law until the deceased can be removed. Miss Twitchell and I will secure the building. You, Captain—Captain—?"

"Ogilvie," the captain had said, wide-eyed.

"You will keep the general public back. Come, Miss Twitchell."

And Ida had marched out into all that light, followed by Sara, suffering madly from stage fright all along the whole route under the lights, all the way to the black front door and through it. Only inside, away from the light, could she begin to relax, to shakily laugh and say, "Did I have to be Miss Twitchell?"

"We don't have much time," Ida said, humorless and determined as ever.

So they marched through the house, recognizing the route from the teenager's photographs, and there was the right room at last, there were the great peach and coral pillows of floral bouquets, giving off their own muted glow and cloying smell. There was the casket on its bier, upper half of the lid standing open like a cubist's idea of a grand piano. And there was Johnny.

They were far from the lights now, deep within The Shack, absolutely alone. Ida opened the doctor's bag atop a small side table and withdrew a camera from it. "You take the first batch," she said.

"Batch?"

"He isn't going anywhere," Ida said. "Just keep taking pictures."

Sara took the camera with its self-contained flash and went over to stand at the foot of the casket and look up its gleaming ebony slope to the open portion, the white silk puffed over the padding, the body in the box. Oh, God, she thought, looking at that helpless cast-off husk. I'm not sure I can do it. Look how gray the jaw is. I'm not sure I can do it.

I have to do it. Ida's right here, Jack's waiting back on Edger Street, I've come this far, I *have* to do it. Let my hands not shake, she thought, and slowly raised the camera.

Conversationally, Ida said, "I suppose you've figured it out that Jack killed Hanrahan."

Sara nearly dropped the camera. She turned her head and stared at Ida, still standing there by the side table, hand on the doctor's bag. "What was that? What did you say?"

"I was hoping you'd let it alone," Ida said. "That's why I shot the gun into your bed."

"*You* did?"

"I knew you were in the other room with Jack," she said. "I hoped he'd convince you then to lay off."

"He didn't— He never—"

"That's because I couldn't ever say anything to him, that was the problem," Ida said. She could have been talking about a missed lunch date. "I didn't want him to know *I* knew he'd killed Hanrahan, because then maybe he wouldn't be sure he could trust *me*. But he can. Absolutely."

"But—" The whole world was melting around Sara, going in and out of focus like the cousins' photographs, slipping and sliding. "But why *would* he?"

"Hanrahan was a private detective."

"I know that."

"Sybille Hamler hired him."

Sara shook her head. "I don't know who . . . I don't know that name."

"George Hamler's widow," Ida said, naming a major rock star who'd died last year.

The name at last made a connection for Sara, who said, "The fire!"

"When we got the body in the box," Ida agreed. "Jack went in as a fireman. Sybille Hamler's mother was in there, she was a cripple in a wheelchair, they didn't get her out in time, she died."

"Oh, Ida," Sara said, feeling as though her heart would break. "What are you saying?"

"Jack set the fire."

"No!"

"Jack set it," Ida said implacably. "It was the only way to get the picture. Sybille believed it was arson, and then her mother's death would be murder. She hired Hanrahan. Hanrahan thought he had the goods on Jack. He went to Florida to be absolutely sure, and Jack didn't have any choice. You can see that, can't you? Why you and I have to stick with him, no matter what? Because he just didn't have any choice."

Sara tried to think, tried to absorb all this, tried to make it make sense. Jack— Hanrahan— Ida firing through the hotel room window to scare her off. The dead man beside the road . . . "No," she said.

Ida watched her, very carefully. "No? What do you mean, no?"

"Jack was already there that morning, when I arrived," Sara said. "He was there all day. He couldn't have gotten rid of the car. He couldn't have gotten rid of the guard. Yes, Taggart, him, too!"

Ida said, "Sara, this is very important. For Jack's sake. He did what he had to do, and we have to stand by him."

"No. It wasn't him, because he ran into me when I stepped off the elevator, he was there all along. And the only other person who knows about it, Ida . . ." Sara looked at this cold and ruthless woman ". . . is you."

Ida's hand came out of the doctor's bag again. This time, it held a gun.

Chapter Ten

They wouldn't let him through. He honked and honked, leaning on the horn, sticking his head out the window to scream, and the slow tidal waves of people barely noticed him at all, moved only when the bumpers and fender of his car brushed their bodies, blinked resentfully in his headlights, moved with that underwater slowness of dreams. "Life and death!" he screamed. "Life and death!" And what did they care? They were barely alive, and death was merely the excitement of Johnny Crawfish.

A state trooper, looking like a man who's gone far too long without the opportunity to exert some authority, pushed his way to the side of the car, lowering at Jack like an incoming storm front, saying, "What do you think *you're* doing? You can't drive through here."

"The Board of Health women!" Jack yelled at him. "I've got to get to them!"

"Why?" the trooper demanded, noting the total civilianness of the car, the lack of identifying uniform on its driver. "Who are you supposed to be?"

"This is life and death, dammit! I'll give you my résumé *later*! Get me through this fucking *crowd*!"

Jack's intensity had its effect, that and his utter disregard for the trooper's authority, suggesting that Jack's own authority was too supreme even to need mentioning. "Follow me," the trooper said, pretending *he* was the one giving the order, and stepped out in front of the car to yell at people to clear this area, keep back there, *move* it. A mounted policeman soon joined him, and they all made their way through the surging billows of denim and polyester and elaborate bas-reliefs of hair, followed by vaguely curious eyes. Is this interesting? It doesn't *look* interesting, but is it interesting after all?

At the main entrance to the compound, Jack clambered from his car and was escorted to a State Police captain identified as Ogilvie. Beyond Ogilvie, The Shack stood out starkly against the night, floodlit. Everyone was back here out of that light, pressed to the perimeter of the estate. Nothing could be seen to move up there; it was as though life itself ended at that doorway.

Captain Ogilvie, a put-upon harried man, stood arms akimbo, fists pressed into hips, jaw thrust forward, as he glared at this new interruption. "Yes?" he demanded. "Just who are *you*, and just what do *you* want?"

Jack opened his mouth. Over the captain's shoulder, the house gleamed and glistened, empty except for Ida and Sara. Am I wrong? Am I crazy? The body in the box! Right now, right this minute, those two are getting the body in the box. Do I lose that? If I open my mouth, the *Galaxy* does not get the Crawfish cover. Am I right? Or am I wrong?

"Well?" the captain insisted, leaning closer.

"The, the-the-the-the-the-the, the Board of Health women!" Jack said.

"What about them?"

"They're— They're phonies! They're really from the *Weekly Galaxy*, they're not Board of Health at all!"

The captain stared. "Are you out of your mind? They've got ID, court orders, they—"

"Phony! Phony!" Jack clawed out his own ID, the *real* ID, and pushed it at the captain. "I'm their editor! I *sent* them there!"

The captain didn't want to believe any of this, and he certainly didn't want to believe anything said by a self-confessed editor of the *Weekly Galaxy*. Brushing Jack's ID aside like a pesky moth, he said, "We'll verify all that when they come out."

"You have to go *in* there!" Jack yelled. "One of them's a killer!"

Half a dozen cops now stood about and gazed at Jack, certain he was crazy. Ogilvie leaned backward slightly, no longer thrusting his jaw out. "Killer, is she? And you're their editor. And we're supposed to go in and—"

The sound of the shot silenced the entire world.

It couldn't have been anything else. It *cracked* out from that big empty light-struck house, and flattened everything in its path like a sonic boom. Captain Ogilvie, slack-jawed, turned to stare. Jack, a great agony pouring through his body, tottered and clutched at the nearest trooper for support. Leaning on that smoothly uniformed arm, staring through grit-covered eyeballs at the house, he said, through a throat gone closed, "I loved her, goddamnit, and I never told her. Goddamnit! Goddamnit!"

CRACK!

The sound of the second shot caused a dozen moving bodies to freeze, just at the edge of the zone of light. In the motionless silence, Jack lifted his head. *Two* shots. "There's hope," he whispered.

Chapter Eleven

When Ida said, "Go through that door over there. Walk," Sara thought: She wants to take me to a basement or somewhere, where the shot won't be heard. Then she'll walk out and say she left me to guard the body, and she'll drive away, and go become somebody else with that cleverness of hers, and they'll never find her. And I'll be dead, in the basement of The Shack. In these shoes!

That was when she took Ida's picture. Not to take Ida's picture, but to shine the sudden flash in Ida's eyes, and *run!*

Ida fired the gun, a terribly loud and shocking sound in this room, and a vase full of flowers behind Sara *shpackled* into an infinity of wet shards and spraying water and collapsing lilies.

The noise of the gun must have startled Ida, too, that and the flash in her face, because she didn't fire again until Sara was leaping deerlike through the door. Sara heard the *chuk* of lead into wood, and she cried out, losing her balance, flailing around, losing the camera, waving her arms, her feet skittering in all kinds of directions until at last she righted herself and ran across this anteroom littered with an obstacle course of Lucite folding chairs. She slapped at chairs as she passed, knocking them over in her wake, trying to slow someone who could merely send a bullet flying *over* every obstacle and directly into her shrinking back.

Even if there'd been time to look behind her, she wouldn't have done it; something *was* gaining on her. Through the next doorway, and the next, and leftward down an endless marble-floored hallway that stretched away to infinity, as in a dream where something's chasing you and you can't run fast enough and the door keeps receding farther and farther away.

CRACK! CRACK!

A bee stung her left shoulder, and her knees wobbled, all strength draining away into the marble floor. The door rushed toward her, an ally at last, and she burst through it, the heavy sensible shoes dragging at her feet, the bee sting goading her shoulder, the LIGHT a hot slap in the face when she spewed across the threshold, stripping away her shadow, stealing her balance, sucking her strength. "Oh, *God*!" she cried, tripping over her own self, and fell sprawling on the gray grass beyond the curving path.

She rolled onto her back, frantic, and Ida came out, all gray and white and remorseless and caring about nothing in this world but the death of Sara Joslyn. Ida raised the pistol, and forty people with handguns cut her to ribbons.

Chapter Twelve

In the ambulance, Jack kept talking, because the doctor on the scene had said to "keep her engaged," that although the bullet graze on her shoulder was unimportant she was "in trauma" and Jack should not let her "go all the way into shock." *I'm* the one all the way into shock, Jack thought, but he kept talking. "I read your letter," he said, "the one you had under your underwear."

She lay on the stretcher, the scratchy blue blanket stretched over her as she stared at him, silent, unblinking. The ambulance swayed, and Jack swayed with it, and the silent state trooper beside Jack on the other stretcher swayed with it, but Sara just lay there and stared at Jack and didn't blink and didn't even sway when the ambulance swayed.

"See, what you had wrong," Jack told her, "was that Phyllis was the only person in your apartment, so she had to be the one to take the piece of paper from over your desk. But *Ida* was in there. I put Ida on the job when I found out Boy had a spy on our team. Ida checked everybody, she found out about Phyllis and *Trend,* she checked you out, too, she was all over that apartment you two had. Ida was better at searching places than anybody I ever met. She came out of there knowing your clothing sizes and your shoe size. She came out of there with your piece of paper. Sara, do you know why she killed the man beside the road? Because I don't."

Sara stared at him, not blinking, not bracing herself when the ambulance swung around a long curve.

Jack nodded, licking his lips. "What I figure," he said, "she was riding out to the *Galaxy* with him, for whatever reason, she got him to stop, she shot him. You drove by. She was ducked down in the car. She saw your brake lights, she figured you'd come back, she moved while you were turning around. She went and hid on the other side of that concrete divider in the middle of the road. What the hell, there wasn't any other traffic. You came back and she watched you. All the time you were there with the dead man, she was watching you from the other side of the divider."

Sara didn't react, didn't move.

"She didn't know you," Jack said. "She didn't see a *Galaxy* sticker on your car, she figured you'd go somewhere else to report it. You left, she put the body in the trunk and drove on to the *Galaxy* and the guard there told her you'd just reported somebody killed in that car. She told him it was just one of our stunts, and why wouldn't he believe it? *Everything* is just one of our stunts."

Sara swallowed. She licked her lips. That was the only change.

Jack said, "She told him she'd need his help with the stunt later, and she parked in the regular parking lot even without the right sticker because the guard knew her, she was a long-term valued employee. Then she came in and established her presence with all that stuff about Keely Jones, and made sure nobody was making a big thing out of your story. Then she went back out and got the guard to come with her, and took them both out in that scrub land out there and buried them. And returned the rental car. And all she wanted was to keep you from doing any follow-through."

Jack gave a bitter laugh, shaking his head. "At the *Galaxy*," he said, "that should have been easy. Who does follow-through on anything *real* there? And you were forgetting it, too, weren't you? Until she started shooting into hotel rooms. All she had to do was wait, trust the *Galaxy* to degrade you, make you forget. She didn't have enough patience, that's all."

The ambulance braked, slowed, stopped. Doors slammed.

Sara sighed, a long susurration. "Hanrahan," she said.

Jack leaned forward. "The dead man? He's Hanrahan? What about him?"

"He thought you set the fire," she said, in a small faraway voice. "He was coming to talk to you. Ida knew you'd both figure it out she was the one. Since you didn't set the fire, she did. And the dead mother was murder."

"Oh, Christ," Jack said, and nodded. "I never wanted to look too closely at that particular piece of good luck. I never wanted to be sure."

The ambulance doors opened, and busy medics were there, ready to slide Sara away. "Just a second," the state trooper said, speaking for the first time since the start of the ride. "Before you take her," he told the medics.

Sara's wide eyes turned toward the trooper. Jack said, "Yes?"

The trooper leaned closer to Sara. "After the first shot," he said, in his colorless uninflected voice, "when Mr. Ingersoll here believed you were dead, he said, and I quote, 'I loved her, goddamn it, and I never told her.' I just thought I should report that to you."

Sara's eyes had somehow grown even wider. She looked at Jack. "Did you? Did you say that?"

Jack gave the blank-faced trooper a look. "Shit," he said. "Now everybody'll know."

THE WAY WE LIVE THIS INSTANT

Chapter One

In his private office at *Trend,* The Magazine for the Way We Live This Instant, special projects editor David Levin had a high view westward over the calculated rubble of the West Forties, and over the broad Hudson River, to the Jersey side with its solitary graceless rectangular high rises here and there at the water's edge as though, county by county and town by town and shire by shire, New Jersey was doing its feeble best to give New York the finger. Beyond these examples of the shame of the architecture schools lay America itself, beneath an ever-changing sky, and to the north a glimpse of the Palisades, and to the south a peek at New York Harbor. It was an enviable view, well earned by David Levin's exertions on behalf of *Trend,* and he liked to stand at his broad windows, hands clasped behind his back, and view that view every chance he got.

He was doing so today, when Myra his secretary came in looking doubtful and said, "Two people out here who want to talk to you. The man says his name is John R. Ingersoll, and you know him from the *Weekly Galaxy*."

The blood drained from David Levin's face. The *Weekly Galaxy*! That astonishing, repellent woman! She'd stolen those tapes, he knew she had but he could never prove it, and he could never find her again, and he would never be able to admit to *anybody* what had happened. So all he'd been able to do was make an editorial decision to the effect that the *Weekly Galaxy* story was too crude after all to be of interest to *Trend* readers, and kill it. Much to poor Phyllis Perkinson's disgust, by the way, only slightly assuaged by his immediately assigning her to the John Michael Mercer wedding (thus giving her a vacation and getting her out of David Levin's hair—or scalp; he was rather bald—in one fell swoop).

And John R. Ingersoll—Jack Ingersoll—had been Phyllis's editor down at that scurrilous rag, Levin remembered that name. What was the man doing *here*? "Certainly not," he said.

Myra extended a tape cassette toward him, saying, "He said I should give you this."

Levin accepted it, with fingers that suddenly shook. It was one of the tapes the woman had stolen, he recognized his own cryptic pen markings. What are they up to? For my own protection, he thought, I'd better find out. And if they want my assurance that *Trend* is not going to blow the whistle on them after all, by God, I'll be happy to give it. "All right," he said. "Send him in."

Myra ushered in a couple, both reasonable looking, the woman young and quite attractive, the man jaunty, with a rolled newspaper under his arm. "Hi," said the man, grinning. "I'm Jack Ingersoll, and this is my partner, Sara Joslyn."

"Hi," said Sara Joslyn, also grinning.

Levin nervously tapped the cassette against the knuckles of his other hand. "Yes? You wanted to talk to me about the *Weekly Galaxy*?"

"Oh, no," Ingersoll said, beaming broadly. "We quit that place."

"Then I don't under—"

"We came to talk," Ingersoll said smoothly, "about going to work for *you*."

"Me? No, really, there isn't the slightest—"

"Just a second," Ingersoll said. Something about the man's calm self-assurance was unsettling. "Sara and I are excellent investigative reporters," he went on, "I can pretty well assure you of that."

"Nevertheless, I—"

"Just to give you an example," Sara Joslyn said, withdrawing another tape cassette from her bag and holding it up for him to see, "here's our first exclusive, just for you, if we're working for the magazine."

Levin peered at the cassette. Unwilling, but helpless, he said, "What is it?"

"You," Ingersoll told him, "in conversation with a woman named

Ida Gavin, a former reporter on the *Galaxy*. You appear to be in bed together. Ida keeps describing what you're doing."

Levin leaned back against the plate glass of his view. He could remember that woman's voice, remember her running commentary. Good God!

"In fact," Sara Joslyn said, with an incongruously sweet smile, "*you* make a couple of requests on that tape, at one point."

"You may not remember Ida Gavin," Ingersoll said, "at least not under that name. This might help your memory." And he unfolded the *New York Post* he'd been carrying, open to page five, and handed it to Levin.

No! The madwoman at the Johnny Crawfish wake! *Weekly Galaxy* reporter, multiple murderess. The cold eyes in the standard publicity photo looking out at him were familiar indeed. Levin was so engrossed in gazing back at those eyes that he didn't notice Ingersoll look approvingly around the office with the air of a man who expects to move into it in, oh, say, no more than four years.

When Levin at last tore his eyes away from the dead eyes of the dead woman in the newspaper, he looked instead at the tape in Sara Joslyn's hand. "How can I know—" he began, and his voice failed, and he started again: "How can I know that's the only copy?"

"What does it matter," Ingersoll asked pleasantly, "as long as we're working for you?"

"Special projects for *Trend*," Sara Joslyn said, and smiled like an angel. "We'll do wonderful work. You'll see."

They would. They could. They had no reason not to. There was a small table handy; Levin put the newspaper on it. He extended his hand, and Sara Joslyn put the cassette in it. His fingers closed on the little plastic box.

Jack Ingersoll, expression serious, said, "None of us will ever mention this again. That's a promise."

Levin looked from one to the other. The scene shifted; he saw them in a different light. These people— These people really were *investigative reporters*! The crew he'd been working with were grade schoolers in comparison. With these people, David Levin could . . . rule *Trend*!

A sudden honest smile lit Levin's face. He shifted the cassette, extended his hand, and said, "Welcome aboard!"

Jack Ingersoll took the hand in a manly and trustworthy grasp. "You won't regret this, Mr. Levin," he said.

Sara Joslyn's eyes shone. "Clean journalism," she breathed, "at last."

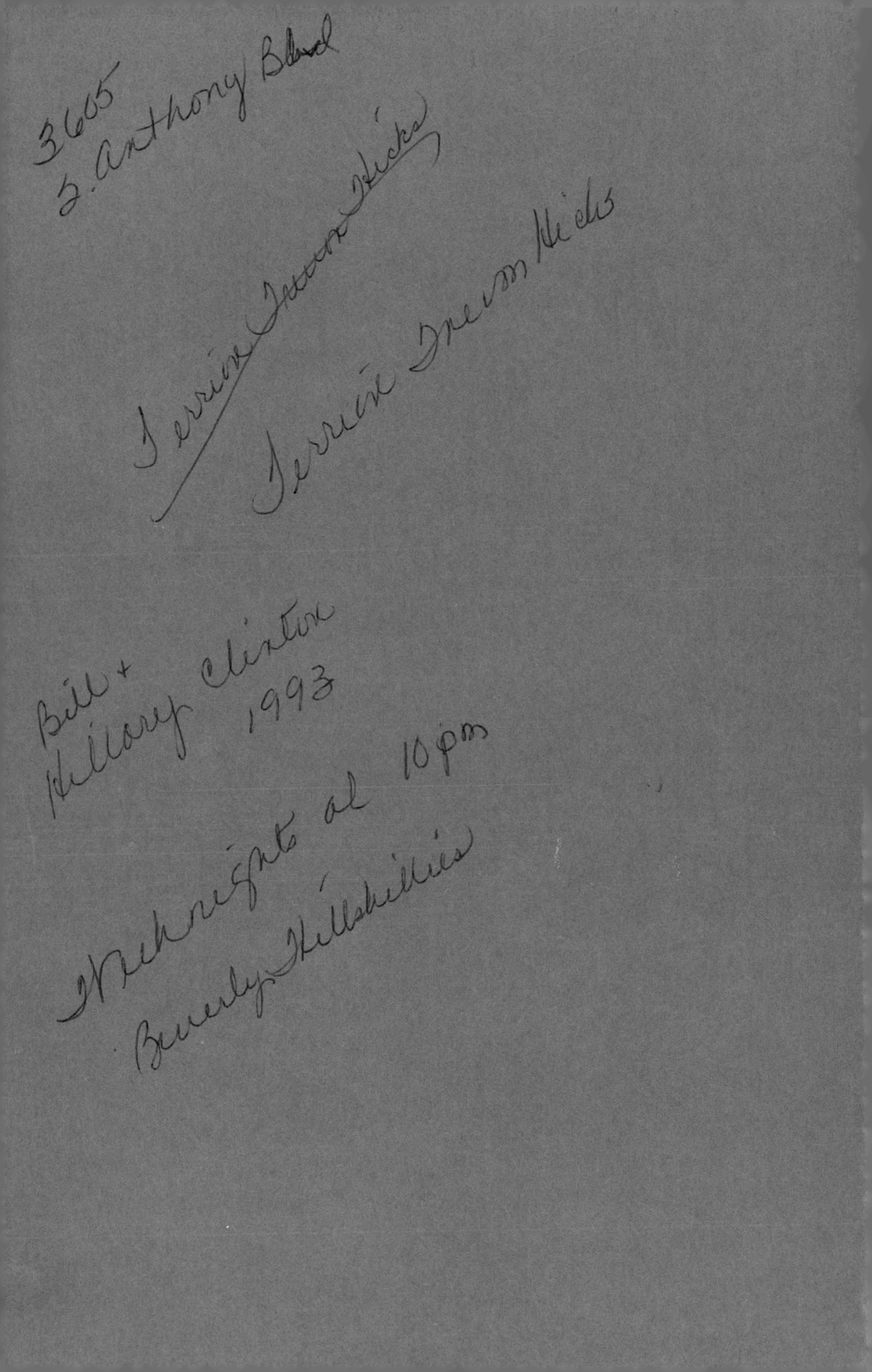

3605
S. Anthony Blvd

~~Terrence Jason Hicks~~

Terrence Dream Hicks

Bill +
Hillary Clinton
1993

Weeknights at 10pm

Beverly Hillbillies